Praise for Renee Ryan

"RT Top Pick . . . Fanny cares for Jonathon deeply, but she won't marry him without his love. At a crossroads, Jonathon will have to choose whether to walk away or be the man that Fanny believes him to be. The elements of Christian faith are superbly woven into the story [*The Marriage Agreement*], and fans of this delightful series will surely enjoy this sweet tale of forgiveness, hope, and redeeming love."

—Susannah Balch, *RT Book Reviews*

"With book two in her Charity House series [*Hannah's Beau*], Ryan writes with passion and love, as always. She knows what readers expect and never disappoints."

—Patsy Glans, *RT Book Reviews*

"Don't miss this wonderful story [*The Marshall Takes a Bride*] about redemption and forgiveness. The characters are lovable, and likable, even at times when they're not nice, and the faith message is interwoven without being overbearing and preachy."

—Patsy Glans, *RT Book Reviews*

"RT Top Pick . . . This sixth in the Charity House series [*The Outlaw's Redemption*] is filled with complex characters and many endearing, familiar faces. It's a fascinating addition to this delightful series."

—Susan Mobley, *RT Book Reviews*

"Ryan outdoes herself with this latest offering [*Dangerous Allies*]—a mix of romance, intrigue, and spies. She writes her characters with strong feelings and heart."

—Patsy Glans, *RT Book Reviews*

"5 stars . . . Perfect for . . . everywhere. Whether you're looking for a book to curl up with for a long evening, during a carpool line, or to take on vacation, you'll want to include *His Most Suitable Bride!*"

—Dora Hiers, *Fiction Faith & Foodies*

ALSO BY RENEE RYAN

Charity House historical series

World War II historical series

Village Green contemporary series

RENEE RYAN

Journey's End

A GILDED PROMISES NOVEL

Waterfall
PRESS

*I dedicate this book to my favorite real-life couples:
Hillary and Bradley Nolan, Kelsey and Dan Halverson.
Your love for one another reminds me that true love
exists in every generation. I love you with all my heart.*

Journeys end in lovers meeting,

Every wise man's son doth know.

—William Shakespeare, *Twelfth Night*

Chapter One

Ellis Island, 1901

"Oh, Caro, look. We're almost there. We're almost in America."

Caroline St. James made a noncommittal sound deep in her throat. Unlike the frail Irish girl leaning heavily on her arm, she knew that arriving at Ellis Island was only the first step in the rigorous registration process.

Frowning at Mary's sickly pallor, Caroline carefully guided her friend into the queue of fellow immigrants disembarking the ferryboat. Cautious by nature, and with a suspicion honed by necessity, she watched for trouble, assessing potential threats in the mass of anxious humanity pressing in from every possible angle.

It would be too easy to lose her friend in this crowd. Where would Mary be then? The girl was already showing signs of exhaustion, and they hadn't even made it off the ferryboat yet.

Lifting up onto her toes, Caroline caught her first glimpse of the imposing stone building up ahead with the endless lines of immigrants stretching from door to dock.

"Almost there," she whispered to herself, and yet still so far to go.

She'd paid close attention to the hushed whispers of other immigrants whose relatives had already passed through Ellis Island. Several tough challenges lay head, starting with the "long staircase." From what she'd gathered, reaching the top did not mean the journey had come to an end.

Each immigrant also had to pass a medical exam and an extensive interview. Caroline's pulse picked up speed. The American authorities could send her back to London for something as minor as a recurring cough or as major as a criminal record.

While she may have stolen food to survive and fleeced an unsuspecting gambler or two, she'd never been caught. And she'd never, *never* harmed anyone worse off than herself.

Given the abject poverty of her fellow passengers, she doubted she was alone in having done whatever was necessary to survive.

Still, in contrast to the other immigrants now moving into the vast hall with her and Mary, Caroline hadn't come to America seeking the promise of a better life. For her, this journey was a means to an end. The first step in a meticulous plan to right a terrible wrong.

The crowd condensed, moving as one solid pack at a pace more suitable for a funeral procession. The foul-smelling web of bodies shoved, pushed, and jockeyed for position, as if their minuscule efforts could hurry along this unending process.

A hard jostle from behind sent Caroline's tattered skirts tangling around her legs. For a half second, she lost her balance, and her grip slipped from Mary's arm. The girl stumbled forward dangerously.

With a small gasp, Caroline reached for her friend, catching her just before she dropped to the ground.

"Thank you, Caro." The words shuddered past dry, cracked lips, a sure sign of Mary's discomfort. Yet her pale, terror-stricken face told the real story. The illness she'd contracted aboard ship last week had grown worse, alarmingly so.

Pressing her lips into a determined line, Caroline put a hand under her friend's arm and hauled her upright.

For a fleeting moment, Caroline allowed herself to close her eyes. Not to pray—she'd given up on that futile pursuit years ago—but to gather her inner fortitude. She would not fail her friend.

Resolve firmly in place, Caroline opened her eyes, swallowed, and forced confidence in her tone. "Don't worry, Mary. We'll get through this together."

Together. How odd it felt to say the word, to have someone to care about and want to protect, when she'd vowed never to do so again.

Half dragging, half pulling, Caroline maneuvered her friend in the direction of the stairwell. Would anyone notice she supported most of the girl's weight?

Casting a quick glance at a uniformed man standing on a small pedestal, Caroline stifled a gasp of dismay. The official's dark, narrowed gaze swept across the slow-moving crowd. Relentless, unyielding, he looked like a hungry predator searching for the weakest in the herd.

Thankfully, he hadn't spotted Mary. Yet.

Caroline released a hissing rush of air. The frantic percussion of her heartbeat sounded loud and insistent in her ears.

Must. Press. Onward.

Taking note of the labored breathing beside her, Caroline looked down at her friend. A burst of affection filled her bitter heart. This sweet young Irish girl, with the pretty auburn hair and delicate features, had become Caroline's first real friend in years. Perhaps ever.

Mary's devotion to God, who had long since abandoned Caroline, should have sent her running in the opposite direction weeks ago. Instead, every time Mary closed her eyes and prayed, Caroline felt an unfamiliar yearning, as if there were a gaping hole in her soul that needed filling.

She brushed the disturbing thought aside and then eased Mary another step forward. At this rate, they would be in these cramped conditions for hours.

The sea of bobbing heads parted, just a bit, revealing a perfect view of the stairwell up ahead.

"Oh. Oh, no." Mary curled her fingers into Caroline's sleeve. "I don't think I can make it."

Caroline craned her neck. The stairwell went up, and up, and up farther still, the incline so steep she couldn't see the top.

How would Mary ever make the climb? How utterly tragic if she didn't. The girl had family awaiting her arrival. People who loved her, as Caroline had grown to over the endless hours trapped together in the hull of the SS *Princess Helena*.

"Listen to me, Mary. You can do this. Just lean on me if you grow tired."

Mary shook her head in defeat. "It's too steep."

Caroline refused to give in to the dread prowling at the edges of her calm. "All you have to do is remember what I taught you. Keep your head high, chin up, eyes forward. Perception is the key."

"Caro." Mary cut a glance to her left, then dropped her gaze to her feet. "If we get separated—"

"Don't say that." Caroline faced her friend and gave her a little shake. "Don't even think it."

"But if we do," Mary persisted, a sheen of tears filling her eyes, "you *must* continue on without me. Go to the address I told you. If Aunt Jane is away, ask for my cousin Bridget. Either one will know what to do. They'll help you with—"

"That's enough, Mary. It's really quite enough." Caroline tried to sound stern, but her voice tripped over every word. "Eyes forward. Yes, that's right. Now. Chin up."

Mary did as ordered. But then her lips trembled, and one fat tear rolled down her cheek. Followed by several more.

Caroline stole a discreet glance in the official's direction. As if sensing something amiss, the man leaned forward, teeth exposed, shoulders bunched.

He caught sight of Caroline. And then . . .

Mary.

No. *No.*

Panic closed Caroline's throat—the sensation felt as though a noose had been cinched and pulled too tight.

She shifted in front of Mary, shielding her from the official's direct line of vision.

But she'd acted too late.

The man jumped off his perch and, for a blinding second, disappeared in the crowd. Just as quickly, he reappeared. Closer. Too close. Less than thirty feet away.

Eyebrows huddled together, he shoved through the knot of immigrants, not caring if he stepped on toes or knocked over children. His eyes were locked on Mary, his purpose clear in his hard gaze.

"Listen to me." Caroline turned to Mary, urgency in her voice. "You can make it. Don't shake your head at me. Yes, you can. Just climb with confidence."

"I . . . I'll try."

"We'll do this together."

Mary gave her a tremulous smile. "All right."

Side by side, they began their ascent and conquered the first five stairs without incident. But then a hole opened in the crowd. A hand reached out, closed over Mary's shoulder, and yanked hard. Caroline lost her grip on her friend's arm.

No.

Helplessness washed over her. She reached out frantically, shouting Mary's name, running her gaze around the surrounding area. To no avail. Her friend was gone. Seized in the amount of time it took to take a single breath.

As far as abductions went, Mary's had been skillfully executed.

Caroline twisted around on the stairs. Wobbling only slightly, she searched for the familiar cloud of red-gold hair.

There she was. Several rows back. Arm clasped in the official's ruthless grip as he hustled her along in the opposite direction.

Where was he taking her?

Caroline started back down the stairs, desperate to catch up with them. But with each forward step she was shoved back two. People shouted at her in a cacophony of different languages. She knew she was heading in the wrong direction. Yet she persevered, careening upstream against the tide of determined immigrants.

She pushed and pushed, until she could go no farther.

The crowd had grown too thick at the bottom of the stairs and was as immovable as a brick wall. And just as unyielding. Caroline had no other choice than to turn around and follow along in the proper direction or risk being trampled to death.

Her heart constricted painfully in her chest.

She'd failed Mary. And now she was on her own again with no one to look after but herself.

Familiar territory, to be sure; the tragic continuation of a tale nobody cared to hear.

Wasn't that the saddest part of all?

Losing her friend was just one more defeat to add to the countless others. A choked sob tripped past her lips.

The sound was so foreign in her ears she staggered slightly to her right and instinctively gripped the railing for support.

Cursing her momentary loss of control, Caroline threw back her shoulders, lifted her chin, and proceeded to the top of the staircase. She made eye contact with no one, resolved to get through the rest of this excruciating process as she had all the other challenges in her life. Alone.

Despite her outer bravado, Caroline entered the designated women's area with a stab of dread. Not because she was worried about passing the medical exam. Years of surviving on the streets of the East End of London had made her fitter and stronger than most. But what if they instructed her to disrobe completely?

Would they search her clothing and find the money she'd sewn into the lining of her skirt? Would they insist she explain where she'd come upon such an outrageous sum?

Caroline breathed a sigh of relief when a nurse in the entryway instructed her to remove only her coat and blouse. She could keep on her chemise and everything below her waist.

Once she removed the required items, a stern-faced woman in a starched white blouse checked her posture, ran her fingers down her spine, then spun her around and examined her eyes, ears, nose, and throat.

A few more pokes and the woman deemed Caroline healthy. According to the big round clock on the wall, the entire process had taken precisely six seconds.

After several more hours of waiting—this time in a large room called the Great Hall—Caroline was directed to a sizable wooden desk, behind which a man wearing wire-rimmed spectacles sat perched on a tall stool. A variety of official-looking papers lay in neat, perfectly aligned piles in front of him.

Like many of the uniformed men she'd encountered today, he had average features, ordinary brown hair, and very small eyes. He'd also planted the requisite bored expression on his face.

Was he truly disinterested, or would that change as soon as the questioning began?

Caroline held her breath as a shiver of trepidation navigated along her spine. If she failed this interview, she could be sent back to London. But if she passed, she would be free to enter America legally.

Wasting no time with pleasantries, the man said in a flat American accent, "State your name, please."

"Caroline St. James."

"St. James." He shuffled through the stack of papers, plucked one free from the middle, then set it directly in front of him. "Age?"

"Twenty-two."

"Tell me, Miss"—he dragged his finger down the page—"St. James. Why have you come to America?"

"To make a better life for myself." The trite answer flew past her lips before she could edit herself. A mistake. She shouldn't have been so vague. Would he think she was trying to hide something?

Thankfully, the official approved of her answer. "That's certainly a noble pursuit." He gave her a surprisingly patient smile. "But how do you plan to actually achieve such a lofty goal?"

"I'll find a job, of course."

"And do you possess any particular skills that will assist you in this endeavor?"

Of course she had skills. Unfortunately, none that would be considered suitable in a respectable young woman of limited means. Thus, she proceeded to do what came naturally to her when caught in a dangerous situation.

She embellished the truth.

"I'm a seamstress." Not a complete lie; she'd sewn on a button once or twice.

"A seamstress," he repeated. "Why, that's excellent. Simply excellent." He made a mark on the document. "And do you have any relatives in this country?"

Her mind rifled through possible answers. Skirting the truth once more, she presented the names Mary had mentioned earlier. "Aunt Jane and Cousin Bridget."

The man's head snapped up. His gaze thinned with suspicion. Had someone else given those names already?

For a long, tense moment, he said nothing. Refusing to buckle, Caroline returned his scrutiny with a confident, unflinching stare.

A beat passed and then another. At last the official nodded. "Very good. How much money do you have with you?"

Even though she'd prepared for this question, her skin turned to ice. *Breathe, Caroline.* In. Out. In. Out. *You must remain calm.*

A nearly impossible feat. If this man discovered how much money she had sewn in her skirt, he could start asking all the wrong questions, the ones not on the document in front of him.

The ones that would get her deported as quickly as any contagious disease.

Breathe.

Smiling shyly, she placed a look of sublime innocence on her face and quoted the exact amount she'd put in her reticule that morning. "I have five pounds."

She lifted the cloth purse strapped to her wrist to punctuate the statement.

"Five pounds." The man's eyes widened. "A tidy sum, indeed."

Perhaps that would be true if she were an impoverished seamstress coming to America in search of a better life. But five pounds wasn't nearly enough for her real plan. And it was only a fraction of what she'd sewn into her skirt.

"I must ask, Miss St. James. How did you acquire such a large amount of money?"

Adding a hint of confusion to her smile, she pulled her bottom lip between her teeth. "I . . . well, I saved it, of course." She lowered her voice and leaned forward. "I have been preparing for this day for a very long time."

Now *that*, she silently reflected, was the truth.

"I see. Then let me be the first to welcome you to America."

"Thank you. You've been very kind, Mr."—she glanced at the nameplate on his desk—"Andrews."

"It's been a pleasure. You may change your pounds into dollars over there." He pointed to a row of teller windows behind her. "Good luck to you, Miss St. James."

Luck. Luck would play no role in Caroline's time here in America. She'd struggled to survive too long in a "hotbed of villainy" to rely on anything but careful planning and meticulous preparation.

After thanking her interviewer for his assistance, she moved to stand in line at the teller windows. Memories threatened to steal her composure—dark, painful reminders of that horrendous day nearly a year ago when her life had been altered forever.

This journey had begun then, with her mother's startling deathbed revelation. When Caroline had been shocked to discover that she had a wealthy grandfather, a man who had abandoned his own daughter because she'd dared to fall in love with someone below her station. A greedy old man who'd ignored his daughter's pleas for help after her husband had been killed and she'd found herself penniless with a small child in tow. It was the knowledge of her grandfather's cruelty that had driven Caroline to America. She'd come to seek justice.

Justice? Or revenge?

Sometimes it was hard to know, even in the privacy of her own mind.

How she wished with all her heart she'd come to this country for the reason she'd told Mr. Andrews—to seek a better life. But there would be no happy ending to her tale. Not like so many others here today.

Standing in yet another slow-moving line, Caroline had a clear view of the famous kissing pole. She watched, strangely disconnected, as families reunited with one another after their separation earlier in the registration process. She knew nothing of the happiness displayed so freely. Hugging, kissing, laughing. What astonishing foolishness.

And yet . . .

An unwanted burst of longing clawed for release, nipping at the edges of her control like tiny little rat teeth. The dreadful emotion tangled inside one word. *Family.*

What did a woman like her know of family?

To Caroline, the word was nothing but a slippery promise that remained permanently out of reach. Nevertheless, her heart . . . yearned.

What would it feel like to belong so completely? To love and be loved unconditionally? To know true security for once in her life?

Mary, bless her naïve little heart, had claimed that Caroline wasn't alone, that she had someone who loved her without question and always would. Her Heavenly Father.

Caroline shook her head at the ridiculous notion. She'd given up believing in fairy tales long ago.

But what if Mary was right? What if the answer was as simple as her friend claimed?

Would God ever truly accept a woman like her?

Caroline shut her eyes against the painful sensation of wanting what she knew she could never have. No matter how many slow breaths she took, no matter how many times she swallowed, her mouth went dry and it felt as though a noose had been fixed around her throat

For the hundredth time since boarding the SS *Princess Helena*, Caroline wondered if she was making a mistake. Was seeking retribution a shameful act, one that would dishonor her mother's memory?

An image of Libby St. James's face flashed in her mind. Not the beautiful, happy, carefree girl who'd sacrificed everything for love. But the pale, broken woman who'd lived in Whitechapel and been forced to turn to begging, and other more horrible pursuits, to feed herself and her young daughter.

The sad, heartbreaking memory of a mother who had ultimately been incapable of caring for herself, much less her daughter, reminded Caroline why she had come to America.

Richard St. James would answer for his sins. Caroline would make sure of it.

Chapter Two

By the time Caroline made her way to the kissing pole, her thoughts had returned to Mary with a vengeance. She admitted, if only in the dark recesses of her mind, that she missed the girl. Dreadfully so. The realization came as a complete and utter surprise. Only a few hours of separation had passed, and already Caroline felt the absence of her friend. The feeling was quite unfamiliar and one she would rather have avoided altogether.

Apparently, the young Irish girl had done the impossible. She'd broken through Caroline's determination to remain distant. Mary's unassuming presence, her unwavering faith, even her persistence in befriending Caroline despite Caroline's attempts to ignore her, all these things had worked together to form a bond between them.

A bond that now had Caroline worried about the girl's future, to the point of making her stomach roil with apprehension.

Where had the authorities taken Mary? Would they refuse her entry because of her current medical condition?

Surely Mary's God wasn't that unjust. After all, the girl hadn't always been frail, not for most of the journey. But seasickness had taken its toll in the final days. By the time the ship had docked, Mary had lost far too much weight thanks to her permanent state of queasiness.

Perhaps now that they were on firm ground the girl's vibrancy would return.

Would it return soon enough?

Caroline moved slowly around the kissing pole, searching for the familiar face of her friend. One time around, two . . . By the third she lost her remaining shreds of hope. She knew that as each moment passed, the likelihood of Mary joining her today became less and less.

She had to make a decision. Stay or go. Both presented difficulties.

A glance to the heavens told her the sun had dipped well past the halfway mark. Three, maybe four hours of light left in the day. If Caroline stayed much longer, she might have to wander the unfamiliar streets of New York in the dark. She'd been in worse spots, true, but not by choice. And always in an at least somewhat familiar neighborhood.

But if she left now, she would be abandoning the only real friend she'd ever had. The thought didn't sit well, which was the most surprising discovery yet.

Tossing her shoulders back, Caroline paced around the kissing pole once again, widening her arc as she went. The crowd had thinned out, making her search easier. And yet far more depressing.

"Mary," she called out, standing on her toes in order to see over the heads of the taller immigrants. "Mary O'Leary, are you here?"

Silence met the frantic question.

Sighing, Caroline pressed her hand to her forehead. The air was too hot, oppressive even, as if the world were closing in on her and she'd lost the ability to breathe. It was altogether possible she might actually cry.

A hand clamped on her arm.

Caroline stiffened, assessed, considered several options, all the while forcing down the instinct to spin around and fight.

Think, Caroline told herself. *Think before you act. You aren't on the streets anymore.*

Balancing on the balls of her feet, she hovered in a moment of indecision. The touch on her arm was light, nonthreatening. Familiar.

Relief buckled her knees and her heart lifted.

"Mary!" Caroline spun to face her friend. "Oh, you dear girl, you made it."

"I did."

As she looked into her friend's face, Caroline realized she'd never been so happy to see another person in her life. When had this girl become important to her? When had Mary become the sister she'd never had?

To Caroline's surprise—and embarrassment—tears pricked at the back of her eyelids. She banished the unwelcome sensation with a hard blink.

"What happened?" Her voice came out shakier than usual. "The last I saw you an American official was leading you away by the arm."

Mary opened her mouth to speak, but then she swayed, the heavy bag in her hand making her list slightly to the left.

Caroline took her friend's luggage from her and then eyed her more closely. Although Mary didn't look nearly as sick as she had this morning, her skin still had a greenish undertone. "How are you feeling?"

"Stop fussing, Caro, I'm perfectly well." Bold words, spoken with an oh-so-confident manner. But then Mary made the mistake of lifting her chin, whereby she promptly lost her balance.

Caroline automatically reached out to steady her. "Perhaps we should call for a doctor."

"No." A shudder passed through Mary. "No more doctors poking at me, or asking their endless questions." She looked over her shoulder and shuddered again. "We should go, before he changes his mind."

Something in the girl's expression, a cross between uneasiness and regret, gave Caroline pause. "He?"

"The doctor who let me through." A faraway smile spread across her lips, making her look almost ethereal, as if her mind was somewhere else entirely. "Dr. Brentwood was . . . very kind."

"Are you saying he bent the rules for you?"

"I don't know." Mary looked over her shoulder a second time. "And I don't want to find out."

Neither did Caroline.

With her free hand, she reached for her own bag and adjusted the weight of both pieces of luggage to even out the load.

"Let's head to the ferryboats. You'll tell me what happened with your Dr. Brentwood later." She spoke in an authoritative tone, making certain Mary understood that Caroline would expect every detail once they were away from Ellis Island.

Mary didn't appear a bit concerned by the warning. In fact, she brightened considerably. "Does this mean you're coming with me to Aunt Jane's after all?"

Although Caroline had never agreed to travel into the city with her friend, much less stay at her aunt's home, she couldn't leave the girl to fend for herself. Not now. Not with her skin leeched of color and her balance still questionable. "Apparently I am."

"Praise the Lord." Mary smiled even brighter. The gesture added a hint of pink to her cheeks, and she almost looked like herself again. Almost, but not quite.

Mouth set in a determined line, Mary reached for her luggage. "Let me take that from you. I'm quite capable of carrying my own bag."

They both knew that wasn't true.

"Of course you are," Caroline said in an appeasing tone. "But I'm perfectly balanced. You'll throw me off if you attempt to assist me now."

Mary sighed, but she didn't argue, which only confirmed Caroline's earlier suspicion. The girl had yet to fully recover.

For a tense moment, Caroline struggled with the need to protect her friend, to do whatever it took to lighten her burden. This, too, was a new sensation, this desire to care for someone beyond herself and her mother. Perhaps she was getting her new beginning after all.

But this was a dangerous delusion, one she must squelch immediately. She'd come to confront her grandfather and to demand an explanation for his years of abandonment. She had not journeyed all the way to America to make friends with a sweet Irish girl, or to find a place where she belonged.

Richard St. James. She repeated her grandfather's name over and over in her mind. *Richard St. James. Richard St. James. Richard St. James.* At last, the familiar anger and consternation returned, flaming to life like a blazing fire.

On familiar ground once again, Caroline led Mary toward an official-looking booth, moving as quickly as possible through the smell of wet wool, sweat, and grease.

Avoiding pleasantries, she asked if there was a map of New York, more specifically Manhattan, available for purchase.

"No. But you may consult that one over there." The bored official pointed absently to a large map posted on the wall beside his booth.

"Thank you."

A quick perusal of the crisscrossing lines and Caroline let out a sigh of relief. She'd assumed the city's layout would be as complicated as London's, and thus it would take her considerable time to learn her way around. But after one long, pointed look at the map, she had the basic design memorized. The streets, avenues, and boulevards created perfectly spaced squares running east to west, north to south, with a large park in the middle.

Mary pulled in close beside her, her gaze on the map as well, her brows drawn together in confusion. "Do you see where we have to go?"

"That's Orchard Street, there." Caroline ran her finger along a line just north and slightly east of the foot of the island.

Mary squinted at the map, cocked her head, and then—finally— nodded. "I see it now."

Dropping her hand, Caroline kept her gaze trained on their destination a moment longer. She resisted the urge to let out a cynical snort.

She'd traveled across an entire ocean only to land right back where she'd started, on the east end of a city that had no place for her and probably never would. The irony would have amused her if it wasn't so terribly tragic.

Would she ever find a place to call home?

Until she completed her task in this city, it was a question she dared not ask herself. Where she ended up after this ordeal was over didn't matter. It couldn't.

* * *

Jackson Montgomery had a long, tedious afternoon ahead of him, one that promised nothing but trouble, assuming his assistant's report proved correct. Since John Reilly was meticulous with his details, often to a fault, Jackson braced for the worst as he rounded the corner of Hester Street on the Lower East Side of Manhattan.

With his assistant following silently beside him, Jackson was able to study his surroundings without interruption or unnecessary input.

Eyeing the general area, he drew in a sharp breath of air and swallowed back a hiss. The oppressive stench of rotting vegetables, day-old fish, and unwashed linens filled his nose. The low, mournful sound of a merchant's shout rang out, followed by several more. Even though the end of the day approached, countless men, women, and—sadly—children continued to conduct their daily business, as if every sale mattered to their ultimate survival. Which, Jackson realized, was probably true.

Various foreign languages wafted through the foul-scented air. Jackson recognized German, Italian, and several Slavic dialects. Even accented English from the British Isles joined the incomprehensible jumble of words as the people haggled over prices.

He'd never seen so many desperate souls jammed in one place. Not even the opening-night crush at the opera compared with such chaos. Careful to avoid knocking someone over, he wove through the market-place at a slow pace. After nearly careening into a cart of radishes, he turned onto Orchard Street, where the five tenement houses he owned were located.

Tapping into the remaining scraps of his self-control, Jackson emptied his mind of all emotions, all thoughts, all intents save one: the landlord of his Orchard Street tenement houses had better be prepared with an explanation.

Despite Jackson's efforts to remain detached, icy anger surged. He swallowed back the emotion and focused on the alleyway to his right and then the one on his left. So many people. So little space available for them.

As if reading his thoughts, John Reilly broke his silence. "So many people, living on top of one another, it's unconscionable."

"Yes, it is." Jackson swerved out of the way of a toddling child clinging to her mother's skirt. "They pack themselves in the tenement houses along these streets, sometimes three generations to a room."

"That can't be comfortable. Nor"—his eyes haunted and filled with distress, Reilly frowned at the overflowing gutters and trash on the street—"sanitary."

Left eye twitching, jaw tight, Jackson fisted his hand with a white-knuckle grip. "No, not without proper ventilation in the apartments it isn't."

Hence the reason he'd given Smythe such a large sum of money last month. He'd instructed the landlord to make long overdue repairs as well as construct a series of interior windows that would allow the outside air to better flow through the individual apartments.

With so many people living in one unit, the airless rooms had to be stifling on a good day, unbearable in the summer. The image brought a heavy dose of guilt. Why had he not come down here sooner?

Jackson had never planned to own real estate, especially not tenement houses, but that was one of the many consequences of his father's selfish actions. Yet, as he looked around him, Jackson's own difficulties seemed trifling compared to the daily struggles these people faced. He was humbled by their fortitude, by their willingness to forge a life for themselves despite their cramped living conditions, lack of consistent employment, dismal wages, and often the inability to speak English.

The least he could do was ensure they had a safe home to return to at night after a long, hard day of work.

Why had he allowed his landlord such autonomy when his gut had warned him the fellow couldn't be trusted?

The question weighed heavy on his heart because, deep down, Jackson knew the answer. He'd been focused on his own troubles and personal agenda instead of the people indirectly in his care.

Perhaps if his father had stayed and faced the consequences of his actions all those years ago, Jackson would have been more aware of the conditions of his tenement houses.

Instead, he'd spent most of his time and energy restoring his family's good name. He'd been so focused on earning his rightful place back in society that he'd ignored his Christian duty to the people who depended on him.

To whom much is given, much is expected.

He'd failed these people. Now he had to fix his mistake before he could move on with his own future.

"You know, Jackson, I've been thinking." Reilly shifted to his left just in time to avoid stepping into the path of a pack of boys rushing past them. "What if Smythe has taken off completely? What if he's run away with your money?"

Jackson tightened his fist again. "Then we'll hunt him down like the dog he is."

What George Smythe had done was reprehensible. No matter what happened here today, the man would be held accountable.

Tuning out Reilly's litany of complaints about the smells and the crowds and the endless jostling, Jackson continued down the street. Listening to the assistant's grumbles, no one would guess that John Reilly had been raised on a street just two blocks over. Reilly's personal knowledge of this area was one of the reasons Jackson had insisted he join him on this particular mission.

Drawn by some invisible force, Jackson found his interest pulled to the left. Two women carefully picked their way through the dense crowd. The taller one was clearly in charge, leading the way with a slow yet determined gait. The smaller one seemed to be struggling with each step and leaned heavily against her companion for support.

Clearly, they were new arrivals to the neighborhood. The luggage gave them away.

Half a block over, Jackson couldn't make out their faces. But they were dressed respectably, and neither wore any adornment on their heads. They were probably from the British Isles, perhaps Ireland if the frail girl's red-gold hair was anything to go by. She reminded Jackson of a wounded bird as she clung to her friend's arm.

The friend, on the other hand, had much darker hair, thicker and wavier, the color of rich chocolate. That hair, that beautiful, untamed hair, captured Jackson's attention and held it. For a moment—for one shocking, inexplicable moment—everything in him eased, softened, and simply let go.

He fought for objectivity, even as he took a step in her direction.

There was something about her, something unique and different that didn't fit with her surroundings. She moved with a regal confidence more suited to a drawing room farther uptown.

Mesmerized, Jackson took another step in her direction, barely registering that his assistant had turned his litany of complaints toward the heat and the smell of rotting garbage.

Jackson focused only on the woman, only on how the glow of the late-afternoon sun cocooned her in soft, golden light. His pulse thundered in his ears.

The woman, she seemed somehow . . . familiar.

Had they met before?

He couldn't imagine when. She was clearly new to America.

And yet . . .

He sensed that he was supposed to know her.

Closer now, he was able to see her face more clearly. The other girl completely forgotten, Jackson catalogued the brunette's features one by one. She had smooth, flawless skin, high cheekbones, and dark, winged eyebrows over sea-green eyes, pale eyes lightened even further by the afternoon sun.

Would her voice match that exquisite face? Would she speak in a deep, sultry alto? Or a higher-pitched soprano?

One thought kept echoing through his mind. *I know her.*

But how? Where had he seen her before? The image wavered just out of reach. And every step he took toward her made him the kind of man he thought he'd never be. He froze but couldn't look away.

She caught him watching her. Lifting her eyebrows a mere fraction, she stared back at him without flinching or demurring.

Despite the boldness of her gaze, she presented a fascinating blend of innocence and purity of character, the perfect image of a woman with limited means doing her best to survive a harsh world.

Therein lay the problem.

The picture was all wrong.

This was no ordinary down-on-her-luck lass seeking a better life in America. Jackson recognized the look in her eyes, the same one he saw in the mirror every morning. This woman with the stunning face and remarkable eyes had plans.

Big plans.

Jackson understood all too well what it meant to pursue life with a specific goal in mind, to work tirelessly to seek a change in circumstances despite the odds against succeeding.

Perhaps he would . . . There was just enough time to go over and . . . do . . .

Nothing. Jackson would do absolutely nothing because, just as he'd sensed in the woman across the street, he had his own plans. *Big plans* that required unwavering focus on his part.

He would not compromise his honor, not even for a seemingly harmless conversation with a beautiful stranger.

Honor and duty, these were the principles he lived by on a daily basis, the very things that set him apart from his wayward father. And thanks to Edward Montgomery's shameful act, Jackson could never forget, not even for a moment, that honor and duty were all that mattered.

Back on track, the brief moment of recklessness gone, Jackson swung his gaze away from the woman and continued on his way.

He had an appointment with a shady landlord to attend to. And now more than ever he relished the prospect of setting matters to rights.

Chapter Three

No longer trapped in the stranger's probing stare, Caroline finally remembered to breathe. Needing a moment to regain her equilibrium, she pretended grave interest in her surroundings. Yet, no matter how hard she focused on choosing the safest route for her and Mary, Caroline's mind kept drifting back to the handsome stranger and their disturbing encounter.

Even from a block away, when she'd first caught a glimpse of him, something about the man had called to her, compelled her even. She'd felt a strange connection, different from any she'd felt before, one that went deeper than mere physical attraction.

Dragging in a sharp pull of air, Caroline cast another quick glance in his direction, just in time to watch him pass by a mere five feet away. The smell of leather, wood, and spice wafted around her, a pleasant distraction from the foul stench of the marketplace.

As if sensing her eyes on him, he turned his head in Caroline's direction—*again*—and their gazes locked—*again*.

She forced herself to remain calm, to consider him with an objective eye, as she would if she were sizing him up across a gaming table. The man was more than handsome. He was devastating. With a little thread of danger around the edges that caused Caroline's heart to thump against her ribs. His hair was dark, nearly pitch-black, his eyes a piercing blue-gray, his features strong and undeniably masculine.

She immediately broke eye contact and tried not to sigh—she was not the sighing sort after all—but . . . *oh, my.*

He was clearly wealthy, as evidenced by his expensive clothing, but he was like no man of considerable means that she'd ever met. This was no self-serving wastrel or bored member of the upper classes. He would make a worthy opponent across a gaming table, or anywhere else for that matter.

Mary stumbled, drawing Caroline's attention back to where it belonged. As she steered the girl around a cart loaded with day-old bread, a disturbing thought arose. What if the rest of the wealthy Americans were of the same ilk as the handsome stranger?

Hoping to gather more information, she studied the other man striding along the street beside him. Slightly shorter than his counterpart, this one was dressed a bit more humbly and had a slighter build. Although equally attentive to his surroundings, the smaller of the two was clearly the subordinate. But no pushover.

If Caroline's grandfather was anything like either man, then she'd made a serious error in judgment. She'd assumed Richard St. James was a weak man, but what if she was wrong?

What if her grandfather proved a worthy opponent with a steel spine and a clever mind?

To go in blind, without full knowledge of what she was up against, would be a mistake. She knew that now.

She must take the time to research her adversary more closely. Only after she uncovered concrete information about her grandfather would she know how to plot out the details of his downfall.

"Caro?" Mary's voice slid through the stale air. "Are we nearly there?"

Caroline smiled down at her friend. "We're less than a block away."

"Oh, good. I'm a bit"—Mary broke off and released a trembling breath—"weary of all these crowds."

Caroline was as well. But where she was merely frustrated with the pushing and shoving, her friend had obviously reached the end of her stamina.

The poor girl looked beyond exhausted. Her pallor had returned, and the purple shadows beneath her eyes were more distinctive than they'd been that morning.

"Lean on me, Mary, just a little longer. I promise, I'll get you to your aunt's home soon."

Tugging her friend tighter to her, Caroline guided Mary down the street, away from the handsome stranger and the man with him. She silently counted off the numbers above each entryway. Number 96. Number 88. Number 75. Number . . .

Caroline stopped midstep. The numbers were descending not ascending. So distracted was she by her encounter with the dark-haired gentleman, she'd led Mary in the wrong direction.

Badly done, Caroline. She couldn't afford mistakes like this. She must be mindful of every detail, no matter how small. No errors allowed.

Aware of Mary's labored breathing and growing need for Caroline's support, she turned them in the proper direction and pushed through the endless knot of people with as much haste as she dared.

A commotion a block away caused her to slow their pace. No stranger to street brawls, she didn't need the rapidly gathering multitude to warn her what lay ahead. She wasn't especially alarmed—for her own safety, at any rate. She knew how to dodge the worst of any dispute, even if she'd been the cause. But this wasn't just about her safety. Mary was far too frail to risk exposing her to a possible surge in the agitated crowd, or worse, a stray fist.

Keeping one eye on the rapidly growing mob and the other on the street up ahead, Caroline angled her friend away from the fray.

Barely three steps later, a round of cheers rose up from the throng. Caroline swiveled her head to get a better look and gasped aloud.

The handsome stranger was right in the middle of the action, moving with ground-eating strides toward the thickest portion of the crowd. Seemingly unconcerned for his own safety, he reached into the tangle of people and plucked out a shabbily dressed ruffian. Spinning his quarry around, he slammed the fellow against the building behind him and then gripped him by the lapels.

Shouts of encouragement echoed off the brick and mortar.

"Glory," Mary whispered.

Caroline's sentiments exactly.

Although outwardly calm and clearly in control of the situation, the elegantly dressed gentleman spoke fervently to the man in his grasp, his tone far too low to be heard above the commotion.

The ruffian gave some sort of response, which only served to make the gentleman's muscular shoulders shift, flex, and then go still. Very, very still. *Deathly* still.

That was one angry man, barely holding his temper in check. Caroline's suspicions were confirmed when she caught a glimpse of his face. His mouth was flat and hard, his eyes determined.

Running from such a man had been a colossal mistake. Caroline almost felt sorry for the ruffian, except somehow she sensed he'd done something terrible enough to warrant the confrontation. The next few moments were not going to be pretty for him. A potentially unpleasant scene Mary had no business witnessing.

"Come away, Mary. We must get you to your aunt's home before darkness falls."

The stubborn girl let go of her arm and moved closer to the drama unfolding before them. Caught off guard by the bold move, Caroline had no choice but to follow her friend.

Not until she reached the very edge of the crowd did Mary finally stop. The gawking, shouting mob had become surprisingly silent, with their heads leaning forward, as if straining to hear whatever would come next out of either man's mouth.

The gentleman's subordinate stood slightly off to the left of the dispute. He looked mildly put out with his bored, uninterested eyes. At one point, he crossed his arms over his chest, released a heavy sigh, and then leaned his shoulder against the building.

Caroline wasn't fooled by the indifferent manner. He was ready to move into the fray if needed.

"What do you suppose that man has done to incur such wrath?" Mary asked in a soft tone meant only for Caroline's ears.

Caroline shrugged. She didn't know for sure, but she had a few ideas. "If I had to guess I'd say money was involved."

When it came to men and their fights, money was almost always at the root of the matter.

Mary clasped a hand to her throat. "Have you ever seen anything like this?"

Actually, Caroline had. Too many times to count. London's rough East End wasn't known as a "hotbed of villainy" without reason.

Intrigued, she waited with the others for the gentleman to make his next move. A pall of silence still hung over the crowd, broken only by the sounds of breathing—the ruffian's rapid and erratic, the gentleman's slow and measured.

With his victim still in his clutches, the gentleman turned to his subordinate.

"Mr. Reilly." The flat American accent was devoid of emotion. "Our friend here is still refusing to cooperate."

"Yes, I see that."

"Would you be so kind as to locate a patrolman while I detain Mr. Smythe awhile longer?"

Mr. Reilly shoved away from the building. "Right away, Mr. Montgomery."

Montgomery. The Scottish name fit the man with the heart of a warrior, who was wrapped in a fine suit but had a quiet, lethal edge to his movements.

"I am waiting for an explanation, Mr. Smythe." Montgomery shifted his hold, drawing the rogue closer to him. "You may tell me now, while it is just the two of us, or you may do so from behind a row of iron bars. Either way, I will have my answer."

A bout of cursing flew out of Smythe's mouth, the words so foul Mary's mouth dropped open. Caroline had a sudden urge to cover her friend's ears.

"That's quite enough of that." Montgomery shoved Smythe harder against the building. "Let us not forget there are women and children present."

"I'm not frightened of you."

"You should be." Scowling furiously, Montgomery leaned in closer, his breathing calm and measured. Even in his anger, he appeared in control. "I will ask you again. What have you done with the money I gave you for the repairs I ordered?"

Smythe snorted in disgust. "I didn't take nothing from you that you couldn't afford."

"You are missing the point entirely. Take a good look around you." Holding tightly to his collar, Montgomery swung the man around to stare at the crowd. "These are the people you stole from—not me, them. The residents who live in this building with you and depend on you to follow my orders."

Smythe blinked, his eyes glassy with hate. "All I see is a bunch of dirty, worthless immigrants."

As one, the crowd burst into angry shouts in differing languages and dialects. Caroline didn't need an interpreter to know what they were saying.

In a precise, cold tempo, Montgomery unleashed his own rage. "These *immigrants* are good, hardworking, honest people who deserve a safe, comfortable home in which to lay their heads at night."

"Ha. Like you care."

The man had a death wish. Caroline was convinced of it. She was also quite certain he was a rat of the first order.

The muscles in Montgomery's shoulders tightened, and his jaw tensed. "You will not question my motives, ever."

Such arrogant superiority, such grim resolve. However much money Smythe had stolen from this man, she doubted the sum was worth making such a fearsome enemy over.

A cold chill swept through her soul. What if her grandfather was like this Montgomery? What if Richard St. James was equally fierce when crossed?

It was a thought that had never occurred to her. Until now. Panic gnawed at her, trying to tear into her like an alley cat pouncing on its prey. She nearly gave in to the emotion, but an image of her dying mother flickered to life in her mind, and she remembered the first lesson of survival: *Never underestimate your enemy.*

Still, Caroline mustn't allow panic to take hold until she had gathered more information. There was no reason to assume her grandfather was anything like this man. Montgomery's outrage was due to his concern for the people in his care. Conversely, Richard St. James had abandoned his daughter without a speck of remorse through the years. His good name and place in society had been more important to him than his own child.

Renewed anger flowed through Caroline; hot and painful, the emotion was strong enough to bolster her need to ensure justice was served.

No more distractions. Especially not from a handsome stranger with strong moral character and a proper sense of right and wrong. Besides, she already knew how this particular standoff would end. Mr. Smythe would either pay back the money he stole or go to jail.

There was no reason to stay any longer.

"Come, Mary, we've both seen quite enough." With one last glimpse in Montgomery's direction, Caroline took the girl's arm and steered her away.

Mary cooperated without a single argument, which was a relief to Caroline. She had a lot of thinking ahead of her. There were plans to sort out. Information to gather. And, if all appeared in order, a trap to set.

No more distractions.

A handful of steps later, Mr. Montgomery and his battle with the charlatan, Mr. Smythe, were all but forgotten. The spasm of regret twisting through her heart was of little consequence—that's what Caroline told herself.

Heading in the proper direction now, she kept her gaze straight ahead. A loud, happy cheer rose up from behind her, but Caroline didn't look back. Not even once.

* * *

Jackson returned to Orchard Street two weeks after his altercation with George Smythe. He'd learned a valuable lesson about blind trust, hence the need to check on the progress of the new ventilation systems himself. Now that his former landlord was exactly where he belonged— behind bars—Jackson was confident his tenants would achieve a better quality of life. If not today, then as soon as the majority of the building repairs were complete.

Jackson was *not* there for another glimpse of the woman with the compelling eyes and self-assured manner. That would be counterproductive and, quite frankly, a complete error in good judgment. They were from different worlds with different goals in life. His future plans did not include a woman like her.

He hadn't been able to get her out of his mind these last two weeks, though. Memories of her beauty had haunted him deep into the late hours of the night. No matter how brief, he couldn't deny there had been a connection between them. Despite her confidence, Jackson had experienced a strange desire to protect her.

His fascination with a complete stranger he knew nothing about, not even her name, took him by surprise. Especially with his future already mapped out, down to the smallest detail. Yet there he was, striding along the streets of the Lower East Side of Manhattan, secretly hoping for a glimpse of a woman he'd only seen once.

He had probably built her up in his mind. Surely that was the reason for this odd obsession to find her again. Yes, this was his chance to prove to himself that she was as ordinary as any other woman. Once he had his confirmation, he would be able to move on with the next step in his life.

With this new goal in mind, Jackson increased his pace along Orchard Street. Rain had fallen in the early morning hours, leaving the streets slick with moisture and a cool feel to the air not usual for this time of year. At this early hour, the vendors and street merchants were still setting up their carts for business. The sun's rays were stuck behind the buildings, leaving gray shadows dancing lazily along the path Jackson forged.

Stopping at the spot where he'd grabbed Smythe from inside the angry crowd, he turned his back to the building and scanned the immediate area. Although this was the last place he'd seen the woman, the odds of crossing her path again were greatly against him.

So what was he doing? He should go in search of his new landlord for their scheduled tour of his tenement houses.

Instead, he dug in his heels, crossed his arms over his chest, and leaned back against the brick wall behind him. The shadows were deeper in the shelter of the building, a perfect place to watch the activity of the streets unnoticed.

Alone with his thoughts, his mind wandered to a disturbing realization he'd only recently made about himself. Before two weeks ago, he'd always thought David and Samson weak men ruled by their flesh rather than the Spirit. He'd thrown his father in their company and had judged all three harshly.

But now, after laying eyes on the beautiful woman with the stunning face and remarkable hair, Jackson had a different perspective. He still didn't sympathize with their sinful behavior, nor was he able to justify their actions—that would make him too much like his father, which he most definitely was not—but Jackson better understood the power of temptation.

The differences between the men of the Bible and his own father were clear. Once they accepted the error of their bad behavior, Samson and David had turned away from their sin and back to God. While Edward Montgomery had embraced his debauchery.

Anger surged. He was not like his father. He was not.

Then what are you doing, seeking out this woman?

The question brought him up short. He was pursuing a stranger because of a momentary sense of kinship, an unwanted one at that.

He pushed away from the wall, resolved to move on, both literally and figuratively. With tight, angry strides he paced to the foot of the steps leading to the front entryway of 227 Orchard Street.

That was when he saw her. Exiting the very building he'd been about to enter.

Jackson froze midstep. The sight of her caused a physical pain in his chest. He wanted to walk away, at the very least to look away, but he could do neither.

Her beautiful eyes widened in surprise, giving her an expression of shocked innocence. She recovered quickly, though, too quickly, as if she refused to tolerate a single moment when she wasn't in control of her emotions.

How well he knew the sensation.

But then, for a brief moment, her lips curved upward. The sudden, lovely smile dazzled him. Common sense told him he was doomed if he let himself be charmed by this woman. Up close, her skin was like cream, her black lashes like rich velvet.

On your guard, Jackson, this one's not like any other woman you've met.

He swallowed just as she took her first step toward him. Stopping halfway down the steps, she allowed her smile to widen just a bit. "You again."

She spoke simply, in a matter-of-fact tone, as if this meeting had been inevitable. Her cultured, sophisticated accent indicated that she hailed from England and had obtained a proper education while living in her homeland. The enthralling alto was exactly the pitch he'd expected and was in complete opposition to the humble, faded green dress she wore.

"Yes," he said, looking soberly into her eyes. Rarely had a girl captivated him like this. "Me again."

"You are the owner of this building, are you not?" She commandeered the next step, the move bringing her eyes level with his. "The one who sent that wretched Mr. Smythe to jail?"

It was Jackson's turn to blink in surprise and, for a full second, he could not make himself respond to her question. He was rarely surprised by anyone, especially a woman.

After a deep breath, he shook himself out of his frozen state of . . . fascination. "Do you live here in this building?"

Although that would explain her presence here this morning, he could not picture this beautiful, elegant creature living in one of his tenement houses.

"No, well, yes, but I am a very temporary resident," she confirmed. "I will be moving out at the end of this week."

Questions tangled in his mind. Why had she come to America? Why New York? Where was she heading next? Farther uptown or to another part of the country entirely? There were many more questions running through his mind. He asked none of them. Everything about this woman spelled trouble, and Jackson had made it his policy to avoid trouble at all costs.

Why wasn't he continuing on his way? Why was he standing there, hoping to prolong their encounter for as long as possible?

"Tell me, Miss . . ."

"Caroline. My name is Caroline."

Aware that she had chosen to reveal her first name only, and bristling at that, Jackson continued a bit more cautiously. "Tell me, Caroline, since you've lived in this building for a few weeks, what do you think of the living conditions?"

She rested a hand on her hip, caution in her eyes now as well. "Do you wish to hear my true opinion?"

"Of course."

"I think you were correct to get rid of Mr. Smythe. He allowed this building to become nothing short of a slum."

Jackson nodded. Why bother arguing the point? "Go on."

"The current landlord is much better, more caring. He is forging ahead with the building's repairs in a quick and timely manner. However . . ." She allowed her words to trail off, as if she wasn't sure if she should continue. *"However,"* she repeated more firmly. "I do believe Mr. Tierney could benefit from the occasional bath or two."

Charmed by the accurate remark, Jackson resisted the urge to throw his head back and laugh. He was not one to give in to his emotions. He maintained his composure for five full seconds. Then a smile spread across his lips.

In a single glance a thousand words passed between him and Caroline, unspoken phrases that Jackson completely understood but refused to decipher.

No matter how captivating she seemed, no matter how mesmerized he felt at the moment, nothing could change the fact that she was the wrong woman, rousing the wrong emotions in him.

A crying shame, really, because Jackson sensed she would have kept him on his toes given half a chance. And he was only just now realizing how much he would have enjoyed that.

Chapter Four

Caroline watched Mr. Montgomery's reaction to her suggestion that his landlord needed a bath. Or rather, she watched his *highly restrained* reaction to her suggestion. More than a little intrigued, she waited for him to give in to his amusement fully.

He did not, of course. She hadn't actually expected him to. They were alike in that. In fact, as she watched him wipe his face clean of all expression, she found herself doing the same.

Despite her outward calm, her heart beat a sporadic rhythm against her ribs, as if something deep within her recognized a kindred spirit in this man. One overly controlled soul to another.

What pain in the man's past had taught him such careful moderation? Even more interesting, what would it take to push him to the limit, to prod him into a loss of his remarkable control, if only momentarily?

Surprised by the direction of her thoughts, she looked away from his handsome face and clamped her lips tightly shut. She had a long day ahead of her at the library and then the newspaper office and, if all went according to plan, at the Waldorf-Astoria. Yet here she stood, neither attempting to push past Mr. Montgomery nor enticing him into further conversation.

He seemed equally caught in the moment.

Needing something to do with her hands, she tucked some of the hair that brushed her cheek behind her ear. His gaze followed the gesture, then just as quickly snapped back to her face.

His eyes narrowed ever so slightly.

Laid bare under the intensity of his stare, Caroline tensed. She forced herself to breathe slowly, forced her mind to settle. But nothing she tried could pull her out of her strangely distracted state. She was entranced and felt painfully alive in this man's presence.

A dangerous, impossible situation when she was so close to finalizing the details of her plan. With the information she'd already gathered about her grandfather—from the way the New York papers hailed him as a highly respected civic leader and businessman to the particulars of his philanthropic endeavors—Caroline was even more driven to disclose his true nature to society.

If, in the process, she managed to avenge her mother's untimely death as well, then so much the better.

The need to right such a terrible wrong was like a sickness in her, having grown far too powerful to be driven out by a momentary—albeit pleasant—encounter with a handsome gentleman.

As if understanding her hurt on a level even Caroline didn't comprehend, Mr. Montgomery gave her a bold, manly smile and then touched her arm. The connection was whisper light and unbearably gentle.

"Thank you, Caroline. I appreciate your candor this morning. You have been a wealth of information."

Had she? She'd barely told him anything at all.

"I stand by what I said," she insisted, leaning forward until she'd closed the distance between them to a handful of inches. "All of it."

He laughed outright, unmistakable humor filling his gaze.

At last, she thought, *I have managed to push past this man's courteous facade at last.*

Still smiling, his hand traveled toward her face but stopped halfway and floated back down by his side. "I . . . That is, thank you again, Caroline." He stepped to his left, clearing a path for her to proceed down the steps unhindered. "I won't detain you any longer."

Dismissed. She'd been dismissed. In a very polite manner, to be sure, but there was no doubt their conversation had come to an end. At least from Mr. Montgomery's standpoint.

Strangely relieved rather than insulted, Caroline cracked a rueful smile. "I'm pleased I could help."

He gave her a sharp nod, then continued up the steps and into the tenement house as if they'd never met. Hesitating just inside the threshold, his hand stilled on the doorknob. He glanced back over his shoulder, looking straight into her eyes.

They exchanged faint, cautious smiles, a silent, yet definitive farewell that communicated a world of regret on both sides.

I will never see him again, Caroline realized with a heavy dose of sadness. It was just as well, she knew, but that didn't stop the sense of loss swelling inside her.

"Good-bye," she said softly, her voice barely above a whisper.

"Good-bye, Caroline." He shut the door behind him with a resounding click.

After the briefest of pauses, Caroline began her descent down the remaining two steps and then turned in the direction of the Astor Library on Lafayette Street.

Her mind was already on the task before her. But unlike her previous encounter with Mr. Montgomery, this time she did look back in his direction. Not once, but twice.

* * *

A half hour later, Caroline completed the eight-block walk to Lafayette Street and Astor Place. Moving quickly, she skirted past a slow-moving carriage pulled by an ancient horse and then a motorcar puttering along the road at an even slower rate. Men, women, and well-behaved children joined her on the sidewalk, but most were en route to some other place than the library.

That meant Caroline had a quiet morning of reading ahead of her, a perfect scenario under any circumstance. If her time were her own, how she would enjoy spending hours on end in the library, exploring all the worlds inside each book and periodical.

Such was not the case. She had much work to do.

At the entrance to the library she paused a moment and took in the magnificent stone and brick structure that stood four stories high. The architecture was quite complicated and spoke of wealth and money. Large glass windows encased inside stone arches were spaced perfectly from end to end on every floor.

Though Caroline wouldn't have guessed it, according to the librarian, the building had been through several renovations and expansions.

The structure appealed to Caroline's love of precision and order. The sturdy stone and red brick gave her a sense of hope for the future, a reminder that there just might be a place where chaos and uncertainty did not exist.

Refusing to allow her mind to dwell on such a notion, Caroline entered the library quickly, her head down. The smell of leather, decades-old parchment, and freshly varnished wood filled her senses—a pleasing aroma that encouraged her to relax her guard a moment, to stay awhile and simply enjoy the literary treasures waiting to be discovered.

But there was no time for that now.

Gaze still focused at her feet, she made her way to the stairs to the second floor. If she allowed herself to look at the shelves of books lining the walls, if she caught even a glimpse of the beautiful marble and elegant walls, her heart would yearn for what she could never have. Stability. A sense of permanence.

Home.

Yet another dangerous fantasy she couldn't afford.

When Caroline had foolishly confessed to Mary her wish for a secure future and a place to call her own, the girl had told Caroline such a thing was possible. "Caro," she'd explained in her gentle voice. "All things are possible with God."

Caroline had promptly changed the subject before Mary could start in on her about surrendering her cares to the Lord or some such nonsense. In Caroline's experience, God was nothing more than a vengeful, distant presence that allowed flagrant injustices in the world. Why would she ever surrender to such a callous deity?

Lips flattened in a grim line, she climbed the stairs to the second floor and paced to the back of the cavernous room.

Stopping at her usual table, Caroline allowed herself a small smile. The librarian had anticipated her today. The morning newspapers were already stacked in neat, orderly piles awaiting her perusal.

Lowering herself into a chair, she chose the *New York Times* to read first. Ignoring all other sections, she turned directly to the society page and ran her fingertip along the words, looking for one name in particular.

Richard St. James.

She found him halfway down the first column.

Alone in the large room, she read the entry in a small, quiet voice. "Richard St. James made a rare appearance at the opera this evening. His beloved granddaughter, Elizabeth St. James, was by his side, looking as lovely as ever."

Hand shaking, Caroline's finger paused over the newspaper. She remained perfectly still for several heartbeats and forced her breathing to slow.

But no matter how many times she told herself to remain calm, nothing could suppress the feeling of despair. Her blood ran hot, then ice-cold, and her stomach churned with—yes, she admitted it to herself—envy. Pure, unadulterated jealousy of the first order.

All because of that name. That name!

Elizabeth St. James. Beloved granddaughter.

Caroline's first cousin. Her own flesh and blood. A young girl barely nineteen years old who'd been named after Caroline's mother.

The irony was like a dagger to her heart.

Elizabeth St. James.

Caroline suppressed the howl of outrage that formed in her throat. She wanted to rip the newspaper into tiny little pieces and toss each one into a smoldering fire, hot as the fury running through her veins. She wouldn't, of course. Caroline had far too much control to give in to such a childish reaction.

Steeling herself, she continued to read in a low, staggering voice that hitched over every other word. "Dressed in a gossamer gown of layers upon layers of white silk, Miss St. James was, as always, the most attractive, accomplished young woman in the theater."

Attractive. Accomplished. Caroline felt the breath leave her lungs. Yet she read on. "Considered the most popular girl in social and musical circles across the city, Elizabeth's trademark blonde curls were swept up in a classic chignon, offsetting her deep blue eyes that have caused many a male to spout poetry in her presence."

This time it was not jealousy that washed through Caroline but a sense of unfairness. While this nineteen-year-old girl had been enjoying trips to the opera and the theater, Caroline had been scraping for the barest of existences, with the fear of starvation driving her every decision.

The blood rushed from her head, making her dizzy. The emotions raging inside her—hurt, longing, loneliness—were so strong, so powerful she bent over in response. She rested her forehead on the table, overwhelmed and heartsick. How could she ever pull this off? How could she waltz into parties and pretend she didn't know who these people were?

No. *No.* Caroline refused to give up when she'd come this far. No sentiment allowed. And definitely no crying.

She squeezed her eyes tightly shut and breathed in slowly. In. Out. In. Out.

Back in control, she sat up and continued reading. She skimmed over the list of occupants in the St. James private box, completely uninterested, until she came upon another familiar name.

A gasp sputtered past her lips. "Among the other patrons in attendance was longtime family friend and St. James business partner Mr. Jackson Montgomery."

Montgomery? Caroline's pulse leapt. Could this Jackson Montgomery be the same Mr. Montgomery she'd met on Orchard Street?

Surely not. Most certainly this was a mere coincidence. *Her* Mr. Montgomery owned tenement houses, while there'd never been any mention of Richard St. James owning that type of building.

Besides, Montgomery was a common enough name. Although . . . Caroline had to admit that the man she'd met on the street that morning would fit in her grandfather's world.

Slowly, resolutely, Caroline read on. "It is believed a match between Mr. Montgomery and Miss St. James is in the making. Will a spring wedding be in order for this fashionable couple?"

Goose bumps rose along Caroline's arms, and her scalp began to tingle. What were the odds? *What were the odds?* She did the math in her head, calculating all the variables, coming up with a disastrous answer.

Resigned, yet determined to be thorough in her fact gathering, she flipped through the other newspapers the librarian had left for her. This time she searched for the name *Jackson Montgomery*.

She came across no fewer than three other stories speculating on the "event about to take place" between the handsome Mr. Montgomery, a young man of excellent standing, and the pretty Miss St. James, a most worthy match for the gentleman.

Caroline waited for some feeling to emerge. Nothing but a cold emptiness swept through her.

What did it matter if Jackson Montgomery was the same man she'd spoken with this morning? This bit of information changed nothing. In truth, Caroline should consider herself fortunate to have discovered the possibility of Montgomery's connection to her grandfather—and cousin—before she worked her way into their world.

Forewarned is forearmed—one of the hardest lessons she'd learned on the London streets.

After reading through each newspaper again, this time more slowly, Caroline decided she had enough information to put her plan into motion. She knew all the names of the important people of New York, who was in town, and who had traveled to the Continent for an extended stay or honeymoon.

The latter was her best option for infiltrating the upper echelons of New York society as quickly as possible. Caroline St. James was about to become Caroline Harding, a distant cousin of the newly married Patricia Harding of Boston, Massachusetts. Patricia had met and married Malcolm Green of Seventy-Second Street in a whirlwind romance. The couple just so happened to be on their lengthy honeymoon in Europe and had encouraged Patricia's British cousin, Caroline, to visit America.

A handful of chance meetings with the right people at the opera and theater, all carefully played on her part, would eventually lead to advantageous invitations to parties and soirees in the finest homes. After a while, Caroline would be accepted as one of them.

Only then would Richard St. James meet his other granddaughter, the one he'd abandoned to a life of hardship and despair. The old man would never be the same. That much, Caroline could guarantee.

Chapter Five

Two and a half weeks after his latest encounter with Caroline of Orchard Street, Jackson arrived at Warren Griffin's home, determined to put the woman where she properly belonged. In the past. Rolling the tension out of his shoulders, he focused on the brownstone mansion with serious intent. To no avail.

Memories of the beautiful immigrant and her dry sense of humor attacked his mind. She'd made him laugh, and by doing so, she'd helped him forget, if only momentarily, why he had to keep himself under control at all times, why his behavior had to be above reproach, no matter the circumstance.

An odd sensation—part longing, part confusion—sent his pulse racing, his head spinning in turmoil. A secret, uncontrollable portion of his soul, the part he'd ruthlessly suppressed for most of his life, wanted to forego tonight's dinner party and return to Orchard Street.

Jackson cursed himself for the direction of his thoughts. Nothing must be allowed to propel him off the course he'd set for his life. Tonight, his attention belonged to another woman, the *only* woman who should ever be allowed in his mind.

At that reminder, certainty took hold. After his meeting with Warren Griffin, Jackson would be free to take the next step in his future. Marriage. To a suitable, proper young woman from one of the finest families in New York.

His engagement to Elizabeth St. James would be the ultimate symbol of all his hard work, the final proof that he'd restored respectability to the Montgomery name.

Jackson braced for a wave of satisfaction but experienced only a hollow, empty feeling. Where was the sense of completion, the pleasure of fulfillment, the glory that came with knowing his father's shame could no longer hurt him or anyone else in his family?

An image of long dark hair and sea-green eyes swept across his mind. His gut knotted. Even now, the wrong woman crowded his thoughts. Dangerous territory.

He must remember why he'd chosen Elizabeth St. James to become his future bride. She was more than the embodiment of kindness, compassion, and Christian charity. She was his friend, a woman who shared his outrage over the conditions of his tenement houses.

Elizabeth would make a perfect wife, he reminded himself, as if thinking it over and over again would make it true. She was sweet and proper and represented everything good in their world. Even knowing all this, a part of him still wanted . . . wanted . . .

Jackson swallowed back the rest of the thought. Jaw set rigidly, he stalked up the stone steps and knocked with authority.

The moment the door swung open, Jackson crossed the threshold with confidence and nodded to the Griffin family butler of twenty years. "Good evening, Winterbotham."

"Mr. Montgomery." The man sketched a short, elegant bow and then accepted Jackson's hat and gloves. "Mr. Griffin is waiting for you in his study."

"Thank you, I know my way."

Jackson fought the urge to rush his steps. An edge of impatience churned in his stomach as his heels struck the marble like hammers on nails. The sound reverberated against the wood-paneled hallway. He wanted this debt settled; only then would he be free of his father's bad choices and able to make an offer for Elizabeth's hand in marriage.

As he entered Warren Griffin's private study, the older man rose from behind his desk and strode toward him with a genuine smile cracking his weathered face. "Ah, Jackson, here you are at last."

Jackson took the offered hand, smiling cautiously at his father's most trusted friend and ally. There'd been a time when Edward Montgomery had been far richer than the man shaking Jackson's hand. In fact, Warren Griffin's fledgling shipping empire—now one of the largest in the world—had been initially funded by Montgomery family money.

Unfortunately, for every wise investment Jackson's father had made as a young man, three bad ones soon followed. By the time he'd fled the country, Edward Montgomery had lost most of his inherited wealth. He'd also left Jackson with the humbling task of paying back his considerable debts. Tonight's payment to Warren Griffin was the last of them.

Freedom was one bank draft away.

Impatience surged once again. Jackson dropped his hand to his side and forced a calm in his voice he didn't especially feel. "I would have been here sooner, sir, but I was unavoidably detained at the office."

"Understandable, my boy." Before Jackson could respond, the older man motioned to his left. "I believe you know my son, Lucian."

Surprised, Jackson spun on his heel to face the other occupant in the room. A host of boyhood memories lurked below the surface, ready to spill forth. Quickly switching his mind's focus, Jackson shot out his hand once again. "Luke, it's been too long. I hadn't heard you were back in New York."

"I only arrived this morning." With a wry grin, Luke strode forward, clasped Jackson's hand, and gave a quick, hard shake. "It's good to see you, my friend."

"And you."

Although Luke's addition to the party tonight meant Jackson had to rethink his strategy with Elizabeth, he was truly glad to see his old friend.

Luke's blond hair had darkened over the years, and smile lines now appeared around his eyes. The man had barely aged since they'd attended Harvard together. Luke had been an excellent student and loyal friend to Jackson—dedicated, strong-minded, and honorable. When Luke had left for London to take over the British branch of his family's shipping business, Jackson had been sorry to see him go.

He was only now realizing just how much. He'd missed their friendship. Luke had been one of the few members of society who hadn't cared what Jackson's father had done, or why.

"What brings you back to New York?" Jackson asked, silently calculating the years since his friend's departure. Three. Three full years had passed.

"I'm here to attend to . . . family business."

Jackson heard something behind the casually spoken words, noticed how Luke and his father exchanged uneasy looks. Watching the odd exchange, Jackson was reminded of the day Luke left. There'd been something in the way his friend had looked, sorrowful and full of regret, yet tight-lipped and uncommunicative. "Luke, I've always wondered—"

"Enough about me." Luke gave a short laugh, his words sufficiently deflecting an in-depth conversation about himself. "Tell me about you, my friend. Are you still working alongside Richard St. James?"

"I am."

"The old man treating you well?"

"Better than well. We have a strong working relationship and see eye to eye when it comes to our shared business interests. I find

Richard's advice spot-on in most cases, and he respects my legal background enough to turn to me before he signs any contract."

Jackson also offered insight into other legal matters, but he deferred to practicing attorneys when the situation warranted a more careful review.

"Sounds like your father's partnership with St. James is turning out to be more beneficial for you than it ever was for him."

"In more ways than I can explain." Jackson had taken over his father's partnership with Richard St. James immediately following the day he'd graduated from Harvard. Armed with a shiny new law degree, Jackson had quickly discovered he preferred conducting business transactions and taking calculated risks to arguing in the courtroom.

Through the years, the patriarch of the St. James family had become more than a partner in their shared ventures. He was the father Jackson had never had and always wanted. He owed much to Richard St. James, more than he could ever repay. He would consider it a great honor to call the man family.

If Elizabeth said yes, Jackson would get his wish.

At Luke's insistence, they discussed Jackson's investments in greater detail. He expanded on his railroad enterprise and his newer interest in steel, as well as his unexpected foray into real estate on the Lower East Side of Manhattan. When the conversation circled to Luke's life in London, his friend's brows dropped down tightly over his eyes, and his lips clamped into a thin, hard line.

An awkward silence followed.

Warren Griffin cleared his throat. "I see the hour grows late. We should join the others before our absence is noted."

Both Griffins seemed in a hurry to quit the room, their clipped steps equally quick. Jackson followed more slowly.

Not until they were at the doorway did he remember the reason for this meeting. "Mr. Griffin, about that transaction I came to make—"

"After the party, Jackson." The older man rested a hand on his shoulder. "It can wait until after the party."

"But I have the bank draft here in my—"

"I promise, my boy, we'll get on with our other business before the night is through."

Though he'd have preferred to settle matters now, Jackson knew better than to force the issue at this point. "Good enough, sir."

What did it matter if they took care of business now or at the end of the evening? The important thing was that Jackson's future would soon be his own. No more family scandal hanging over his head. No more financial obligations left for him to sort out. After tonight, his decisions would involve only what he wanted. And what he *didn't* want.

Swallowing his impatience, Jackson threw back his shoulders and exited the room a step behind the Griffin men.

Just a few more hours, he reminded himself. After all these years of cleaning up his father's messes, he could endure. Another. Few. Hours.

Luke and his father entered the drawing room ahead of Jackson. Luke's broad shoulders blocked Jackson's view of the room. Ignoring the other guests, Jackson maneuvered around his old friend, locked eyes on the woman he would officially begin courting tonight, and crossed the room to her.

He was aware of conversations continuing around him, but he didn't alter his pursuit. Ahead of him was his future, the only reason he'd agreed to attend this party.

His heart beat slow and steady. His breath remained perfectly even. Odd.

Where was the anticipation he was supposed to feel? He continued across the room to where Elizabeth stood near the marble mantelpiece.

His future bride had arranged her hair in a soft pile of golden curls atop her head. Her face held an expression of tranquility, making her seem distant, untouchable, as though she were a fairy-tale princess waiting patiently for her prince to arrive.

Jackson swallowed. No denying the girl was beautiful and elegant, almost too perfect to be real. When he took her hand in his, he braced for the excited kick in his gut.

None came. He felt only a vague sense of unease that left him feeling . . . slightly . . . unfulfilled.

This wasn't the first time he'd noticed this lack of passion for his future bride, but this *was* the first time he'd been left feeling uneasy about it.

Why had he never longed for Elizabeth? Why had he not lain awake at night anxious to make her his bride?

As though she could read his mind, Elizabeth's eyebrows lifted regally above her cornflower-blue eyes.

Strangely disconnected from the moment, Jackson released her hand and stepped back. "Elizabeth, you are looking exceedingly lovely this evening."

He hated that he had to remind himself again and again and again that this solid, predictable woman was his perfect mate.

Elizabeth smiled at him with a soft look in her eyes, the same bland stare she gave everyone she met.

Why was he only noticing this now?

"It is always a pleasure to see you, Jackson."

Her voice held no enthusiasm.

They were like two strangers, only just meeting, when nothing could be further from the truth. They'd known each other since Elizabeth was still in the schoolroom and before Jackson's family had fallen into ruin.

He kept his gaze on her exquisite face, willing his heart to beat faster in her presence.

"Jackson, I don't believe you've met my new friend, Caroline. Caroline"—Elizabeth gestured someone forward—"this is Jackson Montgomery, an old friend of the family. Jackson, this is my friend Caroline Harding."

The name brought him up short, but he kept his eyes firmly on his intended.

"Jackson." Elizabeth angled her head. "Did you hear me?"

He shook his head, swallowed back a wave of foreboding. "Yes, you have made a new friend."

A rustle of silk captured his attention. He swiveled his head in the direction of the noise and froze.

He felt a physical blow in his gut. It was her. The woman from Orchard Street. Caroline. His Caroline.

Unable to look away, he stared in muted astonishment. Her beauty left him momentarily speechless. The dark hair, the creamy color of her skin, the bold blue of her dress—Caroline Harding was . . . she was stunning this evening.

And those eyes. *Those eyes.* They were as vibrant and green as he remembered. Tonight, they also held a sliver of distrust in them, and a hint of hostility.

Interesting.

"Mr. Montgomery," she said in that distinctive British accent of hers that had stuck with him since their previous meeting. "It is a pleasure to meet you."

So she was going to pretend they'd never met. Her voice was low, youthful, yet rich in tone, almost musical.

Something about the way she looked at him drew him forward, toward her, enticing him to destroy all remnants of the civilized, honorable man he'd worked so hard to become. No wonder. The woman was a complete and total fraud.

What was she up to?

One way to find out. He would let her play out her charade awhile longer. Jackson tapped into his renowned patience and waited for her to take the next step. She brazened it out for several long heartbeats and then slowly broke eye contact.

The next move was his.

He took a step in her direction. She lifted her chin at a haughty angle. Hoping to intimidate her, to force her hand, he took another step, stopped, frowned.

What did he care if Miss Caroline Harding belonged at this party? Unless she was here to hurt his future bride, her presence was of no consequence to him.

Turning purposely away from the woman, Jackson motioned Luke to join them. "Elizabeth, I assume you know Lucian Griffin."

Elizabeth's eyes twinkled in recognition. "Well, yes, we are acquainted."

Luke stepped forward and took his time addressing both Elizabeth and her *new friend*.

Jackson found his gaze settling on Caroline Harding's face once again. The stutter in his heartbeat urged him to look closer.

She was dressed more elegantly than when last they met. Her blue gown was cut in the height of fashion. With her hair piled on top of her head in a loose style that left tendrils framing her face. She had an air of innocence and propriety, appearing to be the very image of a young woman navigating her way through the labyrinth of New York society with great success.

The woman standing before him was no regular society miss—that much he knew. But neither did she appear to be a down-on-her-luck immigrant.

Who was the real Caroline Harding? This elegant, perfectly coiffed creature, or the more humble version he'd met on Orchard Street? And why was she befriending Elizabeth?

The best way to find out was to keep the woman close. Jackson liked that idea. He liked it a bit too much.

Chapter Six

Caroline attempted to settle her raging pulse. From the moment she'd caught sight of Jackson Montgomery entering the drawing room, she'd been aware of his uncompromising masculinity. Even dressed in elegant evening attire, he had the aura of a sly predator. Most of his acquaintance would probably consider it harmless. Not so Caroline.

A shiver navigated down her spine. She could not allow herself to be afraid of him. Jackson Montgomery was just another man at just another party among the New York elite. Except . . .

Nothing could be further from the truth.

He'd recognized her. That much she was able to deduce from the cool, narrow-eyed gaze he had fixed on her. At any moment, he would call her out for being a fraud.

Montgomery chose a different route, determined silence. Clever man. Caroline felt a stab of surprise but would not allow him to gain the upper hand.

This scenario was no different than any of the high-stakes card games she'd joined in the past year, where losing was not an option. Better than anyone else in this room, she knew that Jackson Montgomery was a dangerous man.

Lucian Griffin said something that made Elizabeth laugh. The sound was a pleasant, sweet melody similar to Mary's tinkling amusement. Caroline bit her bottom lip in dismay. She missed Mary and made a mental note to visit her friend soon. But, for now, Caroline must focus on her cousin. Nothing could be allowed to distract her from getting to know this young woman.

Elizabeth St. James was nothing like she'd expected. There was no subterfuge or playacting in the girl, no indication she was the spoiled heiress Caroline had expected to meet here tonight. Her obvious goodness, so much like Mary's, made Caroline suffer an unbearable churning of guilt and regret.

Unfamiliar longing touched her heart, a longing to be the kind of person she sensed in Elizabeth and Mary.

"Miss Harding."

Caroline steeled herself as Jackson Montgomery moved into her line of vision, subtly cutting her off from the rest of the occupants in the room. He was standing too close, the pleasing scent of his spicy shaving soap drifting into her nose.

"Your name is vaguely familiar." He spoke in the same flat, emotionless tone he'd used right after he'd slammed George Smythe up against the tenement house wall. "Have we met before tonight?"

Caroline swallowed. He was baiting her, daring her to reveal her hand. It was far too soon for that.

A master at bluffing, she knew what she had to do next, knew how to play this game. "That's hardly likely. I only just arrived in America a few weeks ago."

"I see." He shifted again, all but creating an intimate fête for two. "I missed where you said you were staying."

"At the Waldorf-Astoria." Her unspoken message: go on, check for yourself. She'd rented a room in the hotel for this very purpose. All part of her meticulous plan to become a part of her grandfather's world.

"The Waldorf-Astoria," he repeated, his dry tone hiding none of his suspicion. "A prudent choice."

Tread carefully, Caroline. Give him as little information as possible.

If Mary were here, she'd suggest Caroline pray for guidance. Caroline preferred to use her own wits, a much more tangible commodity in situations such as these.

Trapped in Montgomery's stare, her palms turned moist and hot. Oh, no. She would not be cowed into making a mistake. "Have you been to the famous hotel, Mr. Montgomery?"

"I have dined there a few times."

A none-too-subtle challenge hovered in his words, daring her to prove—or perhaps disprove—her story, much as a proficient gambler might toss out an important card to see how far his opponent would go.

Now they were on familiar ground.

"What do you think of the turtle soup?" She posed the question with a jerk of her chin, fully aware the hotel was known for the delicacy.

"Personally, I found it rather bland." A slow smile spread across his lips as he spoke, while his gaze turned dark and volatile. She knew that look well enough. The cat toying with the mouse.

What Montgomery failed to realize was that she was no mouse. She was a cat as well.

"I found the soup utterly horrid," she said in a conspirator's whisper.

He laughed at that. A low, deep chuckle that slid across the small amount of exposed skin on her arm. Caroline looked away for a moment, squared her shoulders, then landed her gaze on a spot just over Montgomery's right shoulder.

"Miss St. James, would you care to dance?"

Caroline started at the request, then quickly realized the words had come from Lucian Griffin, not Montgomery. Both men had the same deep tone and spoke with similar American accents.

She opened her mouth to respond, or rather to refuse, but caught herself just in time. *You are Caroline Harding,* she reminded herself, *not Caroline St. James. Not yet.*

Lucian Griffin had been talking to Elizabeth, which was confirmed by the becoming blush spreading across her cousin's cheeks. "I'd be delighted to dance with you, Luke."

Smiling in a charming manner, the man took Elizabeth's hand and gently led her away. Heads bent together, they fell into quiet conversation. Elizabeth, clutching his arm tentatively, seemed a bit nervous in the man's presence. He covered her hand with his, and she visibly relaxed. Their interaction was really very . . . sweet.

Elizabeth was the enemy, she reminded herself, though the sentiment fell flat.

With an unreadable gaze, Montgomery stretched out his hand to her. "Dance with me."

Caroline had stalled long enough.

All her planning had led to this night, to this next step in her well-thought-out plan. There would be no getting close to her grandfather if she didn't first get past Jackson Montgomery.

Smiling with the perfect blend of shyness and naïveté, she took the offered hand. "I'd be delighted."

He tucked her hand through his arm and turned her in the direction of the ballroom. They didn't speak as he led her through two more drawing rooms.

Still, Caroline was aware of the man's hand resting lightly atop hers. She could feel his heat through her gloves, could feel the firm pressure despite the thin barrier between them.

Against her best efforts to control her reaction, she shivered.

His gaze snapped to her. She gave him nothing to look at but her serene profile.

The ballroom itself was one floor below them. As they drew to a stop at the top of the grand stairway, she was reminded of her entry into

America through Ellis Island. Though the twirling dancers made quite a different sight than the sea of desperate immigrants.

She shoved aside her trepidation and focused on this one moment, this one man. "What a lovely ballroom." She cast a serene smile in Montgomery's direction. "A bit small, but lovely all the same."

Very softly, almost as a goad, he gave a partial explanation. "We are not in the habit of building houses with ballrooms here in America. Griffin Manor is one of the few homes in New York that possesses one."

Caroline already knew this piece of information from her research. She'd also discovered that her grandfather's home possessed a ballroom as well. There was only one other in Manhattan. "That must present few opportunities for balls."

He nodded, his austere profile unreadable in the low, flickering light. "There are only a few balls a season, which makes each one that much more special."

"How very . . . American," she said, putting a slight note of censure in her tone.

His jaw tightened. "We handle many things differently here in America than you do in England."

She'd hit a nerve. Remembering the way this man had *handled* George Smythe, Caroline sucked in a sharp breath.

Montgomery gestured toward the stairs. "Shall we?"

She nodded.

As one, they began their descent of the stairs.

Considering the limited size, the ballroom was relatively spacious, with shiny parquet flooring and a chandelier so grand Caroline was sure it would eclipse the entire apartment where Mary and her family lived. Such a disparity of situations, no different than in England.

"Do you attend many balls back in London, Miss Harding?"

"At least ten a season," she said without a hint of irony in her voice.

"How about on Orchard Street?" He leaned in close, his voice low and deadly. "Attend any balls down there lately?"

Caroline went very still, the taunt hitting its mark. Her throat tightened as a touch of ice-cold fear made swallowing impossible. Just as quickly, she put a leash on her emotions.

"I . . . no, I have not attended a ball on Orchard Street, as you well know."

"Indeed." Turning her into his arms, he began leading her through the complicated three-part steps of a waltz.

"I say, Miss Harding, you dance very well." His lips curved in a predatory grin. "For an immigrant just off the boat."

Caroline felt a flush of heat creep across her cheekbones. "You think you know me." She forced her jaw to relax. "But you have no idea who I am." *Or why I'm here.*

"No?" He spun her through a complicated series of turns. "Then, please, Miss Harding, enlighten me. Why would a woman like you, one of impeccable manners and dress, take up residence in a tenement house on the Lower East Side of Manhattan?"

Before answering, Caroline looked at Montgomery with deliberate condescension, as if she had every right to be in this home, as if her heart weren't pounding in a chaotic rhythm, as if her nerves were completely under control.

He returned her glance with an innocuous one of his own, patience personified, his hold around her waist casual and relaxed.

She wasn't fooled. The man was ready to toss her out of this home at any moment.

Considering her options, she decided to go with the truth, or at least a portion of the truth. Something in the way Montgomery held her stare, the cool, measured gaze, told her he would accept nothing less.

"I met a girl of limited means on the journey across the ocean." True. "We became friends, of sorts." Again, true. But now came a bit of embellishing. "When I found out she needed money, I hired her to become my maid. I then—"

"You mean to tell me"—Montgomery's eyes narrowed to tiny slits—"you set off for America alone, without a chaperone or a maid in attendance?"

Oh, he was a clever one. No woman of the British upper classes would ever travel alone. She'd nearly given herself away. No more stretching the truth, Caroline decided. Too dangerous. "Of course I already had a maid with me. But Mary needed the money. She was really more a companion than a maid."

"I see." Moving them through the dance at a moderate, controlled pace, Montgomery executed a slow turn, and then another, and one more, sliding them across the floor with expert ease.

Throughout the dizzying dance, Caroline became acutely aware of the man's broad shoulders, lean waist, corded thighs.

And yet. And yet.

And yet, she must remain focused on their conversation.

"Unfortunately, we hit a bad patch of weather halfway into the voyage. The poor girl took ill and never truly recovered. I knew she would have difficulty successfully navigating the registration process at Ellis Island, so I . . . assisted her."

And that, Caroline decided, was all she was going to say on the matter. Let the man draw his own conclusions. The fewer details she presented at this point, the better.

"How very kind of you."

Caroline bristled at the patronizing tone. Sweet, compassionate, gentle Mary hadn't been in need of Caroline's friendship. And despite Caroline's attempts to ignore the girl, they'd made a connection, deeper than Caroline had been willing to admit until now.

Careful, careful, she thought, holding herself in check.

She smoothed her expression free of all emotion. "Mary is not a charity project. She is my . . ." Her chin rose in cool defiance. "Friend."

"This girl, was she—"

"She is not a *girl*. Her name is Mary."

"I stand corrected. This . . . Mary, she was the one I saw with you on Orchard Street a few weeks back?"

"Yes, she lives in your tenement house with her aunt and cousin."

"And you were with her that day . . . because . . ."

"I couldn't very well leave her to find her way to her aunt's home alone. Not while she was still ill."

His hand flexed on her back. "No, you couldn't."

The sincerity in his gaze, the hint of admiration, made Caroline nearly gasp with relief. He believed her story. She was definitely . . . practically . . . *almost* sure of it.

His next words told her otherwise. "That doesn't explain why you chose to move in with her for two weeks."

"I told you, she'd taken ill. Someone had to nurse her back to health."

"Her own family wasn't up to the task?"

"Don't be obtuse, Mr. Montgomery. We both know you are smarter than that."

He didn't respond. He simply held her stare, waiting for her to continue. She sighed. "You've been down to Orchard Street on several occasions. You of all people know the living conditions there, and the necessity for your tenants to work every day in order to survive to the next."

When he still didn't respond, she reached for a calm that did not exist. How could he not know what she was talking about; how could he be so thick? Had she underestimated him? Was he as coldhearted as the rest of his kind, as her own grandfather?

Caroline suffered a moment of total disappointment in the man, which was the biggest surprise of the night.

But then Montgomery's expression softened, and he spoke with a slow, steady voice. "Your friend's family could not afford to take off from work to nurse her back to health. That is why you stayed with her."

His grasp of the situation confused her all over again. "Yes, that is correct."

"You are a rare woman, Miss Harding."

The compliment sent her pulse pounding in her ears and her heart lurching against her ribs. For one dangerous moment the man had made her forget why she was there. A deadly prospect. Caroline couldn't afford to grow complacent.

Jackson Montgomery sent her mind spinning and made her heart yearn for something more. This put her at a large disadvantage. To deal with her grandfather she would need every available weapon in her arsenal—her wits, nerves of steel, and a heart of stone. Mary had already penetrated the latter. No one else must be allowed to breach any of her defenses.

As if sensing her moment of vulnerability, Montgomery pulled her a fraction closer. Her breath hitched, and a powerful sense of safety warmed her blood.

Now, she decided, would be a good time to pray.

Chapter Seven

For several long heartbeats, Jackson stared at the woman in his arms. He'd never met anyone quite like Caroline Harding. On the surface, she looked like every other young woman at the party. And yet, she didn't fully fit in, either.

The same could be said of the woman he'd met two weeks ago near the Bowery, a woman whose humble clothing had done nothing to hide her regal bearing.

Who was she?

Her story about nursing a frail immigrant she'd met aboard ship rang true. He'd seen her with the girl in question and had witnessed the care with which she'd guided her friend through the labyrinth of Orchard Street.

Who was she?

"I have never met anyone like you," he admitted.

His bluntness seemed to amuse her. "I'm afraid, Mr. Montgomery, I have heard that many times before."

He wanted to believe she was at this party for harmless reasons. He could not. "Who are you?"

His tone came out more lethal for its softness.

Her eyes widened a tiny fraction, enough to tell him he'd caught her momentarily off guard. She recovered quickly. "I am Caroline Harding, as I've already said."

He'd meant the question rhetorically. But her reaction had Jackson wondering if he'd been right to question her identity. "In a little over two weeks I have met two Caroline Hardings."

The music stopped, and she slowly stepped out of his arms. Again, an echo of the smile that had dazzled him the last time they'd met slipped across her lips. "That is precisely how I planned it, Mr. Montgomery."

She was admitting to being a fraud? Right here, in the middle of the Griffins' ballroom? Surely Jackson had misunderstood her. "Is it, now? Explain yourself."

Her smile widened. The expression was far less innocent than before but just as beguiling. "Come, now, you can't expect me to reveal all my secrets. A woman must be allowed a certain level of mystery."

He frowned.

"Oh, bother. You Americans are so suspicious." She released a long-suffering sigh. "My cousin is Patricia Harding of Boston, Massachusetts. She recently married one of your own, a Mr. Malcolm Green."

"I'm aware of the match." He'd attended the wedding two months ago, with nearly five hundred other New Yorkers and just as many Bostonians. The blessed event had been one of the most talked about of the year and had been covered by every New York and Boston newspaper.

How convenient that Caroline Harding would show up *after* the wedding, claiming to be related to the bride, a woman from Boston, not New York, who happened to be out of the country on her honeymoon.

Jackson leaned toward her.

He immediately drew back, shocked at his own behavior. Caroline Harding could be in New York for any number of reasons, some innocent, some not at all.

Jackson had worked too hard to allow himself to make an error in judgment. He was close to putting the past behind him. Yet there he stood, in the middle of a ballroom, in front of all of New York society, wanting to uncover every one of this woman's secrets. For all the wrong reasons.

Swallowing hard, he offered his arm to Caroline.

They left the dance floor in silence, neither attempting to speak again. Jackson was a man ruled by his mind, not his flesh.

Before meeting Caroline Harding, he'd never understood how his father could abandon his responsibilities, *his family*, for a woman who wasn't his wife. In his self-righteous anger, Jackson had always scorned Edward Montgomery's actions, had always thought himself better than the man who'd sired him.

Now, with Caroline's hand resting lightly on his arm and his heartbeat drumming in his ears, Jackson wondered if he carried more of his father's blood in his veins than he wanted to admit.

No. Jackson was better than his father. This strange, unwanted attraction to Caroline was a momentary lapse, the proverbial cold feet. No other explanation made sense.

No other explanation would be allowed to make sense.

* * *

Unsure where he was leading her, Caroline let Jackson Montgomery escort her away from the crowded dance floor at a surprisingly fast pace. Just as well they were finished dancing. She was in no mood to concentrate on the complicated steps of the waltz while also matching wits with the man.

Her current opponent was no overdressed, overfed, oversoft wealthy gentleman she could outthink. Caroline wasn't afraid of him. Except, well, yes, she *was* a little afraid of him.

Knowing when to retreat was essential to survival. She started to pull away and make some excuse to leave the party. Montgomery caught her midstep and tugged her back to his side. His scowl told her he'd been thinking during the silence that had fallen between them.

Coming up with conclusions better not pursued.

"Let's find your new friend, shall we?"

New friend? Oh, right, Elizabeth. He meant Elizabeth. He was testing her. Under the circumstances, she had two choices: retreat or continue as though nothing were amiss.

Her gaze cut back to Montgomery's face. His closed expression told her this was not a man easily fooled with clever stories or inane words. That left her one choice.

Go on the offensive. "I noticed the way you looked at my friend Elizabeth. Am I to assume you are courting her?"

Eyes so blue they appeared silver in the muted light locked with hers. "That is not an appropriate question to ask of a gentleman you just met."

Ah, she'd hit her mark. "Perhaps not. But I find that I like Elizabeth and only wish to ensure her"—Caroline paused as if searching for the proper word—"happiness."

Montgomery's grip on her arm tightened. "Why do you care about Elizabeth's happiness? You have only just met her."

"True." Caroline dragged her gaze free of his and put a shrug in her voice. "But she has left a favorable impression."

Not what she'd expected to feel for a woman she hadn't known existed before two weeks ago. Not just any woman. Her cousin. Her . . . family.

A tug of unexpected yearning pulled at Caroline's heart, making her wish for things she could never have. Security, a home, a future free of fear and uncertainty. The air grew heavy around her, suffocating her ability to draw in a decent breath. She fanned her fingers near her face, trying desperately to look bored.

"Elizabeth has that effect on people," Montgomery said at last. "Everyone she meets likes her immediately."

"A fine quality, indeed." Realizing how hard it was going to be to hurt the girl—her cousin—even indirectly, Caroline forced out her words in a steady voice. "She is, I think, a very special woman."

"Yes, she is." Montgomery dropped an unmistakable warning in his voice that left no doubt as to where his loyalty lay.

Refusing to make a mistake now that she'd come this far, Caroline held her ground without hesitation.

Tonight was only one small step in her long-range plan.

Relax, Caroline. Stay focused.

She carefully released the air in her lungs.

"Ah, there you two are." Lucian Griffin stepped in front of them, forcing them to halt. "We were beginning to wonder where you'd disappeared to."

Taking in her surroundings, Caroline realized Montgomery had led her far away from the dance floor and had directed her toward a more private spot. How had she not noticed the route he'd taken?

In a slow, careful move, Montgomery released his hold on her arm. "Thank you for the dance, Miss Harding. It was a pleasure to get to know you better."

A pleasure? Now he became all politeness and impeccable manners, when only moments before he'd oh so subtly warned her away from Elizabeth.

Jackson Montgomery was proving a master at artifice, equal to her own skill. Did he play cards? If so, Caroline didn't fancy a go at facing him across a table. He would be ruthless.

Of course she, too, could be ruthless when it came to executing a plan.

"You are quite welcome, Mr. Montgomery," she said with equal politeness. "I hope we may repeat the experience in the near future."

"Indeed." Bending at the waist, he took her hand, hesitated a fraction longer than necessary, then pressed his lips to her knuckles. Even through the gloves she could feel the firm pressure of his mouth. A shiver worked its way up her spine.

Why could she not remember that this man was a part of the enemy camp, a business associate and friend of the St. James family, and perhaps even the future husband of her cousin?

The thought left her feeling hollow inside.

"Caroline." Elizabeth's voice broke through her chaotic thoughts. "My grandfather is throwing a dinner party at our home tomorrow evening. Would you care to join us? I've already asked Luke"—she tossed the man a shy smile—"and he has graciously accepted the invitation."

This was it. The moment she'd been waiting for all night, the sole purpose of instigating a friendship with Elizabeth St. James. Where was Caroline's joy? Her sense of relief?

She'd come here for this very reason. Yet all she could think about was the man beside her, the way his impossible-to-ignore presence made her lean instinctively in his direction.

"Tomorrow evening?" She scrunched her brows together in a slight frown. "This is awfully short notice."

"Please say yes, Caroline. Now that Luke has agreed to join us we are in need of one more to even out the numbers."

"Elizabeth, my dear, perhaps your friend has other plans for tomorrow night and doesn't wish to break them to join us."

Oh, Montgomery was a smooth one. He'd spoken with such casualness, but Caroline had caught the challenge in his eyes, the kind that told her to keep her wits about her or suffer the consequences.

Why must she keep reminding herself of that?

"Yes, Elizabeth, I would like nothing better than to attend your dinner party tomorrow evening."

"Oh." Elizabeth clapped her hands together. "Oh, how lovely."

The other woman's joy was so genuine, so infectious, that Caroline almost recanted her agreement. For a perilous moment she found herself reconsidering everything.

She could walk away right now, this very night, and never look back. She could return to England before anyone was hurt. When she'd planned her initial strategy all those months ago, she'd thought only of the man who'd abandoned his own daughter and, subsequently, Caroline as well.

She hadn't expected to contend with other family members, hadn't expected to discover she had a cousin nearly her own age.

What had seemed so simple back in London had become far too complicated to sort out in the middle of an overcrowded party.

Caroline needed time to rethink her plan. As if on cue, a tall grandfather clock chimed the hour. Midnight already. A perfectly acceptable time to leave a party of this sort.

Unfortunately, Caroline couldn't leave yet, not without drawing unnecessary attention to herself. Her problem was solved when they were joined by two young women. This was Caroline's opportunity to make her escape.

She eased away with as little fanfare as possible. She could feel all eyes watching her retreat. No surprise there. In open defiance, she lifted her head a fraction higher and carried on as though she belonged in this world.

If all went according to plan, the pretense wasn't even a lie. Or at least, not a complete lie.

* * *

Jackson watched Caroline Harding pick her way through the crowded room, her agile gait reminding him of the woman he'd first seen on Orchard Street. As she ascended the staircase, an odd jolt of longing sent his pulse racing. He shook himself free of the sensation.

He knew nothing about the woman other than the few facts she'd deigned to reveal. She was a mix of contradictions. Bold yet innocent. Wary yet clever. Jackson found himself intrigued. Dangerous territory.

Filled with doubt, he watched her a moment longer. There was an edge to her dark beauty, a sharpness that warmed his blood.

His reaction was not entirely proper. He nursed the suspicion growing in his heart, relishing the fact that he would have another opportunity tomorrow evening to uncover the source of her allure. That left him an entire day to do a bit of digging. He would begin the process tonight.

Only once Caroline had disappeared into the crimson drawing room did he remember Elizabeth's presence. He turned his attention to her, and for a moment, he simply watched his future bride converse with Luke.

Perhaps it would be for the best to wait to begin his courtship. He needed to finish his business with Warren Griffin. And it wouldn't hurt to discover just what Caroline Harding was up to now that she'd befriended Elizabeth.

"Elizabeth, I'm afraid I must leave you in Luke's capable care." He took her hand and again wondered where the spark had gone. Had it been there before? Yes, of course. He was simply battling a case of cold feet. "I will see you tomorrow evening at your grandfather's home."

Gently pulling her hand free, Elizabeth gave him her trademark serene smile. "I look forward to it."

Frowning slightly at the lack of emotion in her voice, Jackson turned to Luke. "And you, my friend, what do you say to luncheon at the Harvard Club?"

"I say it's about time you made the offer."

After agreeing upon an hour to meet, Jackson went in search of Luke's father. He found the older gentleman in the billiard room.

"Ah, Jackson, there you are." Griffin set down his cue stick. "I was just about to come find you."

"I was hoping that might be the case."

"Yes, yes." He motioned for the other man to continue the game without him. "Come along, then."

Side by side, they navigated a labyrinth of hallways only to end up where Jackson had begun the evening—in Warren Griffin's private study.

Once the door was shut and they were settled in their respective chairs, Jackson pulled out the bank draft he'd brought with him.

"This is the last of the payments I owe you." He handed over the piece of paper and waited for Griffin to glance at the amount.

"You know how I feel about this." The older man shook his head, sighed. "I never expected reimbursement. The money I gave your father was a gift."

They'd had this same conversation every time Jackson made a payment on his father's behalf. "He should never have taken the money from you in the first place."

Griffin cocked a brow. "He had his reasons."

"Dishonorable ones."

"Not entirely. And despite what you may think, your father never coerced the money out of me. I willingly gave him what he asked for."

Jackson frowned. "Even knowing he would use it to leave town instead of face the consequences of his actions?"

"Again, all I am willing to tell you is that he had his reasons for what he did."

Of course he did. Jackson swallowed back a disgusted hiss. "Then he should have stuck around and explained himself."

But Jackson knew that would never have happened. Even if he'd wanted the chance to ask for forgiveness, he couldn't have done so. Edward Montgomery had been banished from every home in New York. Not because he'd left America without a backward glance, but because he'd taken his wife's sister with him.

The resulting scandal had been unprecedented. At the time, Jackson had been in his final days at Harvard. It had taken him years to restore his family's name to the point where all the best families of New York once again accepted someone with the last name Montgomery into their homes.

As if reading his thoughts, Warren Griffin cleared his throat. "Your father isn't evil, Jackson."

"Perhaps not. But he's certainly selfish." *And weak.*

Edward Montgomery had never once thought about the devastation he'd left behind. Or the embittered wife who hated all men as a result of her husband's betrayal.

"You are a good man, Jackson." Griffin placed the bank note in the top drawer of his desk. "You have borne more than your share of the burdens for your family and have done so admirably."

Jackson said nothing. His father had left him no other choice than to bear the consequences of his actions. "I appreciate your support, Warren, more than you can know. By opening your home to me, to my family, you taught others in town to do the same."

"You will always be welcome here, Jackson. Not only are you Luke's friend, but you are an honorable man. It is a great joy to include you in our circle of friends."

Jackson shifted uncomfortably in his chair. Did he deserve such praise? Was he honorable? Had he ever truly been tested? An image of Caroline Harding flashed before him.

Was she a temptation put before him to test his resolve, to see what he was made of?

God is faithful. He will not allow you to be tempted beyond what you can bear.

Jackson had to believe that was true. He had to trust that he was nothing like his father.

"Jackson, my boy, I have said this to you before, but it bears repeating. If you ever find yourself in trouble or in need, do not hesitate to come to me for assistance."

"Thank you, Warren. I will keep that in mind."

Jackson rose, said a final farewell, and then left the room without another word. He had no plans of taking the man up on his offer. Because no matter what challenge Caroline Harding presented in the coming days, he would not give in to her charms. He would keep his honor intact, remembering what he would lose if he faltered even for a moment.

Halfway down the hall, the earlier sense of foreboding returned. The sensation grew more distinct with each step he took. Jackson couldn't help but wonder if he was already in over his head.

Chapter Eight

Caroline woke the next day with a ruthless headache. Her dreams had been plagued with dark, watery images she hadn't been able to bring into focus. More exhausted now than when she'd first laid her head on the pillow, she allowed awareness to drift into her mind by degrees. Better that than remember the details of the previous evening.

And the man who'd played a starring role in her dreams: Jackson Montgomery, her cousin's future husband, her grandfather's business partner.

Caroline's own personal nemesis.

She winced but kept her eyes firmly shut.

After a moment, she became aware of the first threads of sunlight filtering through the large plate glass window of her hotel suite, beckoning her to start her day.

Sighing, Caroline peeled open one eye, then the next, then promptly shut both when her gaze landed on the ornate red and gold canopy above her head. How could people live with such decadence when so many others barely scratched out an existence? Not that Caroline didn't enjoy the luxurious room—she'd be a hypocrite to pretend otherwise—but it was the principle of the matter that raised her hackles.

Most of her life she'd hustled for food, always worrying about where she'd find her next meal. Now she had to pretend she came from a world of luxury where her most pressing problem was what to wear that day.

She stretched out her limbs, gave a little sigh of pleasure as the fine linen slid across her torso. The sound startled her eyes open. What was wrong with her? This was not her, this lazy, idle creature. Infiltrating her grandfather's world was already taking a toll on her spirit.

Living among the wealthy, even for a week, carried unexpected challenges. One in particular came to mind.

Jackson Montgomery.

After spending her dream-hours with him, Caroline did not wish to think of him this morning. He'd already proven himself far too clever, too dangerous, and highly suspicious of her. A deadly combination.

It was unnerving how he seemed to look past her exterior and straight into her core. If he showed up at her grandfather's tonight, Caroline could not let her guard down around him, nor could she let him see a moment of weakness in her.

Groaning at the daunting task ahead, she buried her head beneath her pillow. The scent of lavender filled her nose. The pleasant aroma reminded her that she didn't belong in this world. But she didn't belong in Whitechapel, either. In truth, she didn't know where she belonged.

Sighing a third time in so many minutes—*really, that is quite enough of that*—Caroline tossed aside the pillow and stared up at the canopy above her head. She'd fallen asleep counting the seams in the material, her mind a whirlwind of chaotic thoughts. Now she couldn't seem to get out of bed, even when she had a multitude of tasks to complete before tonight's dinner party.

Not for the first time since moving uptown, she wished Mary were here with her. Caroline could use the girl's calming influence. Maybe her friend would pray for her. Or simply offer up words that would provide comfort.

A knock at the door had her scrambling out of bed with a cold start. Looking frantically around, she had to remind herself she'd done nothing wrong. She'd paid for this room already, a full two weeks in advance.

"One moment, please," she called out.

Working fast, she shrugged into a lush rose-colored robe that cost more than her mother had earned in a year. Guilt coursed through her as Caroline let her gaze wander about the bedchamber. Libby St. James would have enjoyed a night in a room like this. Her mother had *deserved* a night in a room like this.

Why hadn't Caroline tried to win vast amounts of money before her mother died, if for no other reason than to lighten Libby St. James's burdens?

Caroline knew the answer, of course.

Because fleecing unsuspecting gamblers, no matter how much money they had in their pockets or how badly they played, could not be justified. Not morally.

Another knock rang out, this one louder than the first.

"Enter," Caroline called out at the same time she slipped her feet into a pair of satin slippers. Satin! What a strange, extravagant luxury that felt beyond ridiculous, yet she knew it was required for the role she'd chosen to play.

The hotel maid assigned to her room poked her head around the door. "You told me to wake you at dawn, Miss Harding."

The soft, lilting American accent sounded more pronounced this morning, as if Sally was taking great pains to speak very clearly, very precisely. Caroline only noticed the small change because she took equal care with her own accent. What, she wondered, was Sally hiding inside that careful inflection?

"Yes, I did wish for you to wake me early. Thank you." When the girl hovered on the threshold, chewing on her bottom lip, Caroline motioned her forward. "Please. Come in, Sally. I would like your opinion on something."

"You want *my* opinion?"

"I do."

Not sure why that surprised the girl, Caroline ushered Sally into the room. The maid wore the requisite hotel uniform, a nondescript light blue dress under a long white apron tied in a neat bow at her back. The cap on her head hid the girl's hair, but Caroline could tell from her fair coloring and light eyebrows that Sally was a blonde like Elizabeth. They were of the same height and build as well.

Unsettled by the similarities, Caroline let go of Sally's arm and moved across the room to glance out the window overlooking the street below. At this hour, activity was light.

Sally cleared her throat.

Caroline glanced over her shoulder.

"You wished for my assistance with something, Miss Harding?"

"Yes. Come with me." Caroline directed the maid to the closet on the far side of the room. "I've been invited to a private dinner party tonight, and I'm mulling over what I should wear."

"You want my opinion on what you should wear?" Sally straightened her spine, looking quite pleased, perhaps even triumphant, as if she'd just succeeded at some secret task. "Truly?"

Caroline bit her lip again, wondering if she was making a mistake dragging the maid into her intrigue, no matter how indirectly. She proceeded cautiously. "If you were ever to attend a private dinner party where you were meeting an important person for the first time, would you wear this dress?" She pulled out a sophisticated crimson gown. "Or that one?" She indicated a blue silk dress with a nod of her head.

As Sally surveyed the choices a moment, a shrewd look filled her eyes. "If I were to attend such a party"—she stepped forward and considered a moment longer—"what impression would I be wanting to make?"

The question proved the girl was far more intelligent and observant than most in her position, traits Caroline had noticed from their first meeting. Sally might be an employee in this hotel, but she had brains. And that knowing look in her eyes indicated that she recognized that Caroline wasn't quite the person she pretended to be. Perhaps Sally wasn't the person she seemed, either. Perhaps, like Caroline, the woman carried secrets hidden deep within her.

Instead of feeling threatened by her suspicions, Caroline felt a connection to the maid, as if she'd known the girl all her life. She'd felt a similar bond with Mary the first time they'd met as well. Two strong connections in so many months. How odd. "The goal is to make the people at the party want to know you better."

Sally nodded. "Would I want to portray"—she glanced at Caroline—"innocence?"

A valid question, one Caroline had considered long before she'd boarded the SS *Princess Helena*. "No, not innocence, not particularly. However, you would want to present a nonthreatening air. Let's say harmless but likable."

Hands on her hips, Sally leaned forward and stuck her head inside the closet. "I'd wear this one." She plucked out a white silk dress with delicate silver lace on the bodice and a satin ribbon of the same color at the waist. "They'll not be able to resist you."

At Sally's declaration, Caroline found herself torn between amusement and a jolt of unexpected longing. "I could never pull off irresistible."

"But of course you could. Not only will this dress set off your coloring, but you will appear sweet and pure, like a . . . like an ingénue." Sally gave an impressive eye roll, the censure in the gesture making her seem as though she knew more than she was letting on. "The wealthy in this country do so love their ingénues."

An ingénue, indeed. Caroline smiled reluctantly. Did she wish to make that particular statement? A pointless question. She could never pull off sweet, youthful innocence.

Despair threatened to overwhelm her. Was she kidding herself? Was she playing at a game that was beyond her skills? Would she ultimately destroy herself rather than her grandfather?

As if sensing the direction of Caroline's thoughts, Sally replaced the dress in the closet with considerable care and set a slim hand on Caroline's arm. "May I speak freely, Miss Harding?"

Caroline nodded.

"I know you are not one of them."

Caroline drew in a sharp breath. She thought she'd been so careful, addressing every last detail. Clothes. Hair. Attitude. "How . . . how do you know?"

"It's not a bad thing." Sally squeezed her arm. "I meant it as a compliment."

Oh, but this was terrible. "How am I giving myself away?"

"You look me in the eye, for one. You also speak to me in a respectful tone." She let out a short laugh. "At this point, due to my impertinence, you should be tossing me out of this room, but instead you are waiting to hear what else I have to say. You are good, Miss Harding, and very kind. Those qualities can't be faked and are rarely seen among the wealthy set in New York. Not from my experience, anyway."

Caroline was many things, but she'd never thought of herself as either good or kind. In her experience, such qualities equaled weakness. And weakness was a death sentence in Whitechapel.

"Whatever you are planning," Sally continued, "you will be better off playing to your strengths."

Caroline tapped a fingertip to her lips, her mind running through the decisions she'd made over the last few weeks. She *had* been playing to her strengths, or so she'd thought. She'd used her keen mind to gather information about her enemy. She'd meticulously planned every detail of her entry into her grandfather's world, down to what clothes to wear and when. But now this hotel maid claimed she'd missed the mark.

"All right, Sally, since you seem to have me all figured out. What are my strengths?"

Not at all insulted by Caroline's flat tone, Sally dropped her hand and stepped back. "You have a unique ability to make people around you feel important, as though they matter."

"I . . . do?"

"You are doing it now, by asking a hotel maid for advice. Anyone else in your position would ignore me completely, but you treat me as someone of worth. No." Sally shook her head vehemently. "You are not one of them. I'd stake my life on it."

Caroline's heart lurched. "But I have to make them think I belong." Her grandfather must not discern her reasons for getting close to them, not at first.

Definitely not tonight.

"Well, then, I suggest you be yourself—charming, kind. Likable. Speak to the other guests the way you speak to me. They will have no other choice but to love you."

Love her. Another sliver of longing slipped past her defenses. No. *No.* She couldn't allow herself to hope for something so out of reach. This pursuit wasn't about love, or acceptance. Or even belonging. It was about righting a wrong, about making a man pay for his sins. A man who'd embraced his granddaughter Elizabeth while he'd abandoned his own daughter to the mean streets of London.

Richard St. James must pay. He must.

What will you do after you've exacted your revenge?

Caroline didn't know the answer to that question. In truth, she hadn't bothered thinking that far ahead. She knew she could never go back to living on the London streets. Where she would go when this was over, she couldn't say.

Thankfully, Sally's voice broke through her thoughts before she could contemplate the problem any longer. "You don't want them to love you, do you? You want something else entirely."

How much should she tell this girl? Cautious to the bone, for very good reasons, Caroline knew better than to reveal her plan to a stranger. Thus, she spoke in generalities. "I simply want them to think I'm one of them. That's all for now."

A thoughtful expression in her gaze, Sally nodded. "There's no denying you look the part. You sound like one of them, too."

Caroline sighed. Of course she looked and sounded like an educated woman of class and substance. Libby St. James had taught Caroline herself, focusing on the various traits one would expect in a highborn lady. A well-worn, beloved Bible had been her primer.

When Sally held her silence, blinking at her with a measured gaze, Caroline took the maid's arm and directed her into the tiny parlor of her suite. "Looking and sounding the part aren't enough, are they?"

"No." Sally shook her head. "Of course, with the right dress and the proper hairstyle you've won half the battle."

Winning half the battle, or even the full battle, wasn't her goal. Caroline wanted to win the war. According to Sally, she needed a new approach, one she should have thought of before now.

This maid was the key. What better way to know how the upper class acted than to learn from someone who witnessed their activity on a daily basis?

"Sally, how long have you worked at this hotel?"

"Nearly four years. I worked in a private home a year before that." A shadow fell over her face. "I was the personal maid for the lady of the house."

There was a story there, but Caroline didn't think Sally would reveal the details if she asked. Not with that closed expression on her face. "Would you say you've had considerable experience with the wealthy men and women of New York?"

Sally snorted in disdain. "I would, indeed."

Definitely a story there.

"What am I doing wrong?" The question was as much an admission of her role as an imposter as if she'd come out and said as much aloud.

Sally smiled then, her wily look reminding Caroline of the young pickpockets in Whitechapel. They had the same happy expression as this girl, right after a successful pinch. "Nothing that can't be addressed over time."

An image of Jackson Montgomery materialized in her mind, and a shiver slipped along her skin. She remembered well the shrewd look in his eyes both times they'd met. He would surely be at the dinner tonight, watching for any mistake she might make. She would have to be smarter than him. "I don't have a lot of time to prepare."

Only a few hours.

Was it too late? Had she already blown her chance to ruin her grandfather before she'd even met the man and discovered his weakness, the one thing—whatever that one thing was—that would destroy him in the same way he'd destroyed her mother?

Caroline wouldn't hurt her grandfather directly; that would make her no better than he. Instead, she would allow him to destroy himself. She would use the same strategy she did with the arrogant wealthy gentlemen who came to gaming clubs, the ones who overplayed their hands and didn't know when to quit. Greed, it was a powerful motivator and at the root of most men's downfalls.

"Sally, do you think you could teach me where I'm making my largest mistakes by this evening? I'd pay for your services."

"I don't want your money, Miss Harding. But I would consider it a joy to work with you."

"You must let me reimburse you somehow. If not money, then some other way."

"Perhaps you could speak with the manager and request my exclusive services during your stay?"

The request had Caroline wondering what the other guests expected from a pretty young maid like Sally. Surely there were some requests, perhaps from the males, that were decidedly unpleasant. She even supposed many of the female guests were difficult as well, perhaps openly rude.

Caroline would ask Sally about the particulars of her job and her life. One day. But now was not the time. The clock was ticking, and they had only a handful of hours to prepare.

"If I make arrangements with the hotel manager, would you be willing to start immediately?"

"Oh, yes, Miss Harding. Absolutely."

"Excellent." She smiled. "Under the circumstances, I think you should call me Caroline."

"I will not." Sally shook her head at Caroline, obviously disappointed in her. "A maid never addresses her mistress by her given name."

"Well, then." Caroline tried to look stern. "We'll call that my first lesson."

That made the girl laugh, just a little, enough to let Caroline know she'd won herself an ally, if not a friend. The realization made her miss dear Mary more than ever.

"You are a quick learner, Miss Harding. I'll give you that."

She had to be. "Thank you, Sally." Caroline tightened the belt around her robe and added a hint of snobbery to her tone. "While I get dressed for the day, please seek out the hotel manager and inform the man I would like a word with him."

Instead of doing as she was told, Sally stood rooted to the spot. When Caroline simply stared at her, the maid angled her head and gave her a look of impatience.

"What now?"

"Miss Harding." Sally blew out a slow rush of air. "A woman in your position would never dress herself."

"But that's absurd. I'm in the privacy of my own room. Who will know?"

"*You* will know."

The point was a valid one. Even alone, Caroline must play her role. With that in mind, she threw her shoulders back. "Allow me to rephrase my request. Once you have helped me dress, you will inform the hotel manager that I wish to speak with him about an important matter."

"Yes, Miss Harding."

Caroline moved to the dressing table and sat. Eyes focused on her image in the vanity, she grabbed her hairbrush without looking down and handed it to Sally over her shoulder.

The maid got immediately to work.

Holding back a smile, Caroline watched Sally arrange her long dark hair into a beautiful, fashionable twist. The girl had considerable skills, and Caroline liked her more as each moment passed. "I will wear the green-striped walking dress today."

"An excellent choice, miss. I will see to it at once."

Before turning away to retrieve the garment, Sally caught her eye in the mirror and winked. The gesture spoke volumes. Caroline was on the right track at last.

She only hoped her efforts would be enough.

Chapter Nine

Jackson arrived at the Harvard Club twenty minutes ahead of his scheduled meeting with Luke. Welcoming the time alone, he strode along the dimly lit corridors, hardly taking note of the décor, his mind hastening through the events of the previous evening. Nothing had gone as planned, not his conversation with Warren Griffin or his interaction with his future bride.

Uneasiness spread through him, and he quickened his pace.

Was he experiencing a case of cold feet? Was that the cause of this sudden void in his heart?

That had to be the reason.

The sooner he made an offer for Elizabeth's hand, the sooner they could set a date. His life would be back on course. Nothing stood in the way anymore, nothing except this odd sense of uneasiness that refused to release him. Bad timing that, since he planned to speak with Richard St. James that very afternoon. He would eventually request Elizabeth's hand from her father, Marcus, as that had always been the plan. But out of deference for his business relationship with Richard, Jackson wanted to approach the elder St. James first. Once he had Richard's blessing, he would seek out Marcus's as well.

Jackson anticipated both conversations going well. After all, the engagement between him and Elizabeth had been understood for years.

Soon, she would become his fiancée. And then his wife.

Uneasiness spread through him again, a sensation Jackson had rarely felt before a month ago.

Before he'd met Caroline Harding with her beautiful eyes, hidden agenda, and secretive nature.

Scowling, he veered into the club's library and settled in a chair next to a small table containing the day's morning newspapers. He couldn't drum up any interest in the news. His mind reeled with thoughts of a woman he hardly knew.

Something about Caroline Harding had captured his attention. Whenever he was in her presence, some indefinable emotion called to his inner nature, a wild part of his soul he'd kept hidden deep within himself since boyhood.

Angry at the direction of his thoughts, he yanked up one of the newspapers and snapped it open. The type blurred in front of his eyes.

The logical course of action would be to seek out more information on Caroline Harding, perhaps verify her story and connection to Malcolm Green's new wife, Patricia Harding. Jackson knew where to start, with her traveling maid turned companion. He knew the girl's name—Mary. He also knew where she lived—*his* tenement house.

So why wasn't he charging down there right now and demanding answers?

Scoffing in frustration, he turned the page with a hard flick of his wrist.

A movement off to his left caught his eye. Turning, he saw Luke striding in his direction. His friend made slow progress, stopping every few feet to address someone wanting to shake his hand or welcome him back.

Smiling ruefully, Jackson set the newspaper back on the table.

A hand clasped his shoulder and Luke came into view, then moved around Jackson and sank in the overstuffed chair across from him.

"The Harvard Club hasn't changed a bit."

Jackson looked around, took in the rows of bookshelves on his left, the brick fireplace on his right, the muted colors on the wall, the masculine furniture throughout. A man's sanctuary, to be sure, all the way down to the smell of cigars and aged leather. "I suppose that's part of its charm."

"Charm." Laughing, Luke's gaze shot around the room. "I don't know about that, but the sameness does provide a sense of homecoming, one I find rather comforting."

"Speaking of your homecoming." Jackson repositioned himself in his chair and leaned slightly forward. "Is your return permanent or temporary?"

"I don't know yet." Luke took another long look around the room. "It will depend on whether I can settle a certain matter with my father."

The evasive answer wasn't typical of the man Jackson had once known. He remembered the awkward tension in Warren's study last night, a tension father and son had rarely shared in the past. Something didn't add up.

Due to their long-standing friendship, Jackson decided to be direct. "Why are you really here, Luke? What brought you home so suddenly?"

"Would you believe me if I said I was homesick?"

"I would not."

"You know me well. But I assure you, nothing earth-shattering has occurred." Luke waved off Jackson's attempt to interrupt him with a flick of his wrist. "I merely find myself embroiled in a small family matter that requires immediate action on my part."

Luke's explanation was evasive at best. Jackson was too much of a lawyer to let the matter drop. "Should I ask the question again?" He rested his forearms on his knees. "Or perhaps I'll redirect my initial query. Tell me, my friend, why did you leave America in the first place?"

Eyes turning haunted, Luke lowered his gaze and picked at a piece of lint on his pant leg. "What can I say? I was bored with my pampered life." He looked up again, his face now clear of all expression. "I needed a change of scenery."

At the cryptic response, Jackson remembered the exchange of anxious glances between father and son last night. "Are you in trouble?"

"I suppose I am." Luke growled low in his throat, a sound of angry frustration. "But not in the way you probably think. I . . ."

When he remained silent, Jackson filled the conversational void. "What kind of trouble are you in?"

Luke's eyes darted left to right, right to left, not quite landing on Jackson's. "I hurt someone very badly, and I won't be forced to repeat my mistake, no matter how passionately my father insists or how noble his reasons may seem on the surface."

The man was withholding vital pieces of information. Jackson knew all the signs: the guarded, wandering expression, the lack of concrete answers. Traits he would never attribute to his friend, a man whose yes always meant yes and no always meant no.

"What's really going on with you? Talk to me, Luke. Maybe I can help."

"You are the last person who would understand the position I find myself in."

Considering his family history, Jackson understood a great many things. "Perhaps you aren't giving me enough credit."

Luke closed his eyes, tipped his head back, and breathed in deeply. "My reason for leaving America had to do with a . . . woman."

Of all the possible reasons for Luke leaving the country, Jackson would never have suspected the cause was a woman. Luke had a reputation for handling women with charm and aplomb. In fact, he was considered somewhat of a legend among the younger men in society.

The tortured look in his friend's eyes did not match the man Jackson knew. "Go on. You were saying you left because of a woman."

Luke scrubbed a hand over his mouth. "I handled our relationship badly. There can be no restitution for what I did to her or how I left matters between us. And that's all I'm going to say about it."

"You can't possibly think—"

"I mean it, Jackson. Don't press me on this matter."

For the span of several heartbeats, Jackson held silent. What could have possibly gone wrong with Luke and this mysterious woman?

You are the last person who would understand.

Jackson braced himself. Despite sensing his opinion of his friend might be changed forever, he did exactly what Luke asked him not to do. He pressed for more information. "Did you become involved with a married woman?"

"No." Luke's temper came fast and hard, making Jackson wonder if he'd hit the mark despite his friend's denial. "I'm guilty of many sins, but adultery is not one of them."

Fair enough. "Well, whatever led to your departure and subsequent return, I'm glad you're back. You've been missed."

"I didn't exactly come home willingly." Luke sighed. "I was summoned by my father. He has decided it's time I marry, for the sake of our family. Words like *legacy* and *duty* were tossed around more than once. I have two months to choose a woman on my own or my father will do so for me."

"Luke, we don't arrange marriages in America."

"Not according to my father. Apparently"—Luke's tone turned bitter—"I am paying for another man's sins. Ironic, really, when you consider I have my own sins to answer for."

"What man?"

"I cannot say."

Noting how his friend kept shooting glances toward another part of the club, Jackson followed the direction of his gaze. There were several men involved in a deep conversation, heads bent. Jackson wasn't friends with any in the group nor, did he think, was Luke. He swiveled back around. "What are you going to do?"

Luke shrugged, the casual gesture at odds with the storm clouds in his eyes. "I haven't decided. If I can come up with no other solution, I will *consider* marriage. But only to a woman of my choice and on my terms. Love will not be part of the equation."

The ferocity in his friend's words had Jackson rearing back in surprise. "You hate the idea of a love match that much?"

Luke's features contorted into a dark, thunderous glower. "Love is the root of chaos and uncertainty and only ends in heartache."

"When did you get so cynical?"

"Do you disagree?"

Jackson had no ready answer. His mother had loved his father. Look how that had turned out. "I'm sorry you're being forced to make such a difficult decision."

"I appreciate that, but don't worry about me. I have everything under control."

In Jackson's experience, when a man said he had *everything under control*, he was moments away from losing perspective. And yet, Jackson couldn't fault the man's resolve to avoid love. Love was messy and turned to bitterness when things went wrong. His mother was proof of that.

Friendship was a far better foundation for marriage than love.

But was it enough?

Of course it is enough. Jackson refused to let doubt settle over him. Elizabeth was going to make him a good, proper wife, and Jackson would be a loyal, dutiful husband in return. The situation was no more complicated than that.

Keep telling yourself that, Montgomery.

Jackson eventually left the club and returned to his office. Thanks to his conversation with Luke, he was feeling unsettled and perplexed. Who was this woman Luke had hurt? Did Jackson know her?

Possibly. Probably.

His friend was hiding a large portion of the tale, but Jackson wouldn't press him for more information. If Luke required his help, he would ask. Until that time, Jackson had his own future plans to set into motion.

Squaring his shoulders, he stopped at his office and informed John Reilly that he was heading straight to his meeting with St. James.

Reilly, his head buried in a stack of papers, nodded absently. "Good enough."

Organizing his argument in his mind, Jackson went up the additional flights of stairs to the top floor of the building. The climb helped settle his mind and strengthen his resolve.

The moment he entered the penthouse suite, Richard's secretary greeted him with a smile. "Good afternoon, Mr. Montgomery. Mr. St. James is expecting you."

"Thank you, Edith." Jackson returned the older woman's smile with a genuine one of his own. He liked the middle-aged woman. She might tuck her brown hair into an ordinary bun at the nape of her neck, but there was nothing ordinary about her. Yes, she had plain brown eyes and plain, unremarkable features and wore plain, nondescript clothing, but her inner kindness radiated out of her like a sunbeam splitting through a dingy cloud on a blustery day.

"You may go on in now."

"Thank you."

Maneuvering around her desk, Jackson knocked twice on the closed door before entering the spacious office without waiting for a response.

His father's former business partner, now Jackson's, sat behind a large desk made of the finest mahogany available. Nothing but the best for the business titan. The high ceilings gave the room a feeling of grandeur and permanence, much like the man behind the desk.

At seventy years old, the older man was in peak physical condition. He wore the aura of power comfortably. He had a full shock of white hair, handsome features that had weathered over time, and a tall, lithe frame. His startling green eyes held keen intelligence and a lifetime of secrets.

Those who worked for Richard St. James considered him a fair man, if somewhat single-minded. There were rumors of a sad tale in the man's past, something to do with his daughter, but Jackson had never been privy to the particulars.

He halted a few feet short of Richard's desk.

The older man's gaze landed directly on his face. In that moment, Richard reminded Jackson of Caroline Harding. They had the same direct stare, the same startling green eyes.

Jackson swallowed.

Wrong woman.

He swallowed again.

Horrendous timing.

He had no business thinking of another woman now, or ever. He was about to ask this man, his mentor and business partner, for permission to marry his beloved granddaughter.

A pair of bushy white eyebrows traveled upward. "You requested this meeting. I assume you had a reason."

Jackson cleared his throat. "I did."

"Well, then, have a seat and let's get to it."

Jackson did as requested, choosing one of the two wingback chairs facing the older man's desk. Not sure where to begin now that the time had come, he cleared his throat again. This wasn't supposed to be so hard.

Why the sudden reticence? he wondered. Jackson adored Elizabeth, had always adored her. He'd known her most of his life and had considered her as precious as a sister.

A sister?

Where had that terrible thought come from? Elizabeth was the woman he wanted as the mother of his children.

And yet . . .

The thought of building a family with her made him mildly queasy.

He blamed his sudden resistance on his conversation with Luke. Love wasn't necessary for a successful marriage, Jackson reminded himself. He admired Elizabeth and her family, especially her grandfather. Perhaps it would be more conventional for Jackson to ask Elizabeth's father for her hand, but Richard St. James was the family patriarch. It made sense for Jackson to speak with the head of the family first.

Yet, still, Jackson couldn't push the words declaring his intentions past his lips.

The older man broke the silence for him. "I understand your school chum has returned to New York."

Grateful for the reprieve, Jackson answered without hesitation. "Luke, yes, I was just with him at the club."

Richard nodded. "I always liked that boy. Can I assume he is doing well?"

"Very." If one didn't count the fact that Luke was struggling with some sort of family matter and being cryptic about the particulars. Jackson wasn't sure what problem his friend had gotten himself into, but this moment wasn't about Luke.

Enough stalling. "Sir, as you are aware, last night I paid off the last of my father's debts."

"I find your actions commendable. You have taken good care of your mother. Not many sons would have been so . . . patient."

He paused, leaving the rest unspoken.

For which Jackson was grateful. His business partner was well aware that Lucille Montgomery was a difficult woman at best, unbearable at worst.

Instead of braving the storm of her husband and sister's betrayal with courage and dignity, Jackson's mother had grown bitter through the years. She took out her anger on those closest to her, most often her son and her God.

Jackson tried to give his mother the benefit of the doubt. The whispers had been hard on her, especially in the early days. But her husband had been gone for five full years now. It was time for her to accept that he wasn't coming back and move on with her life.

"Many men in your position might not have taken the responsibility of family as seriously as you have," Richard continued. "But now that the worst is over, it's time you focused on your own life."

There. The perfect opening. "That's what I wished to speak with you about."

Richard said nothing.

Jackson continued. "Now that there is no more debt, and my family's scandal is all but forgotten, I am ready to marry. I wish to offer for—"

"You want to marry? So soon?" This seemed to surprise the older man. "But you are still young."

"I am nearly thirty years old."

"Like I said, still young. It's only been one day since you paid off your father's debt. Surely you want to take some time to enjoy your freedom."

Freedom was the last thing Jackson wanted. Look what it had done to his father. "You know I have been working toward a specific goal of late." *Respectability.* "Marriage to a woman of good family and fine character is the next logical step."

"No." Richard waved that off with a flick of his wrist. "You should put it off awhile longer. Wait at least a year or more to settle down."

"I had planned on a yearlong engagement."

"That's not what I meant. You should enjoy your life without the responsibilities you've had to shoulder these last few years."

The man wasn't listening. Why wasn't he listening? "But, sir, I—"

"Jackson. My boy." Speaking as a father would to his son, Richard rose from his chair, circled around his desk, and set a hand on Jackson's shoulder. "No one in society has ever questioned your honor. You are considered a man of solid Christian integrity, one who is well thought of and respected. Marriage isn't necessary to enhance your already stellar reputation."

Those were nearly the same words that Warren Griffin had said to him last night. But coming from his mentor and business partner, they seemed to take on new meaning, as if the other man was trying to tell him something else entirely.

But what?

"Sir, I came here today to ask for Eliz—"

"Let's not talk about that just yet." He released Jackson's shoulder. "We need to strategize for our upcoming meeting with Schwartz and Dietrich. I believe you visited them last week about representing our interest in the tenement buildings on Orchard Street."

The none-too-subtle shift in topic gave Jackson pause. "Yes."

"Very good." Richard returned to the other side of his desk, his message clear. Despite all the talk about honor and integrity, he didn't want Jackson to offer for Elizabeth. Not yet, anyway.

He tried to keep the disappointment out of his voice. "I need to retrieve my notes." He rose and turned to go.

"Jackson."

He froze midstep.

"Do not misunderstand what has been said here today. When the time is right, you will make a fine husband. The kind any father, or grandfather, would welcome into his family."

Chapter Ten

Heart pounding wildly against her ribs, Caroline stood frozen in place outside her grandfather's home. *Home.* The word toyed with her outward control, as if teasing her with a spark of hope she could not allow to ignite.

Mouth set in a grim line, eyes fixed on the large monstrosity of a house, Caroline couldn't deny the feeling of enchantment surrounding the beautiful building. Even the stars twinkled above her head, while the silvery sound of leaves rustling came from the bushes lining the perimeter.

Concerned by her fanciful reaction to this house, Caroline frowned. This wasn't the first grand home she'd entered since arriving in New York. Yet this one possessed a haunting beauty that made her breath hitch in her throat.

A chill traveled through her followed by a wave of deep-rooted regret. Why had her mother not tried harder to return home? Why had she not journeyed back to America and demanded her father listen to her side of the story?

Anger, longing, a brief moment of defeat, those were only a few of the emotions warring for supremacy in Caroline's heart. At the moment, she didn't know whom she was angrier with, her grandfather for abandoning his own daughter, or her mother for running off with a man for the ridiculous notion of love.

Love. What a pointless emotion, fraught with dangerous pitfalls. Caroline would never fall in love. Never. She'd seen the devastation left in its wake, knew the pain that resulted when love was lost or stolen away.

Enough.

Lifting her chin, she mounted the first step. And then took the next. *Too many stairs in this country.* She'd never had to navigate so many in her life. Her own humble dwelling in Whitechapel had been ground level, dirty, small—the complete opposite of this grand home.

Anger sprinted through her again, followed by frustration and then sorrow, bone-deep sorrow.

This house, this mansion, was where her mother had lived the first eighteen years of her life. The reality of how far her mother had fallen made Caroline's breath come in hard, quick snatches.

Enough.

She navigated the next three steps, her gaze shifting left to right, right to left. The three-story brownstone was a mammoth structure, filling half a city block. Gaslights from the street bathed the exterior in a golden, welcoming glow. Row upon row of windows sparkled like diamonds in the inky night. A fairy-tale palace come to life, promising safety, comfort, and happily ever after.

Caroline sighed. Happy endings didn't exist for people like her.

Her mother had believed otherwise, and that false thinking had contributed as much to her death as Richard St. James's abandonment.

Swallowing hard, Caroline continued up the final two steps. She lifted her hand to knock, but her knuckles met empty air as the door swung open on its own. A stiff-backed man dressed in a black servant's uniform ushered her inside with a curt nod of his head. Remembering Sally's instructions, Caroline barely made eye contact with him.

Pretending she was above this man's station went against everything her mother had taught her. Libby had been a proponent of the biblical precept: *Consider others better than yourself; look not only to your own interests, but also to the interests of others.* It would seem the lesson had stayed with Caroline. She couldn't take for granted someone else's hard work.

Except for tonight. Tonight she was one of the wealthy. And all that that implied.

Another servant came up behind Caroline and grasped her cape. Although prepared for the move, she had to resist the urge to spin around and slap his hand away.

He is not a street thug trying to steal your property, she reminded herself.

"The others are in the blue drawing room at the top of the stairs."

She gave a brief nod, squared her shoulders, and made her way toward yet another set of stairs. This particular staircase extended upward in a long, sweeping arc. Made of the finest marble, these steps were far superior to the wooden ones at Ellis Island, but just as intimidating.

Caroline's fingers twined in the fabric of her skirt. *Don't fidget.* Sally's instructions from earlier in the day swept through Caroline's mind. *A lady holds her head aloft, eyes cast forward, her spine ramrod straight.*

Caroline dropped her hand to her side and placed a serene look on her face, the one Sally had taught her and she'd practiced in the mirror all afternoon. The new strategy they'd designed was exceedingly different from the one Caroline had originally adopted.

Could she pull this off?

Not if she stayed rooted to the spot. She began the climb.

Halfway to the top, a voice drifted from behind her. "Miss Harding, I see you have arrived a full half hour early this evening."

Caroline froze. A prickling, sharp as knifepoints, skidded down her spine.

The voice grew nearer. "I have to wonder at your eagerness."

A pleasant sensation shot through her, followed by a moment of alarm. She would not—could not—allow herself to be thrown off her guard by a man, any man, and certainly not this one.

She swallowed once, twice, then turned to look over her shoulder. "Mr. Montgomery." She flashed a wry smile. "I see you are an early arrival as well."

"I had business I needed to discuss with the family." He didn't elaborate, not that she'd expected him to. He was a frequent guest in this home, as much a part of the St. James inner circle as if he'd been born into the family. She was the interloper.

A touch of cold dread moved through her. She held Montgomery's stare, well aware that beneath the perfectly tailored evening clothes was a dangerous man, all hard muscle and coiled power, a predator capable of striking at any moment.

He came to a stop on the stair just below hers, bringing them eye-to-eye. Only a tiny tic in his jaw marred the aura of complete control he exuded.

A heartbeat passed. And another. *Trapped,* that was the word that flickered in her mind. But, oddly enough, she wasn't afraid. She was intrigued despite herself. There was a hidden wildness in him she doubted others saw. Perhaps even he didn't acknowledge that part of himself.

Fascinating.

Frightening.

Something about the man made her forget to remain coldly distant. *Beware, Caroline. Beware.*

Montgomery offered his arm. "Shall we conquer the rest of the way together?"

"Certainly."

Stomach in knots, she took his arm, suddenly glad for his support as well as the physical barrier of his sleeve and her glove. It wouldn't do for her to get too comfortable around the man.

They climbed the stairs as one, their steps perfectly in tune with one another. Caroline might have found that odd had she had time to consider the matter in depth. For now, her mind was already inside the blue drawing room. Centered on the man she'd come to meet for the first time.

Richard St. James was in for the shock of his life.

At the top of the stairs, two servants dressed in identical black uniforms and starched white shirts opened a pair of double doors in unison. Most likely a move they'd perfected through years of practice.

Caroline hesitated at the threshold, her skin growing hot, then frigid. Her family awaited mere feet from her. People who shared her blood. Caroline closed her eyes tightly, drew in a slow breath of air.

"Problem, Miss Harding?"

"No, I . . ." She tapped into the trace of stubbornness that had kept her strong through the leanest, most difficult times. "I am ready."

His eyes narrowed. "Interesting choice of words."

Oh, he was a clever one. Taking out her frustration on him, she fixed the infuriating man with a quelling stare.

That earned her a dry chuckle. "I don't know quite what to think of you, Miss Harding."

"Perhaps thinking is precisely your problem."

Dropping his head close to hers, he hovered near her upturned face. For a dreadful moment, she thought he was going to kiss her.

In the next instant, he snapped back to attention. "Perhaps thinking too much is my biggest failing of all."

She doubted that.

Without another word, he led her past the open doors. The room was so grand and sophisticated and dripping with sparkling light that Caroline found herself dazzled. And stunned speechless.

An unanticipated, dangerous reaction. This was not the way she'd planned to enter her grandfather's world. Clutching Mr. Montgomery's arm, she blinked several times, then focused her gaze. She counted a total of three other occupants in the room, her cousin, Elizabeth, and Elizabeth's parents—a middle-aged couple Caroline knew to be her Uncle Marcus and her Aunt Katherine.

She'd seen them before, at the opera and the theater, but they had not seen her. She'd made sure of that.

Montgomery cleared his throat.

All heads turned.

Elizabeth smiled at them both, started forward, then stopped as a collective gasp rose from her parents. She returned to their side.

"Mother? Father?" Frowning in confusion, Elizabeth angled her head and studied the older pair. "Whatever is wrong with you?"

Katherine St. James ignored her daughter's question, her gaze widening with each breath she took. "It can't be. It just can't be."

A glass slipped from her hand and crashed to the floor, the sound reverberating against the ornately decorated walls.

Out of nowhere, a servant rushed forward to clean up the broken shards. Caroline's uncle jumped to his feet and started for Caroline but was tugged back by his wife. "Marcus, wait."

Silence hung in the room like a thick wool blanket.

"I say, Miss Harding." Montgomery drawled the words in a low tone meant only for her ears. "You certainly know how to make an entrance."

She didn't respond to his goading. She couldn't. Her gaze was fixed on her uncle. He appeared shocked by her appearance, and . . . oddly—somehow—pleased to see her.

Caroline hadn't expected that reaction.

But then she remembered that her mother had always spoken fondly of her older brother, even though ten years had separated them in age. If Libby were to be believed, Marcus had loved his little sister to distraction, spoiling her beyond reason. Caroline hadn't believed that. Such a devoted brother would have come looking for his sister when she'd disappeared all those years ago.

Marcus St. James had never crossed the Atlantic Ocean. Not once. Her mother had been clear on this subject, heartbreakingly clear.

Caroline broke eye contact with her uncle, the hair on the back of her neck rising. Another person had entered the room.

She slowly turned and, finally, after all the planning and scheming, locked gazes with Richard St. James.

Heart in her throat, Caroline took a step forward, froze. She hadn't expected to feel this rush of homecoming, this sense of hope mixed with utter confusion. Her grandfather was supposed to be an old man, a frail scrooge showing his age, not this strong, handsome man with broad shoulders, a kind face, and . . . her eyes.

She'd thought she'd inherited her eyes from her mother but hadn't suspected her mother had inherited them from this man.

The color drained from her grandfather's face. "Libby?" His eyes blinked rapidly. "Is, is that you?"

"No. Not Libby. Caroline. My name is Caroline." Her voice came out far too unsteady for her liking. "Libby was my mother."

* * *

Jackson viewed the unfolding drama as if through a tank of murky water. Half his mind focused on the shock racing across Richard's face and the other half on the fact that Caroline Harding was still holding on to his arm. With a death grip.

He realized he should probably peel away her fingers and extricate himself at once. But something about her carefully contained behavior, the way she tried to still her shaking, the vulnerability in her eyes, got to him. It seemed appropriate to suspect her of something underhanded, but an inexplicable need to protect her suddenly shot through him.

She wasn't what she seemed; he knew that now. She'd come to this house with an ulterior motive. Until he knew what she had in mind—precisely—Jackson wouldn't abandon her.

Richard moved toward them, his gaze drifting from one to the other, confusion evident in his eyes. "Jackson, you know this young woman?"

The question was a valid one, especially with their arms linked so tightly together. "Elizabeth introduced us last evening."

As if gathering her courage, Caroline drew in a harsh breath, released his arm, and faced Richard directly. "Do you deny me? Do you deny who I am?"

Her eyes were filled with a mixture of pain and anger, big shining eyes full of fight and spirit. Eyes that were so similar to Richard's there could be no question they were related.

Was she his love child?

No, Richard was an honorable man. By all accounts, he'd loved only one woman, his wife, Constance. When she'd died, he'd vowed never to love again. Thirty years later Richard had never once broken that vow.

Or had he? Who was this Libby?

"Everyone out." Richard's eyes never left Caroline's face. "Everyone but you."

Even though Caroline's breath came in quick, hard bursts, she nodded at the command. "I'm not going anywhere."

"But we are." Marcus rose to his feet. Amidst protests from his wife, he calmly escorted her and Elizabeth toward the exit.

Elizabeth pulled free of her father's grip, her eyes wide with curiosity as she looked from Caroline to her grandfather and back again. "Perhaps I could stay a moment longer?"

"No, my dear, you will not stay *a moment longer.*" Marcus readjusted his hold on her arm. "Come along, Elizabeth. Katherine, you as well."

A sound of dismay slipped from both women's lips. Marcus remained impassive. Before exiting the room completely, he stopped next to Caroline and whispered something in her ear. Jackson thought he heard, "Welcome, my dear," but he couldn't be certain.

The doors snapped closed, leaving Jackson alone with Richard and Caroline.

Richard looked pointedly at him. "You will leave us as well."

Not a chance. "I'm staying."

"This matter is none of your concern—"

"Perhaps not. But we don't know what this woman really wants from you." He dropped a meaningful glance at Caroline. "She could mean to do you harm." He doubted that but wasn't about to risk the possibility.

As if to punctuate his point, Caroline flashed her teeth at him. "I knew you were the one to watch."

Having had her say, she turned her back on him.

Jackson clenched his jaw, baffled at the spurt of anger he experienced from her dismissal. "Are you carrying a weapon on your person?"

"I am not." She released an impatient sigh. "And, no, you won't be searching my *person* to see if I'm lying."

At her saucy remark, Richard made a sound deep in his throat that could have been a snort or a laugh. Either response would have been understandable, given her outrageous behavior.

Jackson's mood darkened as he studied the woman he'd first met near the Bowery and then at the Griffin ball. She was an accomplished liar, that much he knew, but what else was she?

Who was she?

"Caroline." Richard reached out to her, then retreated when she glowered at his outstretched hand. "Where is your mother? Where is Libby?"

Caroline went very still at the question, her eyes unblinking, her tone ruthlessly flat and void of emotion. "She is dead."

"Dead? My Libby is dead?" Richard's renowned calm crumpled, and his knees buckled beneath him. He reached out to steady himself on a nearby chair. "When? When did she die?"

"A year ago, in a filthy, rat-infested hovel in the East End of London." Caroline's voice changed then, the cultured, educated accent completely gone, replaced by a strong cockney inflection.

"So recent." Tears sprang to the older man's eyes, grief etched around his mouth, making him look every bit of his seventy years. "If only I had known she was in trouble, maybe I could have—"

"What? You could have what? Saved her?" Caroline practically spat the words. "Is that what you were going to say? You think you could have *saved her*? When you were the one who destroyed her?"

"No."

"Yes. You abandoned your own daughter to a life of poverty and despair."

Daughter. Libby had been Richard's daughter?

That made Caroline his granddaughter.

"*No.*" Richard's hand shook as he wiped it across his mouth. "I never abandoned her. She disappeared without a word. I searched for her. For years, I searched."

"You lie!"

At the bold outburst, the two stared at one another, neither moving, both breathing hard. The silence stretched between them, thickening by the second, stealing the air.

The doors suddenly burst open, and Luke Griffin sauntered into the room, his easy gait indicating he had no idea a family drama was unfolding right before his eyes. His next words confirmed his complete lack of awareness of the ever-increasing tension. "What did I miss?"

Chapter Eleven

Caroline ignored Lucian Griffin, her eyes trained on her grandfather. The evening was not progressing as she'd hoped. Not by half. When she'd first contrived her plan for Richard St. James's downfall, she'd expected to face an unfeeling man, one who was both greedy and concerned with his own selfish ambitions. This broken, grief-stricken version didn't fit with her preconceived notion.

Her grandfather seemed to have aged twenty years in the matter of so many minutes. His eyes had taken on a world-weary sheen, while anguish etched creases on either side of his mouth.

Baffled, she tugged her bottom lip between her teeth. Her revelation wasn't supposed to affect him this way. He was supposed to be showing his derision at this very moment, perhaps even tossing her out of his home.

He was not supposed to be so obviously . . . devastated.

For all intents and purposes, she'd won. Before the battle had even begun.

Why wasn't she feeling more triumphant? Perhaps because she'd come prepared for a fight, not . . . this. This pain-filled misery.

Of its own volition her hand lifted to her face. A patina of tears wet her cheek. Tears of sorrow, of remorse. Guilt.

This wasn't fair. She was supposed to feel hate. Only hate. Instead, the hole in her soul seemed to widen. She wanted . . . so much, so many things she had no name for.

Her trembling hand dropped to her side.

"Miss Harding." Montgomery shifted in front of her, the sudden move breaking the trance she'd fallen into. "You will leave this home at once. You have nothing more to say to—"

"No." This from her grandfather, the force of the word at odds with the pained, hollow despair in his eyes. "I wish to speak with my granddaughter alone." His gaze landed on Montgomery, then slid to the right to encompass Lucian Griffin as well. "Both of you leave us. Now."

Montgomery spoke up. "I'm not leaving you alone with this woman."

"She is no threat to me."

"I beg to differ." Montgomery kept his gaze fixed on Caroline as he spoke. The tight, flat grimace indicated he was engaged in a careful assessment of her. Of all the people in this room, she sensed he could cause her the most harm.

"Is your name Caroline Harding?" he asked.

Caroline stiffened her spine. There was no need to lie anymore. "No."

"Are you related to Patricia Harding?"

"No." She ground her teeth together to quell the swift kick of fear, an emotion she could not afford at the moment. "My name is Caroline St. James."

"St. James? How . . . convenient."

No, not convenient. Tragic. The source of her mother's greatest shame, and perhaps Caroline's as well. "Back down, Mr. Montgomery, I have not come to harm my grandfather."

Much to her surprise, she realized she spoke the truth. How wrong she'd been about herself and her motives, thinking she could come to America for the sole purpose of ruining this man, her grandfather. Her reasons had been far more complicated than that, something she would explore in greater depth when she was alone.

Of course, none of that meant she was through with the notion of seeking retribution for her mother's death. She had questions. Questions only one man could answer.

Montgomery set his hand on her arm. "Assuming you *are* who you say you are, then you—"

"I am." She had proof, undeniable proof.

His grip tightened, not enough to hurt her, but enough to make his point. "Assuming your story is true—"

"It is."

"Time will tell."

"Yes, it will."

Montgomery was trying to call her bluff. Except, bad news for him, Caroline wasn't bluffing. She was no imposter trying to con an old man. She didn't want a dollar of her grandfather's money. She didn't want his love, either, or his acceptance. She wanted justice. Justice for her mother.

Lucian Griffin made a sound in his throat, reminding all of them of his presence. "I see I have interrupted a private matter." He turned to face her grandfather. "If you will excuse me, sir, I will make myself scarce."

"Take Jackson with you." Not a request, a command. The harsh tone was Caroline's first glimpse of the real man beneath the pallor, the one who ran a business empire that spanned three continents.

Lips flat, Lucian Griffin grabbed Montgomery's arm and yanked, hard.

The stubborn man didn't budge. "I'm not leaving."

"Yes, you are." Though her grandfather's voice was low and strained, the words brooked no argument.

A silent battle ensued between the two men. Montgomery broke first. Letting out a short huff of displeasure, he turned to go but stopped himself and leaned toward Caroline. "I'll be just outside, waiting for you to finish in here."

She felt a little shock at the prospect of facing him after she was through with her grandfather. "Do what you think you must. As will I."

He wanted to respond to her challenge. She saw the truth of it in his narrowed gaze. But he held his tongue, proving himself to be a man of phenomenal restraint.

Impressive.

Terrifying.

She had the sinking feeling she'd just grabbed a tiger by the tail. So be it. Keeping her chin high, she waited for him to quit the room with his friend. A moment later, the soft click of the doors indicated his departure.

Silence fell over the room.

Caroline took the opportunity to study her grandfather. He appeared . . . crushed. There was no other word for the man's complete physical transformation. Was the knowledge of his daughter's death all it had taken to bring him down?

This was not the victory she wanted. Her grandfather should be fighting her. At the very least, he should be proclaiming that he didn't care what had happened to his wayward daughter.

"Come with me, young lady."

Giving her no chance to reply, he headed toward a door at the back of the room. Not sure what he had in mind, Caroline obeyed the curt command and followed him into what appeared to be a private study.

The masculine scent of aged leather and wood confirmed her suspicion. She took in the room with a single glance, her heart sticking in her throat at what she saw. Bookshelves. Rows and rows of them lined the entire wall in front of her, from floor to ceiling, containing books and books and more books.

Caroline felt a moment of joy, followed by such longing her knees nearly gave out. Her mother had taught her to read. But there hadn't been money for books. Libby had saved three of her favorites from her previous life. *Pride and Prejudice, Great Expectations,* and, of course, the Holy Bible.

Caroline had read the Bible with her mother most evenings of her childhood. But on her own time she'd devoured the other two stories over and over again.

Until the pages were in tatters.

What she wouldn't give to explore the titles on the shelves before her now. Her fingertips itched to run across the multicolored spines, to discover the treasures within the pages.

Forcing herself to look away, Caroline turned her attention to her grandfather. His gaze was focused above her head. The same longing she harbored in her own heart was reflected in his eyes.

Intrigued, she spun to see what had him in such a state. Before she could check her reaction, a gasp flew past her lips.

Words failed her, completely and utterly failed her.

She was staring at a life-size painting of a young woman in a white dress with silver-and-blue lace, the garment much like the one Caroline wore now. If she didn't know better, she would say the painting was of . . . *her.*

"It can't be," she whispered. "I don't understand."

But, of course, she did. She was looking at a painting of her mother, a younger, prettier, happier version of the broken woman who had raised Caroline as best she knew how.

Caroline had always known she favored her mother. Their eyes were the same unusual color, the tilt the same upturned angle. But she had only known the woman who'd given up on life. Not this carefree, smiling girl.

"I had that painting commissioned the year before we sailed for London." Her grandfather's voice turned gruff and shook slightly as he spoke. "Your mother had just turned seventeen."

Drowning in grief and sorrow, Caroline drew in an audible breath. "She looks so young. And happy."

"You are the very image of your mother."

"Not the mother I knew," she said, unable to stop the bitter words from slipping past her lips and skidding through her soul.

"I have missed her every day since she left us."

The sentiment was uttered with such sadness, such pain, that Caroline couldn't reconcile the man in this room with the one she'd planned to destroy. Could he truly be grieving for his daughter?

If that were true, why had he not accepted her back into his home? "So you say—yet you returned her letters, every single one of them, all but ignoring her pleas for forgiveness."

"I received no letters." His confusion appeared real, as did his skepticism. Did he think Caroline was lying?

"She sent at least three dozen."

He shook his head, refusing to admit to the truth. "No."

"Yes."

He shook his head again, then redirected the conversation as if staying on the same course would completely do him in. "Tell me what happened to my daughter. I need to know. How did she die?"

"She contracted pneumonia." Caroline said the words without inflection, determined to hold back any emotion that would give away her motives.

"How did she become ill?"

Caroline frowned at the question. What did it matter how? It was the story of her mother's life *before* she died that Caroline had come to tell. She'd made the arduous journey across an ocean for this very purpose, to toss Libby's tragic tale in this man's face, to demand he . . . he . . .

What? What had she wanted from him? Had she come so he would beg for her forgiveness? To watch him crumble in pain and remorse?

Whatever her original reasons had been, she realized now that her ultimate goal had always been to tell her grandfather what had become of his daughter.

This was her chance.

She glanced back at the painting and sighed. She didn't recognize that innocent girl above her head. An image of the last time she'd seen her mother alive materialized. There'd been so much blood, and Caroline had been too late to save her.

Furious at the reminder of her own helplessness, she turned her back to the painting. "You had better sit down for this."

Nodding, he lowered himself into a nearby chair.

When he indicated she take the one beside him, Caroline refused. She couldn't sit and tell her tale. She needed to move as she spoke.

Feeling like a caged animal, she paced through the room. The fancy rug beneath her feet had an intricate design of flowers and coiled branches. A kaleidoscope of color danced before her eyes, blurring her vision.

"Before I begin with my end of the tale, I need to know what took my mother to London in the first place."

His shoulders slumped forward. "When that painting was complete, and I looked at it, really looked at it, I realized my daughter had grown into a woman and would soon have to marry. I decided to take her on a trip to Europe, before I lost her completely."

Caroline glanced at the painting, thought of the young girl in the picture with so much promise before her. "Go on."

"London was our first stop. Your mother had heard about Hyde Park from her friends, and she wanted to experience it as they suggested, on horseback." He clutched the arms of the chair with a hard grip. "She'd never ridden a horse before, so I thought it would be wise to purchase a few lessons for her, before we set out for the park."

Again, this portion of his story matched the one Caroline had heard from her mother.

By all accounts, Richard St. James had doted on his daughter. Why, then, had he refused to open her letters year after year? For that matter, why bother sending them back? Just to be cruel?

"Your mother fell in love with riding. After that first lesson, she returned to the stables whenever our schedule allowed." A smile spread across his lips, the gesture making him look like the loving father after all. "Libby made friends everywhere she went. Everyone adored her, including the boys in the stable."

Caroline's father had been one of those "boys."

"It didn't take long for me to discover there was something more drawing her to the stables besides the horses." Caroline didn't have to check his gaze to know it had grown dark. She heard the sorrow in his voice. Not rage, not judgment, but genuine, heartfelt sadness. "No, not something—someone."

"My father."

"I thought it was just a mild flirtation." He scrubbed a hand down his face. "When I realized it was more, I, of course, had concerns. I—"

"Forbid her to continue seeing my father."

"Yes." His head snapped up. "And I would do so again, given the same circumstances. They came from two different worlds. What kind of life could that boy offer her?"

"One full of love," Caroline whispered. That's what her father had given her mother. Love. The kind of all-consuming passion that had made her reckless, forsaking everything she'd ever known. Caroline would never allow herself to feel that kind of destructive emotion. Never.

"I refused to relent. I thought I was protecting her." The regret in him was palpable, as though he was reliving every argument he'd ever had with his daughter. "One day, after a particularly heated discussion on the matter, Libby went for a walk with a friend, a young woman of good family I thought I could trust. And . . ."

When he didn't continue, Caroline urged, "And?"

"She never came back."

Caroline could feel the rage she'd harbored in her heart all her life dissipating into something far more dangerous. Sympathy. Sympathy for the man she'd come to destroy.

He wasn't so formidable now. In fact, he looked in need of compassion. Her compassion.

She shook away the ridiculous notion and focused on the memory of her mother's last years of life. Most days, Libby had been unable to pull herself out of bed, leaving her young daughter to fend for them both. The memory was enough to harden Caroline's heart. "The day she went for this walk. That was the day she ran off with my father?"

"That's correct." A slow breath of air wheezed out of his lungs. "I immediately hired a private detective to search for the couple. They were never found."

Caroline took over the story then, disregarding the agony she sensed in her grandfather. "My father was far quicker and sharper than any of your hired detectives understood. He knew how to hide in plain sight. He and my mother moved around the streets of London unnoticed."

She paused, gave her grandfather a chance to interrupt or perhaps ask a question. When he remained silent, she continued.

"They were deliriously happy. Unfortunately, my mother wasn't prepared for living on the run, and my father wasn't much better. When they found out I was on the way, they decided things had to change."

This next part of the story was the hardest to tell. "He found work wherever he could, but it wasn't enough. He wasn't educated and had no family connections. Eventually, he went to work with a street gang in Whitechapel."

Her grandfather shuddered but wound his wrist in the air, indicating she carry on.

"As it turned out, Jonathan Archer wasn't cut out for a life of crime any more than my mother was cut out for life on the run." Neither had been like their daughter, Caroline realized, cringing at the reality of who she'd become in order to survive. A liar, a cheat, a woman bent on revenge. "My mother always said my father was a good man, full of honor and integrity."

And that was his downfall, in the end.

Instead of scoffing at this, her grandfather nodded. "My Libby was always a good judge of character."

Not the Libby Caroline knew. Her mother had been a terrible judge of character, as evidenced by the place where she'd died, a dirty, run-down shack in the most disreputable section of London. *Bad company corrupts good morals.* Had that been the true tragedy of her mother's life? The loss of who she was, at the core, because of the company she'd chosen to keep?

"My father was killed several months before I was born, by the man he was supposed to be working for."

Her grandfather's eyes flew open. "You never met your father?"

"No." She held the old man's gaze. "He died, and as far as I'm concerned, abandoned my mother as surely as you did."

"Why didn't Libby try to come home?"

"She did. By the time my father died, you had already left the country. Like I told you, she sent letters, the ones *you* returned unopened."

He rose quickly and stalked toward her. "Where are these letters now?"

At last. This severe, furious man was the one Caroline had expected to meet here tonight. Now they were on common ground, engaging in the battle she'd come prepared to fight.

"I have them tucked safely away."

"I demand you show them to me."

"I thought you might say that. But as you can see, I am dressed for a dinner party." She twirled in a slow circle to make her point. "Where exactly would I stash three dozen letters in a ridiculously overpriced gown worth more than my mother scraped together in a year?"

He ignored the question.

"You will retrieve the letters." Not a question, or even a statement, but a command. "And bring them directly to me."

Caroline bristled at the commanding tone that didn't match the grief she saw in his eyes. Her own emotions ebbed and flowed in several directions, making her dizzy, making her question her goals, her very purpose for being in this room.

She let none of her internal conflict show on her face. "Of course you will want to read them. However, I find this conversation has exhausted me beyond my endurance. I will return tomorrow morning with my mother's letters."

"You will return with them tonight. And then you will tell me the rest of your story, leaving out no detail, no matter how large or small, terrible or tragic."

"And if I don't return?"

"You will." He strode to a door near the bookshelves and pulled it open with a hard tug. "Jackson," he called out. "A word, if you please."

Montgomery materialized in the doorway, his immediate presence indicating he'd known her grandfather would take her to his study rather than remain in the blue drawing room.

So the man was able to anticipate his business partner's actions. A valuable piece of information Caroline tucked away.

"What can I do for you, sir?"

"Escort my granddaughter to her place of residence, wait for her to retrieve what is mine, and then escort her back here at once."

"Very good." He nodded, acting compliant and biddable as any lackey. "I'll have her back within the hour."

"Whatever you do, do not let her out of your sight."

Turning to face her directly, Montgomery displayed a predatory grin. "You may count on it."

Chapter Twelve

Jackson made no effort to speak to Caroline as he escorted her through the St. James home. Soon enough, they would be alone in his carriage, where no one could overhear their conversation. For now, he kept to the less traveled hallways, in the express hope of avoiding an encounter with the rest of the family. Or Luke.

Shoulders tense, Jackson shot a quick glance at the woman by his side. There was something akin to despair showing in her small frame, a look that might be defined as dejection. He should be pleased. Instead, he felt a swift kick in his gut, followed by a desire to ease her sorrow.

In the dim light, she seemed too vulnerable to be completely immoral, even though Jackson knew a healthy dose of suspicion was imperative at this point.

Concealing his thoughts, he directed her to the front stoop and motioned her to his waiting carriage.

"No motorcar?" she asked, scoffing.

"I am a man of simple tastes," he admitted. It was a moment of self-honesty that gave him pause.

Frowning, he took her hand and guided her into the carriage. Her fingers trembled lightly beneath his. An act? Or genuine emotion? He hated that he didn't know.

Moving in behind her, he settled on the seat facing hers. Eyes on her he shut the door and then pounded on the roof with his fist.

The carriage lurched forward, sending her scooting backward to maintain her balance. Her eyes narrowed. "You did that on purpose."

He didn't deny it.

Before she could completely right herself, Jackson swooped forward and placed his palms on the seat cushion on either side of her. He'd sufficiently trapped her, using his superior size to corral her to the spot.

She didn't flinch, or gasp, or even try to slap his hands away. She remained perfectly calm, her expression devoid of all emotion. Impressive control. "I suggest you rethink your route of intimidation, Mr. Montgomery."

She was a cool one. Elusive, mysterious, hard to read. She was also a liar. He leaned a fraction closer. "Who are you?"

Not a single muscle moved in her face. "You know who I am."

Again, he couldn't help thinking her control was impressive. Despite himself, Jackson felt a welling of respect. "Tell me again."

"My name is Caroline St. James." Her hands slid into her lap, twined slowly together. "Libby St. James was my mother."

The aristocratic tone in her voice would convince most people she was exactly who she said she was. But her eyes were filled with too many dark secrets, and something else. Something that could only be described as . . . guilt?

No, something more complicated.

Whatever she had discussed with Richard in his private study had left her feeling remorseful. And sad. The sight of all that pain drew him forward, just an inch. His attention lingered on her face, moving between her eyes and her mouth, both tight with tension. Her beauty enticed him to destroy all remnants of the civilized, honorable man he'd always thought himself to be.

Blessed are those whose ways are blameless.

More than a favorite proverb. A way of life for Jackson.

For a long, dangerous moment, he fought against an unfamiliar yearning rising within him, the one he'd experienced on Orchard Street when he'd first set eyes on this woman. He'd seen her concern for her friend, the way she'd taken most of the girl's weight and had shielded her from the pressing crowd.

Caroline St. James might be dressed in a fine silk gown with her hair twisted in a smart, sophisticated style, but she was no innocent society miss. She was a street-smart woman who had journeyed to America without family or husband and had befriended a frail young woman along the way. That ability to show fierce, unwavering loyalty was the part of her personality that intrigued Jackson most.

Despite knowing she couldn't be trusted, he moved closer still, so close he could see the slight widening of her eyes.

He froze, appalled at his behavior. He was no animal, mastered by his base, fleshly desires.

Yet he couldn't find it in him to move back.

Absorbed in their silent battle, he tapped into his well-honed patience and waited her out. She would soon break under the pressure of his silence. Everyone did.

When she continued holding steady, her gaze unwavering under his, he released a knowing grin.

She blinked but waited him out for several more seconds. Another moment and, *finally*, she pulled back. Away from him.

He heard the small rustle of silk, noted the flicker of battle in her eyes. Sensing her next move, he dropped his gaze in time to see her fingers unwind slowly. One hand moved to the seat cushions beside her; the other curled into a fist and then suddenly shot up.

She was fast.

He was faster.

With a quick swipe, he caught her balled fist right before it connected with his chin.

"Now that isn't any way for a St. James to behave."

She yanked her hand free. "Beast."

That was a new one. In most circles Jackson was considered highly civilized, completely above reproach. He'd worked hard to gain that reputation. He'd restored respectability to his family name by avoiding activities that could possibly end up in scandal. Yet here he was, all but brawling with a young woman raised in a completely different world than he.

It didn't make sense.

He pushed back and settled against the seat cushions.

Tearing her gaze from his, she set both hands back in her lap. She flattened her palms against her thighs and casually rubbed them across her skirt.

Her face showed no emotion, her fine-boned features almost serene. He felt like a heathen.

That didn't mean he was through interrogating her.

"I take it you've been planning tonight's little drama for some time." When she didn't admit or deny her actions, he continued, "What do you want from Richard St. James?"

"That's none of your business." She looked so sad as she glanced out the window that Jackson felt an unexpected jolt of tenderness. Or was it longing? Both? Neither?

"On the contrary, it is my business. I am Richard's business partner." He leaned back and pretended grave interest in his thumbnail. "You won't get a single penny out of him, you know. I'll make sure of it."

"Planning to keep all that lovely money for yourself?" She pulled delicately at her skirt, carefully reset a pleat, and then smoothed her fingertips across the fabric. "Is that the reason you wish to court my cousin? So you can merge your coffers with my grandfather's?"

Air hissed out of his lungs. "You will not bring Elizabeth into this."

"I have every right to do just that." She adjusted herself on the seat. "Or weren't you paying attention tonight? Elizabeth is my cousin. We are family. Something you, sir, are not. Not yet, anyway. Maybe not ever."

"Is that a threat?" He leaned forward, setting his nose inches from hers. "Think, my sweet miss. Think very hard before you answer."

* * *

Caroline realized a moment too late she'd pushed the man too far. Jackson Montgomery might dress like a gentleman. He might walk and talk like one, but his eyes told her a fierce warrior lurked below the surface.

What if he decided to use physical force with her, like the street thugs she'd encountered on the streets of London? What if he tossed her out of the carriage in such a way she ended up . . .

No. She would not panic. Such an attitude was cowardly. There was decency in this man, despite the seething anger brewing beneath the cool facade.

She would not panic. She would not panic. She would not—

"Where is your bravado now, Miss Harding, I mean . . . *St. James*?" His gaze never left her face. "Has the fine clothing stolen the fight out of you?"

Her heart raced, half with indignation and half with an awareness of Montgomery's superior size and strength. "I don't know what you mean. I have no reason to fight you."

Oh, but that was a lie. Somehow, this man of perfect manners and respectability knew he'd pushed her into a corner, giving her no other choice but to give in or lash out.

Either prospect put her at a gross disadvantage.

A dirty trick.

Apparently, they were more alike than he realized. He was here, in this carriage, subtly threatening her, because he felt the need to protect

Richard St. James from her. As Caroline had often done on her mother's behalf.

More to the point, just as it was for Caroline, this battle was a personal one for Montgomery. Because of money? Or was there something more driving him?

Never underestimate your enemy. A lesson she'd learned in far rougher situations than this.

Peering at him from lowered lashes, Caroline took a quick assessment. This was a man who would not be made a fool.

Neither was he a man who would hurt a woman.

She was definitely . . . practically . . . *almost* sure of it.

"You condemn me and my motives when you have no idea why I have come here tonight." She purposely appealed to the honor-bound man she sensed inside of him. "Are you absolutely sure, beyond a doubt, that I've come to fleece my own grandfather?"

His lips pulled into a cold smile. Sitting so close, she could see the mockery in the gesture. He braced his feet on the carriage floor in a casual manner, his position both relaxed and ready to strike. "Don't forget we've met before, Caroline, on a very different side of town."

A valid point.

She caught her bottom lip between her teeth, suddenly at a loss for words. How could she explain the complexities of the situation when he was so determined that he had the particulars already figured out?

Panic gnawed at her again, trying to tear into her control. She shoved the useless emotion aside with a hard swallow and lifted her chin. It was time to reveal a portion of the truth.

This man—this *brute*—had forced her hand. "I am tired of being alone." To her surprise and embarrassment, tears formed in her eyes. "I wish to know my family, to claim them as my own."

He laughed at her. He actually laughed. "Such a heartfelt response, truly you're breaking my heart. Tell me, Caroline, is that the story you told Richard?"

"At the risk of sounding redundant, what I discussed with my grandfather in private is none of your business. And for the record"—she blinked down an array of emotions—"I am not after his money."

"We'll see."

The carriage slowed to a stop, hailing the end of their journey. She expected Montgomery to open the door at once. But no.

"We have arrived," she said, looking pointedly at the door.

He still didn't make a move. Not one single glance toward the exit. "I will stop at nothing to protect Richard and the rest of his family."

"You seem to be under the erroneous impression that they are in need of protection against me."

"Aren't they?"

It was a question she couldn't answer, not anymore. Perhaps a day ago, yes. But now? After her private meeting with her grandfather she didn't know what she wanted anymore.

And that scared her far more than the man sitting on the other side of the carriage.

Another few seconds ticked by. She counted them off in her head. One. Two. Three. The interior of the carriage seemed to grow smaller, suffocating, beyond confining.

Her hand lifted involuntarily to her throat. She swallowed and did so again, but nothing seemed to relieve the dry, parched feeling.

More seconds ticked by. Four. Five. Six. Caroline waited for Montgomery to make his move. She waited. And waited. Seven. Eight. Nine.

He didn't budge, not one single inch.

When Caroline didn't think she could stand a moment more of this infuriating game, he broke the silence at last. "Answer me this . . ." He held the pause for effect. "If someone were to offer you money to leave New York, how much would it take to send you packing?"

She reached up, her hand nearly connecting with his handsome face. She stopped herself just in time. Barely holding back her temper, she hid her furious reaction behind a quick sweep of her fingers across her forehead.

Dripping pure innocence in her manner, she slid across the small space dividing them and settled on the seat next to the odious man. "Why, Mr. Montgomery"—she bared her teeth in a smile meant to irritate—"are you offering me a bribe?"

It was his turn to reach up, but much slower than she had and with a great deal more control. He captured a wayward strand of her hair between his thumb and forefinger. "That depends entirely on you."

Sitting this close to the man, she could smell his masculine scent, could hear the faint drumming of his heartbeat. Or was that the sound of her own pulse in her ears?

His finger looped around the strand of hair, around and around and around. With each slow twine, the distance between them closed. She'd meant to remain perfectly still, but something about this man drew her forward, even as danger radiated out of him.

He wasn't as immune as he pretended. She saw the conflict in his eyes. One move on her part, one shift on his, and their lips would meet.

She pulled in a steadying breath. Montgomery's familiar scent of leather and wood filled her nose. Her anger at him—at herself—at them both—increased tenfold, enough to unleash her tongue at last. "Unhand me, sir."

He simply smiled.

"What do you say, Caroline?" He asked the question without taking his eyes off her hair still wrapped around his finger. "Do you want to handle this standoff the easy way or the hard way?"

Was he referring to the situation with her grandfather, or the undercurrents between them?

"Will you accept a reasonable offer to leave town, or are we to fight to the finish?"

"It's ungentlemanly of you to ask the question at all. What do you suppose my grandfather would think if he found out you were attempting to buy me off?"

For a brief moment, he had the good grace to look ashamed of himself. As well he should. The offer was an insulting one, especially if she'd truly come to find her lost family.

But that's not why you came, Caroline, not originally, and this man knows that. It was her turn to feel shame.

"You are determined to fight," he said, releasing her hair with deliberate slowness.

"Apparently so."

What she saw in his eyes astonished her. She saw . . . Was that respect? Grudging though it was, the man clearly respected the fact that she'd refused his bribe. Caroline would have expected anger from him, perhaps even condescension. But respect? That could mean only one thing.

He'd been testing her.

And she'd passed.

With a slight lift at the edges of his mouth, he reached around her and twisted open the carriage door. He exited first and then held out his hand to help her down to the ground.

Holding onto her longer than was polite, he whispered in her ear. "Do not make the mistake of thinking you have won, Caroline. I plan to prove a most worthy opponent. The most formidable you have ever encountered."

She blessed him with her sunniest smile. "I would expect nothing less."

He dropped her hand and stepped back.

Head high, shoulders back, she led the way through the hotel lobby to an elevator off to their right. In need of an ally, Caroline was grateful Sally had agreed to wait for her return, no matter how late.

After the events of the evening, especially the last few minutes, she needed at least one person on her side.

Chapter Thirteen

Jackson waited for Caroline to enter the elevator before he proceeded to do so as well. During his latest conversation with Warren Griffin, Jackson had wondered if his inner integrity had ever been tested. Until tonight, the answer had been no. He'd taken the moral high ground in all matters.

Fifteen minutes alone with Caroline St. James, and all remnants of the civilized man he prided himself on being had disappeared. He'd fallen to a low he'd never imagined, resorting to emotional and physical intimidation tactics as well as bribery.

Caroline had passed every test.

Jackson had failed.

"Which floor, sir?"

Jackson lifted his eyebrows in Caroline's direction.

"Four," she said, her gaze fastened on the numbers above the elevator door.

"Four," he repeated, which earned him an annoyed glance from Caroline. She was obviously used to fending for herself and didn't take kindly to someone stepping in when it wasn't necessary.

He should have been aggravated at her willful display of independence. Such behavior wasn't becoming in a woman of good breeding. And wasn't that the point? Some hidden part of him, a part he never knew existed before a few weeks ago, admired this woman's courage and fortitude. He admired her spirit. If half of what she'd said was true, and he was beginning to think it was, then she'd had a difficult life at best. Tragic at worst.

If nothing else, her arrival in America brought more questions than answers. Jackson wanted to know more about this prodigal daughter who'd disappeared all those years ago. Surely she hadn't left to marry a London gentleman, as the rumors purported. What other secrets were there? Had there been a scandal, a secret cover-up?

If so, how had Richard prevented others from knowing any of the details?

The elevator ground to a metal-scraping stop. The attendant reached in front of Jackson to slide the door open. Again, Jackson gestured for Caroline to proceed ahead of him.

She led the way down the hall, head high, her bearing perfectly appropriate for any gathering in a New York drawing room. Someone had trained her well. At room 419, she pulled her key from the reticule hooked to her wrist and fit the piece of metal in the lock.

The door swung open with a soft whoosh.

"Sally," Caroline called out as she stepped into the room. "I have returned."

A second later, a young maid dressed in full uniform popped into the room. The girl's smile disappeared the moment her eyes landed on Jackson.

"This is Mr. Montgomery." Caroline made the introductions with ease, speaking to the maid with respect. And a level of trust she'd not displayed in his company. "Please keep an eye on him while I fetch an important parcel I left behind this evening."

Jackson chuckled at the command. "I don't need a nursemaid."

Caroline tossed him an annoyed glare. "Humor me, sir."

"But of course." He sketched a formal bow, then sat in a nearby chair.

After making a face at him, Caroline disappeared through a doorway. Wondering where she'd acquired the money to pay for such a luxurious suite of rooms, Jackson craned his neck to follow her every move. One problem with that—the maid shifted directly into his line of vision.

He straightened in the chair and smiled up at her with an innocent expression.

The girl pressed her lips together, clearly unmoved by his attempt to charm her.

Jackson nearly laughed. He couldn't remember a time when he'd been so distrusted by not one but two females. Before he could decide whether to engage the maid in conversation, Caroline returned with a satchel in her hand.

Jackson had no idea what she carried inside the bag, but he had deciphered enough from Richard's instructions to know the contents were important to his business partner. Important enough to demand Caroline's immediate return to the house tonight.

"We may leave now." *Let us get this over with,* her stiff posture seemed to say, as if she were weary and feeling the weight of the world on her shoulders.

How well he knew that sensation.

He obediently rose from the chair, slid his hands in his pockets, and lowered his gaze across her. "Do I need to check for weapons before we depart?"

"Don't push me, Montgomery."

"Dispensing with the Mr.?"

"Would you rather I call you . . . Jackson?"

Amused by her tart tone, he thought for a moment and discovered that he actually preferred the irreverent name better. "Montgomery will do just fine, Caroline." He angled his head. "Or would you prefer Miss St. James?"

Her mouth twitched. "Caroline will do just fine."

"Good enough." He swept his hand in a wide arc. "After you, *Caroline*."

She nodded, then turned to her maid. "I will be back soon. Please wait for my return."

Eyes gleaming with some silent message, the girl gave a short curtsy. "Very good, miss."

The ride back to Richard's home was conducted in silence, each of them seemingly caught up in their own thoughts.

For his part, Jackson considered the lack of conversation a blessing. He had much to think over, especially now that the lines had been drawn between him and Caroline.

Every battle waged, whether in a courtroom or a boardroom or on Orchard Street, required careful planning and deliberation. He knew he was in for an interesting fight with Caroline St. James and wasn't altogether sorry for it.

He actually looked forward to their upcoming encounters. He hadn't been challenged in a while, perhaps ever, at least not in the way this woman seemed capable of doing.

His next course of action should be to gather information about his most worthy opponent. He knew just where to start.

The tenement house on Orchard Street. Where he'd first met Caroline.

Perhaps it was time he introduced himself to her dear friend, Mary.

The carriage pulled to a halt. Again, Jackson exited first. He turned, only to discover Caroline had already bounded to the ground with her satchel clutched tightly to her chest.

"Allow me to carry that for you."

The glower she shot him was answer enough. He lifted his hands in a show of surrender.

Once inside the house, they were told by the butler that the elder Mr. St. James was waiting for them in his private study. Jackson fell into step beside Caroline, matching her step for step as he had earlier that evening.

Annoyance wafted out of her. "I remember the way."

"Of that I have no doubt. Nevertheless"—he set his hand on her lower back—"my assignment was to keep you in my sight at all times."

She pulled to a stop.

Jackson did the same.

"Do you always do what you're told?"

"Always." The answer came immediately.

She had more to say. He could see it in the way her head angled to the side and how her brows drew together. Her gaze traveled over his face. For a moment, he felt completely exposed under her scrutiny. "Do you never wish to rebel?"

"Never." An absurd question. His father's rebellion had ruined his mother, his family's good name, and very nearly Jackson himself.

"Not even in some small way, when no one is looking?"

"No." He felt his jaw clench tight. "Not even then, especially not then."

For an endless moment she blinked up at him. Slowly, a smile tugged at her lips. "Now, now, Montgomery." She tapped him on the chin. "It's not nice to lie, not even to yourself."

At that she continued up the stairs, the smile still playing across her lips.

The words to defend himself were there, on his tongue, but he couldn't get them past the hard, flat line of his lips. The woman was toying with him, subtly pushing him, poking at his self-control.

Her questions had been simple enough, straightforward even. His answers just as candid. Yet he sensed she'd seen past his words, to the core of who he was deep down, a secret part of him he kept hidden from the world. And maybe even from himself, as Caroline had intimated with that aggravating smile on her lips.

Before meeting Caroline, Jackson had always believed himself above reproach, above falling into mindless temptation. The thought that he was more like his father than he'd ever imagined made his gut roil. He must not falter.

Take captive every thought to make it obedient to Christ.

A timely reminder.

The woman was merely trying to throw him off guard, turning the fight toward his motives in order to avoid revealing hers.

Clever, clever girl.

Continuing up the stairs, Jackson quickened his pace and caught up to Caroline just outside Richard's office.

They entered together, shoulder to shoulder, neither taking their eyes off the man who rose from his desk. The life-size painting on his right caught Jackson's eye. For years, he'd given the portrait little notice. He studied the painting more carefully now, understanding at once why Richard hadn't questioned Caroline's identity.

And why she'd seemed so familiar at their first meeting.

She was the very image of the woman in the painting. Her mother. Libby. Caroline was, indeed, a St. James by blood. Jackson had no more cause to doubt the truth of it. He'd never doubted, not truly. Her eyes had been too similar to Richard's for him to deny the family connection.

But Jackson had always thought Richard's daughter had died in London years ago. The story had rarely been discussed in detail, not in this home or any other. If Caroline's story was to be believed, Libby St. James had been left behind in a foreign country to raise her daughter alone on the mean London streets. For a moment, sympathy for Caroline overwhelmed him.

Then came understanding.

Followed quickly by alarm.

He now knew the woman's motive for journeying to America. She'd come to exact revenge for her mother.

But how? How did she plan to do it?

Jackson would find out soon enough. In the meantime, he said, "You won't get away with this."

She rolled her shoulders, as if ridding herself of an unwanted pest, then spoke the two words he'd used on her earlier. "We'll see."

* * *

Caroline had matched wits with some of the meanest minds in London with a relatively high rate of success. Her very survival proof enough. As such, she should be able to handle one pampered gentleman who, on the surface, was nothing more than her grandfather's lapdog.

Of course, Jackson Montgomery was no lackey. He was his own man, in charge of his own destiny. Smart, insightful, overly clever and, worst of all, honorable.

She didn't know how to battle a man who fought fiercely but without compromising his integrity. Maybe . . . yes, *maybe* that was the key. She would get the man to compromise his integrity.

The thought didn't sit well. If she successfully drove him to sink to such a low, what sort of person did that make her?

Her grandfather came around his desk, his gaze fastened on her satchel. "Is that them?"

"Yes." She handed over the canvas bag, making eye contact with her grandfather as she did. Her heart dropped at his haunted look.

Was he telling the truth? Had he not received any of her mother's letters?

If not, then who had sent them back to London unopened?

Another member of the family?

The idea that a person in this household had wanted her mother to stay away, permanently—well, that was just sinister.

It also meant her grandfather had been as much a victim as Caroline and her mother.

Despite the scowl on his face, his hands shook as he flipped open the satchel's flap. A wave of remorse swept through her.

"Perhaps you should sit down."

He waved her suggestion away, but the moment he pulled out the first letter, he sank back against his desk.

"Richard. Come. Sit here." Taking charge of the situation, Montgomery took the old man's arm and guided him to a nearby chair.

So wrapped up was she in watching her grandfather that Caroline had nearly forgotten the other man was in the room with them. Witnessing the two together, she reevaluated the situation.

Jackson Montgomery was more than a mere business partner. He cared about the other man. And her grandfather trusted him. Apparently, more than he trusted his own son since Montgomery was the one in this room and not Marcus St. James.

After a short hesitation and a deep breath, her grandfather pulled out the batch of letters. He placed them in a neat stack on top of the canvas satchel and simply stared at the pile on his lap.

Silence fell over the room as he traced a fingertip across the writing penned in her mother's own hand.

Caroline moved a step closer, impatience making her shift from foot to foot.

A lady of unlimited means never fidgets; she remains perfectly still. Sally's instructions flashed in her mind. Although she was no longer playing a part, Caroline stilled.

Needing something to do with her hands, she clutched them together at her waist and sighed in frustration. She wanted to scream at her grandfather to get on with it.

Seemingly as impatient as she, Montgomery reached out toward the stack. Her grandfather brushed his hand away, then opened the top letter, the one sent over twenty years ago.

Caroline had made sure to organize them in chronological order.

Tired eyes scanned across the page, her grandfather's face devoid of all expression, or at least none that Caroline could make out. Turning over the letter, he continued to read. After a moment, he checked the postmark, then replaced the letter in its corresponding envelope and set it on a table beside him.

The next letter received the same meticulous attention. He repeated the process over and over again until he came to the bottom of the stack.

When he looked up at Caroline, tears shone in his eyes. Several slid down his cheeks. He made no attempt to wipe them away.

Caroline's mouth went dry, the salty taste of her own tears on her tongue. She'd sat across a poker table from every kind of player imaginable. She could spot a good bluff in record time.

This old man was not bluffing.

And she'd done that to him. She'd brought upon him this unspeakable pain. Revolted by her own behavior, she could no longer hold her own tears at bay. She swiped at her eyes before they spilled down her face.

"Libby tried to contact me." His voice was so full of pain that Caroline's heart clutched. "I thought she ran off with that boy and never looked back. I never understood why. She was happy in this home. Her desertion never made sense."

Desertion. Her grandfather thought his daughter had run off with a man and abandoned her own family when that couldn't have been further from the truth.

"I have never seen these letters before tonight." He drew in a shuddering breath. "I had no idea she was in such desperate need. What she must have thought of my silence."

God help her, Caroline believed her grandfather's sorrow. How well she knew that sort of unspeakable pain.

Her breathing quickened, cutting off her ability to draw in a decent pull of air. She took short, painful gulps. Her skin iced over as wisps of dismay shot through her.

She'd planned this night for months, expecting to meet a hard, ruthless man with no forgiveness in his heart. A man who deserved punishment. She'd told herself she'd come for justice for her mother, and maybe even for herself. But she knew the truth now. She'd come for revenge.

Bile rose in her throat. She was a terrible, terrible person. One who deserved to be tossed out of this house.

A sob rushed out of her.

She dashed to her grandfather and collapsed at his feet. Placing her palms on his knees, she looked at him through her watery vision. "I'm sorry," she choked out. "I thought you abandoned her, *us*. I came to America hating you."

Two strong hands, grizzled with age, covered hers and clasped gently. "What you must have suffered all these years."

The genuine kindness sent the tears spilling down her cheeks. "I . . . you should know why I really came here tonight. I came to make you pay for your sins." Shame clogged the breath in her throat. "Forgive me."

Chapter Fourteen

Jackson didn't belong here. He didn't belong in this room where a fractured family reunited after decades of lost communication and misunderstandings.

No, not misunderstandings. That wasn't the right term for the treachery that had kept a father from his daughter, and a granddaughter from knowing her family. The very same woman who had just begged for forgiveness from the man she'd come to make pay for his sins.

Jackson believed Caroline's remorse. He saw the way she trembled, even as she kept her shoulders stiff and unyielding. The latter was a sure sign she refused to let down her guard completely. He couldn't blame her for that. Someone in this house had deliberately seized nearly three dozen letters addressed to Richard. But who?

Who stood to gain from such a heinous act?

Several people came to mind, all of them present this evening. Jackson would uncover the identity of the culprit.

For Richard. And, perhaps, for Caroline as well.

He owed her that much for his earlier suspicions. Although, as it turned out, he'd been right to suspect her motives. By her own admission, she'd come here to ruin Richard, her own *grandfather*.

Jackson tried to drum up disapproval. He couldn't.

If he were honest with himself, he would admit that he understood the kind of anger that had driven her to seek revenge. Hadn't he dealt with similar feelings when his father had first betrayed his family? Hadn't he struggled against allowing his hurt to turn into hate through the years?

Would Caroline find healing one day? Would she be able to forgive whoever had set out to harm her mother?

Would Richard?

The two were still holding hands, still speaking in splintered sentences, talking over one another. Both were equally emotional. Jackson couldn't hear all the words passing between them and silently accepted that he wasn't supposed to. He was intruding, but he wasn't sure he should leave Richard alone with his granddaughter yet.

Caroline St. James seemed genuinely remorseful. Jackson wanted to believe her reaction, more than he knew was wise. Someone had to keep a clear head. Someone had to remain impartial. And that someone was Jackson.

First order of business, he had to prevent a scandal from igniting over Caroline's sudden arrival. Not a simple task, but doable. Unless . . .

What if she still sought revenge for her mother, if not on her grandfather, then on the one who had intercepted Libby's letters? Would she destroy her own family in the process? News of her initial reason for coming to America would be enough fodder for the gossips.

Jackson knew his duty. At this point, nothing should change. As before, he would keep a close eye on Caroline and reserve judgment pending further information.

The letters were the best place to begin. He needed to get a look at them, perhaps study each of the postmarks. Where they'd originated was important, especially if he was going to keep word of this from getting out.

For now, it was time to quit the room.

Slowly, as quietly as possible, he took a step toward the exit. Richard looked up, a vague expression of surprise on his face. "Jackson, you are still here."

"I am just leaving. Is there anything you need before I depart?" He dropped his gaze to the stack of letters in Richard's lap. "Anything, perhaps, you wish for me to look into for you?"

He was tempted to be more specific but decided against the idea.

"Not at the moment, no." Richard's hand flattened over the stack of letters. "Later, yes, but not now. Not tonight."

Jackson nodded. Before he turned to go, he glanced in Caroline's direction. Her eyes, dark with emotion, met his. She looked so young, vulnerable, and unbearably innocent that his heart dipped in his chest. On some primitive level, he wanted to steal her away from this house, from these people who had caused her such pain.

"Is there anything I can do for you, Caroline?" He remembered the maid awaiting her return at the Waldorf-Astoria. "Anyone you wish for me to contact?"

A thousand words passed between them, none of which he understood.

She lowered her lashes and sighed. "Thank you, no."

"Very well."

Pivoting on his heel, he left the room without a backward glance. Alone in the hallway, he debated whether to wait until the two emerged or go in search of the rest of the family.

There would be questions, most of which Jackson couldn't answer. But they deserved to know Richard was safe in Caroline's company.

Decision made, he headed down the hallway. His steps slowed, then stopped altogether. Another second and reality set in. He'd come here tonight to begin his courtship of Elizabeth. He'd planned to make his intentions known, if not to the family, then to her.

With all that had happened, Jackson couldn't think about courting her now. Following hard on the heels of that thought came the memory of Caroline's soulful eyes, eyes filled with sorrow and confusion.

Something deep within him shifted away from Elizabeth and moved toward Caroline.

No.

No.

"I want Elizabeth," he muttered. She was his perfect match, the woman destined to bear his children one day.

And yet . . . the image didn't fit so well tonight.

Had it ever?

Holding back a growl, he caught sight of the St. James butler waiting for him at the bottom of the staircase.

Jackson took a moment to clear his thoughts, but only a moment, then finished his descent and paused beside the stiff-backed servant.

"The guests are awaiting you in the dining room, Mr. Montgomery."

Somewhat surprised at this, Jackson lifted an eyebrow. "Is that so?"

"Your grandmother and mother arrived not long after Mr. Griffin. When it became clear that not all of your party would be joining the others, your grandmother took charge of the situation."

At this bit of information, Jackson couldn't hold back a smile. Of course his grandmother had taken charge. Even though it wasn't her place and this wasn't her home, Hattie Montgomery would have assessed the situation, taken note of the tension among the St. James family, and then done what needed to be done.

"Will you be joining the rest of your party in the dining room, Mr. Montgomery?"

"Yes, thank you, Aldrich. I know the way."

"Very good, sir."

Quickening his steps, Jackson found himself looking forward to his grandmother's calming presence. Once a great beauty, Hattie Montgomery still possessed a grand style and sophisticated elegance that suited her eighty-seven years. She knew her own mind, never caring what others thought of her *or* her family, not even at the height of the scandal regarding her son's behavior. Jackson had tried to emulate her response through the years.

He entered the dining room, and all eyes turned in his direction. All eyes, that was, except those belonging to Elizabeth and Luke. They had their heads bent together and were embroiled in a low, hushed conversation.

Jackson wasn't sure what to think of that. Was he jealous?

Oddly enough, no.

"Sit down, Jackson, you have missed the first three courses already." His mother's voice held unmistakable censure.

Glancing at Lucille Montgomery's pursed lips and dark, angry eyes, Jackson had the sensation of being caught in the path of a coiled viper. Uncharacteristic rebellion rose up fast and hard.

"I was unavoidably detained." He did not elaborate.

Clearly shocked at his cold response, his mother opened her mouth, probably to express her disapproval, but his grandmother spoke over her. "Do sit down, my boy."

Moving deeper into the room, he took in the rest of the guests. His grandmother presided at the head of the table. Marcus and his wife, Katherine, sat on her right. Because Luke had taken Jackson's customary seat beside Elizabeth on Hattie's left, he chose the empty chair beside his mother.

Elizabeth looked up when he sat. Her cheeks were flushed with emotion. Jackson had never seen the girl quite so animated.

"Is it true?" she asked in a rush, her usual calm serenity replaced with untold excitement. "Is Caroline Harding my cousin?"

He saw no reason to withhold the truth from her now. After the reunion he'd witnessed upstairs, Jackson had no doubt Richard would immediately bring Caroline into the family fold. "Yes, she is."

"Oh. *Oh*. I have a cousin. Not as good as a sister, but wonderful all the same." Elizabeth clapped her hands together happily, then set her gaze on the doorway. "Where is she? Isn't she joining us?"

"And more to the point," Katherine said, her gaze secured to the doors as well, "is Richard joining us?"

"Yes, son," his own mother chimed in, her interest inappropriate since this was a family matter. A *St. James* family matter. "Where *is* Richard this evening? This was supposed to be his party."

Before Jackson could answer, Marcus added his own question. "Do we know the girl is who she says she is?"

"Yes." Jackson nodded. This question was the easiest to answer. "She has proof."

"Oh, how exciting. What sort of proof?" Elizabeth asked, her eager, wide-eyed gaze full of harmless curiosity. At least one person in this house would openly welcome Caroline into the family. The knowledge had Jackson breathing easier.

"I'll let Richard fill you in on the details when it is only family in attendance." Temper primed, he looked pointedly at his mother, willing her to keep from engaging in the discussion any further.

He could see her mind working and knew what she was thinking. The return of a long-lost granddaughter would be the talk of town. The news would spread quickly. If not handled correctly, the rumors could turn nasty. All the more reason to withhold Caroline's original intent for coming to America, even from her own family. *Especially* from her own family.

Best only he and Richard knew the truth.

Dinner continued into the next course. Speculation at the table heated up, centering on what Caroline and Richard could possibly be discussing in private.

Jackson gave nothing away. The story was not his tell.

After dessert, the party congregated back in the blue drawing room. Jackson joined the other guests. He would have preferred to seek out

Caroline and Richard, but he knew the others in this room were waiting for their return as well. Jackson couldn't predict how the meeting between grandfather and granddaughter would play out.

For Richard's sake, Jackson needed to be in attendance for whatever happened next.

Luke settled in a seat between Marcus and Jackson's grandmother. Ever the loyal friend, he proceeded to regale the room with tales from his time in London.

Elizabeth stopped him halfway through the first story. "Did you happen to meet Caroline in London?"

"No." Luke glanced at Jackson a moment. "But I was there primarily to work. I didn't attend many parties."

"But when you did," Elizabeth pressed, "you mean to say you never met my cousin?"

Feeling oddly protective of Caroline, Jackson opened his mouth to redirect the conversation. Luke changed the subject on his own.

Grateful that his friend controlled the conversation, Jackson moved to the other side of the room. Lost in thought, he placed a foot on the hearth and leaned his forearm on the mantelpiece.

He didn't have long to enjoy his moment of peace before his mother joined him. She stood ramrod straight and had the familiar pinch to her face.

He braced himself.

"The news of Richard's granddaughter should cause quite a stir among our friends, especially since she didn't reveal her connection when she first arrived in this country." A distorted smile spread across her lips. "One has to assume there is a reason she withheld her identity, and not a good one."

Jackson said nothing. What could he say? His mother was correct. On all accounts. And if a tale was scandalous enough—which this one most definitely was—then the good people of New York would take their time dissecting every sordid detail. Conclusions would be drawn, none of them good, most of them wrong.

Ugly twists would then be added, especially if word got out about the intercepted letters. Caroline would be rejected from every respectable home in New York before she'd had a chance to prove herself. The unfairness was not lost on Jackson. Someone in this room had deliberately destroyed Libby St. James, and consequently Caroline.

His mother's voice broke through his thoughts again. "If this does get out"—she drew in a harsh breath—"the St. James name will never be the same."

Yes, Jackson knew this, too, and silently vowed to do whatever was necessary to prevent such a disaster from occurring.

"You do realize, son," his mother said, glancing over her shoulder, "that dear Elizabeth, the poor girl, will not come away unscathed."

Hours ago, Jackson would have railed against the injustice of choosing a respectable woman to wed, only to lose her to the very sort of scandal he'd set out to avoid. Of course, that was before he'd witnessed Richard's sorrow over the fate of his daughter. Not to mention his corresponding joy over having regained a portion of her in the form of his granddaughter.

Under the circumstances, there was only one thing for Jackson to do. Protect the St. James family from censure. Not for himself or his own gain, but for the man who had always accepted him in this home. From the start, in those early days after Jackson's father had left town, Richard St. James had shown the rest of society what true grace looked like.

It was Jackson's turn to do the same.

Chapter Fifteen

Caroline shifted her stance, watching silently as her grandfather directed a servant to a table near the bookshelves in his study. While the man set down a tray laden with plates of steaming food, Caroline reflected over the events of the last few hours.

She'd never felt this physically and emotionally exhausted, not even when she'd been holed up in steerage during her journey across the Atlantic. Her entire body ached, her head felt light, and her mouth had gone dry as dust, the consequences of her unchecked tears.

Once the servant retreated, her grandfather motioned her over to the table, where he held out a chair for her. They'd agreed to dine in private, away from the other guests. Caroline had assumed it was for her benefit, but now she wondered. Perhaps her grandfather didn't want to face the rest of his family. Perhaps he wished to avoid the arduous task of uncovering who was behind her mother's returned letters.

As much as she'd like to know as well, Caroline wasn't up to the task, either, at least not tonight. She'd had enough confrontation for one evening.

"I—that is—" She stopped short. "I'm afraid I don't know what to call you."

"Your cousin calls me Grandfather."

"Grandfather." Caroline repeated the name in her head, rolling it silently around in her mind. "Grandfather." The name tasted strange on her tongue. And yet, somehow, it felt right. "I like it."

"Then Grandfather it is."

Caroline smiled. The simple gesture felt right as well.

In silent agreement, they spent the next few minutes focusing on their individual plates. Given the original nature of her presence here tonight, Caroline should have felt uncomfortable in her grandfather's company. She didn't. Much like her smile, everything about this moment, this meal, this private time with the man she'd spent years hating felt . . . right. Even the silence was pleasant.

"Caroline."

"Yes . . . Grandfather?" They both smiled.

"There's something I don't understand." He set his fork down on the table, his smile fading. "Where did you acquire the necessary funds to journey to America and then set yourself up at the Waldorf-Astoria?"

Her stomach knotted at the question, and she slowly placed her own fork on the table. "I didn't resort to stealing, if that's what you're asking."

"Then how did you earn the money?"

"Do you truly want to know?" She eyed him, unsure how much to reveal. "Even if it's a tale you might not wish to hear?"

"I get a sense you are a resourceful woman." The admiration in his voice was real, but he didn't yet know what she'd done. Would his respect turn to condemnation?

Determined to brave this out to the end and to remain as truthful as possible along the way, she forced a smile on her face, then . . .

Stalled a moment longer. "One has to be somewhat wily in order to survive in Whitechapel."

"Whitechapel?" His face crumpled. "Caroline." He reached out to cover her hand with his. "You must realize how sorry I am that you—"

"No." She pulled her hand free and placed it in the air to prevent him from speaking further. "We agreed. No more apologizing, from either of us."

"Right." He shut his eyes a moment, sighed, then continued. "You were about to tell me how you raised enough money to carry out your plan." This time, he held up his hand to forestall her words. "And before *you* apologize again, I understand your motives for coming here. Given the information you had, I don't blame you for wanting revenge on me."

His voice was deep and forgiving. Instead of comforting her, it had the opposite effect. Her shame returned. "It wasn't revenge that I wanted, not precisely. I just wanted you to . . . to . . ." She couldn't say it, couldn't admit the truth.

"Suffer," he finished for her. "You wanted me to suffer as your mother had all those years in England."

"Yes. Oh, Grandfather, I am—" She cut herself off. "*Not* going to say I'm sorry."

"Good. Now. Proceed with your story."

"It took me six months to earn what I needed."

"How much money are we talking about?"

She quoted the outrageous sum.

"That's the equivalent of what one of my factory workers earns over five years." His gaze turned thoughtful, astute, reminding her that this man was nobody's fool, not even his long-lost granddaughter's. "What sort of . . . activity pays that kind of return in only six months?"

"I didn't steal the money," she reiterated. "Not in the truest sense of the word."

"You're stalling, Caroline." He gave her a disappointed shake of his head. "I expect better from you."

She expected better from herself. "I won the money playing cards."

"You are a card sharp?" He sounded oddly intrigued.

"Not by trade, no. Gambling was merely a means to an end, the fastest way to raise the money I needed." She swallowed. When presented in such a candid manner, she sounded quite calculating. "I was—I was . . . on a schedule."

"Are you saying you cheated?"

She gasped. "No. *Never.* I'm just very skilled at reading my opponent."

"No one is that skilled at reading her opponent."

Sighing, she explained further. "I am also very good with numbers. I can calculate any sum, no matter how large, with very little effort. I also have a good memory. I can deduce from the cards that have been played which ones are still in the deck, thereby mentally calculating the odds of my success or failure per hand."

"Truly?"

She nodded.

"What is four hundred and thirty-five times fifty-one?"

She answered without hesitation. "Twenty-two thousand, one hundred eighty-five."

"Eight hundred sixty-three times nine hundred twenty-two."

"Seven hundred ninety-five thousand, six hundred eighty-six."

"Now that is a useful talent." He rubbed his chin, speculating. "If you are that good, why did you wait until your mother died to earn the money it took to come here and find me?"

Caroline sighed. "Because Mother asked me not to play cards."

"Why not?"

"Because, with my particular skill, the way I play cards is—" She swallowed. "It's a . . . sin."

Until the words left her mouth, Caroline had never considered herself religious, certainly not obedient to an invisible God who allowed so much suffering in the world, in *her* world. But her mother had never given up on her faith, or her God, not even in the darkest days.

Caroline had secretly hated Libby for her blind faith. Or so she'd always thought. Now, she realized that she'd admired her mother for her faith. Just as she admired Mary for hers.

"Libby taught you well."

Caroline sighed again. "Mother used to call the way I played nothing more than a sophisticated form of stealing. In the final years of her life, I honored her wishes to earn money honestly."

They'd suffered a harder life than necessary because of that, but Caroline had agreed. Until her mother's death, when she'd experienced unprecedented remorse. And, yes, shame. Why had she bowed to her mother's wishes when she could have earned enough to get them out of Whitechapel years ago?

So much to regret.

"Caroline." Her grandfather's voice held a shrewd note. "There are other ways to use your skill with numbers that don't involve cards. Legal ways that can earn just as much money."

Doubting that, she angled her head. "Such as?"

"What if I told you I could teach you how to calculate the odds for legitimate gain?"

"I'd say you have an interest of your own."

"You'd be right." He gave her an appreciative wink. "But it may not be for the reasons you think."

Intrigued despite herself, she leaned forward. "Explain."

He waved her off with a flick of his wrist. "Tomorrow, at my office, three o'clock, not a second later."

Oh, he was a sharp one, the wily old goat. He'd given her just enough information to keep her interested, but not enough to give her a reason to turn him down. They both knew she would show up precisely at the commanded time. "I'll be there. But be warned, I'm on to your game."

"That, my dear Caroline, is because we are very much alike."

She allowed herself a brief laugh. "So it would seem."

* * *

Caroline climbed into her grandfather's motorcar just after midnight. The night was clear, with the curve of the waxing moon brilliant against the black fabric of the sky. The streetlamps drew long shadows from the house across the hood of the car.

With only half a mind, Caroline glanced at the million stars above her head. She hadn't seen Montgomery since he'd left her alone with her grandfather. Just as well. She was weary and worn to the bone, feeling as though she'd run a long-distance race. She wasn't up for another verbal battle with the man.

A moment after the driver shut the door behind her, it swung back open and a familiar dark form appeared. She knew those broad shoulders well. A sickening knot twisted in her stomach as the car dipped slightly under the man's added weight, then balanced out once he settled in the seat beside her.

She couldn't see his face clearly in the darkened interior, but she knew he had questions. Many of them. All the more reason to release a long, heartfelt sigh. "Look, Montgomery, I'm not in the mood for another battle with you tonight."

"Nor am I."

"Then what do you want?" Her voice sounded as exhausted as she felt. At least her eyes had adjusted to the dark, and she could now make out most of his features. Even in the weak light he was a stunningly handsome man, and far more masculine than most of the men she'd met in society. The unmistakable muscles beneath his perfectly tailored jacket told her he was a physical being. Something she wouldn't have expected of an individual who spent most of his time in boardrooms.

She heard him breathing calmly beside her. Such remarkable control. She closed her eyes tightly while Montgomery leaned forward to direct the driver to her hotel.

Once they were on their way, he returned to his original position. "I am here to formulate our plan of attack to accomplish our mutual goal." He allowed an eloquent silence to punctuate his words, then added, "We will discuss the details now."

Her mind still muddled from the drama of the evening, she opened her eyes and gaped at him. "What, exactly, is *our mutual goal?*"

"Someone in the St. James household intentionally kept your mother and Richard from reconciling through the years." He seemed surprised he had to spell it out for her, and now that he'd explained himself, Caroline was a bit surprised, too.

"We need to find out who that person is and expose him . . . or her," he said.

"*We?* How is this any of your concern? You are only a friend of the family."

His eyebrow twitched at her barb, not enough for most people to notice, but Caroline knew how to read responses others missed. She sensed she'd found this man's weakness, the reminder of his position in the family. Or, rather, lack thereof.

Another valuable piece of information she filed away in her mind.

"Perhaps I am not a St. James but, at the moment, I am the only person Richard can trust completely."

"And why is that? Because you share a few business dealings with him?"

"Because I don't have a personal stake in his inheritance, while others do." The unspoken message was clear. She was one of the *others* he thought wanted her grandfather's money.

Except she hadn't come here for any inheritance. That simple truth hadn't changed over the last few hours. For a moment, she stared at the velvet blanket of stars out the window and decided to let Montgomery think what he wanted. She wasn't going to defend herself yet again to this man.

She did, however, wish to hear his plan. "What are you suggesting?"

"I propose we work together to uncover the culprit."

She wasn't completely against the idea. "You want us to work together when you so obviously don't trust me. And I equally don't trust you."

He had the good grace to look regretful. "Let me apologize for my behavior earlier this evening."

"Pardon me?" She felt her eyes widen ever so slightly. "I must have misunderstood you. You are apologizing?"

"So it would seem."

How was she supposed to reconcile this contrite man with the one who had vowed to watch her every step? "I have never met anyone like you," she admitted. "You are a contradiction."

"As are you." He shifted on the seat. "I feel I should warn you. Given the nature of your original motives for seeking out your grandfather, I am unable to release my suspicions of you completely."

Nor could she release her suspicions of him. "Fair enough."

"What do you say, Caroline? Do we call a temporary truce?"

Her neck muscles tightened, her mind honing in on the word *temporary*. That implied their truce would come to an end, sooner or later. "Let me see if I understand you correctly. You want us to pool our resources, *temporarily*, as much to meet our common goal as to keep an eye on me."

"I knew you were a clever girl."

So they were to be enemies with a common purpose. The thought depressed her more than it should have.

"In the spirit of fairness, I also admit"—he stretched out his legs, commandeering more than his share of the confined space—"my behavior toward you this evening lacked a certain, shall we say . . . finesse."

Grinding her teeth together, Caroline tucked her feet under the seat and forced her jaw to relax. It was hard not to growl at the man.

"However, I stand by my initial assumption about your character."

Smart man.

"And just so we're clear, Caroline." The space between them evaporated to a matter of inches. "I'm watching you. Every step you take, I'll be there."

"How fortuitous for me."

"I won't do anything to harm your reputation, or that of your family. As of now, only you, your grandfather, and I know of your motives for coming to America. It would be wise to keep it that way."

Trapped in her seat, with him looming so close, Caroline considered several responses to his superior tone. A swift kick to his shin, an elbow in his ribs, maybe even a tear or two. She discarded all three, deciding a more sophisticated course of action was in order. Something in her, some dark portion of her soul, welcomed the challenge this man set before her, enough to pretend to consider his words carefully.

"I agree to your terms."

His eyes dropped over her face and, for a dangerous moment, she thought he might set his mouth to hers. A shiver of anticipation coursed through her. Angered at her response, and, yes, a little frightened, too, she did what came naturally.

She fought dirty. "How do you plan to stick ever so close to me when you're supposed to be courting my cousin?"

He drew in a sharp pull of air. "I'll manage."

"I just bet you will."

With deliberate slowness, he moved away from her.

Caroline felt a sudden jolt of shame. Sweet, kind, naïve Elizabeth didn't deserve to be used as a pawn in this battle of wills. By all indications, her cousin was not spoiled or selfish, as Caroline had expected. Her cousin's safe childhood had formed a good, moral, decent woman of character. In short, the girl was everything Caroline was not.

Yet, as hard as she tried, Caroline couldn't find it in her heart to hate her cousin, or even resent her. Elizabeth was too easy to like, much like Mary O'Leary. And Sally.

Montgomery's voice interrupted her thoughts. "While we're on the subject of Elizabeth. As far as I can tell"—he lounged on his side of the car as though he had all night to spend in conversation—"she doesn't know anything about the letters. Or, for that matter, much about your mother."

Caroline remembered the confused expression on her cousin's face earlier that night. "We should keep it that way," she said. "For her protection."

"Agreed."

Silence fell between them. For a brief moment, Caroline wondered what it would be like to be Elizabeth, to be innocent and adored, to have a man wish to protect her from harm. What would it be like to know someone was watching out for her safety rather than watching her every move?

A spasm of yearning trembled through her. Her hand reached toward Montgomery. Just a bit. Shocked at herself, she hid the gesture behind a quick lift of that same hand to her forehead. She pressed down as though pushing at a headache.

The car stopped in front of her hotel, and Montgomery helped her onto the sidewalk.

"I prefer to make my way inside on my own," she said, stepping out of his reach.

"Of course."

She turned to go, but he stopped her with a hand on her arm. "I will contact you tomorrow afternoon, and we will set up a time to discuss our next step."

The suggestion made perfect sense. However, she needed more than a handful of hours to restore her nerves. Thankfully, she had a way out. "I have plans already."

"Cancel them."

"No."

"Caroline, I—"

"Stop, Montgomery, just . . . stop." She blew out a frustrated breath. "Stop questioning me at every turn."

"Until your actions prove sincere, I will—"

"Oh, honestly, now you're just being redundant." She gave him a haughty lift of her chin. "My grandfather requested I meet him at his office at three. *Those* are my other plans."

"Then we will meet at four, in my office, one floor beneath Richard's."

Tired of fighting him, she acquiesced. "Yes, yes, as you wish."

This time, when she turned toward the hotel, he let her walk away. Of the two meetings tomorrow, Caroline sensed the one with her grandfather would be the easiest to bear, and possibly the source of an intriguing proposition. Conversely, the one with Montgomery would be the more challenging of the two and, she predicted, the source of a rather sleepless night.

Chapter Sixteen

The next morning, groggy and in desperate need of her friend, Caroline was up and out of the hotel before dawn. Less than an hour later, she turned onto Orchard Street, free of incident. Her safe arrival was due in large part to the fact that she'd skirted the worst of the Bowery and several other unsafe neighborhoods along the way. Personal safety was not to be trifled with, ever.

Practically alone and on a familiar street, Caroline lifted her eyes to the heavens, opened her arms wide, and breathed in deeply. Dirty, rotten-smelling air filled her lungs and left her gagging. She didn't care. She loved this hour of the day, when night had yet to surrender fully to dawn.

So much to look forward to, more than she'd ever dreamed possible for a woman like her. Heart light, conscience relieved, she almost believed in the loving God her mother had trusted all her life. Maybe miracles were possible.

Maybe Caroline could start fresh.

My joy comes in the morning. The Bible verse made much more sense to her now. In one evening, her sorrow had turned to joy. She'd stepped into St. James House last night prepared to ruin a man, prepared for a fight to the finish. She'd left the building with a grandfather and a family of her own.

She had much to tell Mary.

And she wanted to hear how the girl was settling in to her new country. Caroline rushed up the steps leading into her friend's tenement house, threw open the door, and immediately collided with a hard, unforgiving wall of wool-encased muscle. "Oh."

She teetered backward, arms flailing. "Oh!"

Strong, masculine hands caught her before she toppled down the steps she'd just skipped up.

"Are you all right, miss?" The cultured accent clearly belonged to an educated American, one who sounded somewhat familiar. Where had she heard that voice?

"I—yes, I'm quite all right." She brushed at her skirts, smoothing out the wrinkles while she slid a covert glance at the man hovering over her.

She nearly groaned out loud. Mr. Reilly. The man had been with Jackson Montgomery that first day she and Mary had arrived in the neighborhood. He'd been in the building on several other occasions as well.

Of all the people to run into, literally, this was not the man Caroline would have chosen. She could think of only one worse scenario—if Montgomery had chosen to attend to his tenement house himself.

Mumbling an apology, Caroline pushed into the foyer and promptly tripped over a seam in the concrete.

Again, Mr. Reilly reached out to steady her.

She shrugged off his assistance as politely as she could. "Thank you, I've got it now."

"Very good." He slowly dropped his hand. "Have we met?"

"Not directly, no." But she'd seen him in the building at least two other times, maybe three, with the new landlord in tow, both men carrying official-looking papers in their hands.

"You live in apartment 523," he said, nodding to himself. "I'm quite certain of that."

"No. I don't actually live there. I'm a friend of the family living there."

"I could have sworn . . ." His eyebrows slammed together.

She held her breath, praying he didn't continue. Then she remembered who she was, who her *grandfather* was. She had nothing to hide. She lifted her chin at a haughty angle.

"Caro, is that you?" Mary's voice drifted from a spot on the stairwell just above them.

The girl had absolutely perfect timing. "Yes, Mary, it is I."

"Oh, what a lovely surprise. I'll be right down."

"No need. I'm on my way up now." Caroline looked back at Mr. Reilly and gave him what she hoped was a serene smile. "If you will excuse me, Mr. . . ."

"Reilly. John Reilly."

"Well, then, Mr. Reilly. It was lovely meeting you."

"And you as well, Miss . . ."

"Caroline. Caroline St. James."

The name registered at once, but she didn't give him a chance to ask any of the questions that leapt into his eyes. "Good day, Mr. Reilly."

"Yes, uh . . . good day, Miss St. James."

A quick toss of her head and she was off, hurrying up the first two flights of stairs at alarming speed.

Thankfully, Mr. Reilly didn't follow or call after her. Thus, she completely pushed him out of her mind.

Mary met her on the third-floor landing. Caroline threw herself into her friend's arms. "Oh, my dear girl, I have missed you so."

"And I, you."

They clung to each other a moment longer, then broke apart in unison, laughing.

Hands on Caroline's shoulders, Mary gasped. "Caro, you are"—she shook her head—"changed."

Yes, she supposed that was true. "I have much to tell you."

"Then come along."

Caroline followed her friend up the remaining two flights of stairs, watching carefully for any sure signs of fatigue. Mary looked healthier than the last time they'd met but was still slightly underweight. Caroline had left money with her friend. She hoped she was using the bulk of it to buy food.

Mary looked at Caroline over her shoulder and laughed. "Stop worrying about me, Caro. I'm fine and getting stronger every day."

Was she? Caroline wasn't convinced. Nor was she leaving this building until she knew for certain that her friend was truly on the mend.

They settled into chairs around the small kitchen table. Before Mary could offer her any food or drink, none of which the girl could afford to share, Caroline took her friend's hand. "Tell me how you've been since we last met."

"I've found work in the Garment District as a seamstress."

"Why, that's wonderful."

"Oh, Caro, it is. It truly is." Mary's grasp tightened, and her face lit from within. "I really enjoy sewing, even if the lighting isn't the best and the days are long and hot."

Caroline leaned over the table. "Just how long and hot are your workdays?"

Sighing, Mary let go of Caroline and sat back in her chair. "I'm working no harder than anyone else in the factory."

And that told Caroline far more than Mary probably realized. "I'm going to get you another job in one of my grandfather's companies. I'll make sure the days won't be long and hot or—"

"I don't want special treatment. Besides, I'm learning a lot where I am. I'm told my needlework is impeccable. I've even been given the task of finishing the dresses for my boss, which is quite an honor. One day"—Mary's gaze took on a faraway look—"I'll design and make my own dresses and maybe even sell them at a department store."

Caroline's heart constricted with admiration. Mary was a dreamer and so full of hope. Caroline loved her friend for that. But she knew the harsh realities of the world, especially for women with Mary's lack of education and connections.

Except . . .

Mary wasn't without connections. She had Caroline. And Caroline was a St. James. If she did nothing else, she would at least provide a better life for her friend.

By the time she left 227 Orchard Street, Caroline made sure Mary had an additional twenty dollars in the cookie jar where she kept her money. And Caroline had the beginnings of a plan swirling around in her head.

* * *

On the other side of town, Jackson arrived at his offices before his assistant. With a bit of time on his hands, he went in search of Richard. The door to his mentor's office stood open and unattended. Weak morning light filtered through the large floor-to-ceiling windows overlooking Central Park. The hush on the air seemed magnified at this hour, the silence broken only by the faint sound of a pen scratching across paper.

Richard was already at work. As Jackson had expected.

Last night, after escorting Caroline to her hotel, he'd debated over whether to return to the St. James home or wait until morning. He'd chosen to wait.

Moving through the deserted reception area, Jackson couldn't help but admire the man he'd worked alongside for years. Even in the midst of a family drama, Richard St. James had arrived at work as he did every day, before anyone else.

Jackson knocked once on the doorjamb as he passed over the threshold and entered the office.

Without looking up from the papers in front him, Richard addressed him. "You're early this morning."

"No earlier than you."

That earned him a slight smile. "Have a seat." Richard set his pen on the desk and leaned back in his chair. "We have much to discuss before we begin the day."

"Yes, we do."

Richard placed his hand on top of the satchel Caroline had given him last night, the one holding his daughter's missing letters. For a moment, he gazed at some unknown spot above Jackson's head, his face undergoing a journey from bafflement to remorse. "I want you to keep these safe for me." He pushed the satchel across the desk. "No one in my family can know of their existence."

The request sounded easy enough but was fraught with potential difficulties. "Does that include Marcus?"

The older man's lips pressed into a hard line. "Especially him."

Jackson heard the anger, the regret, and, yes, the dread. The fact that Richard was having this conversation with Jackson instead of his son spoke volumes. "Do you think he's the one who intercepted the letters?"

"I don't know what I think." Richard picked up a pen and rolled it between his fingers. His expression wasn't exactly angry, but close. "My son would benefit the most from Libby's disappearance. And thus is the obvious suspect. Then again, he adored his little sister. He's the last person I would imagine harming her."

Jackson agreed, solely on the basis of the man he knew Marcus St. James to be. Perhaps Richard's son wasn't as hardworking or dedicated to the family business as his father, but Jackson had never seen signs of dishonesty or greed in him, either. Marcus lived a life above reproach. He didn't drink alcohol, never gambled, and was notoriously faithful to his wife. Most telling of all, he'd raised Elizabeth to be a young woman of strong faith and impeccable character. Jackson could do worse for a father-in-law.

There was something else, a key factor that couldn't be ignored. "Since Marcus is the firstborn and your only son, doesn't he stand to inherit the bulk of your fortune anyway?"

"Yes." Richard let out a short sigh. "Marcus hasn't lived up to his potential, but that doesn't make him a bad man."

No, unless he was hiding a secret life. Jackson doubted that, but it wasn't completely out of the realm of possibility and was something to keep in mind.

"When Elizabeth was born," Richard continued, "Marcus insisted they name her after his sister. Katherine was opposed at first. She'd wanted to name her daughter after her mother, but Marcus refused to budge on the matter."

Out of guilt? Or genuine affection for his lost sister?

Frowning at the uncertainty spreading through him, Jackson picked up the satchel and placed it in his lap. "Perhaps there is something in the letters themselves that will help us uncover the truth."

"Perhaps." Richard eyed him carefully, a speculative gleam replacing the sadness. "Tell me, Jackson, what do you think of my granddaughter?"

"Elizabeth is a beautiful, kind, charming woman who—"

"I meant my other granddaughter. Caroline." Richard leaned back and rested his chin on top of his fingertips. "What is your initial impression of the girl?"

Jackson took a moment to gather his thoughts. There was no doubt that Caroline was equally beautiful and charming, perhaps even more so than her cousin because of the aura of mystery surrounding her. The woman made him uneasy, made him feel things he'd never felt before. It wasn't just her physical beauty that put him on guard. Caroline made him question himself, his basic motives, and what he wanted out of life. She made him second-guess who he was at his core.

She was the most confounding woman Jackson had ever met. When it came to describing his initial impressions of her, he was at a loss. "Caroline is a woman with hidden . . ." He fumbled for the right word. "Secrets."

That wasn't entirely what he'd meant to say. He'd meant to say the woman was a complete mystery to him, intriguing and mesmerizing. But secretive? No. Caroline was anything but. She was a woman who spoke her mind without qualms, a trait he admired. There was no pretension in her, no coy games of saying one thing while meaning another.

"Interesting choice of words, Jackson. But everyone has secrets, my boy. Even you."

He bristled. "I have no secrets."

Richard said nothing, a brilliant tactic but wasted on Jackson, who redirected the conversation to the real matter at hand. "I don't completely trust your granddaughter."

More than that. He didn't completely trust *himself* when he was around her. For a brief moment last night in the motorcar, when his face had been inches from hers, he'd had a strong urge to kiss her. Was he more like his father than he wanted to admit?

No. His mind refused to allow such a thought to take hold. "What do *you* think of Caroline?"

"My granddaughter is a remarkable woman with very interesting talents. She's smarter than most women who've had the benefit of a formal education. I find I quite admire her."

That sort of thinking was dangerous. "You've known her less than a day. Don't forget, she came here with the sole purpose of ruining you."

"Which she openly admitted to me, in front of you."

A clever ploy? Or a moment of unbridled honesty? "Words, Richard. Her admission last night was a string of well-spoken words in the midst of a highly emotional moment."

"You don't believe she meant them?"

As a matter of fact, Jackson did believe her request for forgiveness had been sincere. But someone had to be the voice of reason. "I'm reserving judgment."

"Good." Richard gave an approving nod. "Skepticism is exactly what I need from you. I trust you will keep an eye on her for me."

"That's my plan."

"Excellent. Excellent." He gave Jackson a quick appraisal, looking both cagey and wise, a man with a plan of his own. "That frees me to get to know my granddaughter without having to second-guess every action or reaction on either of our parts."

"I'm happy to assist." More than he should be, considering the time he would have to spend with Caroline.

He rose and silently gathered up the satchel of letters. "About these." Jackson lifted the leather case to make his point. "Do I have your permission to read them?"

"Yes." Richard stood and came around his desk. "But be warned, my boy, you may discover information that will change how you view my granddaughter and, perhaps even, yourself."

Such ominous words put Jackson immediately on guard. What, exactly, had Libby written in her letters? What could she have possibly revealed about her daughter that would change how Jackson looked at not only her but also himself?

There was one sure way to find out.

Chapter Seventeen

Richard St. James kept offices on Forty-Second Street. Caroline already knew the location from her extensive research. She'd strolled down this street at least a dozen times, from both directions, but she'd never been bold enough to enter the building itself.

Her reticence had been based on wisdom and, maybe, a dose of age-old fear.

This afternoon was different, her qualms more manageable. Fortified from her visit with Mary and her determination to see her friend's situation improved, Caroline refused to feel anxious. Shoulders square, eyes looking straight ahead, she pushed through the gold-plated doors with quiet confidence.

Her grandfather's office was on the top floor and required Caroline to take an elevator. Before coming to America, she'd never been inside one of the iron cages. She discovered she rather liked them. There was something exciting about giving the attendant her destination and then arriving there within minutes, no exertion required on her part.

Smiling at the fanciful thought, she exited the contraption, turned to her right, and came face-to-face with Jackson Montgomery. *Well, of course.*

In the thundering silence, air whooshed out of her lungs, her heartbeat picked up speed, her shoulders tensed. She sighed. "You just keep turning up at all the wrong places."

"It's one of my talents." He gave her a blinding smile, the gesture unraveling all sorts of unwanted emotions inside her. "You look very—"

"Presentable?"

"I was going to say appealing." He dropped his gaze over her, and his brows drew together in confusion. "That color suits you."

"I . . ." What was she supposed to say to that? "Thank you."

With Sally's guidance, Caroline had chosen a dress that would present a picture of respectability and understated style. Against Sally's advice, she'd left her hair falling in gentle waves down her back. She hadn't wanted to be poked and prodded for nearly an hour just so her natural curls could be tamed in the latest fashion.

"You never cease to surprise me." Still smiling, Montgomery took her hand and drew her down a short hallway.

"Where are you taking me?"

He stopped in front of an official-looking, stately door. "To your grandfather, of course."

"Will you be attending our meeting, then?" She hoped not. She lost track of her senses whenever he was near. Every. Single. Time.

"Sadly, no. I have some important reading still to do this afternoon." He rubbed his thumb over her knuckles, fitting their palms tightly together.

When he continued to hold her hand, she was ever so grateful for the gloves she wore. The thin layer acted as an adequate barrier.

Then why was her pulse racing? And why wasn't she tugging her hand free?

A heartbeat passed, and she realized it was happening again. She was falling into the same trance she did every time their hands touched. She stared into the man's engaging eyes, the dark lashes a brilliant contrast to the blue, blue depths holding her captive.

A masculine clearing of a throat had her yanking her hand free at last. She swallowed back a gasp, even as heat rushed to her cheeks. She didn't have to turn her head to know her grandfather stood in the doorway of his office, watching her interaction with Montgomery. So caught in the moment was she that she hadn't heard him open his door.

Had Montgomery?

She slid a glance in his direction. No, he'd been taken by surprise as well.

"Thank you, Jackson, for fetching Caroline for me." Her grandfather addressed Jackson with a thoughtful expression on his face.

"My pleasure." Montgomery's attention remained cemented on Caroline as he spoke. "We'll continue our conversation from last night once you're finished here."

In spite of the fact that she'd already agreed to meet with him, the independent portion of her soul bristled at the man's assumption she would jump at his bidding. "We'll continue our conversation when it's convenient for me."

Montgomery opened his mouth, perhaps to remind her of their agreement, but her grandfather's booming laugh cut him off. "I say, girl, you sound just like my Constance."

"Who?"

"Your grandmother."

Intrigued, she studied his weathered face. "Well, then, I'm going to take that as a compliment."

"As you should. My Constance was a plucky, intriguing, mesmerizing woman who never let anyone get the best of her."

The affection in his tone was hard to miss. "Not even you?"

"Especially not me." He took her arm and guided her into his office. "For most of our marriage she had me running in circles to keep up with her. I never knew what to expect from one day to the next."

"I bet you hated that," she said, unable to imagine this refined, elegant man at the mercy of any person, much less a woman.

"I loved every minute." A twinkle glimmered in his eyes, as if he was experiencing a bout of very happy memories.

How . . . sweet.

"Keep that in mind, Jackson, my boy," her grandfather tossed over his shoulder, proving he hadn't forgotten Montgomery was still standing in the hallway. "A man needs his woman to keep him on his toes."

The slight flinch of Montgomery's shoulders revealed his reaction to the words. The poor man looked completely stunned. Caroline had the feeling she'd missed something, something important.

Montgomery recovered quickly. "Food for thought, sir." He nodded at them both, his gaze lingering on Caroline a moment longer than polite. "I will see you soon."

She gave a noncommittal response, then followed her grandfather into his office. Again, she noted that he had expensive taste, if somewhat predictable. The dark paneling on the walls, the intricate design of the rugs, the polished wood flooring beneath, and the wingback chairs with the leather worn to a fine patina all spoke of money and tradition and indicated important business was afoot.

Oddly enough, she felt comfortable in this room. The realization set her on edge. Needing a moment to calm her thoughts, she went to the wall of windows and looked out. At this hour activity was high. Horse-drawn carriages, motorcars, businessmen hurrying to their next appointments—just another day in New York City. So high above the ground, she felt disconnected from the bustling world below and yet somehow energized by it at the same time.

"I suppose New York seems different to you than London," her grandfather said from behind her.

Shaking her head, she turned to face him. "Not as much as I expected."

And that put her instantly on guard. This transition into a new life, a new *world* had been too easy, too smooth. Nothing was ever easy. Good things never happened to people like her.

Desperate for some perspective, she remembered how her grandfather had lured her to his office this afternoon with the promise of an opportunity to use her skills for good. Perhaps this was all a big game to him, or maybe even a trap.

Why hadn't she seen that sooner?

Because you want somewhere to belong.

Her secret desire for a home had made her weak, and far too trusting. Inch by deliberate inch, she allowed her suspicion to return.

"You called this meeting," she reminded him, her voice flat and unemotional, exactly as she'd planned. "Perhaps you'd like to tell me why?"

He didn't answer her question directly. Instead, he addressed the change in her demeanor. Because of course he would notice. "I see you've had time to think matters through and have decided not to trust me just yet."

Caroline had to give him points for reading her so quickly, and so accurately. She was starting to like the old man, more than she should given the nature of the situation. "You would be a fierce opponent on the other side of a card table."

He chuckled. "Perhaps that is where we should begin."

The suggestion took her completely by surprise. "Truly?"

The slight lift of his eyebrows indicated he was waiting for her to make the next move.

Recognizing the ploy, she remained steadfast, refusing to back down, then realized the futility and gave up the battle almost immediately. "I thought you wanted to discuss a way to utilize my skills for *honest* gain."

"I do. But it might be to both our benefits if I knew precisely what sort of skills you possess." He took her arm and led her to a chair. "What better way than to see you in action?"

What better way, indeed. "I could simply tell you what you want to know."

"You could."

Was the man never ruffled? As soon as the question moved through her mind, she had her answer. He knew her game. Hadn't he just said that his wife had been wily, immensely clever, and a woman who kept him on his toes.

He'd issued her a challenge.

All right, then. All she had to do was keep the man on his toes. Her mind rattled through several immediate possibilities.

This might be fun, almost as fun as matching wits with Montgomery.

Montgomery. Now was not the time to allow him to crowd her thoughts.

"Let's set aside the card-playing discussion for a moment, shall we?"

She sighed, realizing her grandfather must have interpreted her silence as retreat. Couldn't have that. She lifted her hands in the air and flexed her fingers. "I would be more than willing to play a hand or two of, let's say . . ." She gauged her grandfather's regal bearing, the expensive clothes, the upright setting. No doubt about it, he was probably a whist man. "Poker."

"Later." His gaze shifted away from her, creating a distance as surely as if he'd walked to the other side of the room. "I read your mother's letters again this morning. She mentioned you in almost every one. When read chronologically, I was able to gather a portrait of your childhood."

Oh. Words stuck in her throat.

Gaze softening, her grandfather took her hand in his, creating a sense of safety she'd never experienced, even as harrowing memories fought for supremacy in her mind.

"I was able to glean how you grew from a child to an adult before you were barely eight years old."

Caroline panicked at the gentle tone, her mind searching for a quick escape. She tugged on her hand.

His hold tightened.

"My mother did the best she could." She felt the need to defend Libby. "She taught me how to read and write and, as you may have noticed, how to speak properly. Those skills alone put me far ahead of the game, especially in Whitechapel."

"Those lessons weren't enough, though, were they?"

Tears started to form in her eyes, tears of disappointment and loss. She shoved them away with a hard blink. "I won't speak ill of my mother."

"I'm not asking you to." He squeezed her hand. "I know you were cast into the role of provider for your family before you were ready. You and Jackson have that in common."

Did they? Was there more to Jackson Montgomery than she'd given him credit for?

Of course there was. Hadn't she sensed from the very start how capable he was, how strong and in charge he could be, how determined he was to protect the ones he cared about? Such as that day on Orchard Street when he'd championed his tenants.

"It's my fault," her grandfather said.

What was his fault? Caroline shook her head and focused on the conversation once again.

"If I hadn't pampered your mother, if I hadn't given her everything she ever needed or wanted, maybe she would have been better equipped to take care of herself and you."

"You couldn't have known she would end up alone, with no hope or skills to speak of." Now Caroline was defending him? When she'd been so determined to keep up her guard?

Laugh's on you, Caroline. You're already caught in this man's trap.

She shuddered.

At the same moment, her grandfather swallowed, hard, then let go of her hand. "Let's get back to my original point."

Braiding her fingers together in her lap, she nodded. "Of course."

"Tell me how you managed to provide for you and your mother when you were nothing more than a child."

The question she'd dreaded most.

Needing to move to release the tension in her muscles, she rose and began pacing the room, much in the same way she'd done the previous night in her grandfather's study. "I don't know when the shift occurred, not precisely. Mother started having difficulty getting out of bed in the mornings, rising later and later until she stopped getting out of bed altogether."

Sighing, her grandfather closed his eyes. "Yet she never stopped trying to contact me." There was such pain in his voice.

"No. She never gave up hope. I instinctively knew she was sick. Not in her body, but . . . in her mind."

Her grandfather shuddered.

She closed her eyes and continued. "I was too young to understand. All I knew was that if I wanted to survive, then I would have to fend for myself, and her."

"I'm sorry, Caroline, I—"

She cut him off. "No apologies, remember?"

"Right." He gave one firm nod, his expression blank, but she could feel the sorrow wafting off of him.

Her hand reached to him, but he shook his head at her. "Continue with your story."

"It's probably nothing you haven't read in a Dickens novel." She cringed at the irony. "I found a gang of kids much in the same situation. Some were completely alone, others had siblings, while a few were like me, with a mother incapable of . . . mothering."

"Ah, Caroline. I'm sorr—" He cut himself off. "Go on."

"We worked together at first, learning from each other, adding members, losing some." She lifted her shoulder. "The short version is that I quickly became proficient at making a living with what could be seen as questionable means."

"Such as?"

"Some members of our gang were gifted at lifting wallets, and I could certainly pull my own weight there, but I used my skill with figures to win money at games of chance. Not only could I remember every card played, I could calculate which ones were left in the deck."

"Fortuitous."

Though she sensed her actions had been wrong, she'd done what was necessary to survive. There was no room for dignity and honor on an empty belly.

She turned to face her grandfather directly. Planting her fists on her hips, she silently dared him to condemn her.

He held her stare. "So you initially picked pockets as a means to feed yourself and your mother. When did you start playing cards?"

"A few months after I turned sixteen. I was tired of barely scraping by, yes, but the truth of the matter was I abhorred begging. And detested the idea of stealing even more."

"You had a moral compass even then."

Had she? "I don't know about that." She lowered her hands. "My mother must have sensed I wasn't earning my way honestly, because every evening, she would marshal enough energy to read to me from the Bible. Her favorite chapter was Proverbs 31."

Even now, after all this time, Caroline could still recite the verses. *Strength and honor are her clothing,* and *she openeth her mouth with wisdom.*

In retrospect, Caroline realized her mother had taught her to be a woman of honor who worked hard and avoided idleness.

"I've heard enough." Her grandfather rose and met her halfway across the room. Before she could object, he pulled her into his arms and held on.

She remained stiff and unyielding for all of three seconds. Relaxing against him, she wrapped her arms around him and held on just as tightly. She resisted the urge to cling, feeling herself doing so anyway.

"Caroline St. James." He set her gently away from him. "I'm proud to call you my granddaughter."

The words washed over her like a cool rain on a scorching summer's day. "I . . . Oh, Grandfather."

"Now for my proposition."

Her heart dipped in her chest, anticipation making her tremble.

"I want you to come work for me."

He wanted her to . . . to . . . what? She looked around the room.

"I want to teach you how to run the family business."

"After what I just told you? Weren't you listening? I'm a beggar, liar, and thief." The old man was senile. Nothing else explained his absurd offer. "You shouldn't trust me."

"Probably not. But I do."

No. This was too much to ask of her. She would let him down. She knew nothing of respectable business ventures. And yet, what would it be like to hone her skills under this man's guidance? If she allowed him to teach her how to earn money respectably, she could provide for not only herself but also Mary and others like her. Caroline could actually be in a position to help women like her mother, like Mary, like so many others she'd encountered in her life.

The possibilities were endless.

One idea shot to the forefront in her mind, the same one she'd toyed with after leaving Orchard Street.

Caroline could run a factory, much like the one where Mary worked. She could employ women who had nowhere else to earn a decent living, women like her mother. And Mary—dear, dear Mary. Caroline would ensure the days were not long and hot.

"I see your mind working." He pointed at her. "You already have ideas."

Her cheeks grew hot, hope rising within her. "Perhaps."

"Then you agree?" He pushed for an answer. "You will commit to learning the business from the ground up?"

"I can think of several problems with this idea, one in particular. What will my uncle, your son, think of this unconventional arrangement of ours?"

"I'll handle Marcus."

"And Mont—I mean, *Mr.* Montgomery?" She pictured the man finding out about this arrangement and found herself smiling. Oh, he was going to hate this.

Something lit in the old man's eyes, something that looked both shrewd and mischievous. "Jackson will come around."

She very much doubted that.

"Do we have a deal?" Her grandfather stuck out his hand.

She took it without question. "We do, indeed."

"Now, young lady, about your living arrangements." Disapproval tightened the corners of his mouth. "No granddaughter of mine will live in a hotel. You will move out at once."

Caroline blinked at the unbending tone. "If I refuse?"

"You won't."

This was the man who ran his business empire with an iron fist. For now, she appeased him with a sweet tone in her voice and a perfectly insincere smile on her lips, fully aware she would not be moving out of the Waldorf-Astoria anytime soon. "Whatever you say, Grandfather."

Chapter Eighteen

Jackson scratched out his signature on the final document, then handed the entire pile back to his assistant. "That'll be all for now, John."

The man nodded but didn't budge from his spot on the other side of the desk. Jackson felt a nudge of apprehension. "Was there something else we needed to discuss?"

"I spoke with Mr. Tierney this morning, per your request."

Ah, yes, of course. Wanting to increase his assistant's responsibilities, Jackson had given John Reilly the task of meeting with the landlord of his tenement houses on a regular basis. There was another reason, of course. His assistant's vast knowledge of the area gave him insight Jackson couldn't hope to achieve on his own. "Are the improvements progressing on schedule?"

The man's mouth tightened. "So it would seem."

Jackson waited for his assistant to expand on this, but he remained uncharacteristically silent. "Is there a problem, John?"

His assistant didn't respond immediately. "No," he said at last, drawing out the syllable. "Not precisely."

"Then what, *precisely?*"

"I believe it to be in your best interest to keep a close eye on the man."

"Is Mr. Tierney not proving trustworthy?"

"He might be overly"—he made a face—*"lazy."*

Jackson let out a laugh. "Everyone is lazy compared to you, John."

"True. Nevertheless . . ." He fixed a brooding stare at a random spot above Jackson's head. Clearly, the task of overseeing the tenement houses was making him uncomfortable.

"Go on, John, feel free to speak your mind."

"All right." A pause. "I would recommend that you or I conduct several unexpected visits, aside from our regular meetings, in order to keep the man in check. We don't want to find ourselves in the same situation with Mr. Tierney that we did with Mr. Smythe."

Not a bad idea. "Are you volunteering for the job?"

"Yes." John blinked slowly. "I suppose I am."

Jackson didn't take his assistant's agreement lightly. The last time they'd made the trek to Orchard Street together, Jackson's serious-minded assistant had unleashed a litany of complaints about the horrendous smells, the crushing crowds, and so much more. It was clear the man wanted no reminders of where he came from.

Jackson gave him one last chance to change his mind. "You would be willing to travel to Orchard Street, at odd intervals of the day, solely to ensure that Mr. Tierney isn't cheating me or mistreating my tenants?"

Expression grim, John gave one curt nod of his head.

"Then I will leave the timing up to your discretion."

"Very good." Despite his carefree tone, Reilly's shoulders remained bunched, and again Jackson sensed his assistant's agreement had not come easy.

"If that is all, Mr. Montgomery, I will deliver these contracts to Mr. St. James's secretary at once."

"Thank you, John."

The man turned on his heel.

"Please be so good as to shut the door behind you."

"As you wish." A soft click soon followed.

Proud of his assistant's attempt to rise above his past, Jackson stared at the shut door. He preferred to delegate authority when the situation warranted. Time would tell whether he'd been right to put John Reilly in charge of the tenement houses.

For now, Jackson had other pressing business at hand. He opened the satchel of letters Richard had given him and pulled out the entire stack. He read each letter slowly, carefully, in chronological order. When he finished, he rubbed the back of his hand across his mouth.

Profoundly moved, his throat grew tight, and the corners of his eyes burned. The tone of Libby St. James's words had grown more desperate as the years had passed. He thought briefly of praying, but for what? For whom?

Libby? Caroline? Richard?

All three. He must pray for all three, perhaps Caroline most of all.

Now that he'd read her mother's pleas, pleas for forgiveness, for mercy, for the barest slice of help that had never come, Jackson understood Caroline's desire for revenge. How could he blame her? How could he remain unmoved by the agony of her childhood?

An empty feeling swirled in the pit of his stomach. By reading her mother's letters, Jackson had intruded on Caroline's privacy. Richard might have given him permission to do so, but Caroline had not. And now, Jackson would never be able to look at her the same way again.

He took a slow, calming breath. For all intents and purposes, Caroline had been abandoned by her own mother, left to provide for herself with no help from her wealthy family.

Jackson leaned back and fixed his eyes on a crack in the plaster ceiling. Caroline had forgiven her grandfather without hesitation. She'd displayed the true nature of grace.

Her strength of character humbled him. Would he be so quick to offer mercy if his father returned to New York and begged for his forgiveness?

Jackson wasn't sure. Edward Montgomery was guilty of his sins. A request for forgiveness would not erase that fact. Only now, in the privacy of his mind, did Jackson admit that he'd yet to forgive his father. He still harbored a desire for retribution. The man had abandoned his family. He'd left his son to bear the burden and provide for the wife he hadn't wanted. Jackson had spent most of his adult life paying for someone else's choices. Just like Caroline had.

But where Jackson held on to his resentment, Caroline offered grace.

The door to his office swung open, saving him from further reflection. He lowered his gaze in time to see Richard saunter into the room. "Caroline sends her regrets. She will not be meeting with you today as planned."

Jackson wasn't entirely sorry for this turn of events. "How was your meeting with her?"

The older man sank in a chair facing Jackson's desk. From beneath white eyebrows, Richard's intense green eyes studied him. "It went better than expected."

"I'm glad." And he was. After reading Libby's letters, Jackson understood the pain Richard must be experiencing, the sense of helplessness, too.

Richard released a slow smile. "Caroline is an intelligent, remarkable young woman, with a sharp wit and—"

"Sharper tongue," Jackson couldn't help adding.

"True enough." Richard chuckled. "Always did like a woman who had the courage to speak her mind."

"But do you trust her?" Jackson had to ask the question. Richard was relying on his impartiality, a state of mind that was fast disappearing now that he'd read Libby's letters.

"I probably shouldn't," Richard said. "By her own admission she came here to ruin me. But yes, Jackson, I do. I trust my granddaughter completely."

Jackson did, too. And that posed too many problems to sort through at the moment. "I still plan to keep an eye on her."

"That should be easy. She has agreed to work here."

Jackson opened his mouth, closed it again. Richard was staring at him with something new in his eyes. "What do you mean? She's agreed to work here, in what capacity?"

"I plan to teach her the business."

The man wasn't kidding. "Why?"

Richard lifted an eyebrow. "Is this your way of reserving judgment? By questioning *my* decisions?"

"Yes, as a matter of fact it is." Jackson placed both palms on top of his desk, stood, then rephrased his question. "Why are you bringing your granddaughter into the family business?"

"She's my heir," he said simply.

"*Marcus* is your heir."

"With no sons."

"He has Elizabeth, who is—"

"A dear, sweet girl with no head for business."

Jackson didn't fully disagree, but he felt the need to defend Elizabeth all the same. "You don't know that for sure."

"Of course I do." Richard waved away the objection. "If I want my family holdings to extend past the next generation, I must take matters into my own hands."

"By grooming your granddaughter to take over?"

"If she's half as smart as I think she is, then yes." Richard made an indistinguishable sound in his throat. "Caroline is, quite possibly, the greatest hope for the future."

What Richard suggested was unprecedented. But the more Jackson rolled the idea around in his mind, the more he could see Caroline rising to the challenge. Marcus would have something to say about all this, but that was between Richard and his son.

Or was it? "Why are you telling me this instead of Marcus?"

"Because, my boy." Richard's eyes took on a crafty gleam. "I'm putting you in charge of her training."

Jackson pinched the bridge of his nose. On one level, Richard's idea made sense. Jackson knew more about the St. James business dealings than Marcus did. Plus, half the family's holdings were tied up with his. The wisest thing Jackson's father had done was align himself with Richard St. James at a time when Edward Montgomery had more money than sense. After law school, Jackson had spent years rebuilding what his father had started and had increased the St. James coffers in the process. Their fortunes were interminably linked now. That alone required Jackson's involvement in this particular matter.

"When does she start?"

"In a few days."

Anticipation, dread, wariness—all three emotions warred with one another in his brain. Caroline working beside him, day after day, would certainly make it easier to keep an eye on her. Her close proximity would also provide them with a certain level of privacy as they went about uncovering the identity of the person who had intercepted her mother's letters.

Not a bad arrangement.

However, one last problem still had to be addressed. "How do you plan to present Caroline to society?"

"I don't."

The knots in Jackson's stomach tightened. "Is that wise?"

"The less fanfare surrounding her arrival, the better."

"You can't be thinking to hide her true identity." Lies had a way of coming out, usually at the worst possible moment.

"We will not hide her connection to me, nor will we unveil it in any special way. The truth need not be altered. Caroline has journeyed to America to connect with family."

Jackson shook his head. "Many already know her as Caroline Harding, Patricia Harding's cousin."

"She is also Elizabeth's cousin, and my granddaughter. That is the portion of her tale we will highlight from this point forward."

Seeing the flaws, Jackson shook his head again. "People will still talk."

"Let them."

Richard made it sound so simple. But considering the man's standing in society and the fact that most of the good people of New York owed the majority of their livelihoods to him, the simple approach might actually work.

"She should move out of her hotel," Jackson said.

Richard flashed him a grin. "She left to pack."

"You invited her to move into your home?"

"I did."

"And she accepted?" That didn't sound like Caroline.

"She declined my kind offer."

Now Jackson was confused. "Then why is she packing up her belongings?"

"I only won a portion of our argument." Richard let out a laugh. "She agreed to move out of the hotel but has refused to tell me where she will be residing instead."

Now *that* sounded like Caroline.

"Are you finished with those?" Richard nodded toward the stack of letters.

"Yes."

"Then I'd like them back." Something unbelievably sad came and went in the older man's eyes. "I wish to keep my daughter's words close to me."

Jackson placed the letters back into the canvas satchel, careful to avoid crushing them, then handed them across the desk.

The satchel tucked safely under his arm, Richard stood. "Will I see you at the club this evening?"

"Not tonight. I have other plans." With Caroline St. James. The woman had information he wanted, the location of her new residence at the top of the list.

* * *

Not long after she'd returned to her hotel, Caroline heard a knock at her door. None too happy at the interruption, she waved Sally off with a shake of her head, then moved toward the door herself. She could think of only one person who would come to her hotel room unannounced.

Montgomery.

Although she'd agreed to work with him to uncover the person behind her mother's agony, the emotion of the last twenty-four hours had worn her out. She wasn't up to yet another difficult encounter.

"I thought I told you I would contact you when it was convenient," she said as she yanked open the door with considerable force. "What part of—Oh, it's you. I . . . Please, do come in."

The newcomer hesitated in the doorway, looking more like a frightened street urchin than the sophisticated society miss she was. "I'm not disturbing you, am I?"

"Not at all." Caroline smiled at her cousin. Elizabeth was dressed in a frilly, pale pink concoction that made Caroline think of sugary confections. Her teeth ached just looking at the girl. "You simply took me by surprise."

"I'm a surprise?" Elizabeth practically vibrated with excitement. "I do hope it's a happy one."

"The very best." Feeling a tug on her heart, Caroline guided the girl into the room. Before she could stop herself, she pulled Elizabeth into an awkward hug. "In fact, my dear cousin, I am extremely happy to see you."

Of all her relatives Caroline had met over the last few days, Elizabeth was the easiest to like. Even from the beginning of her quest, when Caroline was determined to hate every St. James, she hadn't been able to rustle up much animosity for her cousin. The girl was just too kind and sweet. Warm, caring, friendly.

Hard to dislike those qualities.

"You are certain you don't mind that I have come to see you without an invitation?" Elizabeth stepped back and braided her fingers together at her waist. "I wouldn't wish to intrude."

Intrude. That might have been true only a day ago—had it only been a day?—but something remarkable had happened since Caroline had confronted her grandfather the previous night and then met with him this morning. She'd forgiven him.

With that forgiveness had come sympathy. Richard St. James, for all his sophistication and polish, was suffering as much as Caroline. Perhaps more.

"I had breakfast with Grandfather this morning." Elizabeth unwound her hands and looked around. "He told me you would be staying in New York for a while and that you were thinking of—" She cut herself off as her gaze landed on Caroline's trunk in the other room. "Oh. Are you leaving after all?"

"Just the hotel."

"Well, good." Elizabeth moved forward. "When I saw your trunk, I thought . . . Oh, never mind what I thought." She spun to face Caroline directly, then shifted from one foot to another. "Would you care to go for a walk with me?"

"I am in the middle of packing, with my maid's assistance." She indicated Sally with a nod of her head.

Elizabeth didn't so much as look in the other woman's direction. "Won't you take a break? I do so want to get to know you better."

Caroline caught Sally's expression. She knew what that eye roll meant. She hid her own responding sigh. Although Elizabeth wasn't intentionally trying to be rude, she spoke as though she and Caroline were the only two people in the room, as if Sally weren't any more important than a piece of furniture.

For the first time since embarking on her journey to America, Caroline recognized that there was one reason to be glad her grandfather hadn't received her mother's letters. If he had, if he'd opened his arms to them when Caroline had been but a child, she might have ended up just like Elizabeth.

Sweet and kind, to be sure—*probably*—but her cousin was also oblivious to much of the world around her.

"Well, Caro, what do you say?" Elizabeth took her by the arm. "Shall we take a walk together?"

Caroline flinched. "What did you just call me?"

"Caro. It's short for Caroline." Elizabeth looked at her oddly, as though she couldn't understand why she would object. "Do you not like the nickname?"

Mary was the only person who called her Caro, but that didn't mean Elizabeth couldn't. "I—yes. Call me Caro."

"So you will accompany me?"

The girl was certainly tenacious.

And there was nothing keeping Caroline from accepting her invitation. She wasn't checking out of the hotel until the following morning, and she was very nearly packed. "Why not."

"Wonderful."

Caroline started for the door with Elizabeth but stopped midstep when Sally cleared her throat. She spun back around, the question stalling on her lips when she noted the gloves dangling from the maid's hand. A hat hung in the other.

Of course.

She'd nearly forgotten where she was and whom she was with. Proper attire was necessary for a walk with the girl. Caroline was suddenly very tired of all the rules. But she would follow them if for no other reason than to get to know her cousin better. She liked Elizabeth, rather a lot, actually. The girl couldn't have intercepted her mother's letters. She was far too young. But one of her parents probably had, and maybe Elizabeth knew something.

Perhaps this walk would prove beneficial for uncovering more information.

Gliding back through the room, Caroline accepted the hat and gloves from Sally, then mouthed the words, "Thank you."

Sally nodded, the silent warning in her eyes unnecessary.

Once outside the hotel, Caroline drew alongside her cousin. Elizabeth looked to her left and then to her right, evidently debating their route. She considered a moment longer, her fingertip pressed to her chin. Eventually, she turned to her left. "I think we should head to Sixth Avenue. I want to see if Macy's has any new dresses on display."

"You buy your clothes at a department store?"

"My goodness, no." She looked surprised Caroline would ask such an absurd question. "I have them custom-made in Paris."

"Why?"

"According to Mother, no woman of fine breeding should be caught in last year's design. And she should never be caught in the same gown twice."

Caroline couldn't imagine such snobbery. "You and your mother buy custom-made dresses from Paris and then wear them only once?"

The expense was astounding.

Elizabeth sighed. "Anything else is considered gauche."

Indeed.

"I'm not supposed to know this, but . . ." Elizabeth glanced around and then leaned in closer to Caroline. "Apparently, my mother's father had a bit of a gambling problem. His fortune came and went depending on his success at the gaming tables."

At the mention of a wealthy man risking his family's livelihood on the turn of a card or die, Caroline's stomach dropped to her toes. She'd fleeced men like Elizabeth's grandfather. Although she often thought they'd gotten what they deserved, she'd also had a twinge of unease at what their losses would mean if they had families.

She should have known better than to pretend consequences didn't exist.

One more layer of guilt to add to her unconscionable behavior on the streets.

"There was a season in my mother's youth when her father had been very unlucky. She was humiliated at a ball because she was called out for wearing last year's gown." Sighing softly, Elizabeth straightened. "So, you see, no dresses from a department store or anywhere but Paris are allowed. But I do so like to look."

Caroline thought about her conversation with Mary this morning, and her friend's dream of creating original dresses to be sold at a department store.

She could just imagine Mary toiling by the low light of her apartment late into the night, her hand stitching a garment that might make it into the display window of Macy's. Her Irish friend was clearly very talented, her needlework impeccable, hence the reason she was given the task of finishing the dresses for her boss. If only Caroline could lighten Mary's burdens.

But, of course, she could. Or she would be able to do so very soon, once she began working with her grandfather. She was suddenly excited over what the coming weeks would bring.

"Is New York much different from London?" Elizabeth asked the question with wide eyes, indicating that she had no idea about Caroline's childhood.

"There are many similarities, I suppose, but the buildings in New York are decidedly younger."

They turned onto Sixth Avenue.

"I think I should enjoy traveling to London," Elizabeth said in a dreamy voice.

After what had happened with his daughter, Caroline doubted Richard St. James would allow Elizabeth that pleasure.

That didn't mean a trip to the British Isles was completely out of the question. "Perhaps you will go once you are married."

Elizabeth slowed her gait, a thoughtful expression in her eyes. "You mean for my honeymoon." She tapped her finger to her chin. "Yes, that would be acceptable."

As much as it pained her to continue, Caroline needed to remind herself of the reality of the situation, of the man who would take her cousin on her honeymoon.

She swallowed hard. The thought of Elizabeth traveling with Montgomery made her sick to her stomach. "Has Montgo—I mean, has Jackson ever been to Europe?"

"I have no idea." Elizabeth turned to study a window display. "Why do you ask?"

"I thought . . . that is, aren't you two . . ." What was the word for almost engaged? "Promised to one another?"

"Nonsense." Elizabeth swept away the thought with a flick of her wrist. "Jackson and I aren't suited at all."

"But I thought . . ." The newspaper articles speculating about the *blessed event* flashed in her mind. "The talk around town is that there's an understanding between you. From what I understand, he will soon begin courting you officially."

Elizabeth lifted her shoulder in a distracted manner. "I can't stop what people say."

Out of some perverse need, Caroline continued to press the matter. "Do you not . . . like Jackson?"

"I adore him. He is a very good man." A slight frown passed across her face. "I am confident he will make some woman a decent husband."

"There is nothing wrong with marrying a good man who will make you a decent husband."

"That is not what I meant." She started down the sidewalk again. "I, for one, do not want a boring, predictable husband."

Boring? Predictable? Jackson Montgomery was many things, but boring and predictable he was not. And, really, what was wrong with marrying a good, solid man who would treat his wife with considerable care? How could any woman not want that?

As if reading a portion of Caroline's thoughts, Elizabeth sighed. "It's not that I don't want to marry, someday, but I want more than safety and comfort."

The very things Caroline most craved.

"Oh, Caro." Elizabeth looped her arm through Caroline's and tugged her close. "I want so much to be swept away by a man. I want . . . I want . . . *passion*." Eyes wide, she pressed her hand to her mouth, as if shocked by her own words.

Caroline was struck a little speechless herself. Her cousin didn't find Montgomery passionate. How could that be?

When confined in the small space of her grandfather's motorcar, with his face pressed close to hers, Caroline had felt the man's pent-up emotions seething just below the surface.

When he'd lowered his gaze over her, she'd known—known without a doubt—that he would kiss with the same expertise he demonstrated in all other areas of his life. And, oh my yes, passion would definitely be part of the experience.

In fact, for one tense moment in the car last night, Caroline had been . . . to use her cousin's words . . . *swept away*.

Chapter Nineteen

Twenty minutes after they'd returned from their walk, Elizabeth left the hotel suite with a promise to visit Caroline once she was settled in her new residence. Ten minutes after her cousin's departure, another knock came at the door.

Caroline had had enough of visitors for one day. Thus, she sent Sally to get rid of the unwanted guest, whoever it was. With surprising finesse, and a considerable amount of charm, Montgomery worked his way into the room past Sally. *He* certainly had no problem paying attention to the pretty maid.

"Caroline," he said. "A moment of your time."

Sally scurried around him, an apologetic look in her eyes.

"It's fine, Sally. I'll take over from here. In fact, why don't you go home for the evening? We'll continue our packing in the morning."

"No, miss." The girl shook her head adamantly as she lowered her voice to a whisper. "You cannot be alone in a hotel room with a gentleman."

"Right." Caroline hid her chagrin behind a taut smile. Would she ever master all the rules propriety demanded? What would she do without Sally's guidance once she moved out of the hotel?

The answer was simple. She would take the maid with her.

Shooting a quick glance in Montgomery's direction, Sally dropped a small curtsey. "I'll be just on the opposite side of that door, tidying up in the other room."

Caroline nodded with the perfect amount of indifference, or so she hoped. "Very good, Sally."

Waiting for the maid to depart, Montgomery looked around the room in silence. His gaze stopped on several points of interest, such as her trunks and bags. "So it's true. You're moving out of the hotel."

"As you can see." Now that she'd played her hand with her grandfather, the Waldorf-Astoria was an extravagance she no longer needed. Although she trusted her grandfather's motives, she'd refused his offer to move into his home. Instead, she'd chosen a female-only boarding house considered suitable for women of unlimited means.

None of which she deigned to share with her grandfather, let alone the man currently taking stock of her hotel room.

Brows drawn together, Montgomery moved to a half-full trunk and ran his hand along the sleeve of one of the dresses. "I wouldn't have guessed you for a woman with such expensive taste."

"We both know that's not why my clothing is of the first order."

He toyed with the sleeve a moment longer, his strong fingers ridiculously masculine against the delicate fabric. "You left no detail to chance."

Why pretend otherwise? "The stakes were too high for me to risk exposure over a forgotten detail, no matter how small."

"You are a shrewd woman, Caroline St. James." Jackson dropped his hand and turned to face her. "I have to wonder what you would have done had you discovered that your grandfather truly had abandoned you and your mother."

Ah. There it was. Proof he was a detail man himself. In order to know her motives now, Montgomery needed to understand her original plan first. Smart. Very smart. "I should think you could figure that out on your own."

"I know you had set out to ruin him, but the question is, my dear Caroline"—he moved a step closer to her—"how would you have done it?"

She shifted behind the trunk, happy for the physical barrier between them. "Does it matter now?"

"You know it does." He picked up a small statue of Lady Liberty from a nearby table and rolled it in his hand. "Of course, I have several thoughts on the matter but can't decide which route you would have taken."

Caroline shrugged. "What would you say if I told you I didn't know how I was going to destroy him?"

He set the statue down. "I'd say you were lying."

She pressed her lips into a tight line. The need to defend herself was strong, too strong to continue to play this game. The situation demanded honesty. "My plan was to get close to him, to study his every move. Once I learned his comings and goings and his likes and dislikes, as well as the particulars of his character, I would have then focused on the best way to exploit his weaknesses."

Something flashed in the man's eyes, something Caroline recognized as surprise.

"Come now, Montgomery, everyone has a weakness, something that can ultimately be used to destroy them."

"Not everyone."

"*Everyone,*" she reiterated, wondering what his weakness was. What would make Jackson Montgomery fall to his knees and beg for mercy?

Her cousin? Elizabeth had intimated that she wasn't in love with the man, but was he in love with her?

She hated that it mattered so much.

"You mean to tell me," he began, "that you traveled to America without a specific plan in mind."

Caroline gave him a haughty look. "I just told you my plan."

He scrubbed a hand down his face, the first sign of his growing agitation. *Good.* If he was going to make her uncomfortable, then he should share in some of the agony.

"Caroline, these games have to stop." His voice came out painfully calm. "If I am to teach you the family business, I need to know how your mind works."

"*You're* teaching me? But I thought Grandfather was going to . . ." Her words trailed off as she tried to recall exactly what her grandfather had said that afternoon.

"Richard will be involved in your education, of course, but I will be instructing you for now since much of your family's holdings are tied directly to the majority of mine."

Perfectly logical. Then why did she sense her grandfather had some unknown agenda here, one that would put her in daily contact with Montgomery? "You don't find it odd that my grandfather has involved you."

"We are supposed to be on the same side."

"And what side is that?"

"Your grandfather's, yours, and, of course, your mother's."

At the mention of her mother, in that soft, gentle tone, her heart stuttered in her chest.

Montgomery's expression softened to match his tone. "Libby St. James is the true victim in all this." He stepped around the trunk and closed the distance between them with three quick, easy strides. "She is the one for whom justice must be served. Don't you agree?"

Caroline managed a nod.

He reached out and laid a hand on her arm.

She should shove him away—she knew she should—but his touch brought surprising comfort. Confused, she took a shuddering breath. Why was he being so kind, so understanding?

Eyes dropped to half-mast, he slid his palm down her sleeve, captured her hand in his, and squeezed gently. Without her gloves there was nothing between them now. At the intimate contact, everything in her calmed. Her heartbeat. Her breathing. Even her thoughts.

It took every ounce of control not to give in to a sigh.

"I read your mother's letters."

"You . . . *what?*" Yanking free of his grip, she stumbled back a step, her heart dipping to her stomach. "You—you . . . had no right."

His tone turned apologetic. "Your grandfather thought otherwise."

Caroline knew what was in those letters, knew how much her mother had revealed not only about herself but also about her daughter. About *her*.

Jackson Montgomery knew more about her childhood than any living soul, aside from her grandfather.

"How could he have shared them with you?" Her words slipped out in a croaked whisper. She felt betrayed and . . . and . . . What was this strange new emotion? Hope? Relief? Was she so tired of being alone she would risk sharing the burdens of her childhood with this man?

"Your grandfather trusts me, Caroline, and so should you." He reached for her again and caught her hand. "I won't hurt you."

It was the worst thing he could have said, the very words that could cut through her remaining defenses. Despite every instinct to run in the opposite direction, she wanted to stop and lean on someone for a change. She wanted to know there was someone who would fight for her, not against her.

Two cords are stronger than one.

Holding steady, Montgomery didn't make a move toward her. Not one step closer. "Caroline, you aren't alone anymore."

He knew. He knew how utterly alone she felt. Oh, how she wished she could trust him. But life had taught her well. She couldn't allow herself the luxury of relying on anyone but herself.

You aren't alone anymore.

Her breath caught in her throat. What if she let this man become her ally? What would that mean? For her, for Elizabeth?

Elizabeth. How could Caroline lean on Jackson Montgomery, knowing he might very well become her cousin's husband someday?

Because this wasn't personal for him, even if it was for her. She didn't want this man in her life; she couldn't want him. Love couldn't be lost if it had never been found.

She smoothed her expression free of all emotion.

"Caroline, I understand what it's like to take on burdens that seem too heavy to bear at times." His fingers twined with hers, creating a bond between them that went beyond the words he spoke. "I know what you have endured. I—"

"How can you know?" She extricated her hand from his, furious at herself as much as at him. For a brief moment she'd allowed herself to believe. She'd allowed herself to hope. *Weak, weak girl.* "How can you dare compare us to one another?"

"I know what loneliness is," he said, his voice full of gravity, his eyes earnest and intense. "I know what it means to be desperate, to—"

"No. Don't say anything more." She refused to be moved by the sincerity in his eyes or the undisguised vulnerability on his face. He could be bluffing. She needed him to be bluffing. "You can't possibly understand what desperation feels like."

"In that you are wrong. So very wrong."

"Montgomery, listen, I—"

"Enough talking." He swooped his arms around her waist and pulled her to him.

Too stunned to move, Caroline held perfectly still as his head lowered toward hers, his blue eyes dark with intent.

Mesmerized, she felt her breath stall in her throat. One word echoed in her mind, sealing her doom. Finally.

Finally.

* * *

Jackson had never given in to his base desires, had never allowed emotion to rule his actions. Of course, he'd never been this moved by another person's pain.

Common sense disappeared, as did all signs of the respectable man he'd fought ruthlessly to become.

Unable to do otherwise, he pressed his lips to Caroline's. Slowly, gently. She softened in his arms. He murmured her name, and she relaxed further still.

He tightened his hold, pulled her flush against him, and then—

Cold, hard sanity returned.

What was he doing? Caroline was Richard's granddaughter. Elizabeth's cousin.

Elizabeth.

Hot tendrils of guilt shot through him. He pulled back. One beat passed, two.

Caroline blinked up at him. Her eyes were glassy, her lips shiny, her breathing erratic. She looked thoroughly kissed.

He'd done that to her.

Sadly, he couldn't find it in himself to be sorry. Disgusted with his behavior, he released his hold from her waist, only just realizing they were still wrapped in each other's arms.

He took yet another step back. Away from Caroline. Away from temptation.

"I'm sorry." He ran a hand through his hair, cleared his throat. "I shouldn't have kissed you."

He'd allowed his control to slip. He'd ignored propriety and had taken what he'd wanted. One forbidden kiss and he'd become no better than his father. *There is none that doeth good, no, not one.*

He'd been kidding himself to think otherwise.

Caroline continued to blink up at him, her thoughts unreadable in her expression. "Have you ever kissed my cousin like that?"

He shut his eyes briefly against the guilt racing through him. "No."

She touched her lips and looked at him strangely, as though taking his measure and seeing him for the first time. "Maybe you should."

"Pardon me?"

Her hand fluttered back to her side and gripped her skirt. "Maybe you should kiss Elizabeth with that same sort of enthusiasm behind it."

He simply stared at her. "You cannot be serious."

She shook her head at him. "That's the trouble with your kind."

"My kind?"

"You gentlemen who play by the rules," she clarified, her tone turning to disappointment. He would prefer her anger. "You are determined to keep your women locked in their perfectly boring, utterly safe little worlds, unaware that these same women might not mind a little rule-breaking every now and again, especially in the areas of kissing and . . . whatnot."

"*Whatnot?*"

"Honestly, Montgomery, do I have to spell out everything?"

"Apparently, you do."

"You are about as obtuse as any man I have met." She stepped forward and poked him in the chest. "If you want to win my cousin's hand, you should start by kissing her like you just did me."

How could the woman speak so casually about this? A long glance in her eyes and he realized she wasn't as casual as she let on. She was shocked and hurt and lashing out at him.

He balled his hands into fists to keep them from reaching out to her again. Madness. This was sheer madness.

"I won't discuss this with you," he said through a tight jaw. Not when he still wanted to drag her back in his arms and soothe away that sad look in her eyes.

"Fine. Ignore my advice, you stubborn man." She tossed the words at him like a challenge. "But don't say I didn't warn you."

He opened his mouth to argue yet another point with her, not precisely sure which one, but she turned her back on him.

"It's time for you leave." She set her attention on folding some sort of shawl and then carefully setting it in a small drawer on the right side of the trunk.

"Caroline."

"Are you still here?" she asked, barely glancing in his direction.

"I'll leave when we're finished." He waited for her to look at him fully. When she didn't, he continued as if she had. "I want to know where you will be living once you leave this hotel."

She sighed. "At a perfectly respectable boarding house on the west side of town."

Her answer didn't surprise him. That didn't mean he found her decision acceptable. Far from it.

"What?" She turned to look at him at last. "No comment on my choice?"

Oh, he had plenty to say. "I have a better idea."

She gave him a quelling look. "I just bet you do."

Holding back a retort, for both their sakes, he continued, "My grandmother lives in a mansion near your grandfather's home, but not too near."

"And your point?"

"My point is that she lives alone, with only her little dogs and her servants to keep her company. Although she would say otherwise, I fear she is lonelier than she lets on."

She studied him. "And that worries you."

"A great deal," he admitted candidly. "I would like for you and your maid to move in to her home."

"She has agreed to this."

"Yes." Or she would once Jackson explained the situation.

Caroline remained rooted to the spot. "What would you get out of this arrangement?"

"Peace of mind."

"Indeed." Lips pressed together, Caroline picked up another shawl and carefully folded it in the same manner as she had the one before.

At the sight of all that control, his anger reared up. "Not everyone is out to hurt you, Caroline."

"So you say." She placed the shawl in the same drawer as the first. "I can't help but wonder. Is this offer of yours an attempt to keep an eye on me, or do you truly wish to provide your grandmother with female companionship?"

Debating how best to proceed, he took her hands and clasped them inside his. "What if I said both?"

"Then I would say this is the first time in our brief acquaintance that you are being completely honest with me."

He laughed, though the sound came out rusty and a little tortured. "Move in to Wayfare House."

"Wayfare House?"

"My grandmother's home."

"Her house has a name?"

"Say yes, Caroline," he persisted. "The two of you will be good for each other."

"You know, Montgomery, I should move in with your grandmother for no other reason than to keep an eye on *you*."

He smiled. "Say yes, Caroline."

"Let me think on it."

"Say yes."

"You aren't going to relent, are you?"

"Say yes."

"Oh, all right, yes." She met his gaze, her hands shaking ever so slightly. "I will move into your grandmother's home, if for no other reason than to torment you with my constant presence in your life."

Chapter Twenty

Now that she'd had time to think on the matter, Caroline questioned the wisdom of agreeing to Montgomery's proposition to move into his grandmother's home. She'd fallen into a dangerous, albeit temporary, state of recklessness, brought on by the man's unexpected, toe-curling kiss. He'd wormed past her defenses, the clever, talented rogue.

Sighing, Caroline touched her lips.

One kiss, nothing more than a simple meeting of lips, and she had lost perspective. The best course of action would be to move into the female-only boarding house as originally planned.

Nevertheless, by early evening of the next day, Caroline found herself settled in a delicious room on the second floor of Wayfare House. Sally was firmly in tow, installed just one room over. This would have been quite unconventional if Sally were truly her maid. The girl should be residing in the servants' quarters in the designated wing beneath the kitchen.

But Caroline needed her closer. She *wanted* her closer, not only for her much-needed advice, but because she liked the young maid and was beginning to consider her a friend. Thus, she'd refused to listen to Sally's arguments on the matter, pressing her own case until the girl had finally agreed to take the room adjoining Caroline's.

As if materializing on cue, Sally entered Caroline's bedchamber.

She smiled at the girl. "These accommodations are vastly different from the ones we left behind at the Waldorf-Astoria. What say you?"

"I agree." Sally ran her palm along the marble mantelpiece lined with genuine gold, her expression thoughtful. "All these bits of finery are far grander than any I've ever seen. Where do you suppose such vast amounts of money came from?"

Caroline shared the maid's awe. There was wealth. And then there was *wealth*.

"I have no idea." She hadn't dug that far into the Montgomery family history. Instead, she'd used her days at the library to focus solely on her grandfather. "Maybe I'll ask Mrs. Montgomery. I wager she'll tell me."

Caroline had liked the matriarch upon their first meeting earlier that day. Despite their age difference, she'd felt a connection with the old girl that had filled her with a unique mix of affection, admiration, and security. A heady combination.

Sally released an audible sigh. "Do you ever listen to anything I say?" The maid planted her fists on narrow hips. "You can't just ask Mrs. Montgomery that sort of question. It's simply not done."

The girl was really quite versed in what was and was not done. Caroline wondered where she'd received her plethora of information but feared her friend wouldn't answer her truthfully if she asked.

"Oh, Sally. Normally I would submit to your superior knowledge on the subject." Unable to resist, Caroline pulled the girl into a quick hug, as she'd done with her cousin just yesterday. Unlike Elizabeth, Sally resisted the warm exchange.

Releasing her, Caroline let out her own audible sigh. "I sense Montgomery's grandmother is different from most society mavens."

Sally pursed her lips. "I suppose we'll find out which one of us is right soon enough."

"No time like the present." Caroline headed for the door. "Are you coming?"

"No. Absolutely not. It isn't—"

"Yes, yes, I know. A maid joining the family for dinner simply isn't done."

"It's not just that." Sally lifted her chin at a stubborn angle. "Even if it was acceptable, I don't want anything to do with these people, especially not your Mr. Montgomery."

"He's not *my* Mr. Montgomery. And what's wrong with him?" Despite knowing how dangerous it was, Caroline was starting to rather like the handsome brute, although she only admitted that little piece of information silently to herself.

This change of heart had nothing to do with his kiss. She simply enjoyed matching wits with an intelligent man.

"I didn't say there was anything wrong with him. And that's the problem. He's really quite perfect. Handsome, smart, broad shouldered—he even looks me in the eye when he speaks to me. But he's also . . . so . . . so . . ."

"Masculine?"

"I was going to say intimidating. All that easy charm, I don't like it." Palms up, Sally backed away as if there were a large snake hanging from the doorway, coiled and ready to strike. "And his grandmother scares me."

"She's a dear." If one looked past the woman's propensity for asking pointed, uncomfortable questions about one's past, as she'd done when Caroline and Sally had first arrived at Wayfare House.

"All those little yappy dogs running around her." Sally visibly quaked. "They bite."

"Only one of them, and that was after you stepped on the poor thing's tail."

"That curlicue is not a tail." Sally sniffed inelegantly, looking as haughty as any person Caroline had met in New York society. "No. I'll not go downstairs with you. I'll just finish unpacking, if it's all the same to you."

"Coward." Caroline softened the accusation with a wink.

"You better believe I am." They both laughed, the gesture relaxing Sally's shoulders and encouraging Caroline to pull her into another stiff hug.

"Well, if you won't join me, then I'm off to converse with the dear lady and her favorite grandson." Caroline added the perfect amount of snobbery in her tone, the way Sally had taught her that first day.

Sally shoved her toward the door. "Go on with you, then."

"Try not to miss me too much while I'm gone." Tossing a wave over her head, she exited the room laughing. The sound died in her throat once she realized she didn't know how to find her way back downstairs. The hallways in this ridiculously large house were a virtual labyrinth of twists and turns.

After five minutes of wandering around aimlessly, Caroline resorted to the trick she'd learned on unfamiliar streets in Whitechapel. Choosing a direction at random, she flattened her palm on the nearest wall and continued forward. If she didn't break the connection, she would eventually find her way out of this complicated maze of hallways.

Just as she'd predicted, after doubling back a few times, she came to the top of the massive staircase at the front of the house.

Montgomery stood at the bottom, looking dangerously elegant in his formal attire. The black trousers, matching coat and tails, and starched white shirt should have made him look less threatening. No such luck.

Even with his arm casually looped over the banister and that easy expression on his face, he appeared alert, awake, a man who knew his place in the world.

That alone should help her keep her guard firmly in place.

Caroline, you aren't alone anymore. His words from yesterday echoed in her mind. He'd found her weakness and had slipped past every single defense she'd so carefully erected around her heart.

You aren't alone anymore.

Could it be true? Oh, how she wanted it to be true. But it was dangerous to allow even a sliver of hope to form in her heart. The stakes were too high. She didn't have a secure place in this world, and there was no guarantee that she would find one.

What if she failed? What if she disappointed her grandfather and he sent her packing?

You aren't alone anymore.

Oh, but she was.

Eyes cast downward, she made her way to the bottom of the stairs at a slow, even pace and stopped on the last step. Eye to eye with Montgomery, she waited for him to say something. Anything.

"You look lovely this evening." His eyes never left her face. "Although, I must admit, I prefer your hair down, the way you wore it yesterday, as opposed to"—he swept his gaze slightly upward—"your current style."

She resisted the urge to touch her hair. "I was told this is the latest fashion." Sally had been adamant, proving her point with a picture from a current American magazine.

"Perhaps, but it makes you look untouchable."

"Then I shall wear my hair this way every day I am in your presence."

A silent battle of wills commenced. Montgomery was good, holding her gaze with studied intensity. But Caroline was equally gifted in this particular skill, holding steadfast under his stare. She might have won the standoff but for the telling breath that escaped her lips.

He smiled at the sound, a flash of even white teeth beneath full, firm lips that had kissed her nearly senseless yesterday. Her heart dropped to her toes at the memory. Jackson Montgomery was a handsome, virile man at any time. But when he smiled like that? He was devastating.

She very nearly sighed but had the presence of mind to hold to her silence.

Still smiling, he offered his arm. "Shall we?"

Caroline took his arm and allowed him to lead her through the cavernous home. The sound of their shoes striking the parquet floors echoed off the walls, the rhythmic staccato matching her heartbeat.

"How are you finding your new home?" he asked, the perfect gentleman in his tone.

So they were back to innocuous pleasantries. She should be grateful. Actually, she *was* grateful. "Your grandmother has been very accommodating, the picture of kindness."

"And what about your maid?" He lifted a sardonic eyebrow, the gesture indicating he was onto their game. "Is she getting on with the rest of the staff here at Wayfare House?"

Caroline pulled them to a stop just outside what looked to be a drawing room. Deciding candor was the best plan of attack, she drew in a slow pull of air. "Sally is not my maid, not in the traditional sense." She angled her head and caught the amusement lurking in his eyes. "But you already know that, don't you?"

"I was wondering how long it would take you to admit the truth."

"You think you have me figured out." She spoke the words in a condescending tone, as if to insinuate he knew nothing about her, nothing at all. Unfortunately, he'd read her mother's letters and thus knew far too much already.

"Not in the least, Caroline St. James." He placed his lips next to her ear. "You are the most confounding, unpredictable woman I have ever met."

She had to work hard at remaining cool, calm, the picture of serenity, when she wanted so much to smile in triumph. "So you say. Montgomery, I—"

"Caroline. Don't you think at this point in our relationship you should call me Jackson?"

"All right, *Jackson*, you shouldn't be saying such things to me." She tried to frown at him. She really tried. "And, while we're on the subject of inappropriate behavior. You must never, never ever, kiss me again."

There. She'd said it. She'd made herself perfectly clear. A gentleman would have no other recourse than to abide by her request.

A voice drifted from the interior of the drawing room. "Are you two planning to spend all evening bantering with one another in the hallway, or are you going to come in here and entertain a lonely old woman?"

Montgomery chuckled. "We've been found out." He whispered the words with his mouth still close to her ear. "Remember, nothing gets past my grandmother." Genuine affection filled his voice. "She is a cagey old bird."

With that warning hanging between them, he straightened and steered her into the drawing room.

Caroline swept her gaze in a quick circle, landing on a woman of indeterminate age with a pinched face, pale skin, and blue eyes several shades darker than her son's. She sat perched on a chair with her back unnaturally straight. She wore all black, a color that leached her skin of any healthy glow and left her with a greenish pallor. With her face arranged in that off-putting scowl, she looked angry and bitter, a woman who had succumbed to the hardships of life.

This had to be Jackson's mother; no other explanation made sense. Caroline had thought her own mother had been a bitter woman, too, but now, with this current example as a measuring stick, Caroline realized Libby St. James had merely been sad. Terribly, irrevocably sad. Yet she'd held on to her faith even in her final days.

Why hadn't Caroline realized that sooner?

Of their own accord, her fingers dug into Jackson's arm. He covered her hand in a show of support.

In the next instant, Caroline felt herself leaning into him.

"Caroline St. James." He pulled her just a bit tighter to him. "I'd like you to meet my mother, Lucille Montgomery. Mother." He spoke directly to the woman with the hard eyes. "This is Caroline St. James, Richard's granddaughter from London."

Face still scrunched in a frown, Jackson's mother acknowledged Caroline with a brief nod.

"Well, girl, don't just stand there gawking. Come, sit over here"—Hattie Montgomery patted a free space on the settee beside her—"and tell me how you're settling in."

As she had earlier in the day, the older woman held court from her oversized chair near the fireplace with at least half a dozen miniature Pomeranians cuddled in around her.

Grateful for the invitation, Caroline released Jackson's arm and made her way toward his grandmother. She waded carefully through the six miniature balls of auburn-colored fur, aware that their small black eyes were focused solely on her.

The moment Caroline sat, one of the dogs crawled into her lap while two more pawed at her skirt at her feet. Smiling at their antics, Caroline leaned over, picked up both animals, and then set them in her lap with the other one.

It was a bit overcrowded on the settee with two grown women and an assortment of dogs, but no one seemed to mind, least of all Caroline. Deciding he'd been ignored long enough, one of the other three leapt up and licked her chin.

Caroline let out a giggle. *A giggle*. When had she ever giggled? But, truly, how could she not? These tiny, sweet-natured creatures were so different from the feral curs she'd encountered on the streets of London.

"They like you," the older woman said, approval in her voice.

Caroline stroked the soft fur of the pampered pets on her lap. "It's a mutual affection."

Jackson's mother sniffed. "They're horrid little creatures."

"Not completely horrid." Jackson grabbed one of the three in Caroline's lap. "They're just miniature fur balls with big black eyes, sharp little teeth, and"—he lifted the dog above his head—"very fat bellies."

His grandmother's booming laugh filled the air while Jackson tucked the dog under his arm as though it were a satchel. The tiny animal didn't seem to mind but rather settled in. Obviously, the creature felt safe in the man's arms.

Caroline knew the feeling. There had been a moment when they'd entered this room when she'd wanted to curl up in his arms and allow him to protect her, too.

He plans to marry your cousin.

Why—oh, why, why, why—couldn't she remember that important piece of information?

Deliberately moving her shoulders so she would no longer be able to make eye contact with the elegant bundle of temptation, she turned her full attention to his grandmother. "Mrs. Montgomery, I've been wondering—"

"Now, girl, there will be none of that in this house."

None of what? "I'm sorry?"

"You will call me Granny like everyone else does."

But the woman wasn't her grandmother. "You want me to call you Granny?"

"I insist upon it with everyone."

"Everyone?" Caroline rather doubted that. Then again, at eighty-seven the woman was entitled to a few eccentricities.

With a twinkle of mischief lighting in her eyes, the older woman glanced at something—or rather someone—standing behind Caroline. *"Everyone."*

"Well, then, Granny, tell me—" Caroline stopped midsentence, remembering what Sally had said earlier about needing to be careful what she chose to discuss with *these people*. "Tell me about your husband. What was he like?"

A faraway, happy look came into Granny's eyes. "He was very much like my grandson."

Caroline turned to look at Jackson, who was conversing quietly with his mother now, his fingers stroking the head of the little dog still under his arm. There was obvious tension around the corners of his mouth.

I know what you have endured.

Perhaps he'd been speaking the truth yesterday. Perhaps he had carried his own set of burdens. Something inside her softened at the picture he made. "How is Jackson most like your husband?"

"The obvious answer is his looks. The boy inherited that full head of thick black hair from his grandfather. The broad shoulders and square jaw, too. Handsome men, the both of them. Sometimes when I look at that boy I find myself lost in pleasant memories from another time."

There was a melancholy in Granny's tone that was hard to miss. "How old was Jackson's grandfather when he died?"

"He didn't make it out of his fifties."

Caroline couldn't imagine what it would be like to love so well only to lose that love to premature death.

The matriarch sighed, as if caught up in a mixture of memories, some good, others sad. She sighed again, nuzzled the dog in her lap, then scowled at something behind Caroline. "That boy is far too patient, just like my Jasper. He offers grace when he should be doling out a bit of hard truth every now and again."

Caroline couldn't help herself. She glanced over at Jackson once again. He'd set the dog on the ground and was now leaning over his mother, listening intently. To an outsider, he looked enraptured. If Caroline didn't know him as well as she had come to in the past few days, she might have missed the hint of annoyance deep in his eyes.

She looked away, shocked at the direction of her thoughts. She didn't know Jackson Montgomery. They were veritable strangers. A shared kiss did not make them kindred spirits.

"He's a good man."

"Yes," she agreed, not bothering to pretend she didn't know who Granny meant. "He is a very good man."

"He'll make some young lady an exceptional husband one day."

Caroline agreed. But since that particular young lady could very well be her cousin, Elizabeth, she kept her opinion to herself.

"That is"—Granny lowered her voice to a whisper—"once he lets go of his need to be the sole protector and restorer of our family's good name."

"I'm not sure I know what you mean."

"You are not acquainted with the story of our scandal?"

Caroline shook her head. When conducting her research, she'd only dug into Jackson's involvement with her family. Now she wished she'd gone deeper. He'd read her mother's letters and thus knew the particulars of her past. Wasn't it only fair she knew something of his?

"The short version is that his father, my son, ran off with his wife's sister."

Caroline gasped.

Granny pulled one of the little dogs into her lap. "My son, Edward, was never a malicious man at heart, just extremely selfish. He lived for the next pleasure. He played hard, drank hard, and took whatever he wanted, never thinking of the consequences."

Caroline had met men like that at the gaming halls in London. They had been the easiest to take money from and yet the hardest as well, because she always walked away feeling as though she'd taken advantage of them. But more than that, she'd been aware that those men probably had families who were the real victims of their carelessness and excess.

She understood Jackson's mother better now.

"Edward's charm usually smoothed over any feathers he might have ruffled along the way—until he did the unthinkable and fell in love with the wrong woman. Jackson was barely twenty-three years old at the time and was left to pick up the pieces his father left behind."

I understand what it's like to take on burdens that seem too heavy to bear at times.

Oh, Jackson. She'd been wrong to scoff at him.

"I offered to help, to pay whatever debts Edward left behind, but Jackson would hear none of it. He wouldn't allow me to bear the shame, so he did. He took over the business and set out to restore the Montgomery good name."

"By living his life above reproach."

"I see you understand him."

"Yes." Oh, how she understood him. Jackson wasn't boring, as Elizabeth had claimed. He was honorable and wise, a protector and a man of great integrity. He was a . . . a . . . hero.

"As you can imagine," Granny said with a sad look in her eyes, "Jackson walks the straight road every day of his life. Ever since his father abandoned his mother, honor and duty have ruled the boy's every decision. And that's the worst tragedy of all."

Was it? "Why do you say that?"

"I married Jackson's grandfather because the Montgomery men were known for their unconventional ways. They were the quintessential rebels. Godly, yes. Moral, without question. But until Jackson, they never allowed society to dictate their behavior."

How . . . intriguing.

"Jackson comes from a long line of men who did what they believed was right, not what society told them was right." She smiled fondly at her grandson. "The first Montgomery came to America before the Revolution. He was a smuggler during that war, as were his ancestors during the Civil War. Turns out transporting contraband and supplies during wartime is not only a patriotic duty to a Montgomery, but a very lucrative business as well."

Ah, that certainly answered the question about where the family money came from.

"Montgomery men have always lived life to the fullest. They play hard and work harder."

Jackson joined them just as his grandmother finished having her say. "Not all Montgomery men play hard, Granny." Frowning furiously, he added, "Some of us do know the meaning of honor and duty."

"Yes, Jackson." The older woman patted his arm. "Some of you understand a great deal more than you should on the subject."

Chapter Twenty-One

Jackson made the decision to exit his grandmother's house before dinner was served. Not merely because her comments about Montgomery men had left him unsettled—although that was reason enough—but also because he was fed up, stretched to his limit, and wasn't in the mood for more verbal combat.

His mother had been in rare form all evening, complaining about the New York winters and lack of quality people left in town to attend the theater with her. He'd suggested she travel to Florida this year, whereupon she began a rant on the heat and insects and various other points of contention.

Shaking his head, he refocused on his grandmother. She was whispering softly to Caroline again, the topic of discussion the décor of the room. Their ease with one another was evident in their hushed tones and bent heads. He liked seeing the two get on so well, liked it a little too much.

He was supposed to tutor Caroline in business, not bring her into his family fold.

Their kiss. He blamed his lack of better judgment on that earth-shattering kiss.

Once his grandmother came up for air, he made his excuses for the evening.

The women fell silent, each looking a bit guilty, as if they'd been caught telling tales. What had he missed? What secrets was his grandmother revealing to Caroline? "I see I've interrupted, again."

"Well, yes." Caroline spoke in that straightforward manner he was beginning to appreciate. "But that doesn't mean it's an unwelcome intrusion."

His grandmother let out a chortle. "Oh, well played, Caroline. Well played, indeed."

Caroline gave her an affectionate look, then smiled up at Jackson. "Please, join us."

"I've only come to make my excuses," he said again. "I have another engagement this evening."

Caroline lifted an eyebrow, the question in her gaze clear. She thought he planned to spend the evening in the company of her cousin. Which, considering the fact that he was supposed to have already begun courting Elizabeth, was where he should be going.

He couldn't drum up the enthusiasm.

"My plans are with Luke." He elaborated for his grandmother. "You remember my friend, Lucian Griffin—he was at the St. James dinner the other evening."

"Ah, yes, a lovely young man."

Jackson stifled a smile at his grandmother's wording. Lovely young man. Luke would shudder at the fanciful description. "I'll be sure to give him your regards."

"Yes, yes." She waved him on his way. "Go on, go on. As you can see, I'm in the middle of a very important discussion with your friend."

"Indeed." Caroline shot him a challenging stare. "Just before you made your way across the room, we were discussing the origin of your family's fortune."

He scowled. "That is not an appropriate topic of conversation among polite society."

"Good thing we aren't in polite society." Caroline released a short laugh before focusing her attention on his grandmother once more. "If I'm not mistaken, Granny, you mentioned something about . . . smuggling?"

The woman was baiting him, very effectively, too. It took every ounce of his self-control to laugh off her words and address the matter as if every good New York family had such an infamous beginning. "The important part to remember is that my forebears played a patriotic role in two wars."

"So I've been led to understand."

Caroline reached out and placed her hand on Jackson's sleeve. "It takes courage and strength of character to rebel against an unjust system of rules and regulations."

She thought she was so clever. He knew precisely what she was about, openly challenging him to question the rules of society.

From the amusement in his grandmother's eyes, Jackson wasn't the only one to notice the ploy.

The floor shifted beneath his feet. Caroline St. James had gained another ally while Jackson had lost considerable ground.

Hoping to communicate his displeasure, he captured Caroline's gaze for longer than was polite. For one insane moment he experienced a sudden urge to pull her into his arms and kiss her again. Right there in front of his mother and grandmother.

He resisted.

Barely.

Remembering himself, he broke eye contact and took his grandmother's hand. "I will stop by tomorrow morning at our usual time." Without looking directly at the other woman, he said, "Good night, Caroline."

"Good night, Jackson." She used the same intonation as he had, mocking him with her answering civility.

The tight rein he had on his control snapped. Unable to stop himself from giving in to his temper, he hauled her to her feet. "Walk me out," he said. "I have something I wish to discuss with you in private."

"Sounds ominous."

"It will only take a moment."

Without giving her a chance to argue, he pulled her out of the room.

She didn't resist, not even a little, her wary expression communicating that she knew she'd pushed him too far.

Good. She should be wary of him.

Striding quickly through the house, he bypassed the foyer and went straight for a small alcove beneath the stairwell.

"Jackson, this isn't necessary. You have made your point quite successfully." Eyes wide with apprehension, she pressed herself against the back wall of the cubbyhole. "You must know I was only trying to antagonize you earlier."

"You succeeded brilliantly." He stepped into the shadows with her, braced his hands on either side of her. "Maybe it's time you learned what happens when you push a man to his limit."

"I . . . I don't think this is a good idea. Maybe we should—"

He cut off the rest of her words by pressing his lips to hers.

As if she'd been expecting the move, she gripped his lapels and . . . pulled him closer.

Her unexpected reaction sent his control slipping all the more. He furiously tried to remember that he was a man of integrity, one who lived by the solid Christian precepts of behavior, a man who honored women, who protected them from . . . *this*.

He had to pull back, had to stop kissing Caroline right this very minute. He had to remember he wasn't his father.

Fighting for the last remnants of his control, Jackson yanked his head back. He dragged air into his lungs, one hard gulp at a time.

Even with the shadows curtaining her face, he could tell his behavior had stunned Caroline. Though she didn't appear entirely upset about this turn of events.

The woman made him crazy. She made him act completely out of character. And, God have mercy on his soul, he liked the sensation. Liked it enough to know he'd completely lost his mind.

What had he gotten himself into?

* * *

What had she gotten herself into?

That's the thought that ran through Caroline's mind as she stared up at Jackson. He was breathing as hard as she, gasping for air as though his life depended upon it. The wall sconces in the foyer illuminated him from behind, casting him in a halo of light. Ha. The man was no angel. And Caroline was starting to like that most about him.

From the start, she'd underestimated him. As had Elizabeth. For her cousin's sake, Caroline must send Jackson on his way.

"Weren't you leaving?"

"Caroline." His gaze softened, his voice thickened, and he was making it very difficult for her to remember that he didn't belong to her. "I'm not usually such a brute."

"Only when you're around me."

He speared a hand through his hair, the gesture leaving the thick tufts slightly disheveled. It was a good look for him, one that matched the hint of wildness in his eyes. "Apparently, I am at my worst in your company."

If that was his worst, she couldn't imagine what he was like at his best.

She had no right to think such things.

"You should go," she whispered.

"Yes." His hand reached for her, as if of its own accord, then slid back to his side. "Will I see you at the VanDercreeks' party later this week?"

"As I will be attending the small, private party as my grandfather's personal guest, yes, I'll be there."

"Then I'll say good-bye." He placed his palm on her cheek. "Good-bye, Caroline."

She leaned into his hand. "Good-bye, Jackson."

He turned to go, then spun back around. "I know you do it to annoy me, but I like the way you say my name in that street urchin accent."

Before she could shove him away for his impertinence, he withdrew from the alcove and walked to the exit without a backward glance.

With her fingertips pressed to her lips, she stared after his retreating form.

That man. Oh, that infuriating, honorable man who'd borne his own share of family burdens. Why did she have to know that about him? Why did she have to care?

Dropping her hand to her side, she slumped against the wall behind her. Trouble. Jackson was turning out to be trouble, and not in any way she could have conceived.

"Miss St. James." Her grandmother's butler peeked into the alcove. "Dinner is being served in the main dining room."

She rose to her full height and snapped her shoulders back. "I must have lost track of time."

"Yes, miss, that happens rather often in this house."

That response made her smile. "Where, exactly, is the main dining room?"

"Down that hallway." He indicated the corridor to her left. "Third door on the right."

In silent defiance, or perhaps to prove she was still the same Caroline she'd always been, she looked the man straight in the eye and smiled brighter. "Thank you, Burke."

"You are welcome, Miss St. James." He returned her smile. "Might I say, miss, it's a pleasure having you with us."

She touched his arm in a moment of solidarity, then set off in the direction he'd indicated. She entered the room in time for Jackson's mother's next complaint.

"Really, Granny, cranberries? You chose to serve cranberries when you know I cannot tolerate them."

Seemingly unmoved by the woman's hard tone, Granny lifted an elegant shoulder. "Eat around them, Lucille." She smiled up at Caroline. "Please, my dear, take your seat."

Caroline settled in the chair opposite Jackson's mother. Had Granny not shared the story of her husband's desertion Caroline might have been less likely to put up with the woman's incessant criticizing of every little detail of the meal. But now that she knew the source of Lucille Montgomery's discontent, Caroline simply smiled and nodded.

"I trust Jackson got off all right?" Granny asked.

"He did."

Not to be ignored, Lucille entered the conversation with a snarl. "What was so important that he couldn't speak in front of his own mother and grandmother?"

"Yes, dear, what did the boy want with you?" Granny's eyes sparkled in a way that said she knew exactly what *the boy* had wanted from Caroline.

She contemplated telling them both that he'd kissed her until her eyes had nearly rolled back in her head. But that would be pandering at best, petty at worst. Caroline was not in the business of hurting people intentionally, not even a confounding gentleman who couldn't seem to remember he was supposed to be courting Caroline's cousin.

"Jackson wanted to discuss our schedule next week. It seems I'm to spend part of my time inspecting the tenement houses with him."

She didn't know if that was true or not, but now that the idea had surfaced she wondered why she couldn't make that happen. The tenement buildings were where she'd first met Jackson, where she'd witnessed the portion of his personality no one but she knew existed. Now that they knew each other's secrets, it seemed fitting they should begin her business education on the Lower East Side.

Best of all, she would get another opportunity to see Mary.

"I wasn't aware Jackson made a habit of inspecting the tenement houses." His mother's voice held decided disapproval.

Caroline pretended grave interest in smoothing her napkin across her lap. It was either that or say something she would regret. An arm reached around her and set a plate in front of her.

Tired of pretending she was someone she was not, she lifted her eyes to the server before he retreated. "Thank you," she said.

His eyes widened at her boldness, and he quickly looked away, evidently embarrassed by the brief interchange.

Caroline performed a mental shrug. One step at a time. Looking up, she noted two pairs of eyes staring at her from opposite ends of the table. Both appeared shocked at her behavior. *Oh, for goodness' sake.* She hadn't done anything wrong or criminal or even immoral. She'd simply thanked a man for serving her a dish of soup.

She sighed. Did no one but Caroline think the rules of upper-class society were utterly ridiculous?

At least Granny seemed more amused than condemning. Sensing a supporter in the older woman, Caroline cleared her throat and brought up a completely different topic. "I saw you have a well-stocked library on the second floor."

Granny set down her spoon. "It was my husband's pride and joy. Jackson has kept the titles current."

"Has he?" Caroline leaned forward, her food all but forgotten. "How wonderful." Excitement made her voice shake. Not just a library filled with old books, but new ones, too. Oh, the joy.

"Jackson has been diligent in his duty," Granny said. "He adds important works as they become available. A library must keep up with the changing times, don't you agree?"

"I do."

Jackson's mother sniffed indelicately. It was not an attractive sound. "How very progressive of you both."

Granny ignored the jab. "Jackson spends hours up there when he can find the time."

Another thing they had in common. She could envision them in the library at night, reading, a fire crackling in the hearth, a comfortable silence filling the space between them.

She shook away the fanciful thought. "Would you mind if I explored the contents of the shelves myself? I won't take any book beyond the library, but if I could read one or two"—*or ten*—"I would be in your debt."

Again, Granny gave her that look of approval. "You may enjoy the library anytime you wish."

"Thank you, Granny. I—" She clasped the older woman's hand and squeezed. *"Thank you."*

Conversation turned to the unseasonably warm weather, whereupon Jackson's mother began another listing of complaints.

Deciding it was best to remain silent on the matter, Caroline focused on her food. Her mind took her upstairs, to the library full of books she had yet to read. It would take her a lifetime to work her way through all the choices available. What should she read first? A biography? A travel story? An adventure tale, perhaps?

"Now, my dear, do tell." Granny's voice wove through her thoughts, bringing her back to the table. "Have you decided what you will wear to the VanDercreeks' party? It will be somewhat of your official debut as Richard's granddaughter."

Caroline hadn't thought of the party in quite that way. She would have to be careful with her choice. Consulting Sally would be her first order of business. For now, she admitted, "I haven't decided yet."

"May I add my opinion?" Granny asked.

"Please, do."

"You should wear blue, a deep, rich shade of blue with, perhaps, ivory trim."

Caroline had a gown that met that description. She hadn't worn it yet, so no one at the party would have cause to criticize her choice. Elizabeth's words came back to her. *A woman of fine breeding should never be caught in the same gown twice.*

Had Caroline become so much a part of this world that she was becoming a snob like Elizabeth's mother? She shuddered at the prospect.

This wasn't about her, she reminded herself. For her grandfather's sake she didn't want to draw unwanted attention her way. "I have a dress that color."

Satisfaction filled the older woman's gaze. "Splendid. Then that is the one you will wear."

Granny seemed so certain that Caroline couldn't hold back her curiosity. "Out with it, Granny. Why should I wear my blue gown?"

"I should think it quite obvious." The gleam in the older woman's eyes turned calculating. "Blue is Jackson's favorite color."

Chapter Twenty-Two

Jackson arrived at the Harvard Club with his mind still entrenched at his grandmother's house. Or rather, his mind was still in the alcove in his grandmother's house—firmly fixed on a certain raven-haired beauty with exotic green eyes, a mesmerizing voice, and a propensity to sneak beneath his well-laid defenses.

Whenever he was alone with Caroline St. James, his control slipped, every time, whereby he found himself acting out of character. Pulling her into his arms.

Kissing her.

He pushed into the foyer of the club, shoulders tense, head down. He'd worked too hard to make his life his own, had struggled too long to restore his family name to continue down this path. Ruthless discipline was the only thing keeping him in line. He was already on shaky ground If he continued to give in to his selfish desires where Caroline was concerned, he might end up on a path from which there was no turning back.

One false step had a way of leading to another, and another, until one day Jackson would become a man no better than his father, a man who took what he wanted without considering the consequences or thinking beyond his own selfish desires.

Caroline St. James was a menace. A frustrating, annoying, beautiful, heart-stopping temptation he couldn't seem to keep at arm's distance. She would be his downfall if he didn't get a handle on his renowned control.

Regardless of what his actions had shown in the last few days, Jackson still wanted a calm, respectable marriage to a calm, respectable woman whose serene manner exemplified the best of his world.

Caroline St. James was not that woman. She was the consummate rule-breaker, the absolute opposite of her cousin, Elizabeth.

Elizabeth.

Jackson hadn't thought of her since Caroline had materialized at the top of the stairs in his grandmother's home.

In desperate need of a distraction, he strode into the billiards room and searched out a possible opponent. He found just the man at the back of the room, propping up the wall with a broad shoulder.

Jackson approached his friend. "I wasn't expecting to see you here this evening." He studied Luke's scowl, wondered at it. "Shouldn't you be at a party or the opera or some such formal event, choosing your future bride?"

Luke's expression turned murderous. "Mind your own business, Montgomery."

"The hunt going that well, is it?"

Clearly frustrated and spoiling for a fight, Luke shifted his stance to one full of aggression.

Jackson simply smiled.

"Word's gotten out as to the reason behind my return."

Jackson nodded gravely. "How'd that happen?"

Not a blink. Not even a shrug. "My father made a public announcement at the opera the other night." Luke's lip curled. "Now, every event

I attend, I'm swarmed with women—and their calculating mothers—within minutes of arriving."

Jackson almost felt sorry for his friend, but he remembered their days back at Harvard. Luke had never had a problem drawing female notice, nor had he turned any of that "notice" away, quite the opposite in fact. Lucian Griffin liked women—he'd never pretended otherwise—and they liked him in return. "How is now any different than before your father's public announcement?"

Luke gave him a hard glare, the unspoken message just as loud and clear as before. *Mind your own business.*

"I see." Chuckling, Jackson craned his neck, looked side to side, then lowered his voice. "I assume you are hiding out from all that unwanted female attention?"

"Laugh if you will." Luke shot him a smug glower. "We both know you're here for the same reason."

"I'm not hiding."

Luke gave him a bland look.

"All right, maybe I am." A table became open. Jackson jerked his head in that direction. "You want to play a game of billiards or keep propping up that wall?"

"You break first."

Jackson shoved around Luke and made a grand show of choosing a cue stick. Hard on his heels, Luke followed suit, aiming another smug grin in his direction. "You can lie to yourself but not to me. You, my friend, are having your own woman trouble. And we both know who I mean."

With slow, deliberate movements, Jackson rubbed chalk on the edge of his stick and then tossed the cube in the air.

Luke caught it midair. "What? No response? No ready denial?" He arranged the balls inside the wooden triangle, shuffled them tightly to the top. "No pretense that you have no idea to what woman I'm referring?"

Pretending grave interest in their game, Jackson placed the white cue ball on his end of the table, pulled back his stick, and then smacked the ball with a hard tap.

Three stripes and one solid fell into separate pockets at varying speeds.

"Perhaps you should just say what's on your mind." Jackson sauntered around the table, chose his next target, pointed to the far right pocket, then struck the white cue ball again. "Who, exactly, are we talking about here?"

Jackson knew, of course. But did Luke?

He lined up his next shot, missed.

His friend moved into position, opened his mouth, glanced around to see if anyone was listening, then said, "I'm talking about the woman Richard St. James has hired to work in the company office."

Jackson stilled. "How did you know about that? Are people talking?" *Already?*

"Not that I'm aware, no." Luke took the shot. "I only know about Richard's arrangement with his granddaughter because her cousin told me."

A hot ball of dread stuck in the center of Jackson's chest. Elizabeth had discussed Caroline with Luke? "Was anyone else around when you two had this particular conversation?"

Eyes on the billiard table, Luke circled to the other side. "I haven't heard any gossip if that's what you're asking."

Relieved, Jackson let out a slow breath. After all she'd been through as a child, Caroline didn't deserve to be weighed and measured, condemned even, before she made her own way in society. She ought to have a chance to prove to the good people of New York that she was smart and talented and moral, despite her rough upbringing.

"Are you going to keep staring over my shoulder with that cornered look on your face, or are we going to play billiards?" Luke pointed to the table. "It's your shot."

Shaking his head, Jackson moved slowly around the table, choosing the most likely avenue for success. He placed his cue stick between his fingers. "Have you heard *any* talk about Caroline?"

"A bit, and before you ask, it's all been relatively positive at this point. Her grandfather wields considerable power in this town. No one would dare openly criticize her in public."

But in private would they be so kind? Jackson hated that he didn't know the answer, hated that he couldn't control what was said behind Caroline's back.

Luke leaned on his stick. "That's not what I meant, you know, when I referred to your woman troubles."

"I know."

"It's the way you look at her, Jackson. Dead giveaway to what's on your mind."

Jackson's wrist jerked, sending the cue ball at an odd angle and straight into the pocket on his left.

A look of supreme satisfaction filled Luke's eyes as he reached in the pocket and retrieved the ball.

"What is it you think you see?"

Luke smirked. "Do I really need to spell it out?"

There was something in Luke's tone, something that had Jackson setting down his stick. "Why do I get a sense you have a stake in this?"

"We aren't talking about me."

"Maybe we should."

Luke shifted uncomfortably from one foot to the other. "Don't avoid the issue, my friend. You have your eye on Caroline St. James."

Jackson's stomach roiled, dread making his breathing slow and awkward. Luke had to be fishing. "You ascertained that from witnessing a few brief encounters between Caroline and me."

"I'm observant."

"Not that observant."

Avoiding eye contact, Luke sank the next three balls. "I should warn you, Jackson, Elizabeth noticed, too."

For the second time that day, the floor shifted beneath his feet. His feeling of dread morphed in to guilt. "You spoke of this with Elizabeth?" His tone was razor-sharp.

Setting his stick on the table, Luke crossed his arms over his chest and stared hard at Jackson. "She was the one who pointed it out to me."

The revelation staggered him. Everything in him turned hot then ice-cold. Elizabeth. He'd all but betrayed the woman he'd been planning to marry, with her own cousin. He was no better than his father. In fact, he was worse. Unlike Edward Montgomery, Jackson had known from the start the consequences of his actions. Yet he'd ignored caution and had rationalized his behavior. He'd acted selfishly and had hurt a woman he cared about deeply.

For as long as Jackson could remember, Elizabeth had been his future. *Had been.* As in past tense. He was thinking of Elizabeth in the past tense and had been for some time, as if his intentions had changed toward her long before tonight. His friendship for Elizabeth hadn't been enough to keep Jackson from reaching for something . . . more.

For several long seconds he couldn't speak, couldn't breathe. He felt his world shattering around him, splintering into pieces he would never be able to put back together.

Luke continued to hold his stare, a challenge in his eyes. The man knew. He knew Jackson was having second thoughts about marrying Elizabeth. But how could he know, when Jackson had only come to the conclusion in the last few minutes?

Breaking eye contact, Jackson glanced around the room. Noticing they'd drawn unnecessary attention, he motioned Luke to follow him to the library, where they could continue their conversation in private.

Once they were settled near the fireplace, with only a handful of elderly gentlemen smoking cigars and drinking port on the other side of the room, he restated his earlier question. "Elizabeth noticed my interest in Caroline?"

"Actually"—Luke dug the toe of his boot in a crack in the stone hearth—"she thinks you two are very much alike in nature." He held up a palm to ward off Jackson's objection. "Her words, not mine."

"Elizabeth thinks Caroline and I are . . . alike?" The assessment took Jackson by surprise. They were nothing alike.

Or were they?

Another wave of unease clogged his throat.

The fact that Elizabeth had made her own assessment of his relationship with her cousin was disturbing enough. But to discover she'd discussed the situation with Luke? Jackson found that far more troubling.

Elizabeth had shared her intimate thoughts with a man other than Jackson. *And you were kissing her cousin. What does that say about you?*

Jackson swallowed back a growl. "When did you and Elizabeth discuss this matter?"

"At the opera last night."

Last night. Elizabeth had been at the opera with Luke.

Had they gone together? No, Luke's parents owned the box directly across from Marcus's.

Without Jackson's encouragement, Luke went on to explain. "I was bored out of my mind," he said. "Like I always am at the opera. I noticed Elizabeth staring up at the ceiling. I couldn't figure out what had captured her attention." Luke shrugged. "I decided to find out."

"By joining her in her father's box."

Luke gave him a grin. "Naturally."

There was something of the old Luke in that smile, in that droll tone.

"Go on," Jackson urged when his friend remained silent.

"Turns out, Elizabeth was counting the seams in the plaster on the ceiling. Did you know she hates *Figaro* as much as I do?"

Jackson pinched the bridge of his nose. "Elizabeth told me she loves that particular opera."

That had Luke falling into silence. Jackson did so as well. Elizabeth had told two different stories to two different men. Had she lied to Jackson, or to Luke? Either way, Jackson realized he didn't know Elizabeth St. James as well as he'd thought.

Tonight, it would seem, was a night for revelations.

"Jackson." Luke sat in the chair across from him and set his elbows on his knees. "I have to ask you a question, and I request that you tell me the truth."

"All right."

"Are you going to ask Elizabeth to marry you?"

"I . . ." Was he? "No." It was as if a huge weight had been lifted off his shoulders. "I am not."

Luke's shoulders tightened and his eyes narrowed to tiny slits. "She deserves to know. You should tell her immediately."

Yes, he should. Jackson splayed the fingers of his right hand and shoved them through his hair. "I will."

"When?"

"Soon."

Luke leaned forward. "See that you do."

* * *

The invitations began arriving faster than Caroline could keep up. Sorting through them was a daunting task, one Granny had no tolerance for and Sally claimed was beyond her talents. Thus, the following morning, when Elizabeth and her mother appeared on Granny's doorstep with a request to join them for tea, Caroline welcomed the distraction.

"Granny and I were just about to ring for a pot before you arrived," she confirmed, thinking that now was as good a time as any to question her aunt about her relationship with Libby. "I'm sure she won't mind two more."

Of course, it would be the height of impoliteness to assume such a thing without checking first. She excused herself.

Her aunt's voice stopped her.

"No, dear, I didn't mean here. We shall go to the Waldorf," she declared. "That is where all the best people take tea. I have already made the arrangements."

Caroline hesitated, turning slowly around to face her aunt once again. Despite her aunt's imperious tone, if she was honest with herself, the suggestion was not an unwelcome one. Perhaps a public setting would be a better place to try to trick her aunt into revealing something important. Not that she believed Katherine St. James was guilty. So far, the older woman had treated Caroline with nothing but kindness.

Then again, that could all be part of her game.

"What a lovely idea," Caroline said. "Let me see if Granny wishes to join us." As soon as the words left her mouth, she realized she'd spoken as if the older woman was her first priority, as if Granny were her *real* grandmother.

Caroline should be so blessed.

Unfortunately, her suggestion was met with a hint of disapproval from her aunt. "The invitation only includes you, Caroline." Her voice was firm but not completely unkind. "Seeing as this is our first chance to get to know one another, I would prefer today's outing only include immediate family."

Family. Her aunt said the word with such warmth and acceptance, as if Caroline was truly one of them, as if she truly belonged. Under the circumstances, she found herself warming to the older woman and quite unable to argue the point.

Elizabeth had no such qualms. "But, Mother. What does it matter where we take tea? I had hoped we would do so here, with Granny and her little dogs."

"Those horrid creatures?" Katherine visibly shuddered. "They are a nuisance. If they are not nipping at one's toes, they are shedding upon one's dress." Her lips pursed in displeasure. "I think we can all agree on that point."

Caroline didn't mind the dogs—they were really rather adorable—but if her aunt considered them a *nuisance*, then perhaps she should make her excuses with Granny.

Caroline teetered on indecision.

It was Granny herself who solved the problem. "Is that my dear Elizabeth's voice?" She entered the foyer with her chin lifted and one of her little dogs tucked under her arm. "Oh, Katherine, you are here, too. Do come in and join me in the parlor. Caroline was just about to ring up some tea."

Katherine shook her head. "We were just heading out."

A moment of tension fell over the two women. Was there to be an argument, then? Over something as innocuous as where they were going to drink their tea?

Who knew something so frivolous could turn into a battlefield. Caroline would never understand society. Never. She wasn't altogether sure that was a bad thing, quite the opposite, actually.

Of the two, Granny was the most strong-willed. "Nonsense, Katherine, I won't hear of you and Elizabeth leaving now that you are here. Now, follow me."

The older woman spoke with such authority Katherine St. James had little recourse other than to relent. So polite, her manners so impeccable, she even gave in to Granny's request with a gracious bob of her head.

Almost as soon as the four of them were settled in their chosen seats in the parlor, the tea tray arrived.

"Be so kind as to serve, Caroline."

"With pleasure, Granny." Caroline performed the ritual of pouring the fragrant brew into four matching teacups. A plume of steam wafted over her hand as she passed them around their tiny group. A cheerful rattle of spoons followed as each woman added varying amounts of sugar and cream and, in Caroline's case, lemon.

"Well, my dear," Katherine began, setting her spoon on the edge of her saucer and looking Caroline in the eye. "How are you settling in?"

There was no subterfuge in the question, just general curiosity. "Quite well, thank you."

Smiling, Caroline passed a plate of shortbread around. A marmalade-hued dog jumped on the table and began nosing around the tea service.

At Katherine's disapproving scowl, Caroline quickly picked up the furry troublemaker and set him back on the ground. In the ensuing silence, she worked the next round of conversation through her mind. This was her chance to find out who had commandeered her mother's letters. Surely her aunt knew something.

In fact, Katherine St. James might have been the one to commit the tragic sin herself, although that seemed unlikely. Her aunt had been kindness itself to Caroline. And yet, there was something not quite right in the way she treated her. It was as if Katherine were intentionally trying to appease Caroline. But to what end?

If only Caroline had prepared herself better for this opportunity. "Aunt Katherine, would you tell me about my mother? You were friends with her, yes?"

"Your mother and I were great friends." Katherine set her cup and saucer on the table beside her and smiled. "The very best."

Despite the smile, the grief was there, in her eyes, in the catch in her voice. Caroline couldn't fault the woman's sincerity. And yet . . .

"You miss her," Caroline said.

"I do." She sighed. "Oh, but I do."

Elizabeth frowned. "But, Mother, you never speak of her."

After a long hesitation, Katherine waved a dismissive hand at her daughter. "That is because it is too difficult to speak of her."

And yet, her aunt seemed to have no problem speaking of Libby now. The contradiction between the woman's words and her behavior kept Caroline alert. "How did you know my mother?"

"We went to school together." Her eyebrow twitched before she turned her back on Caroline and focused on her daughter. "Libby is the one who introduced me to your father."

"Oh, I didn't know that." Elizabeth's sigh turned all heads in her direction. "How romantic."

Romantic? Caroline was thinking how odd it was that at nineteen Elizabeth was only now hearing this important piece of information about her parents. Once again sensing something not quite right, Caroline leaned forward and studied Katherine's face closely, looking for any signs of subterfuge. She found nothing but a hint of embarrassment in the flutter of Katherine's eyelashes, in her slightly pink cheeks and stiff posture.

Caroline tried to recall her conversation with Elizabeth during their walk along Sixth Avenue. Due to her father's gambling, Katherine hadn't always been treated well by society. She'd been openly humiliated by her peers for wearing a dress more than once.

Libby St. James would have been kind to Katherine despite how others treated her, perhaps even *because* of how others treated her. Sadly, Libby's soft heart had led to her downfall. No woman filled with that much tenderness could have survived the mean streets of Whitechapel.

"It was indeed romantic." Katherine released an airy laugh, giving nothing away of her pain as a young girl. Caroline couldn't help but be impressed. She knew what it meant to be on the outside looking in and felt a moment of kinship with her aunt. "Your father was very sought after. Many young women wanted an introduction."

"But you were the one who managed to gain his notice." Elizabeth clapped her hands together in excitement, her dreamy gaze full of wonder. "Tell me how he asked you to marry him."

"You have heard the tale a thousand times."

"I adore the story. Tell it again. Please, Mother, for my cousin's ears, as well as mine."

"Oh, very well." Although Katherine's voice was full of impatience, Caroline sensed that her aunt was happy to tell the tale of how she became Mrs. Marcus St. James. Caroline wasn't nearly so eager. She would rather hear more about her mother. She desperately wanted to question her aunt about the years prior to and then after Libby left for London. She would have to find a way to do so before the visit was complete.

Biding her time, she listened to her aunt's story with the hope of gleaning more information about Libby. Perhaps Katherine would reveal something important, some small bit of information that would lead to another, and still another, continuing until Caroline found the missing piece she was looking for, the nugget that would tell her who in her family had wanted Libby St. James out of their lives for good.

Chapter Twenty-Three

Several days after having tea with her aunt and cousin, Caroline woke to the sound of rain scratching against the windows. She'd learned nothing overly helpful during their time together, other than the fact that Marcus St. James was a consummate husband and father. Her aunt had been adamant on those points, a little too adamant, which left Caroline quite suspicious of the man.

It was a good thing she would be meeting him again in a few hours, since today was to be her first day of work at her grandfather's office. Unable to sleep any longer, she rolled out from beneath the covers and padded barefoot to the fireplace.

She tossed on a few more logs, grabbed the poker, and proceeded to stoke the fire back to life. Hot orange flames exploded upward, the wood cracking and popping. It never occurred to her to wake Sally to help her with the task. She'd spent too many years taking care of the basic household chores on her own that she would never burden another person to do what she could easily do for herself.

Besides, Sally was more advisor now than maid. Caroline had been fortunate to find her at the Waldorf-Astoria, more fortunate still to talk Sally into joining her at Granny's. Sally was a plethora of information about the inner workings of New York society. Yet, no matter how many times Caroline pressed the girl about her background, Sally never revealed where she came from or how she'd gleaned her working knowledge of this world.

Once the fire burned on its own, Caroline pulled a soft-backed chair closer and considered the stack of books on the nearby table. Last night, she'd padded down the hallway to the library after dinner and, with Granny's permission, had chosen a few to bring back to her room.

Unfortunately, none of the titles caught her interest this morning. She opened a book, read the first two pages, then immediately lost interest. After repeating the process two more times, she gave up on the idea of reading.

Her mind wanted to wander. She let it. Memories from her time aboard ship mingled with images from her first days with Mary on Orchard Street. Much had changed since those days. Caroline had changed. Her *heart* had changed.

She closed her eyes and leaned her head back against the chair and let her thoughts tangle over one another. She'd come to avenge her mother's death and had yet to do so. Her grandfather hadn't ignored her mother's letters, as she'd thought, but someone had intentionally kept Libby from reuniting with her family. Possibly her uncle. Maybe her aunt, despite their pleasant interaction the other day. Or someone else in the household? A servant, perhaps?

No, that didn't make sense at all. What would a servant hope to gain?

She was more confused than ever.

At least Jackson had agreed to help her uncover the identity of the traitor. They would begin their quest in earnest today. She would insist on some time with her uncle.

"You look peaceful."

Accustomed to Sally's light steps, Caroline opened her eyes slowly and smiled. "All part of the illusion."

Eyes concerned, Sally belted her robe with a hard yank. "You want to talk about him?"

Caroline didn't insult either of them by pretending to misunderstand who Sally meant. "There's nothing to discuss. Jackson Montgomery will soon be courting another. It's really that simple."

It had to be. For her cousin's sake.

"Simple?" Sally picked up the poker and moved around the dying embers until flames burst forth once again. Her long, golden hair fell in waves down her back. "Hardly. You're going to be working alongside him every day."

Yes, that was true. "It changes nothing."

Gaze averted, Sally moved to the window and looked out. "Rain's stopped. Dawn will be here soon."

"I suppose I should begin dressing for the day."

Picking up a hairbrush off the vanity, Sally directed Caroline to the chair in front of the mirror and pressed her into the seat. "Let me help you with your hair."

Caroline captured the girl's hand. "I'm perfectly capable of brushing my own hair."

"I know." Sally smiled at her in the mirror, her light blue eyes shining in the glass. "But I want to do this for you. And you should let me. It's what you pay me to do."

"No, it's not." She squeezed Sally's hand. "You are here because you're my friend."

Something came and went in Sally's eyes. "Humor me, Miss—"

"Caroline."

"Humor me, Caroline."

Their eyes met a moment longer. Caroline released Sally's hand. "Thank you, Sally. I would like nothing more than to have you brush my hair."

With a hard swallow, Sally nodded and promptly got to work.

Two hours later, dressed in a dark green skirt and high-necked, cream-colored lace blouse with a cameo pinned at her throat, Caroline stepped into the elevators of her grandfather's building.

"Good morning again, miss." The attendant seemed to recognize her from her previous visit. He'd been running the elevator that day, too.

"Good morning." She smiled at the older gentleman. He struck up a conversation about the weather, which gave her an opportunity to study him more closely. He had a full shock of white hair, matching handlebar mustache, and the kindest eyes she'd ever seen. There was wisdom in their depths. She doubted much got past him. "Is Mr. St. James in his office yet?"

"Yes, ma'am, he arrived at seven o'clock as usual."

A full hour ahead of her. She made a mental note to arrive earlier tomorrow morning. If her grandfather could get himself to the office at the crack of dawn, then so could she.

"And Mr. Marcus St. James? Is he here as well?"

The attendant's lips pulled together in a tight smile. "No, miss, he doesn't usually arrive for several more hours." He focused on the elevator door. "But Mr. Montgomery is here."

The comment confirmed what Caroline had already suspected. Jackson and her grandfather ran the company, not father and son. How would she ever get to know her uncle, and thus find out whether he was behind the intercepted letters, if he wasn't in the office on a regular basis? Perhaps she should have taken her grandfather up on the offer to live in his home after all.

No, that would have been the very worst beginning. If she was to build a lasting relationship with her family, she needed to do so carefully, slowly, deepening the connections over time.

The thought pulled her up short, and she twisted her hands together at her waist. Did she want a lasting relationship with her grandfather, with any of her family?

Yes, yes she did. Desperately.

Somewhere between her entry through Ellis Island and the discovery that Richard St. James had not abandoned his daughter, Caroline had discovered a desire to open her heart, just a little. To find a place where she belonged.

Home. Family.

Permanence.

What did she know about any of that? She knew she wanted all three.

You do not receive because you do not ask. Was Mary right? Was the secret to Caroline's happiness as basic as a prayer? No. God hadn't answered her prayers before. She dared not hope He would do so now.

The elevator bounced to a halt.

"We're here, miss. The fifteenth floor." The attendant reached across her to pull back the metal gate.

"Oh, yes, I . . ." Caroline shook her head. "I realize I don't know your name."

"It's Harold, miss."

"Thank you, Harold."

"Go on, now." He nudged her out of the elevator. "The boss is waiting."

Refusing to give in to the sudden bout of nerves, she brightened her smile, adjusted her attitude, and stepped onto the landing.

Jackson stood waiting for her. Of course. The man always seemed to arrive just when she needed an ally. Solid. Handsome. Present. When had the fragile line between enemy and adversary transformed into something more like comrade and friend?

Here we go again. As was becoming their habit, they spent the next few heartbeats staring at one another. The memory of their remarkable kisses—not kiss, *kisses*—had her releasing a shaky sigh.

Her heart picked up speed. Her mouth went dry. Her thoughts collided together into one big knot of confusing, unrelated words.

Smiling, Jackson reached out his hand to her. She took it, felt something akin to pins and needles shoot through her.

"You're early," he said, tucking her hand around his arm, a hint of respect in his voice.

A pang of guarded tenderness spread through her lungs. "You're earlier."

"So I am." From beneath his dusky lashes his gaze moved across her face. The contemplative pull of his eyebrows made her wonder if he even realized he was studying her so closely.

"Since we have the same destination"—he turned her in the direction of her grandfather's office—"we might as well proceed together."

Proceed together, as if they were a single unit heading toward a common goal. They were, of course, if only on a temporary basis.

A sense of belonging swept through Caroline, making her feel as though this was exactly where she was supposed to be at this very moment in time.

Home. Family. Permanence.

Dare she hope all three were within her reach?

Oh, Lord, please, I so want . . .

She had no idea how to finish the prayer. What did she want? And from whom? Jackson?

Alarm tripped along her spine, stealing her breath. She wasn't supposed to be this connected to a man who was so completely out of her reach.

Even without her cousin in the picture, they weren't well suited. Yet, for now, at this brief moment, their steps were in sync, each of them moving in silent accord with the other, as if they'd walked this path before. And would do so again.

Caroline cast a quick glance in his direction, not at all surprised to find that he was equally lost in thought.

Jackson pulled them to a halt outside her grandfather's office. "Ready for this?"

With his solid presence by her side, she was ready for anything. "I am."

He smiled, a tender sweet lift of his lips. "I believe that you are."

After a cursory knock, Jackson twisted the knob, and they stepped inside the office together.

Despite her earlier calm, her feet turned to lead and her thoughts were riddled with doubts. Her life changed today. Her entire future hung in the balance. The only thing that helped her take a step deeper into the room was the knowledge that she wasn't alone. She had her grandfather on her side. And Jackson.

She had Jackson on her side, too.

* * *

Out of the corner of his eye, Jackson watched Caroline closely. Sensing her nerves, he kept his arm linked with hers. A silent show of support. She'd grown uncharacteristically quiet since they'd entered Richard's office.

Richard set down his pen and stood. "I see you two have found one another."

An odd choice of words. "I ran into Caroline by the elevators." Jackson didn't add that he'd been awaiting her arrival, thinking she might need, perhaps even want, his support this morning.

He hadn't been wrong. She was still holding on to him, and he wasn't about to let her go, either.

Richard smiled at his granddaughter. "I'm pleased by your punctuality."

She didn't try to brush aside the compliment but accepted it with a nod of her head. "What can I say? I'm eager to begin."

"Then it's fortuitous you ran into Jackson." Richard leaned back against his desk and waved the two into the matching chairs facing his desk. They extricated themselves from one another and took their seats.

"He'll be in charge of your orientation today," Richard continued, "assuming that's satisfactory with you both?"

They each nodded their agreement.

"Does this mean I won't see you at all today?" Caroline's shoulders slumped slightly forward, the only sign of her disappointment. "I had hoped to spend at least a portion of the day with you."

"As had I, but something has come up, an issue with a client that needs my personal attention." He straightened to his full height. "I will make it up to you tomorrow."

"That will be fine." She sounded disappointed.

"Do you have any particular thoughts as to where I should begin Caroline's education?" Jackson asked.

Richard lobbed the question back at him. "What would you suggest?"

He'd been thinking on the matter for some time and had decided on several plans of attack. He quickly sorted through them in his head and then made his decision. "An overview of all our holdings would be a wise place to start, then perhaps a tour of—"

"The tenement houses on the Lower East Side," Caroline finished for him.

He wasn't surprised she'd want to start there. Of course, now that John Reilly was making unannounced visits on Jackson's behalf, it wasn't necessary they go there today. But if Caroline wanted to start her tour of their properties on Orchard Street, then that was where they would start. Jackson looked at Richard and lifted a questioning brow.

The older man glanced out the window. "I see the rain has let up. You might as well start with the tour first, before the streets become too crowded. You can review the holdings after lunch." He turned to Caroline. "Do those plans meet with your approval?"

"Yes, perfectly."

"Then you two better be on your way." Richard all but physically pushed them into the empty hallway. The door slammed neatly behind them.

"Well," Caroline said with a laugh. "That was certainly succinct."

Yes, Richard had made himself perfectly clear. But Jackson wasn't sure he was ready to listen to what the man had to say, least of all the words that hadn't been spoken. "We should head out. We have a long day ahead of us."

She pivoted to her left and paced toward the elevators once again. Jackson placed his hands on her shoulders and turned her in the opposite direction. "We have to stop by my office first."

"Oh."

"It's that way." He gestured to the left.

Without further objection, she set out. He felt his mouth kick up in a grin as his gaze landed on the back of her head. She'd twisted her hair in one of those complicated styles that made a man want to spend hours unraveling each and every knot. These were not the thoughts he should be having about this particular woman.

Treat her like any other ordinary employee.

Right. Good, solid advice. Except he didn't have that much imagination. Caroline St. James was the least ordinary person of his acquaintance.

"Wait here," he told her outside his office.

Now that he thought about it, Jackson decided that touring their properties first *was* the wisest course of action. The last thing he needed was time alone with this woman in his office, or any other confined space.

Even if Elizabeth wasn't the woman for him—and he was fast accepting that foregone conclusion—that didn't mean he was meant to be with Caroline, either. With her continued devotion to her mother, and her easy acceptance of her grandfather, she demonstrated a strength of character that left Jackson in awe.

Caroline St. James knew more about mercy and grace than Jackson ever would.

Somewhere, in the deepest, darkest recesses of his mind, he accepted that she deserved a far better man than him.

Chapter Twenty-Four

It wasn't until they were a few blocks from Orchard Street that Caroline requested a change in their itinerary. Since Mary and her family would have already left for work, there didn't seem much point in starting the day there.

"You know, Jackson, I've been thinking. I already have an intimate knowledge of the tenement houses." She'd lived in one for two weeks, after all. "Perhaps we could tour the garment factory first."

Jackson's well-cut lips curved, his molten, sky-at-midday eyes lighting with interest at her request. "Any particular reason for the change?"

His presence filled the tiny confines of the motorcar. His scent, his voice, his intensity, and those eyes. Full of genuine curiosity, as if he truly cared to hear her answer.

Deciding honesty was the best route, Caroline lifted a shoulder. "Mary is employed as a seamstress at a competitor's factory." Remembering her friend's sickly pallor, she tried to put a cool, carefree note in her voice but failed miserably. "I wish to see the sort of environment in which she works."

More to the point, if Caroline discovered her grandfather ran a business like the one where Mary worked, then she would see to it that better conditions were put into place at once.

"You might be surprised by what you see."

"I hope so." She certainly didn't want to discover that her grandfather took advantage of his employees, most of them immigrants like Mary and her family.

Seemingly satisfied with her answer, Jackson gave a brief nod. "Very well, then, as you wish."

Hand on the partition, he leaned forward and redirected the chauffer to take them to the garment factory he and Richard owned. Caroline kept her head lowered so neither man would see the flash of worry in her eyes, worry over what she would find.

Prepared to confront unhealthy working conditions, she was pleasantly surprised to discover quite the opposite inside the four-story building complex on Walker Street. Bypassing the store on the first floor, Jackson led Caroline into the factory.

"Due to the unbearable heat inside this building, we have our employees work on rotating shifts. The idea is for them to take alternating breaks every two hours." He escorted her to the edge of the work floor. "We allow our workers to come and go, and we never lock the doors."

Caroline looked around. Men and women worked in tandem, some sewing, some ironing, some pinning paper patterns atop fabric. A host of different languages filled the air. For the most part, everyone seemed rather . . . cheerful. "I was expecting—"

"Abysmal conditions?"

She lifted a shoulder.

"In other factories that might be true. But your grandfather and I have discovered that a lenient, comfortable work environment results in overall higher output."

"I'm pleased." Mary had told such a harrowing tale. That was it, then. Caroline would put Mary and her family to work in this factory as soon as humanly possible. She would make it her life's mission to learn every facet of the garment industry and find ways to improve this factory.

With Jackson making the introductions, Caroline spoke to several workers, moving through the building at a slow yet systematic pace. At the end of the tour, she felt herself relax. The factory did, indeed, provide a clean, safe environment for the workers.

Back outside, Jackson took her hand as he directed her toward the motorcar. He held on casually, as if it was the most natural thing in the world to do. Her heart took a quick extra thump.

"Where to next?" she asked, her voice a bit shakier than usual.

"The Duchess Illustrated Magazine of Fashion."

"My grandfather owns a women's fashion magazine?"

Jackson nodded. "It is one of the many joint ventures our families own together."

How absolutely fascinating. Caroline hadn't come across that piece of information in her research. She knew the periodical well. Sally had bullied her into poring over several issues, as well as a few *McCall's*.

"Around 1876 our individual grandmothers founded the magazine together," Jackson explained. "They saw it as a way to promote their fledgling dress-pattern business."

"My grandmother was friends with Granny?"

Jackson helped her into the car. "The best."

Why hadn't Granny told Caroline this? She would have to ask her when she returned home that evening.

Since they both seemed lost in thought, the ride to West Thirty-Seventh Street was accomplished in relative silence. Neither Caroline nor Jackson made any attempt at conversation. After being so in tune with one another earlier in the day, the strained atmosphere left her uneasy.

Perhaps strained was a bit overly dramatic. Caroline wouldn't call the mood between them uncomfortable, precisely, just—maybe—perhaps—a bit—melancholy.

Where had this change come from?

Setting aside the question, she allowed her excitement to build as she exited the car outside a nondescript building and waited for Jackson to lead the way. The wind kicked up, ruffling the dark hair around his ridiculously handsome face. A single, shuddering breath escaped her lungs.

He guided her into the building with a hand at the small of her back. "The printing facilities are on the main floor, the pattern-division offices and mail-order department one below." He urged her toward a stairwell. "We'll begin our tour at the top this time and work our way down."

"What's on the top floor?" she asked, beginning the climb with Jackson by her side.

His smile turned indulgent. "It's where the staff artists create the drawings for the magazine's current fashion spreads. The same artwork is then translated into patterns, as well as prototypes of the individual dresses."

Caroline drew to a stop. "You seem to know a lot about the daily operations of this magazine."

"I know a lot about the daily operations of all our businesses."

His answer didn't surprise her. "Why is the art department on the top floor?"

"It gets the best light. Or so I've been told." He pressed his palm flat on the metal door and swung it open. "After you."

Caroline entered the long, narrow room and immediately noticed the wall of windows on either side. Slanted desks, or easels as they were called, were lined up in two rows twenty deep. Mostly men worked at the desks, with the rare woman peppered throughout. The employees all wore neckties. Their shirtsleeves were rolled past their elbows, as if to avoid getting them smudged. Seemingly focused on their work, they concentrated on adding color to their drawings.

At the end of the room, two men studied a handful of the finished drawings.

Caroline watched the work, enraptured by the process.

"Come." Jackson took her hand. "Let me introduce you to the art director."

Hand still clasped with hers, Jackson pulled her to the back of the room. "Monsieur Lappet, this is Caroline St. James, Richard's grand-daughter from London. She only recently arrived in America and has come to tour our magazine."

Lappet proceeded to circle Caroline slowly. "But you are dressed all wrong." He came back around to face her directly. "You must never wear that hideous shade of green. It is worse than gray and makes you look matronly."

Caroline tried not to be insulted.

"You are too beautiful for such a dour color. You will come with me. We have much work to do." He took her hand and dragged her through the room. He stopped at a shut door and turned to frown at Jackson. "You will leave us now."

Jackson shrugged at the dismissal. "I want her back in an hour."

"*Oui. Oui.*"

Still holding her hand, Lappet pulled Caroline into a large, airy room with high ceilings and open rafters and shut the door behind them. Jackson's chuckle wafted through the layers of veneer and wood, the sound making Caroline smile.

She glanced around her and gasped. On display were beautiful gowns of varying shapes, styles, and colors, draped over tables, hanging on the wall, placed over dress mannequins. A woman's dream come true, especially a woman who'd spent most of her life scraping for food and barely surviving.

Rendered speechless, Caroline moved through the room, then stopped at a pink-and-white concoction. She touched the intricate col-lar, circling around the mannequin in a similar fashion as Monsieur Lappet had done with her.

"Not that one." Lappet directed her to the middle of the room. "This one."

Caroline gasped again. The dress before her was made of a rich, silky blue material the color of Jackson's eyes. "It's . . . I have no words."

Lappet beamed at her. "Shall we try it on?"

Understanding that *we* meant *her*, Caroline hesitated. It didn't seem right to do anything but look at the lovely creation. The garment was a work of art. She was a survivor of the mean streets of London. They didn't belong together, she and this beautiful dress.

"Indulge me."

Caroline gave in to temptation.

Lappet disappeared from the room while two of his attendants worked silently, their hands fast and skilled as they helped Caroline out of one set of garments and into another.

They soon stepped back and studied their handiwork. A few more pokes and pulls and then . . .

They sighed in unison.

"It is a perfect fit," one of them whispered, while the other called out to Monsieur Lappet.

The art director sailed into the room and slid his narrowed gaze up and down. He said nothing for several long moments.

When she could stand the suspense no longer, Caroline broke the silence. "Well?"

A slow smile slipped past his lips. "*I* am a genius. And *you* are utterly flawless."

"May I see?"

"But of course." He escorted her to a freestanding mirror.

Caroline blinked at her reflection. And blinked. And blinked. She'd been transformed.

"You must have that dress," Lappet declared.

She'd come to America to seek justice for her mother, not to take advantage of her birthright. "I . . . thank you, Monsieur, but I cannot possibly accept your generous offer. This dress belongs to the magazine."

He brushed her argument aside with a sniff. "And your family owns this magazine. The dress is already yours."

She dropped her head and sighed. Of its own volition, her hand slid across the smooth silk. Maybe . . . just this once . . .

Lappet placed his hands on her shoulders. "Miss St. James, all of New York knows your family owns this magazine. When you are at the opera or the theater or perhaps a private dinner party, you will be expected to dress in the latest fashion."

As she turned back to stare at her reflection, Caroline remembered what Elizabeth had said the other day about her clothes coming from Paris. Whatever was the girl thinking, when such talented craftsmanship lay so close at hand? "Why do you not have Elizabeth wear your creations?"

Lappet's gaze darkened. "She allows her mother to choose her clothing." Head lowered, he smoothed a nonexistent wrinkle from the skirt. "You will do this for me, yes? You will wear my creations around town?"

Oh, he was good. *Very good.* Putting this on her as though she were the one doing him the favor. "You make a compelling argument, Monsieur Lappet."

He patted her hand in a fatherly manner. "Then say yes."

"You have convinced me." She withdrew her hand and patted him on the cheek. "I will wear this dress tonight at a private party I am scheduled to attend with my grandfather. However, I walk out of here today in my original ensemble."

"But of course." Lappet's eyes turned sharp and measuring, his gaze narrowed in calculation. "On one condition."

She lifted a single eyebrow.

"You must promise to burn that ghastly green monstrosity the moment you arrive home today."

Chapter Twenty-Five

Jackson escorted Caroline off the elevator. "I don't understand why you won't tell me what you and Monsieur Lappet discussed during your time together."

She tried not to smile at his annoyed tone. He sounded almost jealous. Wasn't that something?

"I told you, Jackson, it's a secret."

His mouth curved downward, making him look far too boyish and appealing. "Secret, indeed," he muttered. "I can only imagine what sort of secrets you two shared."

Now he really sounded jealous.

She started to take pity on him and tell him about the new dress she was to wear that night but was interrupted by the sound of footsteps heading their way.

Her uncle came around the corner, caught sight of her, and quickly turned back around without breaking stride.

Oh, no. No, no. He was not getting away that easily.

"Uncle Marcus, wait." Caroline trotted after him. "I would like a word with you, if you don't mind."

"Sorry, my dear, no time at the present." He kept his head down, his feet pumping, his tone curt. "Important meeting and all that."

"But surely you could spare a few minutes."

"No, not even one." He brushed aside her request with a flick of his wrist. "As it is, I'm already late for my meeting."

Yet he was heading in the opposite direction of the elevators. Caroline was no fool. No question, her uncle was avoiding her and walking so fast she would have to break into a run very soon if she wanted to keep up with him.

Giving in to defeat, for now, she stopped her pursuit. "Another time, then."

"Certainly, my dear, another time. Most certainly. Most certainly." He shut his office door with a bang. Had she managed to keep pace with him, she would be fishing wood out of her teeth this very minute.

Furious and frustrated and . . . and . . . *furious*, Caroline waited until Jackson joined her in the hallway, then spun around to face him. "Did you catch all that?"

"Every word." He took her arm and drew her down the hallway, away from her uncle's office.

Although her uncle's avoidance of her didn't necessarily make him guilty of anything, it certainly made him appear suspicious. She glanced at Jackson, saw that his mind was working as quickly as hers. "That was quite the telling encounter, wouldn't you agree?"

"It most certainly was, my dear." Jackson lowered his voice to a growl. "Most certainly. *Most certainly.*"

* * *

Jackson arrived at the VanDercreek home early, precisely as he'd planned. Although he would like nothing better than to confront Marcus St. James about his odd behavior this afternoon, Jackson had a more important task to accomplish first. To do that, he needed to be inside this house before any of the other guests. If by chance someone spoke ill of Caroline or Richard or any of the St. James family, Jackson would hear and be better able to stop the gossip before it spread.

Giving himself a moment to organize his thoughts, he looked up at the mansion. He wished Granny would have come with him tonight, if for no other reason than to provide another ally for Caroline. But the old girl had been fighting the sniffles—her word—and Jackson hadn't pushed.

Much rode on this evening. More, perhaps, than Caroline realized. One person. All it would take was one person to decide she wasn't who she seemed, and the gossip would begin.

This need to protect her good name was familiar territory for Jackson, a role he'd played since the day his father had sailed for Europe with his wife's sister on his arm. And his pockets full of Warren Griffin's money.

Jackson braced for the familiar rage that came with thoughts of his father. Nothing came. No rage. No shame. No desire to confront the man who had made his life nearly impossible to bear at times. He felt no more animosity toward his father. And he knew the reason why.

Caroline St. James.

Her influence had left a mark on him. Knowing her, spending time with her, had changed him at his core. His anger, his attitude, even his heart had begun to soften. What had started as a desire to live a life above reproach had nearly turned him into an unforgiving, judgmental man. In his attempt to avoid becoming his father, he'd almost become a bitter, hard-hearted person like his mother.

Jackson had never longed to experience the thrill of the unknown. He'd preferred the comfortable rhythm of a scheduled, mapped-out existence. But now, he wanted more than routine. He wanted surprises. Spontaneity. In short, he wanted Caroline. In his life. For the next seventy-five years, for a start.

He planned to tell her just that. *After* he had a long-overdue conversation with Elizabeth.

Accepting what he must do, he entered the VanDercreek home. Tonight every St. James would be in one room together. It would be the perfect time to watch them interact and maybe—God willing—Jackson would uncover which member of the family had wanted to harm Caroline's mother and, by default, Caroline.

After being directed to the drawing room on the second floor, Jackson stopped cold at the threshold. Despite his early arrival, several of the VanDercreeks' guests were already in attendance, including Marcus, Katherine, and Elizabeth. All three were in conversation with their hosts.

The elderly couple was as elegant and poised as Jackson remembered, dressed impeccably in complementary black and gold. Their position as pillars of New York society had made them the perfect dinner hosts for Caroline's unofficial introduction into society.

As if sensing his arrival, Elizabeth shifted slightly toward the doorway, caught sight of him, and released a sweet smile, the same one she'd always given him. Tonight, as he had at the Griffin ball, he noticed the blandness in the gesture, the almost vacant look in her eyes. No, not vacant, just distant, cool, uninterested. In him. Elizabeth was completely uninterested in him. As he was in her.

Had that lack of connection always been there between them? Had Elizabeth's blue eyes always incited only a mild reaction in him? In comparison, Caroline's direct, unwavering gaze had a way of accelerating his heartbeat, giving him glimpses of what could be—what *should* be—between a man and woman planning to spend the rest of their lives together.

Elizabeth was no different tonight than she'd ever been. Jackson was the one who'd changed. He still adored the girl, as a man might adore his sister. Looking at her with new eyes, he realized she was as pretty as she'd always been, in a girlish sort of way, and perfectly respectable, which were some of the reasons he'd chosen her for his bride.

A mistake he had to rectify tonight.

Now.

He started toward her. "Ah, Jackson, there you are." Marcus gestured him over. "We were just discussing *Figaro*, one of your favorites, I understand."

"It is," he agreed, taking note that Elizabeth looked everywhere but at him.

Luke had been right. She hated *Figaro*.

For the next few moments, Jackson suffered the usual pleasantries, then—*finally*—once a lull occurred in the conversation, he focused his full attention on Elizabeth.

"You are looking especially pretty this evening."

"Thank you, Jackson. That is very kind of you to say."

More tedious pleasantries ensued before their hosts wandered off to greet a handful of new arrivals. Marcus and Katherine joined them, leaving Jackson alone with Elizabeth.

This was by no means the first time the two of them had been left on their own. Yet tonight Jackson found himself at a complete loss for words. If Caroline had been the one standing beside him, he would have come up with any number of topics to discuss. Unfortunately, he had so little in common with Elizabeth there was simply nothing to say now that the usual topics had been exhausted.

Who was this young woman standing before him?

Dressed in a white gown, she wore some sort of a mesh shawl artfully wrapped around her shoulders. The gauzy effect was spectacular, the perfect frame for her flawless face and deep blue eyes. She looked utterly untouchable, a living, breathing work of art.

And Jackson found himself completely unmoved.

It was time to set things right. He took her hand and guided her to a settee.

"Tell me about your day," he said, hoping to ease into the topic for her sake. A man didn't tell a woman he didn't want to marry her without some sort of preamble.

Elizabeth simply blinked at him, owl-eyed, as if he'd asked her to mentally calculate a complicated mathematics equation. "I . . ." Her face fell. "I don't know how to answer your question."

Remorse squeezed his heart, and he gentled his tone, redirecting the question. "What did you do with your time today?"

"Well, I . . ." She stopped and thought a moment, her lips pulling together in a frown. "Are you sure you care to hear?"

"Most definitely."

"I, that is, I—" She cut herself off and shook her head. "Honestly, I didn't do anything worth mentioning."

Sensing her anguish, he took her gloved fingers in his hand and squeezed gently. "Surely that can't be true."

"But it is." Despite her obvious despair, her expression changed to chagrin, which quickly turned to irritation. "I"—she jumped up— "need to walk."

"I'll accompany you."

"Fine." The irritation in her eyes settled in her voice. "Come along, then, if that is what you want."

He took her arm and guided her to a plant-filled balcony just off the drawing room, but still in sight of the other guests.

Elizabeth's agitation grew with each step. Once they were out of earshot of the rest of the party, he urged her to sit again, this time on a brocade-covered settee. "Elizabeth, I apologize. My question about your day was not meant to upset you."

"Oh, Jackson, you haven't upset me."

He raised an eyebrow.

"Well, yes, I suppose you did. But not in the way you might imagine." Looking even more disturbed than before, she rubbed her palms together in an absent manner. "This conversation has been coming on for some time."

Everything in him stilled. "Has it?"

Gaze darting around the room, Elizabeth avoided direct eye contact with him. "The realization that my life is meaningless is only part of the problem."

"Your life isn't meaningless."

"Don't patronize me, Jackson. We both know my days have no real purpose." A sheen of tears filled her eyes. "I spend most of my time at teas, luncheons, parties, or getting ready for one of the former. I do nothing of consequence."

"I thought you liked attending teas and luncheons and—"

She glared at him, effectively stopping the flow of his argument. "Did you know Grandfather has asked Caroline to work with him and learn the family business?"

"Yes."

A choked sob slipped past her lips. "He's never asked me to come to the office with him, not once."

There was a reason for that, of course, one Jackson needed to gently point out without hurting her feelings in the process.

"Elizabeth." He placed his hand over hers, effectively stilling their agitated wringing. "Would you have gone to the office if your grandfather had asked it of you?"

"I . . ." She released a humorless laugh. "No, I don't suppose I would have. But now, I am rethinking . . . everything." She pulled her bottom lip between her teeth. "Maybe I should go with him to work. Maybe I should at least try to be interested in what you men do all day long."

"Elizabeth. Where is all this coming from?"

Looking at him with a pained expression, she drew in a shaky breath. "My mother reminded me that *I* was the one Grandfather adored before Caroline showed up. It's not fair that she should be given favored treatment over me."

Jackson's left eye twitched at the words, words that didn't sound anything like Elizabeth. Her mother had been influencing her opinions, her thoughts, urging the poor girl to view her cousin as a rival, in a way she wouldn't have done on her own. Until this turn of events, Jackson had suspected Marcus of ruining his own sister's life. Had it been Katherine all along? Or had the two worked in tandem?

"Do you resent Caroline?"

"No. Oh, Jackson, that's the strangest part of all." She pulled her hand free and clapped it to her heart, shaking her head vigorously. "No matter what Mother says, I like my cousin. Very much. I think we could be great friends."

"I believe so, too."

A look of gratitude filled her gaze. "Thank you for saying that."

"I mean it. You two would be good for each other." It was true. Caroline would teach Elizabeth the value of knowing her own mind. And Elizabeth would help Caroline enjoy the simpler, less serious things in life: teas, parties, perhaps a shopping trip or two.

Wishing to communicate his sincerity, he took Elizabeth's hand in his and felt . . . nothing. He loved Elizabeth too much to continue allowing her to think there was more in his heart for her than affection. He had to tell her the truth.

"Elizabeth, you should know, I won't be asking you to marry me."

The relief that came with the words staggered him.

"Oh, thank you." Elizabeth pulled her hand free, lifted her gaze to the heavens, and breathed a heartfelt sigh. "Thank you, Lord."

"You are not upset?"

She let out a tinkling laugh. "You have no idea how much I don't want to marry you."

He should have felt insulted, and maybe he did a little. No man wanted to be told he was an undesirable mate, even by a woman he had no desire to marry.

His face must have shown a portion of what he was feeling, because Elizabeth placed her hand on his arm and laughed again. "You should see your face. I didn't mean to be so blunt. I suppose my cousin has worn off on me."

"So it would seem."

Frowning, Elizabeth pulled her hand back into her lap. "It's not that you won't make someone a good husband, but that someone is not me. We are very ill suited, you know."

He did know. It had been a mistake to think otherwise.

Now that she'd gotten a taste of speaking her mind, words tumbled out of Elizabeth's mouth at breakneck speed. "We will always be friends, Jackson, you believe that, yes?"

"Yes. Always."

"And you know that I love you very much." She lifted her hand to keep him from interrupting. "As a brother, of course."

"Of course."

She continued speaking, barely taking a breath. "I only wish for you to be happy."

"I wish the same for you."

"We will never speak of marriage between us again."

"Never." Free. He was *free*. He hadn't felt so light, so awake, so completely himself in a very long time. Maybe ever.

Elizabeth continued talking, asking questions at a rapid-fire rate that required an occasional one-word answer from him.

Only half listening now, Jackson became acutely aware of his surroundings; every sound, every scent, made him feel more alive than before.

"Jackson, did you hear what I said?"

"I . . . no."

"I said"—her hand clasped his arm and squeezed—"you have been looking for a wife in the wrong place, in the *safe* place."

Her words jolted him because they were completely, unexpectedly, irrevocably true.

Dropping her hand, she continued. "I think we both know whom you should marry."

"We . . ." He swallowed. "We do?"

Looking very pleased with herself, Elizabeth nodded sagely. "It's Caroline, naturally. Oh, Jackson, you must marry my cousin, Caroline."

Chapter Twenty-Six

Caroline arrived at the VanDercreek dinner party in the best possible way, on her grandfather's arm. He looked very handsome in his elegant evening attire, the white bow tie a perfect foil for his thick silver head of hair.

After a bit of a debate with Sally, Caroline had chosen to wear the blue silk creation Monsieur Lappet had delivered personally to Granny's an hour earlier. Not because the color was Jackson's favorite, but . . .

Oh, all right, yes, she was willing to admit, if only in the secret recesses of her mind, that turning Jackson's head had been the main reason she'd donned the exquisite gown. She'd never felt more confident and beautiful than at this moment.

As if her grandfather had planned a spectacular entrance, they were the last to arrive at the party. They entered the drawing room where the other guests had already assembled for the evening. She knew most of the people in the room—family, friends, with only a smattering of strangers.

A second glance told her there were two people conspicuously absent from the room. Her heart stalled in her chest, clenching in a brief moment of pain. Where were Jackson and Elizabeth?

Was tonight the night? Would he declare himself to her cousin at last?

No, he wouldn't do such a thing, not here. Not at a dinner party given in Caroline's honor. That would be a serious breach of etiquette, something he would never do.

For once, she was grateful for the man's rigid adherence to society's rules. It would be hard enough to watch him openly court her cousin, twice as wretched if he started tonight, after they'd shared such a wonderful day together.

She knew she would have to face the inevitability of his marriage to Elizabeth. But not yet. Not tonight.

Misreading her slight tremble, her grandfather patted her hand encouragingly. "Think of tonight as a game of chance." He pulled her closer to his side. "And you have an unbeatable hand."

The analogy did nothing to soothe her nerves but rather served as a reminder of how she'd gotten here, the sins she'd committed and could never take back.

"Breathe, Caroline, you have gone quite pale."

"Have I?" She tried to appear surprised by the comment. "It's a bit hot in here, don't you think?"

"I'm sure that must be it. Come." He directed her to their left. "Allow me to introduce you around."

They made their way through the room, stopping every so often to trade meaningless conversation with various members of the dinner party. When they arrived at her aunt and uncle, she reminded herself why she'd traveled to America in the first place.

To seek justice. For her mother.

Caroline had allowed herself to become distracted by a hope for a future that could never be hers until she settled the past.

Schooling her expression into a serene smile, she focused on the likely culprit. Her uncle. His suspicious behavior that afternoon had left little doubt.

Her uncle's returning smile seemed genuine tonight, as did her aunt's. But one of them—or perhaps both—had betrayed her mother in a most horrible manner.

As if to add to her anxiety, the hair on her neck prickled. Out of the corner of her eye she noted Jackson's return to the center of the room. Elizabeth clung to his arm, smiling warmly, placidly, as if she hadn't a care in the world. Why would she? She had Jackson by her side.

A white-hot surge of jealousy rose so suddenly, so vividly, Caroline was afraid it must show on her face. Ashamed at her reaction, at the ugly emotion running through her, she reminded herself that she had not come to America to find love, or a place to call home, or anything that felt soft and warm and permanent.

Knowing that her mind needed to be on her goal, Caroline was unable to stop herself from glancing at Jackson again. Their gazes locked, and even from this distance it felt like a physical blow. Her breathing deepened; her stomach dipped.

But, really, he shouldn't look at her like . . . that.

And yet, *and yet* . . . nothing. Caroline forcibly returned her attention to her aunt and uncle.

In the same moment, the dining room doors were thrown open in a dramatic fashion.

"That's our cue," her grandfather whispered in her ear with the tenderness and affection she'd craved all her life.

She lowered her gaze and sighed. Home. Permanence. Both were within her grasp, she realized, not in the form of a physical structure, or even a city, but in her grandfather, in her own flesh and blood.

Her mother had always claimed Caroline was very much like Richard St. James. Caroline had thought that a great insult, a reminder that she was a sinful, naughty child who refused to listen. Now, she realized, her mother had been giving her a compliment.

Once inside the dining room, when it became evident they weren't sitting beside one another, Caroline went in search of her place.

Her uncle came up beside her, took her arm, and directed her to the opposite side of the table. "It would appear," he said, indicating the placard with her name on it and the one next to it, "that we have been placed beside one another."

"What a happy coincidence," she said. An invisible fist squeezed her lungs, but she pasted a smile on her lips. "Now we may most certainly get to know one another better."

More to the point, this was her opportunity to see if he would reveal his hand. The office would have provided more privacy, but that hadn't worked out well for her.

While the first course was served, they spoke of inconsequential things. Several times Caroline caught Jackson watching her from the other side of the table. He sat several chairs down, next to her aunt, his gaze tracking in Caroline's direction far more often than was polite.

He was different tonight. Or rather, the way he watched her was different—bolder, less inhibited, as if he didn't care if anyone noticed that he couldn't keep his eyes off her.

Her breath caught in her throat.

Caroline wasn't making much of an effort to avoid his gaze, until she looked directly at her cousin. Her stomach knotted. Elizabeth simply smiled at her, a silent message in her eyes.

What was she trying to tell Caroline?

Her gaze drifted back to Jackson. Still smiling, Elizabeth looked from one to the other. And then, to Caroline's complete and utter shock, her cousin winked at her.

Caroline looked quickly away, wondering what *that* had been about.

"With all the chaos of the last few days," Marcus said. "I haven't told you how sorry I am about your mother."

Caroline wanted honesty, not contrition.

"I'm sorry for the way she died."

At the sound of Marcus's voice breaking over the words, she turned her head to look at him directly. His face held no signs of emotion. None she could decipher, at any rate, and that concerned her. She could read a total stranger's motives within minutes. Her uncle was proving a different matter entirely. Was she looking too hard? Had she lost her objectivity?

Terrifying thought.

"Thank you. I admit, I miss her. So very much." For some reason, she was unable to hide her sorrow from this man. "More so with each passing day."

"I . . ." He pulled in a hard breath. "I miss her, too."

Caroline swallowed audibly. She heard the pain in her uncle's voice, and the regret, and believed his sincerity. "Were you two . . . close?"

"Very." His eyes closed a moment. "When she ran off, the loss was unbearable at first. With time, it became less so. Never easy, but tolerable."

She could sense his agony.

"Even when it seemed she wanted nothing to do with us, I still insisted we name Elizabeth after her. Did you know that?"

Caroline had assumed it had been her grandfather's idea to name her cousin after Libby. Now, Marcus claimed it was his.

Was her uncle speaking from his heart or his guilt? Suspicion crowded into her thoughts, but for the moment, she pushed it aside.

She was here to uncover the truth, not offer absolution. Why could she not remember that? What was it about this man's evident pain that made her want to give him comfort?

"It must have been devastating to think your sister had abandoned her own family for a life in London." She spoke in generalities, in case someone at the table deigned to eavesdrop on their conversation.

Shoulders slumped, Marcus pushed his plate slightly forward, the gesture a clear indication he couldn't stomach food right now. "It never made any sense to me, her staying behind when she loved her life here."

His sincerity only added to Caroline's confusion. She felt the first stirrings of doubt, and her instincts told her to believe her uncle. She knew better, of course. But still . . .

"I knew about the man she chose to love, but what of it?" Sad, baffled eyes turned to Caroline and, like her, Marcus kept his voice low. "We would have weathered the scandal if she'd wanted to come home."

Caroline filled her lungs, the effort a challenge. She didn't want to speak of this anymore. But she'd started them down this path. "I . . . It's hard to be here," she admitted, lowering her voice to such a soft level he had to bend his head to hear. "Walking in the world where she once lived, wondering what she would have been like had she been allowed . . . had she returned."

"You look like her, you know." There was a ragged edge to his words now. "It's very unsettling."

Understanding dawned at last. "Is that why you have avoided me, because I remind you of her?"

"Yes. I'm sorry for this afternoon, my dear. My behavior was rather . . . cowardly."

The honest answer made her bolder. She'd caught her uncle at a vulnerable moment. What better time to ask the inevitable question. "Are you the one who intercepted my mother's letters, the ones she wrote to your father?"

Taken aback, eyes blinking rapidly, Marcus looked at her, confused, angry, and maybe a little lost. "Libby wrote home?"

Never taking her eyes off his, Caroline nodded. "She penned over three dozen letters through the years. All of them were sent back, unopened."

His gaze hard and unforgiving, Marcus narrowed his eyes. "Who would do such a thing?"

Who, indeed?

There was only one possibility left. As if drawn by some invisible force, Caroline's gaze met her aunt's from across the table. A momentary flicker of hatred swept into the other woman's eyes, so venomous Caroline nearly gasped aloud.

In the next instant, she felt a flood of fury. By her own admission, Katherine and Libby had been friends. Why had her aunt intercepted her mother's letters? Why?

What had she hoped to gain?

* * *

The moment Jackson saw Caroline's gaze lock with Katherine's he knew she'd discovered the truth. She'd been mere seconds behind him. Katherine had given herself away with a seemingly innocuous observation. *Libby made the ultimate mistake of choosing love over position.* When Jackson had asked her to explain what she meant, she'd hesitated a fraction of a second, then muttered beneath her breath that Libby had gotten what she deserved.

The rest had fallen into place from there.

Angered on Caroline's behalf, wanting to react, to lash out, to right this terrible wrong, Jackson swallowed hard and clamped his back teeth together.

This was not the time or place to exact justice.

Katherine St. James would answer for her sins. Jackson would see to it.

But not here. Not tonight.

Tonight belonged to Caroline. This was her official debut into society as a St. James. Nothing could be allowed to compromise her success this evening. Caroline deserved her moment of triumph, for all the hardships she'd endured as a child. His heart bled for the frightened street urchin she'd been, courageous enough to band with others like herself, doing whatever was necessary to survive.

He admired the woman she'd become. Believed in her. Loved her.

He *loved* Caroline St. James.

The realization hit him hard at first, then settled into an all-consuming need to protect her. Her aunt had better have a good explanation for what she'd done.

The rest of dinner proved endless. The food, as expected, was of the first order. The conversation maddening, thanks to the seating arrangement. He listened to Katherine St. James with cold, hard restraint, nodding when appropriate, wanting nothing more than to see her pay for what she'd done to Caroline and her mother.

A portion of his restraint slipped.

Clearly unaware of his internal battle, Katherine smiled at him benignly. No guilt in her eyes, no remorse. The woman had nerve.

"Did you and Elizabeth have a nice conversation?" She asked the question in her saccharine-sweet timbre that made the cream cake seem bland.

Why had he never noticed the grating sound of her voice before? Why did no one see what she truly was? Katherine St. James had always seemed the epitome of elegance and charm, a woman greatly admired among her peers.

Appearances could be deceiving. Jackson knew that now. In this new light, he noticed so many things about the older woman, things he'd missed or ignored before—the way her lips flattened whenever she looked in Caroline's direction, the angry angle of her shoulders.

"Yes. Elizabeth and I had a most interesting conversation. We discussed our future."

Her eyes widened at his blunt declaration, as well as the inappropriateness of tackling the topic at the dinner table, where anyone could hear their words.

A week ago, he wouldn't have brought up the subject at all, much less in such a public arena. Tonight, propriety took second place to the truth. "Or rather"—he leaned his head close to hers and lowered his voice to a deep, menacing pitch—"the lack of our future together."

Her spoon wobbled in her fingers, the only sign of her reaction to his words. "But, you can't mean—"

"Oh, but I do. Elizabeth and I will not become betrothed."

Her face paled. "But you are so well suited—a merger of our families would be advantageous to us all and—" Her mouth slammed shut.

But the damage had been done. Katherine had considered him a desirable match for her daughter because their marriage would have merged two business empires into one.

Jackson's stomach roiled in disgust. His plan to marry Elizabeth had never been about money or business. His pursuit of respectability had been genuine, if somewhat misguided.

Compelled, his gaze sought out Caroline's.

"*No.*" Katherine spat the word under her breath, ever mindful of keeping her voice low enough so only Jackson heard her. "Do not tell me you have thrown over my daughter for that . . . that . . . horrid creature."

Jackson balled his hand into a fist, then forced his fingers to relax and addressed the less volatile of the two accusations. "If you must know, Elizabeth rejected me."

"My daughter would never—"

"She would. And she did." And that was all he was going to say on the matter. "While I have your attention, let's talk about Caroline and her mother."

"I refuse to speak about either." She glanced around the table, lowered her voice to a hiss. "Not here."

"No, you are right. Not here. But know this"—he captured her gaze—"we will have the conversation before this night is through. I—"

A tinkling of silver to crystal cut off the rest of his words. Richard's voice lifted above the sound. "I wish to propose a toast."

Resigned to the interruption, Jackson picked up his glass and watched as everyone else followed suit, Katherine the last to join the others.

Smiling broadly, Richard pushed his chair back and stood. "To my granddaughter, Caroline."

"To Caroline," the rest of the dinner guests said in chorus. Everyone, that was, except Katherine.

Caroline smiled up at her grandfather with genuine happiness in her eyes. Her cheeks had turned a becoming shade of pink, and Jackson knew why. For all her bravado and tough exterior, for all the outward pretense of not caring one way or another, Caroline wanted to be a part of her grandfather's world.

Jackson would see she was given the chance to succeed.

With his glass still raised, Richard continued his toast, speaking directly to Caroline. "You have brought me hope for the future. Although I will never have my Libby back, I do have you." Richard paused, wiped at his moist cheek unashamedly. "It is my supreme joy to welcome you to the family, my dear. Welcome home, Caroline."

Jackson lifted his glass high in the air. "Hear, hear."

Conversation erupted around the table. Caroline dabbed at her eyes.

"How long are you to stay in America?" someone called to her. "Will you be attending the opera tomorrow evening?" came from another diner.

Caroline answered each question one at a time, her composure in place, her poise undeniable. Only the slight tremble of her lips gave away her nervousness.

Jackson watched her with pride, his love for her growing by the minute. For all intents and purposes, Caroline was a raging success among the good people of New York. For her sake, he would make sure that never changed.

Chapter Twenty-Seven

When she'd boarded the SS *Princess Helena* back in Dover, Caroline had done so with one goal in mind, to seek justice for her mother. Now, in hindsight, she realized she'd been lying to herself.

There had been a deeper reason for her journey to America, a longing so strong she'd shoved the need into the very corner of her mind, afraid to hope for a future that could never be hers. Now, in the aftermath of her grandfather's toast, she allowed the truth to settle over her. Desperate for a place to call her own, she'd come to America to find where she belonged.

At first, her arrival in this country had only highlighted her loneliness—her aloneness—making her wish for something just out of reach.

Welcome home, Caroline.

With those three words, uttered by her grandfather, she'd found her place. She'd found a family, *her* family.

Her heart swelled with joy, and she remembered one of her mother's favorite Bible verses. *For I will turn their mourning into joy, and will comfort them, and make them rejoice from their sorrow.*

Caroline's eyes stung from the tears she held firmly in place. This was not a time for crying. This was a time for rejoicing.

Her gaze sought and found Jackson.

He smiled that confident, beautiful smile of his and tipped his glass in her direction, a silent salute to her. Her breathing slowed as another moment of truth hit her. Jackson's good opinion mattered to her. *He* mattered to her. More with each passing day.

Was she in love with him? she wondered, already knowing the answer. *I love him.* No, no, no. *I love him.* No. Love was dangerous. It could be used against her as a weapon, one that could destroy her, and others close to her.

Including Elizabeth, especially Elizabeth.

Her cousin had made it clear she didn't love Jackson or want to marry him. Was that still how she felt? Caroline could never consider allowing her feelings for Jackson to spread into her heart, into her life, until she knew for sure.

She would never hurt Elizabeth, not intentionally. But before she could focus on her own happiness, and that of her cousin's, Caroline needed to finish what she'd come here to do. Tonight.

The dinner drew to a close, at last. Their host rose from his chair and addressed the table at large. "We will adjourn to the music room, where my wife has arranged a performance of Bach's Brandenburg Concerto Number Five."

Under normal circumstances Caroline would enjoy a private concert of a beautiful piece of music. But these were not normal circumstances. Caroline wanted the past laid to rest.

She wanted justice for her mother.

She wanted it now.

Holding to her patience as best she could, she took the opposite route to the door as Jackson did. She wasn't ready to speak to him. Not yet, not with her emotions still raw and her love for him still so new in her heart. She needed her mind clear.

Jackson seemed to have other ideas. He circled the table, heading straight for her, intent in his every step. He looked masculine and determined and very appealing. Caroline fought herself, lost.

She started toward him.

Elizabeth stepped into her path. "You will sit by me, dear cousin." She twined their arms together in a sisterly embrace. "I wish to speak with you about something rather important that cannot wait another minute."

The urgency in her cousin's voice had Caroline's eyebrows traveling upward. "Truly, it can't wait one more minute?"

Elizabeth laughed. "You are teasing me."

How she adored her young cousin. "Only a little."

"I will not be distracted." She glanced over her shoulder, looked at Jackson, and smiled. "My news simply cannot wait."

No. Not good. Had Jackson made his intentions known to Elizabeth? Had she misread his glances during dinner?

Wanting to know, needing to know, Caroline allowed her cousin to pull her into the VanDercreeks' large, airy music room.

They settled in the back, which suited Caroline perfectly. After a bit of shuffling and the requisite introduction of the quartet, the program began.

Elizabeth remained silent throughout the opening bars. But as soon as the music began in earnest, she leaned her head toward Caroline's.

Caroline braced herself for the dreaded announcement, torn between happiness for her cousin and sorrow for herself.

"You will be pleased to know I told Jackson I didn't want to marry him."

"You . . ." Caroline swung her gaze to her cousin, her mouth falling open. "You . . . what?" she hissed.

"I told Jackson I didn't want to marry him and he—" Elizabeth paused when the music hit a series of soft notes.

Caroline waited for the movement to hit a crescendo, her mind racing. "I must know, Elizabeth. How did he take the news?"

"That's the best part." Elizabeth smiled. "He was in perfect agreement with me. Oh, he loves me, in his own way, but he thinks of me as a sister, nothing more."

A sister. Jackson loved Elizabeth like a sister. And her cousin appeared perfectly happy with that. He wasn't going to court her cousin. He was free to seek out another.

Would he attempt to pursue Caroline now?

Did she want him to?

Yes. Oh, yes.

Joy surged through her, followed by a hard twist of reality. The man was attracted to her, of that Caroline had no doubt. But thanks to her conversation with Granny, she knew Jackson valued respectability more than any other quality in a woman. He would want a wife who had always lived her life above reproach.

Caroline was not that woman.

Her past sins were too great and varied. She'd stolen food, picked pockets, fleeced unsuspecting gamblers. Dignity, honor, *respectability* didn't fill an empty belly. A reminder of how little she fit in this world, in Jackson's world.

Eyes burning, she dropped her gaze to her hands tangled together in her lap. Emotion constricted her chest, making her breath come in short, hard puffs.

"Caroline." Elizabeth covered Caroline's hands with her own. "Are you not happy at this news?"

What an odd choice of words coming from her cousin. Curious despite her growing agitation, she lifted her gaze to meet Elizabeth's. The wise look in the girl's eyes had Caroline reassessing her cousin. She knew Caroline's secret. She knew Caroline cared for Jackson, and not in a brotherly sort of way.

Elizabeth's next words confirmed her fears. "I have seen the way you look at Jackson." The girl's voice held wisdom beyond her nineteen years. "And he at you."

"I would never . . . that is, if you had wanted him for yourself I wouldn't have . . ." Unsure how to proceed, she pressed her lips together and gave Elizabeth a helpless shrug.

"Oh, Caro, I know that." She took Caroline's hand as if it was as natural as breathing. "You and Jackson are entirely too good to ever intentionally harm anyone, especially me."

Caroline wasn't good, far from it. And she definitely wasn't a suitable wife for a man who desired respectability and correctness above all else.

"If a man ever looked at me the way Jackson looks at you . . ." Elizabeth released a dreamy sigh. "I would be the happiest woman in the world."

On cue, the music ended with a dramatic rise, then fall.

More shuffling ensued, preventing Caroline from responding to her cousin's words. Elizabeth released her hand, stood, and then, after a hasty farewell, left Caroline alone.

Two blinks later, Jackson filled the seat her cousin had just vacated.

"I haven't had a chance to speak with you all evening." He dropped his gaze over her in a slow perusal. "You are the most beautiful woman in the room. Though I doubt I'm the first to say so."

The appreciation in his eyes sent a tremble of hope through her. "Perhaps not the first," she whispered, "but certainly the most longed for."

That earned her a wide smile, and she found herself relaxing for the first time all evening. When had this man become her rock?

And, oh, the way he was looking at her. Not for a very, very long time had she felt so . . . special, so accepted for herself. The loneliness of recent years waned under a strange, soothing calm.

"Is that the dress Lappet raved about this afternoon?"

Her stomach fluttered. "Monsieur declared no other woman should have this exquisite creation but me."

"The man is a genius."

She couldn't deny that particular truth. "He does seem to have an eye."

Reaching to her, touching her arm softly, his face grew suddenly very serious, his gaze troubled. "Caroline, I—"

At the same moment, she said, "Jackson, I—"

They laughed, then fell silent.

After a moment, he began again. "You first."

"No." She shook her head. "You."

Impatience rolling off him in waves, he glanced to the other side of the room, frowned, then returned his attention to her. "I noticed . . ." He stopped, seemed to rethink his words, began again. "That is, I noticed that you and Elizabeth were in deep conversation during the musicale."

She flinched. "We weren't intending to be rude."

"You misunderstand my meaning." He brushed a hand down her arm, his touch casual and intimate and highly inappropriate in such a setting. "I doubt anyone else noticed. I merely meant to comment on the closeness you two seem to be building."

"We have become friends."

"I'm glad."

A sense of recklessness, the one she usually stifled, poured through her reserve, loosening her tongue. "We discussed you and her and your future and . . ."

She couldn't quite finish her thought.

"And . . . ?" he prompted.

Caroline opened her mouth to relate the rest, to tell him she knew he wasn't going to marry Elizabeth, when she caught sight of her aunt scowling at them from across the room. No, not them—Caroline.

Katherine St. James was looking at Caroline with unmistakable contempt in her eyes.

"And." She answered her aunt's glare with one of her own. "I know who intercepted my mother's letters."

"Yes." Jackson followed the direction of her gaze. "As do I."

* * *

Jackson felt the first stirrings of concern when Caroline swiveled her head and simply stared at him with a blank expression. He'd expected her eyes to narrow with anger, rage, maybe even hate. But this calm, careful focus? No, he hadn't expected that from her. Although now, in the face of her icy control, he realized just how much alike he and Caroline were.

He'd experienced the same need to keep his emotions in check when he'd confronted George Smythe outside his tenement houses. John Reilly's presence had been invaluable that day, a silent physical reminder for Jackson to keep a tight rein on his temper.

He would offer the same service to Caroline. "We should confront your aunt together."

She said nothing.

"Tonight. We should make our move tonight."

Still, she said nothing. She didn't move, didn't blink, didn't react at all. She merely waited. On him. Keeping a firm hold on her emotions. *Phenomenal control.*

"We will speak plainly and only in absolutes," he said. "There will be no hysterics, no pointless accusations, just an adherence to the truth as we know it."

She blinked at him, her brows slightly lifted, withholding her opinion until he finished.

"It would be best if we avoided involving Richard, at least during our initial confrontation."

At last, she broke her silence. "Agreed."

"Let's go." He stretched out his hand. She took it without question.

Her fingers were cold, even through her gloves. A primitive urge rose inside him, a powerful need to soothe, to comfort, to defend and protect. "Remember, you aren't alone anymore. I won't leave your side."

A single hitched breath warned him of the storm brewing beneath her calm exterior. "You had better do the majority of the talking."

"I planned to allow you the honors."

She grimaced. "You said no hysterics. No pointless accusations. I can't promise to refrain from either. In fact"—her icy stare skimmed across her aunt—"you may have to physically restrain me before I am through with her."

"Then who will restrain me?"

His words elicited a short laugh from Caroline. "We'll just have to be each other's better judgment."

He liked that suggestion, liked knowing she was not only accepting his assistance but counting on it.

She offered him a brief, nervous smile before her lips pressed into a hard line. "My uncle has retrieved their coats. They are leaving."

"We'll maneuver a ride with them in their carriage."

Frowning, Caroline disengaged her hand from his. "That will present a problem. I came with my grandfather. He will expect me to leave with him."

Holding steady, Jackson considered their next move but then caught sight of their hosts heading their way. "I'm afraid we've missed our chance."

Caroline turned her head and sighed. "So we have."

He turned her to face him, spoke quickly before their hosts arrived. "First thing in the morning, before work, I'll fetch you at Granny's. By the time we travel to St. James House, Richard will already have left for the office."

She didn't have time to reply before the VanDercreeks requested her company. It seemed they wanted to introduce her to the quartet.

Watching Caroline interact with her hosts, her smile only slightly strained, Jackson decided that perhaps this turn of events was for the best. A good night's sleep would help cool her temper.

Tomorrow would bring its own set of problems. And rewards, if Jackson had his way. Tonight, he would have to be content with knowing they would soon confront her aunt for her treachery.

Jackson relished the idea.

Chapter Twenty-Eight

Caroline woke the next morning with gritty eyes and a heavy heart. Now that she knew who had kept her mother from returning home she had mixed emotions. On one hand, she wanted her revenge. She wanted to make Katherine St. James suffer, in horrible ways that would make her mother's life seem like a glorious, easy existence.

On the other hand, if Caroline exacted revenge for her mother, wouldn't that make her equally as guilty as her aunt?

Vengeance is mine. The Scripture had jumped off the page of her mother's worn Bible when Caroline had flipped through it last night in her attempt to seek solace. Frowning, she'd flipped random pages and had come upon a similar verse. *Vengeance belongs unto me.*

Could Caroline trust justice for her mother to the Lord? She had no practice, no proof that she could count on good winning over evil. And, yes, what her aunt had done had been evil.

What had possessed the woman to intercept the letters and then send them back, unopened? Wouldn't it have been equally effective to destroy them? Her mother would have been left questioning her father's silence.

Perhaps that had been the point. It was the return of the letters that had killed Libby's hope of ever being accepted back into the family fold.

Could Katherine have been that devious? That calculating? But why? Why had she wanted Libby never to return?

Caroline would know soon enough.

No matter what happened this morning, she would not leave her grandfather's house without knowing her aunt's motives.

And she would have Jackson standing by her side, offering his strength and support.

Tossing the bedcovers aside, Caroline climbed out of bed and reviewed her clothing choices. Monsieur Lappet had sent three other dresses with the blue silk. The pink would be a good option, the pale green a better one. Yes, the soft color would work perfectly.

When she was halfway through her preparations, Sally shuffled in the room, her movements slow, her gaze sleepy.

"You should have woken me," she said, rubbing at her eyes.

"You were restless last night." She'd even cried out at one point. "I wanted you to sleep in this morning."

Sally shook her head. "I can sleep as soon as you leave for the day." She lowered her gaze over the dress Caroline had set out for this morning's altercation. "Pretty."

"The color spoke to me." Caroline eyed the garment. "I need to look my best today."

"Then allow me." Sally took the hairbrush from her hand.

No longer willing to argue over whose job it was to dress Caroline's hair, she allowed her friend to take over the task.

By the time Caroline made her way to the stairwell, Jackson was already standing at the bottom, waiting for her, his arm casually leaning on the banister.

A slow smile spread across his lips.

That smile. It devastated her as always, and her steps faltered. She couldn't think of anyone she'd rather have by her side this morning, not even her grandfather.

Her confidence soared. She took the stairs one at a time, her resolve growing by the second.

A flash of intent filled Jackson's gaze right before he pulled her into his arms and kissed her soundly on the mouth. No preamble, no hesitation. A promise, a silent assurance that he was on her side and ready to slay any dragons that threatened her.

When he drew away, she released a sigh.

"Ready?" he asked.

"Ready."

Since Granny was still abed, they left the house without fanfare. Once they were both settled in the carriage facing one another, Jackson gave the signal to the driver to set out.

Caroline leaned back in her seat. "I have been thinking about how we should proceed this morning."

He inclined his head. "I'm listening."

"I am much calmer than I was last night." She pulled in a soothing breath, glanced out the window, breathed again. "Considering what Katherine did to my mother—"

"To you, Caroline." Jackson set a hand on her knee. "What she did to *you*."

"Yes, well." She chewed on her bottom lip. "I think I should be the one to do most of the talking after all."

His gaze perused her face at a slow, studied pace. He had something to say, she knew it by the angle of his head and the parting of his lips. Would he agree to her request? Or try to talk her out of the idea?

Eyes softening, Jackson took her hand and pulled her into the seat next to him. "Caroline, I'm here to support you, not take over."

"I . . . thank you."

"But know this." He brushed his fingertips along her forehead, down her cheek. "I won't allow Katherine to hurt you. If she tries, either by word or deed, I *will* step in. And I won't apologize afterward."

And there it was. The reason she loved this man. He was willing to allow her to take the lead, but he wouldn't sit back and watch harm come to her. "Thank you, Jackson."

Now that he'd had his say, now that they both had an idea of the other's intentions, Caroline knew she should move back to her side of the carriage. They were unreasonably close, especially if they were to remain above reproach.

Unfortunately, Caroline didn't want to remain above reproach. She didn't want to move away from Jackson, not one single inch. Her ears filled with the sound of her frantic pulse.

Jackson seemed to be caught with the same affliction, neither moving away from her nor making any attempt to put distance between them.

Sitting this close to him, she could see the deep blue rim circling the lighter blue of his irises, could smell the clean scent of his soap. He'd recently shaved, his jaw as smooth as she'd ever seen.

He was so handsome, so painfully masculine, and so dear to her now.

Unable to resist, she pulled off her glove and cupped his face with her bare palm.

Smiling slightly, tenderly, he closed his hand over hers.

"Caroline." He turned his head ever so slightly and placed a kiss on her tender skin.

This couldn't be proper, what they were doing in the privacy of the carriage, yet Caroline couldn't stop herself from wishing he would kiss her again. Like he had in Granny's foyer. Just . . . one . . . tiny . . . kiss.

She whispered his name.

He placed his hand at the small of her back and pulled her close. No words came out of his mouth, no promises or declarations or even warnings that this was a bad idea. Instead, he communicated his heart with the gentle pressure of his lips against hers.

One moment stretched into two.

Caroline's eyes began to water. She'd found where she belonged. In this man's arms.

His head pulled away, inch by measured inch. The light caught his eyes. What she saw in them took her breath away.

He loved her.

But did he want her for his wife?

Would she accept anything less from him?

No, no she would not.

The carriage drew to a halt. Needing a moment to organize her thoughts, she scrambled to her side of the carriage before the coachman opened the door.

Still looking at her, his heart in his eyes, Jackson reached for her again. "Caroline, I lo—"

"No." She placed the missing glove back onto her hand. "Don't say it yet. Wait until after we have confronted my aunt."

He frowned, clearly unhappy with her request. "If that's what you want. But when this is over, I'm going to have my say, and you're going to listen." His tone brooked no argument.

A little thrill slid down her spine. "I understand."

He exited the carriage first and then helped her to the ground. They ascended the stoop together, matching their steps as always. From the very first day, at the Griffin Ball, even before she'd met her grandfather, Caroline and Jackson had been in step with one another. It seemed only fitting that he was the one to stand with her now.

The butler opened the door before they had a chance to knock, looking appropriately bored and put out. Behind the man, Katherine St. James stood frozen in place.

Gone was the kind, Christian demeanor she portrayed to the rest of society. In its place was a pinched display of bitterness. And hate. Such hate. Caroline shuddered under the powerful emotion.

Cold wind swept across Caroline's soul, followed by a hot ball of anger in the pit of her stomach. This woman, a member of her own family, her mother's *friend*, had plotted and schemed to keep Libby St. James from returning home.

Needing a moment to calm her temper, Caroline studied her aunt with a critical eye. Under the bold, unforgiving light of morning, her age showed in every line upon her face. Balancing slightly on her toes, with her shoulders hunched forward and her arms stiff by her side, the woman looked like a snake ready to strike. Even her mean, narrowed gaze had the requisite predatory sheen.

This was no ordinary foe but one who had proven herself willing to fight dirty.

Ah, yes, *this* was the battle Caroline had come across the ocean to fight.

"You know why I'm here," she said, unashamed by the rage that sounded in her voice.

Her aunt lifted her chin, her beady eyes narrowing to tiny slits. "Oh, I know. In fact, I've been waiting for you to make your move for some time now. I'm surprised it has taken you so long."

Realizing they were in the foyer, where anyone could hear their conversation, Caroline suggested they move to a more private room.

"With your lack of breeding, I would have expected you to prefer a more public venue." Katherine lowered her gaze over Caroline, her lips curling into a sneer. "You might walk and talk like you belong in our world, but we both know you are nothing more than a grubby street urchin."

The insult hit its mark, filling Caroline with a moment of humiliation. How could Katherine be so mean-spirited, when she herself had experienced what it meant to be an outsider?

Caroline felt Jackson tense by her side. She placed her hand on his arm and shook her head, willing him to adhere to her silent request not to interfere. Yet.

Her aunt had spoken the truth. Two months ago Caroline had lived in a one-room shack with a dirt floor and only a threadbare blanket for warmth against the cold. Her idea of dressing for "the occasion" had included a borrowed dress from a prostitute and a tedious brushing of her hair.

As if sensing she'd drawn blood, Katherine shifted her gaze to Jackson. "I assume this private confrontation was your idea?"

The implication was clear. Caroline would never have had the natural instinct to behave in a respectable manner.

Jackson started to speak, but Caroline shook her head at him again.

"You've made your point, Aunt, but now it's time we addressed the matter at hand."

"Whatever you wish, *Niece*." As if she had all the time in the world, Katherine led them into the parlor and chose a chair near the window, lowering herself with practiced elegance. It was no wonder the woman was considered a sought-after guest in all the elegant homes in New York. Her manners were impeccable, which made her behavior seem all the more evil.

For several beats, silence cloaked the room.

When neither Caroline nor Jackson moved to break the silence, Katherine wound her wrist in the air. "Do proceed with your questions."

The perfect society maven was there in her manner.

For a dangerous moment, Caroline wanted to rush across the room and shake the woman hard and remind her how it felt to be found lacking by her peers Praying for calm, hoping the Lord heard her, Caroline sat on a brocade settee instead and spoke in a cool, even voice. "We know you're the one who intercepted my mother's letters."

The woman didn't even blink at the accusation.

"You don't deny it?" Caroline had expected a cursory denial at the very least.

"Why would I? Quite frankly, I'm surprised it took you so long to discover it was me."

The nerve of the woman. She acted as if she'd had every right in the world to destroy another woman's life, *her friend's* life. Anger surged, demanding release. Caroline swallowed—once, twice; on the third she curled her fingers into Jackson's sleeve.

He covered her hand in a show of comfort but remained silent. As she'd requested.

She swallowed one more time. "What I don't understand is why."

"Why?" Katherine raised her voice, the first real sign her composure was slipping. "*Why*, you ask? Isn't it obvious?"

Caroline had no answer to the question. How could she know this woman's mind?

As soon as the question roared through her thoughts, Caroline realized Katherine's game. The woman wanted her to cry, to beg for an explanation.

Caroline would do neither.

In such matters, silence was a most effective weapon.

Drumming her fingers on the arm of her chair, Katherine released a snakelike hiss. "I intercepted your mother's letters because I never wanted her to return. She had no understanding of the true meaning of sacrifice."

"On the contrary, my mother sacrificed everything for love."

"No." Katherine's face contorted into a look of pure hatred. "She *chose* love. She chose to ignore her position and duty to her family. She didn't deserve a second chance."

So much meaning was tucked inside those words, so much ugliness. "She was your friend."

"She was never my friend. The day she ran off with her *one true love* was the day I learned to hate her."

Caroline gasped, struck momentarily speechless. Katherine despised Libby because she chose to follow her heart? But that made no sense, especially when Libby's choice didn't directly harm Katherine.

What was Caroline missing?

Jackson squeezed her hand. "Why go to the trouble of returning the letters," he asked in a deceptively calm voice. "Why not destroy them instead?"

Katherine's gaze snapped to him. "I wasn't stupid. I knew she had to be growing desperate. If she thought there was the slightest possibility that her letters hadn't made it to her father, she might try to speak with him personally. I could not allow that to happen."

Confused by the Machiavellian response, Caroline looked helplessly at Jackson. He shrugged, equally at a loss.

"What threat could my mother possibly present to you? Your husband is the firstborn son, the heir. His inheritance would have been secure whether my mother returned or not."

"Don't insult either of us by playing stupid. Your mother was always Richard's favorite. Libby could do no wrong in her father's eyes, while Marcus could never do enough right."

Caroline couldn't let that remark go. "That's not true. My grandfather thinks very highly of his son. I've seen them together, at the office. There is great affection between them."

"Affection?" She spat the word. "Richard has always held Marcus to an impossible standard, while Libby was given anything she wanted, whenever she asked."

A range of bitter emotions crossed Katherine's face.

"Do you know? When your mother ran off with that stable hand, Richard was as livid as I've ever seen him. I thought, finally, the man sees his daughter as she really is. Was Marcus rewarded for staying home, for staying true?" She slammed her fist against the chair's arm. "No. Nothing changed. While Richard searched for Libby, Marcus was still expected to work hard and earn his way in the world."

"There is no shame in earning one's way," Jackson said. "It's that which makes America great."

Katherine ignored him. "I knew if Libby returned, Richard would welcome her back in the fold. He would throw her a party, the prodigal returned and all that." She snarled at Caroline. The woman actually snarled. "Once again, Libby would be rewarded for doing everything wrong, while Marcus and I would be punished for doing everything right."

Caroline had heard the Prodigal Son story countless times from her mother. The parable had given Libby hope that one day her father would forgive her, as the father in the Bible had forgiven his son. But to hear Katherine's interpretation, it was clear her aunt had missed the message of the story.

Before Caroline could say as much, the doors swung open with a loud smack of wood meeting wall. Eyes murderous, jaw clenched, her grandfather strode into the room and stopped next to Katherine. He loomed over her, every bit of his rage evident in his bunched muscles and angry expression. "You are forgetting the most important portion of the story, my dear."

Katherine stumbled back a step. "Richard, you must understand, I—"

"You have forgotten the part where the father must decide whether to forgive the offense"—he held her frozen in his stare—"or not."

Chapter Twenty-Nine

Katherine jumped out of her chair and shoved past her father-in-law, panic in the move. "Richard. You're supposed to have left for the office."

"Obviously, I am still at home." Their stares met, clashed. "I want you out of my house. Today."

"I . . . please . . . no." Her hand went to her throat. "I can explain. Truly, I can."

Hoping to defuse Richard's anger before it snapped, Jackson went to him. "Let her finish explaining her actions."

Richard turned his head, black thunderclouds in his gaze. "Why should I?"

"For Caroline's sake." Jackson willed the older man to hear what he was saying. "Your granddaughter deserves to hear the entire story."

After a slight hesitation, the older man nodded. "Go on, Katherine." His tone turned cold. Ice-cold. "I believe you were relating your version of the Prodigal Son story."

"I've always hated that parable," Katherine admitted.

"It's always been my favorite," Caroline said, reminding them all of her presence. And why they were having this conversation. "As well as my mother's."

"Do you know why I hate the story?" she asked Caroline. "Because the Prodigal Son is welcomed back by his father, no questions asked, as if he'd done nothing wrong and would suffer no consequences for his actions." She spun to glare at her father-in-law. "While the *good* son, who has done everything his father has requested, is scolded for complaining."

"That's where you're wrong, Katherine." Richard's tone was low and menacing. "The father said to the faithful son, *thou are ever with me and all that I have is thine.* He was still the heir and still received his full portion, as will Marcus."

Smiling benignly, Marcus sauntered into the room. "What about me?"

Lightning fast, Richard spun to face his son. "Your wife is the one who intercepted your sister's letters."

His face stunned, Marcus stared at his father. "She . . . *no.*"

"I'm afraid so."

Blinking in confusion, he turned to Katherine, who had the gall to smirk at him. It was the wrong thing to do. His eyes growing as hard as his father's, Marcus strode to her and gripped her shoulders. "How could you?" He pulled her close, so they were nose to nose. "How could you, when you knew how much I loved my sister."

"Oh, believe me, I knew." Katherine sneered at her husband in disgust. "As soon as this one showed up, all you could talk about was your sister. Libby this and Libby that." Her tone turned mocking. "It was as if Libby had returned, instead of her hideous, simpering daughter who—"

"Katherine," Marcus said, his tone as rigid as his glower. "That's enough."

She wrenched free of his hold and stalked over to Caroline. "You are nothing. Do you hear me? Nothing."

Caroline blinked at her aunt, clearly shocked. In one move, Jackson was back by her side, pulling her close. He opened his mouth to defend her, but Marcus beat him to it.

"She is my niece," he said. "Libby's daughter."

"What of *our* daughter? What of *my* sacrifice? I gave up everything to be a part of this family, to live in this house."

"What did you sacrifice?" Richard asked. "You have enjoyed a life of privilege since marrying my son."

"You. This is all your fault." She jabbed her finger at Richard. "You tossed Elizabeth aside for this . . . this . . . harlot. Now she must go. She must disappear from this family. I will not stand for any other outcome."

Eyes glazed over with rage, Katherine reached up and yanked Caroline's hair before anyone could stop her.

With a quick swipe, Caroline clutched her aunt's wrist. "Release me, this instant."

"Or what?"

"Or this." A smile, icy and lethal, spread across her lips as she tightened her hold. Katherine cried out and lost her grip, stumbling back several steps.

"Don't ever touch me again." Caroline moved toward her aunt, eyes intent. She slowly raised her hand, but stopped herself. "You aren't worth it."

Caroline's hand lowered slowly to her side. Her eyes were filled with horror. But somehow she remained calm and in control, her rage firmly held in check.

She was better than all of them, Jackson realized.

Unconsciously regal, she crossed the room to stand by his side again.

"Marcus. Son." Richard's voice quivered with emotion. "Please escort your wife out of my sight."

"Yes, Father." Marcus grabbed Katherine's arm and dragged her toward the foyer. Before quitting the room, he stopped beside Caroline. "I'm sorry, my dear. Please know I wasn't part of my wife's treachery."

His eyes swam with a mixture of shock and disillusionment, a mirror image of his father's expression.

And Caroline's. "I know, Uncle. I know you would never harm my mother, or me."

Looking like a beaten man, Marcus left with his wife firmly in hand. The moment the door shut behind them, Richard sank into a nearby chair.

Caroline rushed forward and collapsed to her knees in front him. "Grandfather? Are you all right?"

"I'm fine, child. I just need a moment to take in the events of the last half hour."

The older man looked as downtrodden as his son. Caroline began speaking softly to him, in a low, gentle tone. Jackson couldn't hear her specific words, but whatever she was saying seemed to soothe her grandfather's grief.

Now that the truth was out at last, the two could begin the process of healing the past and forging ahead toward the future.

Satisfaction filled Jackson. He longed to tell Caroline how he felt about her, that he loved and admired her and wanted to spend the rest of his life by her side.

But now was not the time to declare himself. Caroline needed to be alone with her grandfather.

Jackson slipped out of the room, shutting the door behind him quietly.

Elizabeth met him in the foyer. "Is it true? Did my mother ruin Caroline's life?"

For years, Jackson had protected the people he loved, sheltering them from anything unpleasant. He'd told himself he was giving grace, but grace without truth was dangerous.

"Yes, Elizabeth, your mother is guilty of a very grave sin."

Grimacing, she wrapped her arms around her waist. "I can hardly believe anyone would do something so treacherous. It seems so intentionally wicked."

Jackson saw the despair in Elizabeth's eyes but had no idea how to help her accept the truth of her mother's character, a woman as bitter as his own, just far better at hiding it.

In many ways, Lucille Montgomery had been the more honest of the two. It was time Jackson honored her for that. He owed his mother an apology, for not trying harder to understand her pain. "I must leave."

Elizabeth nodded absently, her gaze darting between the closed doors of the parlor and the stairs leading to her parents' room.

"Elizabeth."

"Yes, yes, good day, Jackson."

No, it wasn't a good day and would probably get worse before it got better. Change was never easy and always carried a cost. "Good-bye, Elizabeth."

Without another word, he walked across the foyer and let himself out.

* * *

Less than an hour later, Jackson entered his childhood home and immediately went in search of his mother. As expected, he found her in the sunroom just off the first-floor parlor. Although she claimed the early morning light hurt her eyes, she'd never once altered her daily routine, not even in the first few weeks after her husband's betrayal.

What she must have suffered, Jackson thought, as he positioned his shoulder against the doorjamb and studied his mother's bent head. The pain and humiliation must have been unbearable, especially in those early days. Surely far worse than what he'd endured himself.

Heart in his throat, he watched his mother a moment longer, trying not to sigh at the picture she made: her back ramrod straight, head bent over her needlework, face scrunched in her customary scowl. Anger and bitterness rolled off her in waves. This was the mother Jackson had known all his life. The difficult, demanding woman with expectations so high no one could ever meet them. Not her husband. And certainly not her son.

Disgrace hadn't made her bitter, he realized with a jolt. Nor had it made her hard, or unforgiving. The sour condition of her soul had been a part of Lucille Montgomery long before her husband had run off with her younger sister.

For as long as Jackson could remember, his mother had wallowed in a constant state of unhappiness, wielding her disappointment in others as a weapon.

The familiar disquiet he always battled in his mother's presence arose, urging him to leave before she took notice of him. He stayed firmly planted in place and forced himself to sort through what he would say to her, what he *needed* to say.

He predicted an uncomfortable conversation.

Pushing to his full height, he stepped into the room. "Good morning, Mother."

"So, you *are* going to acknowledge me." She kept her head bent as she spoke, while her displeasure sounded in her voice and showed in her tense neck muscles. "I was beginning to wonder."

So had he. Prepared for the battle ahead, he moved deeper into the room. "I have just come from St. James House."

"What business called you there so early in the day?" She poked her needle into the material with considerable force, then stilled, as if a thought had just occurred to her. "Is it official, then?" She lifted her head to gaze at him at last. "Have you asked for Elizabeth's hand in marriage?"

"No. I won't be proposing to Elizabeth. However, I will be making my—"

"But the match has been decided for years." She gripped the needlework in her hand, wrinkling the fabric beyond recognition. "The girl was to bring respectability to our family, once and for all."

A month ago, Jackson would have agreed. That was before he'd fallen in love with Caroline, before he'd realized his priorities had been skewed. "Is respectability so important?"

"You know that it is." Her outrage shot through the room like a well-aimed dart. "It is what we have worked for ever since your father left town with that"—she paused, sneered, narrowed her eyes—"that *woman*."

At the fury in her tone and the murderous rage in her eyes, Jackson went utterly still. He'd seen a similar look in Katherine St. James's glower that morning, had noted the same need to hate. But where Katherine's wound had been forged from a false impression of an unknown wrong done to her, his mother's had been founded in truth.

Hurting for her more than he ever had in the past, he went to her, lowered to his haunches, and took her hands in his.

"Mother." He chose his words very carefully. "I know Father hurt you—*I know*—but at some point you must find it in your heart to forgive him. For your sake, if not his."

"No." Eyes wild with a mixture of hurt and anger, she snatched her hands free from his. "I will never forgive that man. And you shouldn't, either. What he did was wrong. He has made both our lives unbearable."

It was true. They had both suffered. But Jackson knew the time had come to forgive, before the hurt permanently gave way to hate.

Closing his eyes, he took a deep breath, swallowed hard, and let go of the anger, the pain, the offense he'd harbored in his heart through the years.

He simply . . . let go.

Jackson knew there would be more work to do. There would be times he would fall back into old habits. But today he had taken the first step toward freedom. He must help his mother do the same.

"Mother." He spoke softly, slowly, urging her to hear him as she'd never heard him before. "Understand, I'm not advocating you deny any wrongdoing on his part, or that you cease to feel the pain of his betrayal, but if you want to take your life back, you have to forgive Father. It won't be easy and it won't be fast, but it will come with time."

"He doesn't want my forgiveness." The resentment in her tone spoke of a stubborn, insidious avoidance of the real matter at hand.

"How do you know that?"

"He has never asked." And there was the real crux of the problem before them. She was waiting for an apology, one that might never come.

Jackson looked at his mother as if coming out of a five-year trance. He would never win this battle with her. Reason would certainly never work. Lucille Montgomery was happy in her misery. She was comfortable in the knowledge that she was the wounded party. The victim.

No matter what words Jackson used, no matter how hard he tried to help her, he couldn't bring her to a place of healing. She would have to arrive there on her own.

That didn't mean Jackson wasn't willing to give it one more try.

"The most Godlike thing you can do is forgive the unforgivable." He let out his breath very slowly, very carefully. "Father is gone and isn't coming back. Even if he does return, he might never apologize for his actions or ask for your forgiveness. You have to decide to do that on your own."

She flattened her lips in a grim line, mutiny in her eyes. "Nevertheless..."

Yes, nevertheless...

Jackson stood, disappointment making his limbs heavier than normal, his movements slower. Regardless of his failure here today, Jackson loved his mother. "I want you to be the first to know. I plan to ask Caroline St. James to marry me."

Her face went slack, then pulled into the familiar scowl he'd grown to expect. "It was inevitable, I suppose."

"What was inevitable?"

"That, in the end, you would choose an unsuitable wife." Still frowning, she smoothed the wrinkles from the crumpled fabric in her lap, stabbed the needle into a random spot, and yanked hard on the loose thread. "It is as I've always feared. You are just like your father after all."

Jackson was nothing like his father. Except perhaps he *was* like the man who'd sired him, at least in this particular instance.

The truth hit him with a force that nearly dropped him to his knees. After spending years working to restore his family's good name, Jackson was going to buck tradition and follow in the footsteps of his rebel ancestors.

He wasn't going to marry for propriety's sake, or to please his mother, or anyone else for that matter. No, Jackson was going to marry for love.

Chapter Thirty

Caroline didn't see Jackson again that day. When her grandfather had decided to stay home from the office—who could blame him, really?—she'd requested to do the same, hoping to spend some private time with him. They'd talked for hours, just the two of them, mostly about her mother and the various memories each of them had of the woman who'd been taken from them far too soon.

The day had brought its form of healing, a healing that had been coming on for some time, at least in Caroline's case. Finally, with each story her grandfather told, she could think of her mother without the raging guilt or regret for what might have been. The sadness—oh, the sadness—that would be a part of her always. Such was the nature of grief.

In time, Caroline knew she would have to find it in her heart to forgive her aunt, but not today. Today, the pain was still too raw, the hurt too new, and Katherine's lack of remorse too maddening.

Back in her room at Granny's, with the sun finally setting on the day, Caroline began the arduous task of preparing for an evening at the opera. She was tired, emotionally wrung out, and really not in the mood for interacting with New York society. She had tears in her eyes again and, now that she was alone, she allowed them to spill down her cheeks.

She stared at herself in the mirror through her watery vision, her mind still in the drawing room at her grandfather's house.

There had been a tense moment near lunchtime, when Marcus had interrupted. He'd only stayed awhile, using the opportunity to apologize for his wife's behavior once again, as well as make a personal request of Caroline. "Would you do me the honor, my dear, of attending the opera with the rest of the family this evening?"

Caroline had gaped at him, quite unable to formulate a response. She could not bear—she really could not *bear* the idea of attending any function with her aunt present.

As if sensing where her mind had gone, her uncle had hastened to add, "It will be a small, intimate party. You, me, Elizabeth, and, of course"—he nodded to the other man in the room—"you are welcome to join as well, Father."

With that additional information, and her grandfather's quick acceptance of the invitation, Caroline had agreed to attend the opera with her family.

My family.

She lifted a shaky hand to her throat and sighed. How far she'd come from the girl who'd stoically endured the merciless registration process at Ellis Island. Angry at the world, and at God, Caroline had come to America to seek vengeance for her mother.

She'd found forgiveness instead. And love, familial love, with her grandfather, who in a very short time had become the earthly, albeit flawed, model of her Heavenly Father's perfect love. She would treasure every year she had with Richard St. James and make up for the time they'd lost.

Caroline picked up her hairbrush and twirled it around in her hand. Heat rose to her cheeks. Could she dare to hope that she'd also found romantic love with a man who knew the worst of her and still seemed to accept her as she was?

Yes, *yes*, she dared to hope. And that was the greatest blessing of all.

Beauty from ashes. So much to be grateful for in her life these days, so much to thank God for.

Thank you, Lord. Thank you.

Her heart pounded with satisfaction. Although she was tired, she was looking forward to attending the opera with her family. Her family!

"Truly, Caroline." Sally wrestled the brush from her hand and gave her a quick appraisal. "I cannot decide if you are a slow learner or just plain stubborn."

She grinned at her friend, realizing how much she'd grown to care for the girl. "Perhaps I am a little of both."

"Now *that*, I believe." Setting her hands on Caroline's shoulders, Sally turned her around to face her directly. "You've been crying."

Sighing, Caroline wiped at her eyes. "Only a little."

"You are sad."

She forced a smile. "Only a little."

Sally pursed her lips and let her eyes wander over Caroline's face. "Perhaps you should stay in tonight."

The thought had merits. The events of the day had worn her out. But Caroline wanted to spend the evening with her family, even if that meant enduring the rest of New York society as well. If she was to embrace this new life of hers, she must learn to appreciate all the various facets, and that included attending the opera in her uncle's private box. Where the good people of New York would watch her every move.

No matter. She would have her family with her tonight, and perhaps Jackson, too.

She gave a small sigh and turned back toward the mirror. "I'll be fine, Sally. But thank you for your concern."

Nodding, Sally began pulling the brush through Caroline's hair. As she'd done many times over the last week, she watched the maid arrange her dark, unruly curls in a sophisticated knot atop her head, marveling at the girl's skill.

Hair coiffed, Caroline rose from the table. As Sally tugged and smoothed each layer of clothing into place, anticipation spread through her. A new beginning. She was embarking on a new beginning, starting tonight. The Lord had provided her with a second chance when she'd done nothing on her own to earn it.

Mercy, grace, she understood both so much better now. She would not squander this unexpected blessing in her life. She would cherish every moment of the adventure that lay ahead.

Dressed and ready for her evening out, Caroline bid Sally good night and made her way to the long, arching stairwell at an inappropriately hurried pace.

Laughing at herself, she placed her hand on the banister and froze. Oh. *Oh.*

Of course.

Jackson stood at the bottom of the stairs, handsome and immaculate in his formal attire, looking up at her with that confident smile she so adored. He inclined his head in a half bow. Taking the steps on wobbly knees, heart leaping wildly in her chest, she managed to navigate her way to the bottom without crashing headfirst at his feet.

She looked at him fully and . . .

Oh.

His hand took hers in a firm, warm clasp. Her stomach dropped, and she felt half suffocated from the sheer physicality of his nearness. She felt a welling of . . . something. Joy, peace, completion? She had fallen unequivocally in love with this man, with his honor, his integrity, his sheer masculine beauty. Her life and her future lay with him.

She whispered his name.

"Caroline. My sweet, beautiful Caroline." His voice and expression were fierce as he pulled her into his arms, seemingly uncaring that he was crushing her dress.

After a moment, he pulled away slowly, as if reluctant to do so. He cupped her face in his hand and smiled. There was something different in his eyes, a raw vulnerability she'd not seen before.

"I love you." He said the words so simply, so easily, as if falling in love with her had been as inevitable as breathing.

Perhaps it had been.

"I love you, too, Jackson." The ache of tears in her throat made her voice hoarse, but the words had come out strong. Real.

For a moment they simply stared into one another's eyes, both speechless, still holding on to one another for dear life. There was no mention of the future, no promises made, but Caroline knew this was no game to Jackson. He would make an offer soon. He was that sort of man.

"We had better go," he said, stepping back, dropping his hands to his sides. "Before I take you back in my arms and ruin your dress beyond all hope of repair."

She cast a glance at the green silk creation. It was in fine shape. But he was right. Any more kissing would bring certain disaster. Then again . . .

"I have other dresses."

His eyes turned soft, amused. "Don't tempt me. We are already late—another few moments and we'll be the talk of the town."

He said the words in jest. Caroline knew this. She heard the humor in his voice. But she was well aware of how hard he'd worked to earn the respect of his peers, to end the humiliation of his father's betrayal. She would not be the cause of a single blemish on his good name.

"You are right." She smoothed her hand down her skirt. "We should go at once."

Not giving him a chance to respond, she swept past him and out into the night. He had no other recourse than to follow.

The short ride to the Metropolitan was made in relative silence. Jackson might not wish to wrinkle her dress, but he had no qualms about holding her hand or running his thumb across her palm.

"I had an interesting conversation with Marcus this afternoon."

Unable to keep from sighing, she dipped her head and waited for him to continue.

"He has decided to send Katherine away." He tightened his hold on her hand, the gesture communicating his support as surely as any declaration would have. "She will reside in their home in Florida indefinitely."

To a woman like Katherine, being sent away was the worst sort of punishment, the equivalent of banishment.

More to the point, Katherine was one of the most influential women in New York society and enjoyed her position greatly. Surely she wouldn't submit to this without a fight. "My aunt has agreed to this? She has agreed to go without a fight?"

"So it would seem."

Caroline had her doubts. Before she could voice any of them, Jackson brought her hand to his lips. "She leaves at the end of the week."

"I suppose that will have to be good enough." If Caroline had her way, her aunt would depart sooner.

"How is my uncle?"

"Angry, sad, confused—all the things one would expect of a man in his situation." Jackson released her hand. "Tonight will be difficult for him."

Caroline's throat constricted on her uncle's behalf. What must it have been like for him to discover his mate had carried such evil in her heart? Even now, after only a short acquaintance, Caroline could hardly reconcile the woman she'd thought she'd known with the one that lay underneath the gracious facade of perfect manners and custom-made gowns.

"The way I see it," she began. "It is up to us to make the evening a pleasant one for my uncle."

"Yes, it is up to us." Admiration filled Jackson's eyes. "You are a good person, Caroline, a woman of compassion and tenderness."

"Please, Jackson." Her cheeks heated. "I'm none of those things. I'm a ruffian from the streets of London. Just a few months ago I lived in a—"

"It doesn't matter where you came from, or how you lived before that day I saw you on Orchard Street. Everything I have just said about you is true, all of it." His mouth came to hers, and he kissed her, gently, slowly, appreciatively. "You are good, very good, in your heart, in your soul, where it counts most."

"I . . ." She pulled slightly back and stared into his eyes, eyes filled with admiration. "Jackson, you . . . you're making me blush."

Of all the responses to his words, she would have never expected that one, which made her cheeks heat even more than before.

"I love you," he said simply, effortlessly, as if it had been true for him forever.

She had no time to formulate a proper response. They had arrived at their destination, and Jackson was helping her out of the carriage before she could think to speak.

Arm linked with hers, he escorted her through the lobby. Heads turned in their direction. Greetings were called out and returned with pleasantries. It was all so . . . easy, comfortable. And yet, Caroline felt a sense of foreboding wash through her. It was the kind of cautionary sensation that had kept her alive in her other life back in London.

The mad crush of people on the stairs leading to the private boxes reminded Caroline of her first day in America. Much like now, she'd been pushed and shoved from every angle.

Her apprehension thickened with the pressing crowd. Tension spread across her shoulders. She put up her guard at once. Her gaze darting back and forth, right to left, she watched for trouble, assessing potential threats one by one.

They made their way to her uncle's private box just as the lights flickered.

"Right on time," Jackson whispered.

Relief tickled a trail along the base of her spine and, finally, she relaxed. But then Jackson moved aside the curtain, and she came face to face with her aunt.

Chapter Thirty-One

"You." The word rushed out of Caroline's mouth in a cold, harsh whisper. Her gaze turned fierce and unbending. A woman prepared to stand and fight. She would not run away from her aunt. She would not back down. Cowardice was not in her nature.

Alert, watchful, cool on the surface with violent ripples of rage and tension beneath, this was the woman who'd survived the vicious streets of Whitechapel. Katherine had no idea who she was up against.

Still, Jackson felt a driving need to protect Caroline. She should not have to be in this position.

His own anger kindled, the pain of it obscene, like sharp, burning daggers stabbing into his chest. All but snarling at the woman who had caused so much suffering in his beloved's life, he swept his glance around the box—the very *empty* box—then returned his attention to Katherine once again.

She was looking her best tonight, dressed in a crimson silk gown fashioned in the latest Parisian style. Her blonde hair was perfectly coiffed atop her head.

She should not be here.

Marcus had promised. Something must have happened.

"Where are your husband and the other members of the family?" Jackson asked, aware that Caroline still stared at the woman, frozen in shock.

Katherine answered the question, her eyes never leaving her niece's face. "Richard insisted on taking the family carriage. I came on ahead of them in the motorcar."

"How very . . . resourceful." Caroline looked as chilly as she sounded. For a moment, a haunted expression filled her gaze, a sorrow so deep Jackson wanted to bundle her in his arms and hasten her away to a safe place where no one could hurt her again, especially not this vicious woman.

But this wasn't his fight, and he knew Caroline wouldn't appreciate him interfering or insisting she leave. Nevertheless, he stayed right where he belonged, by Caroline's side.

Strains of discordant music drifted from the orchestra pit below the stage as instruments were tuned. The lights flickered again, a warning the show would begin in fifteen minutes.

Still standing with her back to the stage, Katherine looked over her shoulder, noted the packed theater behind her, and released a very small, very maddening smile. "I believe that's my cue."

"I'm not having this conversation with you here." Caroline spun on her heel and exited the box.

Katherine rushed after her, intent in her gaze, Jackson hard on her heels.

Out in the hallway, Caroline slid him a glance, a plea really. "You should go, before she makes a scene." She looked frantically around her. "Before someone notices you're here with me."

"I'm not leaving you, Caroline." He wrapped his arm around her and pressed a kiss to her lips, uncaring if anyone witnessed the intimate exchange. "Now and forever."

"Oh, how sweet." Katherine's lips curved in a sarcastic twist. "But, Jackson, are you that unaware of your surroundings?" She raised her voice loud enough to gain the attention of the people in the nearby boxes with only a thin curtain hanging between them. "We are in a very public arena tonight."

"I'm aware."

"Oh, look." Katherine cast a glance behind her, glaring pointedly at the handful of theatergoers tentatively popping into the deserted hallway. "I do believe we are drawing attention from the patrons who have yet to find their seats."

"Jackson," Caroline hissed. "Please, go. Now, before it is too late."

He tightened his hold on her waist, the silent gesture communicating his intentions. "Together, Caroline. We are in this together."

She looked unconvinced and very concerned he was making a mistake. He couldn't blame her for her reaction. For years he'd avoided a moment such as this, had worked tirelessly to maintain his good standing in the community. But he'd only been playing at being a righteous man, following the principles of good Christian behavior. He'd been working for man's favor. Not the Lord's.

He knew the difference now. Caroline had shown him the way of genuine integrity. She'd shown him what real courage looked like. His life had found its rhythm with her by his side.

"As you can see, Katherine, I am officially courting Caroline now." He spoke in a strong voice, uncaring if others heard his declaration, hoping in fact that they would.

Katherine looked duly flustered, irritated, and as if she were spoiling for a fight. "You are making a mistake. She doesn't belong in our world. She isn't one of us. She's an imposter, raised on the dirty streets of London."

He felt a quick flash of rage, tapped it down with a hard swallow. With sharp-edged clarity, he folded his anger deep inside him. His ambition had one focus now. Protect the woman he loved. At all costs. If Katherine didn't have the decency to leave, then he and Caroline would.

Unfortunately, Caroline seemed to have other plans.

She cast him a quick look, silently begging him to depart before she unleashed her temper.

His heart tumbled in his chest. She was obviously trying to protect him. Warmth, admiration, undying love, all three swam through his head. There was something inevitable about this public confrontation, an unavoidable moment in time they'd been careening toward for weeks. The point of no return.

None of them would walk away unscathed.

So be it.

"If you stay," he said to Caroline, "I stay. I won't abandon you."

Frustration sprang into her eyes. "Stubborn, *stubborn* man."

"It's why you love me."

Shaking her head, she turned back to her aunt, her expression turning gun-metal cold. "I may not be from your world, it's true. But what do you suppose people will say when they find out what you did to my mother? A woman you claimed as your friend?"

"They will congratulate me for protecting my family from a scheming, greedy harlot."

Caroline gasped at the insult, a sound so strong with emotion Jackson reached for her to soothe her, calm her.

Prevent her from leaping at Katherine's throat.

Jaw tight, teeth clenched, Caroline shook him off. "We end this, tonight," she told him. "We end it now."

"Excellent idea." Katherine released a skeletal grin so filled with vicious purpose that Jackson instinctually shifted in front of Caroline.

With a dangerous look in her eyes, Caroline skirted around him and braced her feet in a fighting stance. "I am immune to your poisonous machinations. All that you have managed to do, *Aunt Katherine*, is hurt the people I love. For that you will pay."

"Are you threatening me?"

"As a matter of fact, I am."

A gasp rose up from the crowd.

Katherine looked around her and grinned with satisfaction. Their audience had grown tenfold. She nodded to several people she knew. The encouraging smiles she received in return didn't bode well for Caroline. "Threatening me with bodily harm is exactly what I would expect from a girl like you. Your very existence is an abomination to the St. James name." She snarled. "Who was your father? A lowly stable hand."

Another gasp rose from the crowd. Katherine nodded again, this time in satisfaction. She had the *good* people of New York society on her side. They didn't know who the woman was, not at the core. They only knew who she pretended to be. If this confrontation continued, it would be a case of Caroline's word against Katherine's.

Enough. Jackson gripped the older woman's arm and turned her toward the stairwell leading to the lobby below.

"Jackson, you don't have to do this." Caroline drew alongside him, then lowered her voice. "You can still walk away before it's too late, before your reputation is—"

"Hang my reputation," he said, disgusted with himself for allowing matters to get this far. "I won't allow harm to come to you."

Half dragging, half pulling, he continued to maneuver Katherine in the direction of the stairwell. People yelled at him to let her go.

He ignored all their pleas.

Clawing at his hand, the woman narrowed her dark, angry gaze at Caroline like a hungry predator seeking to devour her prey.

Caroline didn't look the least bit intimidated. Quite the opposite. She looked prepared for a fight. A fight to the finish.

Jackson couldn't have been prouder of the woman he loved, or more determined to protect her from her aunt's evil intent.

Unfortunately, he was probably too late.

Scenting a good scandal brewing, theatergoers spilled into the hallway, coming from every direction, closing in on them at an alarming rate.

Katherine had succeeded in whetting their appetites for a juicy story. They wouldn't leave without hearing the whole sordid tale of Caroline's childhood and resulting struggles since.

Jackson refused to make this easy for them.

He continued to pull Katherine toward the exit. The sea of bobbing heads parted, just a bit, revealing a perfect view of the stairwell up ahead. Only a few more feet to go.

Seizing her chance, Katherine lifted her voice over the buzzing crowd. "Caroline St. James, you are a disgrace to our family and a sinful, wicked creature. You came to town pretending to be a relation of Patricia Harding, which is a lie. A lie!"

Caroline went very still, and her face drained of all color. She looked like a cornered animal, uncertain whether to flee or fight.

Jackson moved between her and Katherine, his body a physical barrier. Slick, sharp, dangerous, his anger became a tangible, breathing beast inside him. The part of himself he had always kept under strict control clambered to be set free.

"Katherine, I'm warning you." His words came out low and deadly. "Do not continue down this path."

His warning fell on deaf ears.

Having gained the undivided attention of the onlookers, the woman played to her ever-growing audience. "This woman who claims to be Caroline St. James," she said, jabbing her finger toward Caroline, "is a fraud. A thief and a liar and a cheat. Not two months ago, she lived in the worst part of London, in squalor, earning money God only knows how."

"Not another word, Katherine. Not. One. More. Word." The statement came from behind them. Jackson lifted his gaze over the crowd and caught sight of Marcus hurrying up the stairs. His approach stalled halfway due to the thickening fray.

Katherine swept her eyes over Caroline. "Do you deny any of what I have said?"

Her features unreadable, Caroline lifted her head at a regal angle, not an ounce of shame in her bearing. "I deny none of it. Everything you said is true."

"There. You see." Katherine cast a smug smile over the crowd of onlookers. "This girl, *this fraud*, doesn't belong in our world. She is uneducated and an embarrassment to the St. James name."

A chorus of agreement wafted from the onlookers. As Jackson had feared, they believed Katherine's version of the story. His throat closed. It was over. News of Caroline's background would spread across town by morning. No doubt an ugly twist would be added to her woeful tale with each retelling. She would be rejected from every good home in the city.

He ached for her, for what she had lost. As for him? Jackson didn't care what the rest of the world thought of Caroline. He loved her. Adored her. Was humbled by her courage to speak the truth, no matter how ugly.

She was the embodiment of Christian integrity.

"Caroline might have come from humble beginnings," he said. "But she is the best woman I know. Better than all of you combined." He made his declaration in a loud, firm voice, daring anyone to speak out against her, willing her to hear the pledge in his words, to see the promise in his eyes.

But she had already turned away and was pushing frantically through the crowd.

Jackson rushed after her, shoving through the tangle of people, uncaring if he stepped on toes or crushed dresses.

His eyes were locked on Caroline's retreating back. The crowd let her pass far too easily, but then closed in behind her. Helplessness washed over him.

He conquered the stairs two at a time. He nearly caught up to her in the lobby but lost sight of her again. He darted through a small gap in the throng and then pushed through another, searching desperately for her familiar cloud of dark hair.

There she was. At the revolving doors. One last shove and she disappeared into the night, out into the streets.

Alone. She was all alone.

Panic eating at him, he quickened his pace, pushing hard, shoving anyone who got in his way. So many people. Several shouted at him to turn around. He knew he was heading in the wrong direction. Yet he persevered. All the while, one thought echoed in his mind. One terrible, dismal thought.

He'd failed Caroline. He'd failed to protect her from her aunt, from the terrible repercussions of a scandal she'd done nothing to deserve. And now she was alone on the streets of New York, with no one to stand by her side. Not even him, after he'd vowed never to abandon her.

He only hoped he wasn't too late to make things right.

Chapter Thirty-Two

Thanks to a hired carriage and a clear night, Caroline arrived back at Granny's in record time. Avoiding the clever matriarch required considerable stealth and skills Caroline had honed through the years. Quiet steps and calm, silent breathing, avoidance of the light while keeping to the shadows. The moon was bright that night, making her journey all the more difficult.

Her smooth, unhindered arrival to her room only magnified the reality of who she was at her core. A woman destined to be alone, always alone.

Katherine St. James, for all her malice and spite, had been brutally correct. Caroline didn't belong in this world.

She didn't belong anywhere.

Holding back her emotions awhile longer, just a little bit longer, she shut the door behind her, leaned her back against the smooth wood, and finally broke.

Hiccuping sobs quaked through her body.

"Jackson, oh, Jackson, what you must be suffering because of me." She raised her hand to her throat. "I'm sorry." She whispered the apology into the moonlit room. "So very sorry."

Eyes shut, she slipped to the floor and buried her head in her hands. The tears that had been burning in her eyes since she'd left the opera house spilled unhindered down her cheeks.

She cried for all that was lost. Cried for ruining Jackson's sterling reputation, which he'd worked so hard to build. Cried for the love she'd almost had within her reach.

Love. What did Caroline really know about love? She only knew how to be alone, how to guard her heart and push people away. She knew how to fight and, *now*, she knew how to run.

She fought back another onslaught of tears, a useless indulgence when courage was needed.

"I will not feel sorry for myself. I will not." A sob tried to work its way past her throat. She gulped it back with ruthless control. "I *must* be strong."

She rose quickly to her feet, too quickly. Her head grew light, her vision blurred, and she stumbled several steps forward. Reaching out, she steadied herself on a nearby table. Once she had her balance, she looked down, noted the book beneath her palm.

Her mother's worn Bible. Libby St. James's one great treasure that she'd carried with her to every shack and hovel in which they'd lived. Her words of advice came back to Caroline, words she'd dismissed until now. "This is a guidebook for life, Caroline, but only if you choose to listen to the Holy Spirit's urgings."

Was her answer here, in this tattered Bible? Were the answers to life really so simple?

Hands shaking, Caroline opened to a page at random, skimmed the words in the dim moonlight, and stopped at a verse that caught her eye. *Greater love hath no man than this, that a man lay down his life for his friends.*

Love, real love, was about sacrifice. She knew that, had understood it in her heart for most of her life.

If she truly loved Jackson, Caroline had to let him go. She had to leave New York. If she stayed, Jackson would be shunned from all the good homes in town, as would the rest of her family.

She wouldn't do that to the people she loved.

Despite her conviction, a wave of despair crested. Caroline had been certain she'd found her home, a place to call her own. The dream had been within her reach.

But only for a little while.

Holding back the tears, she flipped to another page of the Bible. Her mother had underlined a verse in Deuteronomy. *The LORD thy God, he it is that doth go with thee; he will not fail thee, nor forsake thee.*

Was it true? Would Caroline never truly be alone? Would God go with her, always, no matter where she went next?

So simple, yet so very difficult to put into practice.

Hands still shaking, she set down her mother's Bible and went in search of Sally. She found the girl in her adjoining room, in a chair, reading, with a pair of spectacles perched on her nose. She looked unnaturally still, as if her mind was somewhere else and the words weren't quite registering.

"Sally, I need you to help me pack." Caroline blurted out the request.

"You want to pack?" Sally pulled her brows together. "Tonight?"

"Yes, tonight. Right now."

"But, Caroline." She closed the book and set it on the table beside her. "Where are you going at such a late hour?"

"I"—she looked wildly around the room—"don't know. A hotel, I suppose."

"You're upset." Sally came to her and took her hands. "Tell me what's happened."

Caroline stared up at the ceiling, attempting to sort through her thoughts, to order them in a proper sequence. Unable to make sense of the last few hours and needing a friend desperately, Caroline revealed what her aunt had done at the opera.

When she came to the part about hiring a carriage to rush home on her own, she stopped talking. The ache in her heart was too great to continue.

She'd found the love of a good and decent man, only to have it ripped away from her in a matter of minutes. A tremendous void of loneliness—no family, no future, *no Jackson*—that was what lay ahead.

No. She would not give in to self-pity. She must take action, must put a plan into motion. Must. Press. On.

Squaring her shoulders, she drew in a fortifying breath. "I'll begin sorting my clothes while you retrieve my trunks from storage."

Sally opened her mouth to argue the point, but Caroline spoke over her. "Please. No advice. No questions. I just need your support."

"All right, then." The girl gave her one firm nod. "If this is what you want, I won't just help you pack. I'll go with you."

"Thank you."

"Granny will be disappointed."

Caroline sighed. "I'll explain it to her as best I can."

They moved back into her bedchamber, through the adjoining door, and stopped dead in their tracks at the sound of insistent knocking. "Caroline, open up."

Jackson. He had followed her after all.

She stared at the shut door, frozen in place.

In the next instant, the door swung open and slammed into the wall with a loud bang.

Jackson stood in the doorway, hair windblown, clothes disheveled, eyes a little wild. Caroline's pulse fluttered, but she fought to stay calm. But, oh—*oh my*—even in his unruly state, he radiated power, with a slight edge of danger. This was the man she wanted by her side, forever, but Caroline couldn't have him, not without hurting him.

An impossible situation with no easy resolution in sight.

Gaze locked with hers, Jackson swept into the room. Trapped inside all that intensity, Caroline felt overwhelmed, disoriented. A sound of dismay slipped past her lips.

Sally, ever the faithful friend, moved directly in his path. "Mr. Montgomery, you cannot be here. It isn't proper."

"Propriety is not my first concern." The desperation in his words had Caroline's throat constricted with emotion.

What was he saying? That he didn't care what others thought of him, *of her?*

Hope kindled in her heart. She suppressed the sensation with a hard swallow.

"You will leave us now." Eyes hooded, Jackson took Sally's arm and escorted her firmly, yet gently, toward the door. "Do not try to return until you are called for."

"Now wait just a minute." Sally pulled on her arm. "Mr. Montgomery, you cannot show up in a lady's bedchamber and demand a private audience."

"Not to worry, Sally. I have no plans of harming Caroline."

Doubt flickered over the maid's pale features. "If you do, you will answer to me."

He nodded. "Fair enough."

Touched by their mutual concern for her, Caroline couldn't look at either of them a moment longer. She moved to the window and gazed out into the night. The big silver moon gleamed over the city. Stars glittered like ice crystals in the sky.

A soft click told her Jackson had shut the door behind Sally.

They were alone. Just the two of them. In her bedchamber. If word of this *private audience* got out, the damage done at the opera would be magnified, irrevocably so.

"You shouldn't be alone with me like this." She clasped her hands together at her waist. "It can only make matters worse for you."

"Caroline." He managed to make her name an apology, which made no sense at all. What did he have to apologize for when she was the one who had brought disaster into his life?

"Please, my sweet girl, turn around and look at me."

When she didn't do as he requested, he placed his hand on her shoulder. She felt his frustration in his touch, and his guilt. His guilt?

She turned to face him.

The look in his eyes—the unspeakable love and devotion, the hint of sorrow—it took her breath away. The truth hit her square in the chest. Jackson was going to fight for her, *for them.*

No. Caroline couldn't let him destroy himself like that. "I want you to leave."

A muscle shifted in his jaw. For a tense moment, he didn't speak, just simply looked at her. "Not until I have my say."

"There's nothing more to be said." She laid a hand on his arm and forced herself to speak the words they both needed to hear. "We can't be together, not after what happened tonight."

Even to her own ears her voice was thin and high-pitched, filled with the sound of her misery.

"I beg to disagree."

Clearly, the man was as stubborn as she was. "The damage has already been done to my reputation, but yours can still be salvaged if you disassociate yourself from me at once."

"You think I would walk away from you, from us, from what we could have together, because of a little gossip?"

Wouldn't he? "You've worked so hard to restore your family's good name. I won't be the cause of—"

"Caroline St. James, you have a lot to learn about your future husband." He pulled her into his arms then, held her tightly against him when she struggled. "I don't care what the gossips say about you, me, *us.*"

The first stirrings of hope fluttered to life, sweeping through her despair like a cool, soothing breeze. "The gossip will not be kind."

"No, it won't. But I know who you are, Caroline, at the core of your very being." He tightened his arms around her. "You are a precious child of God who makes me want to be the best man I can be."

She sighed against him, petrified he didn't know what he was saying, praying that he did.

"Hear me," he continued. "I know what I'm getting myself into. I've weathered this particular storm before and will do so again gladly. Because, this time, I enter the fray by choice. And I promise I will do whatever it takes to ensure the road is as easy for you as possible."

Pressing her cheek against his chest, she closed her eyes and sighed again. Yielding, trembling . . . hoping. So much hope building inside her. "You have to be absolutely sure. There cannot be any doubt in your mind." Her throat cinched around a sob. "Or we will be doomed to failure."

Slowly, carefully, he set her away from him and stared into her eyes. The light of the moon gilded his face, revealing the raw emotion in his eyes. "I love you, Caroline. I want to spend the rest of my life with you."

"Oh, Jackson."

He lowered to one knee and took her hand. "Will you do me the honor of becoming my wife?"

Looking down into his honest, handsome face, Caroline felt a conflicting rush of fear and pleasure, coupled with a tingling in her toes.

"I love you," she whispered. "So very much."

He smiled in response, making it difficult for her to breathe. "You haven't answered me yet. Will you, Caroline? Will you marry me?"

"Yes." She pulled her hand free and cupped his face. The beginning of stubble on his jaw was rough against her palm. "Yes, yes, yes. I will marry you."

He stood. "As soon as possible?"

"As soon as possible," she confirmed, liking the idea very much. Very much, indeed.

"I'll ask your grandfather for his permission first thing in the morning."

Touched beyond all reason, she couldn't help but tease him a little. "That's all very *proper* of you."

He stilled, every muscle in his body tense and unmoving. "This has nothing to do with propriety." His face grew serious, all brooding energy and suppressed power. "It's about treating you with the respect you deserve."

"Ah, there he is. The good, decent man I fell in love with that day on Orchard Street." She smiled at him. "It's true, you know. I have loved you from the first moment our eyes met."

"Another point on which we agree." He drew her close, wrapped his arms around her waist. "I have loved you from that first moment as well."

Joy burst in her heart. "Thank you, Jackson, thank you for wanting to go to my grandfather and ask for my hand properly. I can't think of a more fitting way to begin our life together."

"I can." With masculine intent in his eyes, he pressed his lips to hers in a long, thorough, and really quite scandalous kiss.

Epilogue

Caroline and Jackson were married exactly two months to the day after the scandal broke. Their wedding was the most talked-about event of the season and, paradoxically, the least attended. Despite the convenient hour of the ceremony, and the lack of any other scheduled events that day, the good people of New York refused to grace the church with their presence.

By the morning of the blessed event, Caroline had been discussed, scrutinized, and ultimately deemed unworthy to enter every drawing room in their fair city. Katherine St. James had done her damage but was unable to enjoy the spoils of her efforts as she'd been unceremoniously banished to the family estate in Florida.

According to her husband, she was fortunate to have a home at all.

No one was more surprised by Jackson's nonchalant attitude over the gossip and subsequent turn of events than Caroline. For a man who had once insisted on living above reproach and who had followed the rules of society to the letter, he'd become quite indifferent to his peers' good opinion of him, or rather lack thereof. He told anyone who would listen that he was madly in love with Caroline, and she with him. No amount of talk could sway either of them from their devotion to one another, or their families.

Caroline thanked God every day for her blessings, of which there were many. The Lord had filled the dark places in her soul with light. She vowed to honor Him in every facet of her life, her marriage, and even in her work at the magazine and garment factory.

Waiting for her cue from the reverend, Caroline stood in the back of the church and peeked into the sanctuary. She looked past the rows and rows—and rows—of empty pews and fixed her gaze on the farthest two up front.

She smiled at the sight of the assembled guests dressed in all their finery. Immediate family and a few dear friends had arranged themselves in a haphazard manner on either side of the aisle, guests of the bride intermixed with guests of the groom.

It was incredibly nontraditional of them and really rather perfect, to Caroline's way of thinking.

Thank you, Lord, she whispered silently in her heart, embracing the sheer joy of the moment. The most important people in her life had come to share her most important day.

Mary and her family were there, sharing a pew with Caroline's uncle and Monsieur Lappet. Granny and Jackson's mother sat just one row behind them.

On the other side of the aisle was Jackson's assistant, John Reilly, looking exceedingly handsome in a dark suit and tie. Warren Griffin sat on his son's left, while Elizabeth had commandeered the empty spot on Lucian's right. In his casual manner, he'd looped his arm over the back of the pew behind her.

Elizabeth seemed tense, more so than usual. Ever since her mother had left town, the poor girl had struggled with finding her way. Everything she'd ever known and believed in had been shattered.

Caroline sent up a silent prayer for her dear cousin.

Opening her eyes, she noted that her groom and grandfather were nowhere in sight. Wondering where they could be, Caroline leaned forward for a better look.

"Get back here, this instant," Sally hissed. "No one can be allowed to see you before the ceremony begins."

"Why not?"

"It'll ruin the moment." Sally physically pulled her back into the foyer of the church.

Hands working at a frenzied pace, her former maid buzzed around her, picking at invisible threads and smoothing out nonexistent wrinkles. Caroline stifled a laugh. The girl was acting as if she'd made the dress herself, which wasn't too far from the truth. Sally now worked at the magazine with Caroline, helping Monsieur Lappet design the finished looks for each template.

She'd been the one to choose this white satin bridal gown. The girl certainly had an eye and worked well with Monsieur Lappet. Caroline felt like a fairy-tale princess in the layers of satin, lace, and hand-sewn crystals.

"Ah, my dear, there you are." Her grandfather materialized in the foyer and placed his hands on her shoulders. "Let me have a look at you."

Smiling, Caroline held steady under his inspection.

"You are a vision," he declared. "Simply beautiful."

"Thank you, Grandfather."

He was looking quite handsome himself, dressed in cream trousers and an emerald-colored coat that brought out the green in his eyes, eyes that were a little watery. She adored working by his side and learning the business from the ground up, as he put it. Soon, Caroline would be ready to take over the garment factory. She had lots of plans, all of which Jackson would help her implement.

"I couldn't be prouder of you than I am right now," her grandfather said with deep affection in his tone.

"Nor I, you." Overcome with love for a man she'd come to America prepared to hate, tears of happiness flooded to the very edges of her lashes. She swiped at them with an unsteady hand and lifted her chin at a brave angle.

They'd come so far since that first encounter in the blue drawing room of his home. The grandfather she'd once planned to ruin was about to walk her down the aisle and give her away in marriage.

After a brief dab at his eyes with his knuckle, he offered his arm. "Shall we?"

"Oh, yes."

Sally gave the dress a few more unnecessary tugs and pulls, then deemed Caroline perfectly arranged for her trip down the aisle. "Godspeed, my friend."

At the girl's serious tone, Caroline kissed her friend on the cheek. "Thank you, Sally."

"It's been my pleasure." Sally stepped back, the tears in her eyes turning the blue a shade lighter.

At the back of the church, Caroline's steps faltered and her stomach tumbled to her toes. Jackson stood at the end of the aisle in a dove-gray morning suit with long tails. He made a dazzling and glorious picture.

And, oh my, he was hers, all hers, her present and her future. *My bridegroom.* Truly, the Lord had blessed her beyond measure.

Only slightly watery-eyed, she took a step toward him, and another, and finally another. Her progress was slow, but she couldn't seem to make her feet move any faster. She wanted this moment to last forever.

From his perch beside the altar, Jackson gave her a brazenly intimate smile. Her knees nearly gave out at his boldness. This daring version of the man she loved took her breath away.

As if understanding she needed a moment, her grandfather patted her hand and waited. Her feet began moving again.

When they were halfway down the aisle, Jackson left the altar and came to her. In a complete break from tradition, he said to her grandfather, "I can take it from here, sir."

Throwing his head back, the older man let out a booming laugh. "Yes, my boy, I believe you can." He relinquished his hold on Caroline's arm. "Take care of my granddaughter."

"I will, every day of our lives. Always and forever."

In the next instant, Caroline's hand was wrapped inside Jackson's.

He dropped his head to whisper in her ear. "Ready to get married?"

"Yes, please."

As one, they turned toward the altar. Slowly, they released each other's hands.

And then . . .

Jackson swooped her into his arms, spun her around, and kissed her straight on the lips. All things considered, it was an ideal end to her journey to America, and a perfect beginning to their life together. Their marriage would be built on a strong foundation of faith in God, trust in one another, and love.

Most definitely love.

About the Author

Photo © 2012 Caroline Akins / One Six Photography

Renee Ryan is the author of eighteen inspirational, faith-based romance novels. She received the Daphne du Maurier Award for Excellence in Mystery/Suspense, inspirational romantic division, for her novels *Dangerous Allies* and *Courting the Enemy*. She is currently serving as the secretary of Romance Writers of America. Ryan currently lives in Lincoln, Nebraska, with her husband.

For more information, please visit www.reneeryan.com.